Men Without Hate

Gene Lee

ALL THINGS
THAT MATTER
PRESS

ISBN 13: 9780999524381
Library of Congress Control Number: 2018955348
Cover Photos: Unsplash.com

Cover design © by All Things That Matter Press
Published in 2018 by All Things That Matter Press

For my mother, Betty Lynn Promenski, who I am sure, had she lived to read it, would have approved.
And for my wife, Donna, who has always been there for me.
And for my daughter, Allison, who never seems quite sure what to think of her father.

Acknowledgments

I wish to thank Phil and Deb Harris for providing a home for this book, as well as all thanks to Suzanne Fox, who showed me where the real story lay, and without whose steady prodding and suggestions this novel would not exist.

And also, many thanks to my longtime friend, Lucinda Merritt, for offering a fresh set of eyes when they were sorely needed.

BOOK ONE ~ LEWIS

Part I: War

For two days in July of 1863 the troops on both sides fought and died under an overcast sky. The smoke of the guns in the valley hung like a pall over the rocky field, the grasses trampled by the movements of men in battle while the ridges and bluffs were ruffled by a wind coming out of the south. For the most part, the temperatures stayed mild beneath the gray skies. On what was to be the third day of the conflict, the sun began to break the clouds apart, an honest-to-God summer heat starting to rise. Perhaps not as hot as a July day in southern Georgia where Lewis Raines and a good portion of the men with him, hailed from. But still, a summer day all the same, hot and muggy, made even more so by the presence of thunderheads regrouping in the west as Raines and his battery struggled to get the guns into position.

With the heat and the hard work, some of the men had taken off their shirts and uniform jackets, those who still had them, and Lewis envied those men. As a second lieutenant—the only one the battery had had since First Lieutenant Osgood fell at Chancellorsville—he didn't believe it suited his rank to do as they did. And though he had no problems putting a shoulder to a resistant wheel or a sharp blow with the edge of a ramrod to the backside of a balking mule, Lewis sometimes felt envious of Captain Harker, who by courtesy of rank, was exempt from such duty.

Atop his favored roan gelding, the commanding officer strode alongside the limbers pulling the cannons, carefully keeping pace with the wooden wagons as he oversaw the placement of the battery that morning. In his gray jacket, worn and faded from lack of care, was his Colt Dragoon pistol lacking a holster lost in some prior battle. Captain Harker appeared pleased with what he observed. Catching the captain's eye on occasion, Lewis noticed a certain guarded stare, one belying the officer's confident style. It seemed out of place, a little disturbing, like the sunlight breaking between the parting clouds to light up the ridge while the captain barked out orders. But not now. Noticing Lewis looking at him, the captain gave him a harsh turn of the head, a silent command to pay attention to his own business. Lewis was reminded again, if indeed he had even forgotten, that peace that day was not to be expected; a reminder bolstered by the cries of the wounded coming from the hospital tents to the rear, cries mingling with the smell of fired powder wafting in the air.

The edge on some of the men's faces as they carried out the demanding orders of their captain removed any envy Lewis might have felt for his superior officer. A nagging thought of how any one of the men he was working with could be dead before day's end surfaced in his thoughts. Unlike the way they regarded Captain Harker, Lewis believed the men in the battery held a certain respect for him, begrudgingly as it may be. He found small comfort in this as the thought of dying amongst men who hated him disturbed him greatly.

"Lieutenant Raines!"

It was past mid-morning when Harker reined up and called back to him. The last three hours had been a constant of men grunting and cursing in the morning heat, the creaking of stiff leather, and the groaning of wheel and axle beneath the burden of their loads. The cases of powder, shell, and shot; the tins of canister—that terrible ordnance Lewis hated to use—were all there. If one were to believe the sounds of the morning, he'd think it had to be more than wood, leather, animal and man, could bear. And yet, he had seen it done repeatedly, certain if he lived through the day he'd see it repeated the next.

"Sir."

Leaving the limber he was in charge of, Lewis joined the captain in the shade of an elm tree.

"Are your men ready for what the day may bring?"

After a crisp salute, one the captain didn't return in a crisp fashion, Lewis answered, "I believe they are, sir." He tried to smile, having to wipe away a trail of sweat and dust from his lips with the back of one hand. "And if they're not, they will be when it's time."

"That's good, then, Lieutenant."

And now the captain returned his smile. When he did Lewis was reminded that the commanding officer was still a man like the rest of them, rank and West Point training aside. Beneath the shock of curly blond hair trickling out from under the brim of the captain's hat was an individual not much older than he was. *My age, maybe younger.*

"We've seen very little of the fighting so far, sir," Lewis said, prodding the captain for a clue as to how the day was going to go. "The men are itching to be in the thick of it, today. Before any chance of glory disappears altogether, I suppose."

For himself, Lewis didn't believe in the 'glory' part of his statement. In his two years of fighting, precious little of that aspect of war had been revealed to him. Some of those who had been alongside of him at Fredericksburg the previous winter, up on Marye's Heights pouring canister into the oncoming Union troops, had thought glory was there. Lewis had seen only murder and carnage. For the greater good, he wanted to think. He still had dreams of how it was on the Heights that bitterly cold December day. The true victory of Chancellorsville in the spring had erased some of the bad taste from his mouth. Maybe because the battery hadn't had to resort to canister, but instead could inflict long range damage with the heavier guns and shells. But no. When "glory" was mentioned in the same sentence with what he and the men were involved in now, for him, at any rate, it meant nothing. Lewis had said it to the captain only for the men. Not for him.

"Good," Captain Harker repeated absentmindedly as he surveyed the ridge ahead and the progress of the battery's limbers along the rocky trail. "Glory, is it?" The captain was back with him now. "Well, Lieutenant, they'll have plenty of opportunity today to cover themselves in as much glory as they want. You can rest assured on that."

"Thank you, sir." For the men, he wanted to add, as if to distance himself from their emotions and because of a certain light in the captain's eyes. "That'll lift their spirits some. Especially after the hard work of this morning."

"The work's not over yet, Lieutenant Raines. I expect it's just beginning." Harker turned back to the ridge and the groaning men and wagons up ahead. "As for thanking me? You can do that later. If you still care to."

The weariness in the captain's voice took Lewis aback, it sounding so unlike the confident officer atop the prancing roan overseeing the movements of the units beneath his command.

"We're almost in position, Lieutenant."

The captain took a thin cheroot from inside his jacket and lit it, the sudden bitter sweet smell of the smoke a reminder for Lewis of other times: of his father sitting in the shade of the front porch at home, relaxing with the same kind of cigar at the end of another hard day's work in the fields.

"Best you return to your men and wait for further orders," the captain said.

"Yes sir," Lewis said and saluted. The captain's weary salute and tired smile weighed heavily in Lewis' mind.

In less than another hour the battery was in place. Lewis and the tired men of his command having found a second wind, hurried to complete the final tasks of unlimbering the cannons. They stacked shells and secured the horses away from the guns in preparation for battle. The tension in the officers, men, and even animals was proof that today was to be a big fight. The men would need whatever rest they could find before it began.

Captain Harker rode up one more time as the last of the howitzers was unlimbered, tiny rivulets of sweat glistened beneath his eyes.

"All right, Lieutenant," he said, reining up the roan in front of the muzzle of the last unlimbered piece. "You and your men have done a fine job this morning. Much deserving of their rest over yonder." The captain pointed towards a group in the trees squatting over a small fire and a pot of chicory coffee. "Wait now," he continued, "for the signal to engage. You do remember the signal, yes?"

Comments such as this were what caused the rancor Lewis felt toward the captain. West Point or not, able commander or not. He was capable, too. Despite his rural upbringings, so different from the ease of being a plantation owner's son and enjoying the best schooling money could buy, his capability under fire was well known to his men. To the captain, as well, though he certainly ignored the truth of it whenever convenient for him to do so.

"Yes, sir, I do remember, sir." His anger kept Lewis from saluting the captain who smiled tightly back at him in recognition. "Two cannon reports from Colonel Alexander's position, sir."

"Indeed, Lieutenant. When you hear those reports pour it into them."

"We will, sir. We'll give them hell."

"Make sure you do, Lieutenant. Lest they return the favor."

Harker continued down the ridge toward the next battery where Lewis imagined a similar conversation between similar men would occur. Foreboding as his last words had been and weary as Lewis knew the captain was, he had shown a renewed sense of excited energy, an energy Lewis hadn't seen since Chancellorsville. Smoke from blazing guns had hung hot and heavy that day, the field before the battery strewn with dead Yankees blown down by the captain's gunners. Harker, busy racing up and down the line of cannons, had turned once to Lewis and his battery, light blazing from his eyes as hot and heavy as the guns firing.

The captain's battle energy was all his own. Lewis didn't imagine anything similar radiated from *him* in the heat of battle. Battle was mainly hard work, hot, dirty, and muscle-straining. He tried to leave the excitement to the others, never sure if what he felt during a fight was excitement or fear.

Lewis was tired. They were all tired. They were battle-grimed. Ever since Chancellorsville, when it seemed they would never stop firing, loading, and firing again, stopping only to cool guns down, opportunities for the men to wash had been few. But washed or not, Lewis knew that if a looking glass were handy, the black hair and lean features of his face, the sharp nose, thin lips, the grey eyes, would only be faintly visible through the dust and sweat.

The thought brought back how his mother had told him that he possessed the face of a poet. Lord Byron was the poet Ella Dixon Raines had in mind, as she told her son on those occasions when she read to him from the great lord's works. She kept a faded picture of the poet, clipped from a periodical shortly before her son was born, in a scrapbook of doilies, poems she had written as a young maid, and letters from family members living and dead. As a boy sitting at his mother's feet, Lewis could never picture a resemblance between him and the poet, could not understand why she called him "her own little Lord Byron." With age that resemblance might come, he had thought, wanting only to please his mother. But the only thing that had come with age had been the withering illness consuming her. By the time Lewis was ten there was no more reading of poetry at his mother's knee. Only the short and scattered conversations held when she was feeling "up to it," which consisted of him doing most of the talking as he held her hand, telling her of his day while she stared into his face with eyes that once shone brightly but now didn't seem truly alive.

Why he thought such a thing now was beyond him. Nothing seemed very poetical to him at the moment. Nothing resembled anything his mother would've been a part of.

As he took a pull of tepid water from the canteen Sergeant Cuthbert passed him, Lewis looked over the lip of the leather container at the faces of the other men with him: privates Dixon, Boggess, and the Jewish man, Zink. Lieutenant Osgood had been the last of the original unit, though original may be misleading as Lewis only counted back to the men who had been with him since Marye's Heights the previous December. Osgood was missed and his death during the glorious victory of Chancellorsville had yet to sit well with Lewis. The Lieutenant had been a real friend and his death left an empty place, one Lewis hadn't experienced before. The nights playing chess until late in front of the fire, the talk of the poets Keats and Lord Byron, their mutual despair that the war might never be over, and their increasing doubt that if the end did come it would be with victory for the South. These had been the core elements of their friendship, ideas and feelings Lewis couldn't talk of with Cuthbert or the others.

"Ye think we'll see some good fighting today, Lootenent?" Sergeant Cuthbert put the canteen back on the bed of the limber next to the powder cases held in reserve. "Seems like them other fellers," he gestured with one hand at the far edges of the line spread down the ridge and in the peach orchard below, the rocky outcrops way across the valley where the enemy positions were, "been having all the fun lately."

Cuthbert was a good man, quick to volunteer for the hard work, equally quick to laugh at a good joke, especially one played on himself. He was famous for somehow coming up with whiskey for the evening entertainments, but never willing to divulge his secrets of how he managed to do it. After a while the men quit asking, Lewis, too, all of them just grateful for Cuthbert and the relief his whiskey and jokes brought. The sergeant seemed so relaxed—even with the threat of the upcoming battle before him—as he leaned back against the limber in the shade of the trees, legs and feet splayed out before him on the ground, the slight breeze coming across the ridge roughing the few strands of red hair falling across his face.

"So, Lieutenant?" Cuthbert asked again. "Ye think today's our time for all that fun?"

"Yes, Sergeant," Lewis answered the grinning man. "I do." Just as he had asked the captain earlier Lewis, too, was being asked by those below him, a ripple effect down the chain of command being played out all along the lines that day. And as the captain had said to him, he said to Cuthbert now, "Concerning the 'good' of any fighting we do today, Sergeant, I imagine that will be decided by others."

"It'll be good, Lieutenant," Cuthbert told him, brushing the wayward hair off his forehead. "Good and hot for them boys in blue across the valley."

The laughter of the men vanished once it left the shade of the trees, drifting into the hot air rising above the valley. Laughter produced by nerves as not all of the men shared the same enthusiasm for battle as Cuthbert did. Lewis didn't see how any sane man could. But perhaps that was why God created men like Sergeant Cuthbert. It seemed as good an explanation as any, he supposed.

At any rate, it was done now, the battery in place, everything ready, down the line of the ridge, as well: the rest of Colonel Alexander's batteries in position. Blackened gun snouts looked out over the valley toward the far hills and the targets waiting there. The nervous coughing of tethered horses mingled with bursts of human laughter drifting on the breeze coming down from the hills. Some of the men were eating a make-do lunch of hardtack and chicory coffee, not much considering the fight ahead of them. This was standard fare for Lewis and the soldiers of Lee's army who were learning to fight and survive on very little of anything.

It was shoes. Lewis had heard from those who were here when it began that the little town they were marching past might have shoes.

What the town had instead was a small force of Union cavalry coming in on the other side, the two opposing forces meeting suddenly in the middle. Lewis felt a twinge of sad disgust at such a thought. Shoes for troops who had none, who had marched long miles in bare feet, grateful that it was summer. Many of them had marched in the snows of the previous winter in the same condition. Not the Yankees, though. There had been no barefooted corpses in blue in the snow below the heights outside of Fredericksburg. None that Lewis had seen at any rate. Those in the Confederate lines without shoes on their feet had swarmed out at first light in search of them, Lewis included, the men yelping with joy when they found a suitable enough pair. It hadn't taken Lewis long to find ones for him and the sturdy brogans he had stripped from a dead Yankee that day covered his feet now.

The sun pushed higher in the clearing sky and he hoped it wouldn't be too much longer before the signal came. Of course, that was up to Colonel Alexander's discretion, *his* sense of the right moment to begin a rain of destruction on the enemy forces on the other ridgeline. Lewis and his men, the others up and down the line, had done all they could do. All but the waiting, at least.

He blinked his eyes against the glare of the sun, pulling the bill of his cap lower over his forehead to improve his vision in the harsh light. Yes, so far, his men had done their part well.

***

It was a long ways away. This hot and hazy July day in Pennsylvania with nothing to do but be patient until all hell breaks loose

And very cold that February morning as Lewis drove the family buckboard to town for supplies. The hard winds from the north whipping through the pines and oaks bordering the rough wagon road leading from Ruskin to Pendleton only served to intensify that cold. Lewis didn't mind the trip; it gave him the opportunity to spend time with his good friend, Jack Hewitt and the Hewitt family. Unlike the Raines family dwelling on the edge of the Okeefenokee Swamp ten miles south of town, the Hewitts lived within the city limits of Pendleton. Lewis especially enjoyed these visits now that his interest in the Hewitt family had recently come to center more on Jack's younger sister, Mamie, than on Jack himself.

As he sat on the hard buckboard seat bouncing along the uneven road, Lewis's thoughts drifted from the cold of the morning to the warmth of Mamie Hewitt's skin the last time he had held her in his arms. Not to mention the flush on her face, the heat of her hands in his the first time he had kissed her. This wondrous event had occurred just two weeks before in the garden out back of the house after the Saturday meal was done. Yet it seemed like a lifetime ago to Lewis and he had thought of little since—couldn't help but think of her now as he let the horse take the wagon along a route they knew well. He remembered clearly the wonderment of her face, the way her lips opened slightly for his kiss. How different that had been—holding her tight against his chest, their lips pressed together—than when they had danced together at the Christmas Cotillion. He had thought dancing with her that night was as close to God and Heaven as he might ever get.

The Hewitts seemed fine with Lewis at their table for Saturday dinner, and afterwards, staying the night. The Reverend Hewitt clearly was equally glad to have the young Raines boy attend service at the First Baptist Church of Pendleton come Sunday morning. Lewis knew that the Reverend prided himself on his church and the faithful flock who attended. He did his best to provide them with an enlightened version of the Good Book's teachings, one suited to the modern times they were living in. Much better suited, the Reverend declared over dinner one night, than the harsh teachings of the Primitive Baptist Church on the outskirts of Ware. An equally primitive town, the Reverend went on to say. For it was common knowledge that on the rare Sunday Edwin Raines *did* take his family to church, it was there. But if his daughter, with her comely looks and flirtatious manner, was the reason for young Lewis's increasingly frequent visits, then the more power to the Lord. There was more than one way to skin a cat, Lewis heard the Reverend say. And in the Lord's armaments more than one way to bring another lost soul under his wing.

He'd have to marry Mamie Hewitt, Lewis thought. That was plain enough to see. Marriage was a lasting proposition. According to Edwin Raines, at any rate, who had said so when Lewis asked his opinion on the matter. "Best be sure from the start," his father had continued, "that what you're thinking of is the right thing."

And there was a problem. Lewis wasn't exactly sure that marrying and starting his own farm and family was what he was looking for. He wasn't sure, except when he was near Mamie. At those times the idea of *not* being with her the rest of his days seemed to be wrong. He didn't know much, Lewis was willing to admit, but of that he was sure.

The horse in the stays whinnied and blew, pulling up short as they came to the fork where the one road headed on to Pendleton and the other veered west towards Ruskin. The wind had picked up, blowing harder and colder in steady bursts through the pines, the trees too thin along that stretch of road to make much of a buffer against it. Lewis was glad for the wool jacket he wore, a handmade Christmas gift from his mother. Pulling it tighter around his shoulders, he thought again of his father's prediction through the *Farmer's Almanac* of an early spring. *Cold wind from the north says no to that, he thought. If it keeps blowing like this it'll be winter all the way through April.*

He turned the horse's head toward Pendleton, but the old mare snorted out a blast of hot air, lips pulled away from her teeth as she stamped her hooves in the clay. Lewis slapped the reins hard against her rump to no avail. Bears were not uncommon in these parts, Lewis well knew. They were prone to moving out of the deeper woods in the first days of spring to make their way to the edges of the swamp on the other side of the Raines farm. Fresh water and easy meals of marsh rabbits and young deer were the draw, especially after the leaner days of winter. It seemed early for bears, but perhaps his father was right, and spring was coming. That wind from the north could be blowing scent of a bear's presence. Pulling his father's rifle, loaded and primed before he set out that morning, Lewis slapped the mare's rump again hard with the reins.

"Giddap now!"

Bears, early spring or no, something or someone awaited him in town, a feeling he hadn't been able to shake of late. Wasting time on thoughts of Mamie Hewitt and a nervous horse were getting Lewis Raines no closer to whatever it was.

"Giddap."

***

Lewis's father, Edwin "Tiny" Raines, along with his brother Dawes, farmed 2,000 acres in southwest Georgia. It was good, fertile soil just east of the little town of Ruskin, and just west of the edges of the Okeefenokee Swamp. It was the nearness of the swamp, Edwin Raines claimed, that made their acreage so productive. Every year for the last fifteen they had planted and harvested crab-grass hay, sweet potatoes for themselves and their hogs, tobacco, and corn. Though hard pressed by others who did, they grew no cotton. "Tiny" Raines was a funny nickname for his father, considering the man stood at 6'4," and weighed 245 pounds of hard muscle. Lewis, along with his sister Cordelia, had heard the stories of family lore many times. The original Edwin Raines—once court poet for the English king and who, by a series of bad investments in the Dutch East Indies, had landed in debtor's prison. When given the chance the first Edwin had sailed with Oglethorpe to the Colonies. Edwin and his family had flourished on the coast of Georgia, through hard times and good and the American Revolution. Tiny Raines would have been there still but for a land grant given him by the United States in gratitude for his service in the Indian Wars of the 1820s and then again in 1838. That was back when under Andy Jackson's leadership good God-fearing Americans were able to finally rid the area of the Creeks and Cherokees and do something productive with all that land the Indians were letting go to waste.

Or so Dawes Raines believed and always took the chance to declare when he and his brother sat out on Edwin's front porch and enjoyed a bottle of their favorite bourbon. As a boy and even as a young man, Lewis would sit in on these discussions of the latest going-ons in the area: crop forecasts; so and so over to Ruskin had some head gone missing; Mr. Waite's son had run off to Atlanta; all the idle talk of men that Lewis didn't understand but was happy to be a part of. He was only privy to the talk, though, not the men's whiskey. A situation that changed suddenly one Friday evening shortly after his eighteenth birthday and his father turned to him after taking a long pull off the bottle.

"I guess you're old enough for this now, son," he said and passed the bottle to Lewis.

When Dawes finally stopped laughing he told his brother, "Well, hell, Edwin, it's been way past time for that boy. Two years, easy, if you ask me."

After Lewis took that first hot sip of liquor he had choked but held it in. Then he took another, thinking how it was sure a mystery why men liked the stuff. But wanting badly to be a man, he was damn sure going to learn to like it, even if it killed him in the trying.

Edwin had never joined in, though, when the talk turned to war and how it had been going up against the Indians, allowing his brothers to do most of the talking. That was like his father, Lewis had always thought, quiet and deferring to others. Of his own deeds he spoke little. Strangely enough, whenever the talk did turn to the Indians, Lewis could've sworn that the look coming across his father's features seemed to be one of disgust, not the pride in glorious deeds that showed on the face of Dawes and young Lewis eager to hear more.

It had been more of the same last night, Lewis had thought, as he pulled the buckboard around front of Crueller's General Store. Hard whiskey and talk. Though the talk of war this time had not been of those in the past, but of one looming in the future. Lewis was wondering how long it would be before the raw taste of bourbon would be gone from his mouth, a taste so strong he had gagged on it.

The town was certainly quiet for a Saturday, a day when the streets and sidewalks should be busy with farmers in buckboards and their wives going in and out of the stores. It was that cold air out of the north, he bet. That kept the lady shoppers home that day. He shouldn't have been there either, he thought. Should be slopping the hogs with what was left of last night's dinner and helping his father with the sharpening of plowshares for the demanding work to come. And normally that would have been the case, he would have been doing this town chore the first of the following month. But his father, a man who considered himself not only an astute, but also a scientific farmer, had read in the almanac how an early spring was to be expected that year. Being a firm believer in the almanac, Lewis's father had taken its prediction to heart. To have everything in place, fields plowed and tilled, and seeds in the ground when spring came, he had sent his youngest boy to town that morning.

With so few townspeople out and about, Lewis had an easy time of getting his orders filled. Being the only customer in the store, Mr. Crueller was eager to help Lewis with his list, expressed regrets that he was short on lead for musket balls, and assisted Lewis with loading the supplies into the buckboard, something the storekeeper wouldn't have been able to do on a Saturday morning. Lewis was happy for the help and the ease of the trading as it would allow him to spend more time at the Hewitts.

"Ye be going off soon to fight them Yankees, I suspect."

Still dwelling on thoughts of Mamie and almost finished with the loading of the wagon, Lewis didn't hear old Dag Shorter addressing him. Though Lewis had acknowledged the man when entering the store, the business of buying and loading supplies put the man out of his mind. He hadn't even realized he was spoken to as he hurried along with his thoughts, a situation Dag corrected by grabbing hold of Lewis's coattails as he was heading from the wagon into the store.

"Now hold on there a minute, boy. I'm a-talkin' to ye."

Lewis obliged the older man, his eyes still on the last sack of flour on the counter of Crueller's store, Mr. Crueller himself waiting now patiently behind the counter for his money. The effort of raising his massive bulk out of the rocker to catch onto Lewis's coat caused a low grunt to escape from Shorter's throat.

"I know Tiny Raines never taught his son to go disrespectin' his elders that'a way."

"Excuse me, Mr. Shorter?"

He was relieved Shorter had released his coat. A streak of grime and oil shone against the dark wool where the old man's fingers had been. Lewis realized now that Shorter wasn't alone on the store's front porch. Jase Hinkins sat next to him in the other rocker, grizzled, and obviously besotted from the previous night's activities. In his trembling fingers Hinkins held a copy of the "Atlanta Constitution," the only newspaper available.

"I'm sorry," Lewis said. "My mind was elsewhere. I didn't catch what you were saying."

"I know where yore mind was, boy," Dag Shorter grunted, his head tilted down the street toward the church where Reverend Hewitt preached come Sunday. "But what I was sayin' was, will ye be leaving soon for the fightin'?"

"What fighting would that be, Mr. Shorter?"

"Well goddammit boy, don't you folks out by the Swamp keep up with national e-vents a-tall? 'What fightin'?' Fightin' them goddam Yankees and that infernal Abe Lincoln what wants to take our niggers away is what fightin' I'm talking about."

"That's right Mr. Raines," Jase Hinkins spoke up. Lewis was grateful for the intrusion. Further speaking on Shorter's part seemed liable to lead to an attack of apoplexy, judging by the redness of the old man's face and the way his breath came short and gasping the longer he went on.

"Says right here in last week's paper," Jase continued. "Our fair state of Georgia done gone and seceded from the Union. Yes sir. Says it right here." The red-eyed man rattled the newspaper in Lewis's direction as if Lewis, who had said nothing, might doubt him. "Says right here," Jase Hinkins repeated, to drive his point home.

"Well, Mr. Shorter, Mr. Hinkins, I believe that's government business," Lewis told the two men. He wasn't real sure how to take this piece of news. If it weren't for the newspaper in Jase Hinkins's trembling hands, Lewis wouldn't have believed either one of the two old-timers. "Best left to our elected men in the state legislature, I'm sure. And the Governor." He pushed by the men on the porch politely to open the door of Crueller's store. "Not my concern, I don't imagine."

Dag Shorter erupted into a fit of loud laughter so sudden and violent Lewis worried that the quaking of the big man's body in the rocking chair might send him flying off the porch.

"None of my concern, he says." Shorter stopped the violent laughter as suddenly as he had begun to crook a sober finger at Lewis in the doorway. "When them Yankee's come looting and killing and letting them niggers go raping your momma and sister, you just might reconsider what is your concern and what ain't."

These were extraordinary things Dag Shorter spoke of, ones Lewis's mind couldn't fathom. White American men waging death and destruction on their fellow Americans? And not only that, but allowing black men to commit the acts of depravity the old man on the porch predicted? Not being able to comprehend the depth of the issues, Lewis tipped his hat to them, finished his business in the store, and escaped to the sanctuary of the Hewitts. He hoped he wouldn't find the same sort of disturbing talk there.

As he snapped the reins to the mare's rump and the wagon started down the street, an image of Dawson came suddenly into his thoughts. Dawson, the son of the Hewitts's house Negro, Abraham, was a big strapping black man perhaps ten years older than Lewis. It was Dawson's coal-black arms that Lewis suddenly imagined wrapping Mamie up in his. But doing what? he asked himself. Lewis couldn't stand taking it any further, the cold chill ripping down his spine enough to bring him back to the reality of the dusty main street of Pendleton, the safety of the parsonage looming ahead, and the friendly spire of Reverend Hewitt's church next to the house.

***

February passed, March came on, and Lewis, tired of the continued cool weather, hoped spring was not far away. Then the bitter cold *did* ease off, and as it could in that part of Georgia there came several days when the sun had risen in an endless clear sky. No clouds were present to break the intensity of the light streaming in the fields of the Raines property and the men sweated profusely as they worked. The un-seasonable heat was such that one morning, Dawes mentioned to his brother, "Damn, Edwin, you said that almanac called for an early spring. Seems to me it was summer that it meant." But the hot days didn't last long and though the hard cold was gone, it wasn't quite spring yet. The weather stayed perfect for working in the fields, and for the hunting of turkeys along the edges of the pine stands at dawn.

The subject of war didn't come up and Lewis had put it well from his mind. It resurrected once again a few weeks after his trip to town — a resurrection that occurred one night in late March over dinner at Jared Dancy's house.

Sitting at the Dancy dinner table that night, laden with its complement of gleaming crystal, sparkling china, silver cutlery, and lily-white tablecloth, Lewis was reminded again that Jared Dancy was the wealthiest man in Ware County. The Dancy plantation, as Chandler Dancy, the family patriarch, was eager to inform visitors spread out over ten thousand acres of prime farming and grazing land. Tobacco, corn, crab-grass hay, and sweet potatoes for hogs were the staple of the plantation. Unlike the Raines, though, the Dancys also farmed cotton. With the cotton came slaves—and with both, great wealth. It wasn't long before Chandler and his family rose in status above his neighbors. Though the Dancys came from the same humble beginnings as the Raines, Mixons, and Hewitts, Chandler Dancy had no problems in adapting to his new situation. He had named his plantation Blackshear Landing and as he grew wealthy and old, he relished his status of gentleman planter. He greatly enjoyed the rewards of being considered the man who grew the best Sea Island cotton in the state of Georgia, if not the entire South. Equally evident to Lewis, Jared reaped the rewards of both prestige and money with little effort on his part.

Chandler Dancy died suddenly in the fall of 1856, the result of a minor scandal in Atlanta concerning a gambling debt and the senior Dancy's assertions that the debt occurred because of marked cards and was therefore not binding. As Dawes Raines cheerfully observed on the Friday evening following the receipt of this interesting news, Chandler might have won his case had he been better with dueling pistols. Two years later Jared began paying court to Cordelia Raines. Whether or not this had anything to do with Chandler Dancy's death, Lewis didn't know. What he didn't understand was why his sister put up with the man's suit, it being common knowledge in Ware County that the younger Dancy was much the same as his father, interested more in cards and strong drink than anything else life had to offer.

Because of the holdings of Edwin Raines, his wartime fame, and good name in Ware County, Cordelia was certainly a proper match for the heir of Blackshear Landings according to Ella Raines. Lewis sat in the corner of the living room by the fire pretending to read the book *Uncle Tom's Cabin*, a work that his mother had asked him to read because, as she said, "It sure seems to be causing quite a stir around here." What his parents were talking about at the time was much more interesting than the actions of Simon Legree.

"Besides," Ella said. "The girl loves him."

"Well," Edwin Raines growled. "That makes her a damn fool, then."

"Perhaps," Lewis's mother said in those soothing tones Lewis was familiar with her using whenever she needed to press a point with her husband. "Fool, or not, that doesn't change how she feels about Jared."

Despite Edwin's further argument that sooner or later the scoundrel would break Cordelia's heart, he gave in to the pressure exerted on him by his wife and daughter. On a beautiful June afternoon at Blackshear Landing, with nary a cloud in the sky and Reverend Hewitt's warning to "let no man tear asunder" ringing out beneath that blue sky, Jared Dancy was wedded to Cordelia Raines. Edwin lost a daughter, but gained a son, feeling ill-used in the bargain all the way around— sentiments that he sourly expressed to his son and two brothers as they gathered around the punch bowl after the ceremony to drink to the union.

Now, three years later, over dessert and before the men retreated to the parlor for cigars and brandy, Jared Dancy brought up the question: Would there, or would there not be, war?

"The Yankees should know we're going to fight to protect our rights under the Constitution. Protect our homelands. But they keep pushing us into a corner."

Dancy's fair skin, made fairer by the shock of red hair falling down his forehead, seemed flushed in the light of the chandelier above the big table in the dining room. The candles overhead reflected off the china and glassware into his eyes, giving him a slightly crazed look, Lewis thought, as he watched his brother-in-law swallow the last bite of apple pie on the plate before him.

"And yet," he continued, after washing down the pie with a gulp of coffee. "They keep telling us that we cannot leave the Union. That there will be serious consequences. Hell yes, I say. Hell yes there will be consequences!"

"Calm yourself, Jared." Cordelia, seated next to her husband at the head of the massive table, her own face and arms grown pale from a life no longer lived in the hard fields and housework of the Raines farm. "Do we really have to talk about this now?"

She was smiling, but it was forced. Lewis could see the strain of it in his sister's eyes as she glanced around the table at her family. Her once lustrous black hair had faded since becoming Dancy's wife. From the soft living, was Lewis's guess. From being mistress of the large plantation. And from the recent miscarriage, the second in as many years. Not only was her hair fading, she was going gray around the temples. With a start he realized his sister was growing older. Apparently much older than he was, though only two years separated them in age.

"Well, sir," Edwin Raines said from the other end of the table, his face ruddy and alive in the light of the chandelier. "You'll have your war, no doubt, and soon enough. Then you folks can settle your differences with Mr. Lincoln once and for all."

Like his sister, Lewis's father smiled. Unlike her, he appeared perfectly at ease in his broadcloth jacket and white Sea Island cotton shirt. Called his "Sunday Best," they were the only jacket and white shirt Edwin owned.

"My war? It'll be your war, too, Mr. Raines," Dancy said as he rang the little bell by his place set for the house man to come clear the table. "Make no mistake about that."

"Oh no. Not my war at all. There's no stake in it for me. Freedom to own slaves or not, it's all the same as far as I'm concerned. The Negroes have been a curse on us in the South for long enough."

His father's words reminded Lewis of when, as a boy and not yet five years old, he had seen Negroes for the first time. "Look, Daddy," he had said as he rode in the wagon with his father past The Landings on their way to Ruskin for supplies. "Look Daddy," he had implored again, pointing at the black people bent over the cotton growing up from Chandler Dancy's lands. It was all new and the boy needed an explanation. Needed to know who these people were that were working so hard. The women, all of them in plain muslin dresses, colorful scarves hiding their hair, and dark features from the sun. The men in loose pants, made of cotton as well, most of them shirtless, and the boy wondering at how the black skin of these men could glisten so in the sunlight. And the boy, unaware that his first request had been lost to his father's ears in the clatter of the harness and the wagon wheels, tugged at his father's arm and said one more time, "Look, Daddy."

"Negroes, son," his father answered, without looking. "Niggers, as some call them. Either way you say it they're still slaves." Edwin Raines turned to look at the boy. "Some folks like to live, boy, with a plentitude of possessions, alive, or not."

The words answered the boy's questions and staring into his father's grey eyes steady on the road ahead, the boy knew not to ask again. Knew enough of the man by then to accept what his father said. He didn't understand; supposed he might when he was older, say like his Uncle Dawes, who seemed to know everything. It was a knowledge the boy was fairly certain his father possessed, even if it wasn't always forthcoming. This suspicion was neither confirmed, nor made less confusing by what his father said next.

"But that ain't our way, son. Not the way any Raines I ever knew of looked at the world. A good roof over our heads, food on the table, and faith in the Lord, that's our way, son. The way I was taught. And don't you ever forget it."

That day had been a long time back, Lewis thought as he sat at the Dancy dinner table. And yet, the Negroes were still there and his father still felt the same.

"It's past time to set them free and rid ourselves of it," Edwin said then, as if to underscore what Lewis had been thinking of.

"That's dangerous talk, sir."

"Is it?"

Lewis guessed that everyone at the table felt the sudden chill in the room, saw how both men's eyes narrowed now at one another across the distance of the white linen tablecloth. But Dancy, and to his credit, forged ahead.

"It is, sir. You might ask Tom Lee over in Pierce County about what that sort of talking did for him. Except that he's dead. Someone came along one night and burned him and his family off their farm. Hung poor Tom from the oak tree in his front yard after he was heard spouting off in a similar way."

Lewis noticed the satisfied look coming over his brother-in-law's features as he related this gruesome tale; wondered, as well, how much more in detail the happenings of that terrible evening Dancy might have witnessed firsthand.

"Spouting off? Is that what you think I'm doing?"

"No, sir, I don't."

Now it was Lewis's turn to feel satisfied by the hard tone in his father's voice and the chastened look spreading across Dancy's face.

"They'll play hell trying to do that sort of thing to a Raines. I can guarantee you that, sir."

"Yes, sir, I believe you can." Knowledge of Lewis's father's skill with knife, tomahawk, and pistol was written all over Jared Dancy's face as he echoed Edwin Raines's words, "Yes sir, I'm sure you *can* make that guarantee."

Jared looked around the table for confirmation of his opinion or just to break away from the grey eyes held steady on his?

"Well, that's enough of that sort of talk for one night." Edwin pushed away from the table and stood up. "I believe a cigar and some of your late father's fine brandy are in order after such an excellent meal, Jared. Wouldn't you agree?"

"Yes, I most certainly would."

As always, Lewis was amazed at how his father seemed to be many men in one: hard-working farmer, doting father, loving husband to an always ailing wife, fierce warrior, and when necessary, a gentleman in society. All qualities Lewis admired, as well as wonder if someday they might be a part of his makeup, too.

"We'll miss you, though, Jared." Edwin stopped at the parlor door and turned to his host. "When the war comes."

"Miss me, sir? I don't understand." The innocent questioning in Jared Dancy's eyes was astonishing to Lewis. He was no scholar or serious student of man and his ways, but he still knew what his father was getting at. "Am I going somewhere?"

"No, I guess not," Edwin answered his son-in-law. There was no more talk of war that night.

Rumors all that month of April—of the newly formed Confederacy of Southern States and of young men leaving to join militias to defend their "country" — reached even the remote Raines's farm. To all of these Edwin Raines and his two brothers made no comment other than that they wished the young men "good luck."

On the day the news of Sumter came, Edwin and his son were busy preparing the front section by the hog pens, turning the soil up and getting it ready for sweet potatoes. The almanac's prediction of an early spring had been proven correct, so much so that Edwin worried aloud that they might not get the tubers and other seeds in the ground in time. Lewis wished the almanac had gone on to say how that early spring was going to be short lived; that summer would follow hard and fast on its heels. For the last three weeks the sun had borne down relentlessly on the men in the fields and the lack of cloud cover in the bright skies added to the men's misery as they worked. The red clay seemed to reflect the worst of the sun's heat back at them until by the end of the day Lewis felt as hard-baked as the soil he had been working. The only relief to be found was in the noonday break and the bucket of cool spring water kept ready in the shade of an oak tree on the edge of the field.

Lewis was in the process of putting a dipperful of water to his lips when he heard the shouting of a man coming from the woods on the back side of the house. The man burst into view, coming out of the pines and scraggly oaks, spurring the horse carrying him across the clearing toward the Raines house. Lewis saw his mother come out on the front porch, waving towards her men. In almost the same instant as Ella Raines lifted her arm to wave, the man jerked hard on the reins, turning the horse in the direction of Lewis and his father in the field.

As the rider drew closer, Lewis saw that it was John Dixon, one of the many young men of the Ruskin Dixons who was also a distant relative. He was coming hard, his face lathered with sweat like that of the horse's when he reined up in front of them. "It's war I tell ye," he yelled out. "By God we're at war!"

He dismounted, eagerly accepting the dipper of water Edwin Raines offered. Once regaining his breath, John Dixon explained himself. "We blew that fort to smithereens, sir," he said before gulping down another long drink of the spring water. "Forced 'em Yankee soldiers to surrender lest they get blown to pieces with it."

"Who are the 'we' you are speaking of?"

The look on his father's face was like the one that crossed it whenever his children did something not to his liking.

When his father lifted his hat back from his head and ran the cloth across his brow, Lewis saw that his father's hair had thinned so much that he was practically bald, the skin of his exposed skull glistening from the sweat in the noon sun. Ella Raines would soon be ringing the outside bell by the front door, Lewis thought, calling them all in for dinner. He was very hungry from the morning's work. The cold biscuits and ham and redeye gravy would go a long way toward alleviating that hunger. But when his father spoke again Lewis knew there'd be no eating yet, that the hunger would have to wait until John Dixon answered the question put to him.

"Slow down a minute, son, and tell me. Who are the 'we' that did all this fort busting business? South Carolina has a force capable of defying the Federal Government? Under whose command and by what authority?"

"Why, it was P.T. Beauregard, sir, leading the troops." The young Dixon seemed taken aback. "By the authority of the governor of South Carolina, I imagine." Judging by the expression on his face, Lewis saw his cousin assumed this part of the story to be common knowledge. "The state militia up there showed 'em Yankees all right. Showed 'em good that the South ain't gonna be under Lincoln's goddamn thumb no more. No sir. And pardon my language, sir."

Edwin Raines put his hat back on and turned to the house where his wife still stood on the front porch. She was a faint figure in the gingham dress she wore for housework, shimmering in the heat rising up from the ground before the house.

"It's a damnable business, then," Edwin Raines said. As if in agreement, two crows hidden somewhere in the maze of oaks and scraggly pines called out to one another in their mocking way. Lewis stared at his father as the young Dixon boy remounted his horse. Having heard the boy's news, Lewis saw that it was time for him to ride on to the next farm, to Pendleton and beyond, until the word was spread to all.

"A damnable business is all I can say," Edwin repeated as his wife rang the dinner bell again, the clanging tones peeling across the field to the hungry men. "Care to stay for a bite to eat?" Edwin said, as if suddenly remembering his manners. "Before you head on, son?"

"I thank ye kindly, sir but I must get goin', I reckon. And beggin' your pardon, sir, but you're wrong."

"Wrong? About what?"

"'Bout it being a 'damnable business', sir." Dixon put a finger to the brim of his hat in respect for his older relative before putting the spur to his horse and heading on. "It ain't damnable at all, sir. It's war."

***

When Uncle Dawes told him he was thinking about heading off "to see what all the fuss is 'bout," Lewis knew that when his uncle left he'd be riding along with him.

"Besides," Uncle Dawes continued, "I could use me a break from all these durn chores around here. What 'bout you, boy? Think ye might like a little respite from these endless labors your daddy's always got us doing?"

The two men were shoring up a section of the hog pen where one of the big sows had managed to dig her way out, in the process creating the potential for the entire pen to collapse. It was just another of what apparently his Uncle Dawes considered to be the endless work of a farm, the only life Lewis had known since he first drew breath. But something rang true inside of him when his uncle asked about the "respite." Something he hadn't known one way or the other until right then when it was plain as the nose on his face. That yes, he could use a little respite. Between the uncertainty of Mamie Hewitt, and what may, or may not happen with her, and the unknown excitement of the distant war, his life was in an uproar. One that was threatening to consume him. On that hot morning Lewis suddenly wanted to see what lay beyond Pendleton, and Atlanta. The furthest north, or west, he had traveled so far in his young life. And if he had to run the risk of being shot to find out, well then, so be it.

"I guess, Uncle Dawes," he answered. "But do ye think the hogs'll get along without us?"

"Well now, boy, if I didn't know ye better I'd think ye just made a joke." Dawes's face cracked in a wide grin as he leaned back against the fence post he was holding upright while Lewis shoveled mud around the bottom. "I didn't know a serious lad like yourself to be capable of such a thing." The older man looked at the pigs rooting happily away on the far side of the pen. "But to answer your question, nephew o' mine, I'd say, yes. I imagine them porkers'll get along jus' fine in our absence."

"What about my father?" And there was no jesting when Lewis asked this question, the seriousness of it felt in the set of his teeth as he shoveled the last spade of mud. "And my mother?" he added. "They won't like it. Neither one of them."

"No. No, they won't." Dawes let go of the post and with an agility that always surprised his nephew, jumped clean of the fence and pen in one swift movement, to stand—as if by magic—on the other side of the fence laughing. "Mebbe I'd best remind your father of how it was when him and I took off to fight Indians with Ol' Hickory and how our daddy went on 'bout it. That old man of ours like to bust a gut and then some. But he seen it was useless after a bit. Resigned himself to getting some of the neighbor kids not old enough to fight to come help him out around the spread. Your daddy'll do the same."

Dawes opened the gate of the pen for Lewis, clapping the boy on the shoulder as together they walked toward the pump on the far side of the cabin.

"Them were some days, boy. Yessir, I need to remind old hardass Ed of that. Yessir, I do."

"Are we really going, Uncle Dawes?"

"I'm thinkin' 'bout it, boy. Thinkin' hard 'bout it fer sure."

***

Hardly a month after the Dixon boy—the Ruskin Dixons, mind you, he could hear his mother correcting him—rode up to him and his pa working in the fields to give them the news about Sumter, Dawes trotted into the front yard on Sunday. Dawes was dressed in worn buckskins, canvas field duster, a brace of pistols slung across the saddle horn, musket in the scabbard by his right thigh, and his eyes alive with eagerness beneath the rugged beaver pelt hat atop his head. It was clearly evident Dawes Raines wasn't on his way to church that morning, and it was probably clear to Edwin Raines that his son was about to go with him.

Of course, any doubts Lewis's father might have held were dispelled as soon as Dawes had called out, "C'mon boy. If you're a-goin' with me let's get. We're burning daylight here, son."

The remembrance of that morning stayed fresh in Lewis' mind for a long time: of his Uncle Dawes waiting for him in the dusty front yard and his father's scruffy pointer crawling out from beneath the house to sniff at the horse's hooves. He thought of Edwin Raines stepping out into the sunlight, hatless, face and arms damp from the brief scrubbing up he had done after killing a chicken for the Sunday meal. Still fresh in Lewis's mind was Ella Raines's voice asking her husband, "Why didn't you tell me Dawes was coming for dinner?" He remembered the leather bag containing his two other clean shirts, another pair of pants, two pairs of wool socks, the Bible his father gave him when he was learning to read, a small daguerreotype of Mamie Hewitt, and pretty much everything else he could think of he might want from home when he went off to war.

The packing had all been carefully thought out beforehand, the only thing left out of his planning was how he was going to tell his mother and father he was off to fight for his new country, the Confederate States of America. But now that Uncle Dawes was waiting impatiently out in front of the house, the time for careful planning had passed. Only the straight up telling of it remained. That, and getting on his horse, and riding out.

"What's all this about, Dawes?"

Edwin reached out to shake the hand his brother offered and as Lewis came out of the house to get his horse, he saw how the two men seemed reluctant to let go of one another's hands.

"Where are you and my son off to?"

"Well hell, Ed, I figured the boy told ye by this time."

"Lewis has told me nothing."

"Then we best leave it to him now, Ed."

"Surely you're not planning to take my boy off to that trouble of the planters?"

"Like I said, Ed. Best leave it for the boy."

Of course, there could be no doubt in Edwin Raines's head of Dawes's intentions when Lewis came around to the front of the house leading the pale gelding saddled up and ready to go.

His father offered Lewis the old Kentucky long rifle he had used in the Indian Wars, along with a Colt Dragoon pistol a fellow farmer had bartered with three years back for a season's worth of crab-grass hay. Lewis didn't know whether to take the gun or not—was mainly aware instead, of the strangeness in the warm air and the impatience of the gelding beneath him, who was always anxious to go. He looked to Uncle Dawes for help. But seeing nothing in his uncle's eyes to guide a decision one way or the other, Lewis Raines went with his gut.

"You'll be needing this rifle, sir," Lewis handed the finely crafted weapon back to his father, "come varmint hunting time. I reckon the army will give me one to use." He went to hand the pistol back as well, then thinking better of it, strapped the worn leather belt and holster containing the gun around his waist. "I'll take the pistol, though, sir. With your permission." Lewis was grinning as he continued, "I've had my eye on this beauty for some time now."

It was the first time since Dawes had ridden into the yard that morning that Edwin Raines smiled.

"I've seen that eye, son," and father and son laughed.

"You take care of my son, Dawes." Smile and laughter were gone from Edwin Raines as he turned to his brother. "He's a fine boy, fine man, really. I'll need him to be in one piece when this foolishness is done."

"I'll do what I can, Ed."

Dawes was the only man Lewis had ever known to call Edwin Raines "Ed," a name that just didn't suit the man Lewis knew as his father and something that Dawes was evidently well aware of.

"Ye might want to petition them Yankees some, though, Ed. Seeing as how they'll be the ones doin' the shooting at us."

"This is no time for your jokes, Dawes Raines."

His mother's voice, though cracking a little with the effort, was stronger than Lewis thought possible since she had been down the past week with another of her "attacks." Yet she stood now on the front porch, holding onto one of the three wooden posts supporting the overhanging roof, glaring at the three men. Her dress hung loosely from her narrow shoulders and wisps of thinning gray hair slipped free from the bun she had hastily pinned up before coming outside.

"And I'm petitioning you, Dawes," Ella Raines continued. She stepped forward as if to get closer to the man she was affronting but stopped and held onto the wood post harder instead. "It was you who talked my son into this and it's you who'd best bring him back."

"Now, Ella," Dawes began, but Edwin cut him off.

"You boys get going now. Savannah's a far enough piece as it is without you wasting any more time here."

"Yes sir," the two mounted men answered in unison and that was the last Lewis had seen of his parents in two years. He couldn't forget the look on his father's face as he went to slap the rump of the gelding and hollered, "Giddap, now." Nor the way his mother seemed to waver for a moment on the porch as if the wooden column she held onto for dear life were no longer there. The way his hat felt in his hand as he lifted it jauntily from his head to wave a courageous farewell to his family, his spurs goading the gelding along. The wet air of the summer morning seemed to break open for them as the horse broke into a gallop to catch up with Dawes.

***

His Uncle Dawes perished early in the war, less than a year after Lewis and he went to sign up at the parade grounds up in Savannah. Dawes' experience fighting Indians with Andy Jackson had earned him a position in the new Confederate army as a scout, not to mention the fact that he flat refused to give up his horse and become a foot soldier. The young officer in charge of the recruiting suggested Dawes might be more comfortable joining the cavalry. This lieutenant sat nervously at a rickety table set on the lawn, a thick ledger book open on the table in front of him where he recorded each man's basic vitals. Every so often the officer would lift his head from the book to look out past the man answering his questions, at the sea of eager men stretching out beyond the edges of the canopy erected for a makeshift recruiting station.

"Sir," the lieutenant repeated. "I said, why don't you join the cavalry, then. If you're so attached to your horse."

"Well, of course, as ye say, boy, I'm attached to my horse," Dawes exclaimed, his voice rising loud and clear over the general commotion on the parade grounds. "That don't mean I'm a-going to join no cavalry. I came to fight. Not prance around waving a saber and wearing a sash and looking good for the ladies. Not, mind ye," and his voice dropped to a loud conspiratorial whisper as he leaned in toward the young officer behind the desk, "I have anything against looking fine for the womenfolk. But war is serious business, son." He stood up tall then, his voice even louder than before. "Yessir, war is serious business."

The men in line stretching out beyond the station roared out their approval at Dawes's loud assessment. The young lieutenant had to wait for the loud yells and clapping to quiet down before he could speak.

"Now see here sir, we are all here for the same reason: to defend our homeland from those who would usurp her sovereignty."

"I don't know about that," Dawes replied. "Like I said before, I just came to fight."

"The South needs all of her sons for just that purpose, sir."

"Son of the South, is it?" Dawes turned to the men behind him and Lewis could see on his face the fun he was having with the young officer. All of it brought forth a wide smile so big and wide across Dawe's weathered face that it threatened to split his features open. "Hell, lad I'm old enough to be her father and ye want me to go riding cavalry for her? I'm liable to get myself killed doin' that."

This was too much for the crowd of rough men and boys waiting to put their names, or X's, down in the ledger book held open on the table before the lieutenant. The sudden loud burst of laughter and rude yells echoed back and forth across the parade grounds from the red brick walls of the tanneries to other factories on the waterfront. Even up amongst the carriages thronging the sidewalks around the grounds, where the young dandies of the town stood and watched, Lewis could see the occasional lady put a hand to her face, perhaps to stifle a giggle. Lewis wished very much then that his father could be there, to see the effect his brother had on these people. It would have brought a smile to that old man's face, too, maybe enough to erase the sadness that day his brother left for war and took one of his sons with him.

By this time two officers at a similar station on the far end of the parade grounds had become aware of the commotion. Putting down what they had been doing, they came to the aid of their beleaguered fellow. "Come along you men," one of these officers said as he came striding up in business-like steps, sword drawn, his face tight around a dark bushy mustache. "We don't have time for this sort of foolishness. Not when the Yankees are breathin' hard down our necks like they are. Get back in line immediately. All of you." To punctuate the fact that he meant what he said, he and the other officer began prodding at the men with the tips of their drawn swords. Grumbling, the men did as they were bid.

Except for Dawes, who upon seeing his fun had come to an end, slapped his faded hat back on his head and turned toward his horse waiting patiently at the hitching post.

"And where do you think you are going sir?" the dark browed officer called out.

"Why hell, man," Dawes answered over his shoulder. "I just came to see what all the fuss was about with this war of yours. Now that I seen," and Dawes paused for a moment before continuing, "I have to tell ye, it don't look like much. Certainly nothin' like the fun I had with Andy Jackson back in '38. But hell, like I told ye, I just came to see. Now I'm goin' home."

In a move Lewis had seen more than once before, Dawes broke into a mad run for his horse, stopping briefly to snatch the reins from the post before jumping over the haunches, into the saddle, and with one quick spur to the horse's sides, galloped out onto the parade grounds.

"Yes sir, boys," he addressed the crowd of astonished men, "I do believe I've seen all I need to see and I'll be on my way."

Oh yes, Lewis thought, as he clapped and cheered along with the others for his uncle. Dawes certainly made a grand sight as he waved the worn hat over his head once or twice, galloping the horse in a wild circle around the edges of the parade grounds.

***

A year later Dawes was dead, shot down at the battle of Shiloh and by his own side. For though he never formally joined the Confederate Army, he rode off to the northwest. Of course, in war, as Lewis came to learn well, nothing is as ever simple as that, other than a sudden death. But the chain of events leading up to Dawes's end in the pine woods of Tennessee began with his actions on the parade ground in Savannah, a chain furthered along by the sudden appearance of another officer on the field. This officer was of high rank, judging by the grandeur of the new uniform he wore, the saber he carried, and the fine-looking quarter horse he rode that pranced and side-stepped across the grounds. A hush fell over the crowd when this officer rode out towards Dawes and his mad careening gallop around the field. Suspense suddenly hung heavy in the air, a feeling rising from the silent men that reminded Lewis of those dew-wet summer mornings of his childhood when anything seemed possible if he could only be patient enough. Even Dawes must have felt it, Lewis decided later, when recalling the events of the day, for he, too, brought his horse to a slow trot. Then the officer was trotting alongside him, the two men conferring with one another with words no one could hear, lost as they were in the suspense of the moment and the sounds of the factories, the boats' horns, the cries of sea birds wheeling for food.

At least, that was how Lewis remembered it that night, sitting alone in his Army tent by the water. Nothing of what Dawes and the fine-looking officer had to say to one another could be heard, but it must have been good, and important, for Dawes rode off with that officer and Lewis never saw him again. He learned of his death from the letter his father wrote to inform him. Dawes was dead. Edwin Raines went on to convey how his brother had been killed by a musket ball in the back fired by Confederate pickets. Apparently, Dawes had forgotten the password and, in his haste to get word back to General Johnston, he attempted to overrun the pickets. Before he died Dawes managed to tell the man who shot him that the Yankees were coming, that he needed to let the General know that they were coming fast with a surprise attack. What Dawes didn't know, and the rest of the Confederate soldiers still sleeping in their tents would find out, was that the Yankees were creeping even now through the pines to descend upon the just rising southern troops.

Your mother would have written this to you, son," the letter concluded, *"but her sadness is much too great at this time. I have never been good with the pen and hope that you will be able to read this. Just know that both your mother and I pray fervently for your safe return. God willing, this war will soon be over, and any day after that we will see you coming up the road towards home. The place has changed some since you left. I had to let the far fields go fallow because of lack of healthy hands to work them. It will be just you and me to put them ready again for planting when you return. I am hopeful that, again, with the Lord's help, we will be up to the task.*

I look very much forward to the time when I will again see your face. Not only would that do me much good, I am sure it would be more than enough to bring your mother past this last obstacle in her path to good health. Take care of yourself, son, and do not expose yourself to more danger than you have to. I do not believe that I could bear the loss of another.

Your loving father,
Edwin Raines.

"A damnable business?" as Edwin Raines had said. Though Lewis Raines hadn't known the answer then, he surely did now as he waited atop the ridge while July morning turned into July afternoon. And even after telling both his father and mother he'd never be a part of it, here he was, two years later, ready and willing to unleash death and destruction on an enemy waiting across the lovely grass meadow spreading out below the ridge and up on the rocky hills beyond.

God yes, he thought, the meager lunch of hardtack and hot chicory coffee over and his stomach calling for more, whether from real hunger or just nerves, he was never sure when battle loomed. *God yes that day seemed more than a lifetime ago.*

He didn't want to leave the coolness of the shade the oaks provided. Looking back toward the limbers, he saw the horses and one mule grazing contentedly on the grass. He wondered if the animals felt the same, wondered if they knew there was reasonable doubt as to the length of time left for any of them. No, he decided. That was ridiculous. Beasts of burden were all they were, happy for the moment there was still some grass. Happy to be free of the chafing harnesses and hurried men prodding them along.

Something moving to the left of the battery caught his eye. It proved to be Captain Harker coming back up the line. For most of the morning, except for the sporadic firing of the men on the skirmish lines and occasional burst from an enemy field piece, the valley had been quiet. Now, coming along the line with Captain Harker, Lewis could hear the muffled sounds of musket and small arms fire on the far end of the Confederate position. With a start he realized some kind of fight had been raging there all that morning, a battle kept from his consciousness, caught up as he had been in daydreaming of how his life had once been. He didn't know what surprised him more, the battle he hadn't been aware of, or how lost he had been in the past.

"It's pushing one o'clock, Lieutenant. If not later."

Captain Harker reined up in front of Raines and the rest of the battery. The afternoon sunlight, having found a gap in the gray clouds, shone with an intensity that almost obliterated the captain's features in its glare.

"Should be starting any time now."

"We're ready, sir."

"Past ready, Cap'n," Sergeant Cuthbert added, as he came up behind Raines and snapped to attention.

"I know you are," Harker said. "At ease, Sergeant. Save your energies for the Whitworths today."

"Whitworth, sir," Lewis corrected him. "We lost the one at Chancellorsville. Blown to pieces along with Lieutenant Osgood. If you remember, sir."

"Beyond repair," Cuthbert jumped in. "A cryin' shame, too. Guess the Yankees are allowed a good shot on occasion."

"The *rare* occasion." The captain's eyes were alight as he shared the joke with the sergeant. "Hopefully, today won't be one of those occasions."

"Not if I have anything to say about it, sir."

Cuthbert spat another stream of brown juice on the ground. From need, or disgust for the loss of the cannon and for the Yankee gunners who destroyed it? Lewis decided it was both.

The light hardened in the captain's eyes. "And I *do* remember, Lieutenant. Both the loss of the Whitworth *and* Lieutenant Osgood. He was a good man, the lieutenant. A very good man.

"So we have only the three guns, now, Captain," Lewis said, pointing with one hand at his battery in the shade of the oak trees. He didn't want to think of Osgood's death, the taste of gunpowder, lead, the bits of bone and flesh he had spat from his mouth after the explosion of the Whitworth. It was not the time to be thinking of that now. "Two Napoleons and the remaining Whitworth," he continued. "I was told the lost gun would be replaced but it hasn't been done."

"No, I expect it hasn't," The Captain said. "This war keeps on much longer not much of anything will be replaced."

"If Johnny Rebs grew on trees like them Goddam Yankees seems to, we'd a won this war a long time ago." Cuthbert spat out the entire wad of tobacco this time, the brown lump of chewed mass looking like an animal dropping in the sparse grass at the sergeant's feet. "But we'll do fine with what we have. Don't you worry about that, Captain."

"Yes." The Captain loosened his grip on the reins to free his horse to graze. "I would expect nothing less. I'm sure those men below would agree with me, too. Make sure you remember how they're the ones depending on you. More so than me."

Captain Harker waved a gloved hand toward the peach orchard and the road below the ridge. Lewis hadn't noticed, but the troops he had seen there earlier had been reinforced. A pale mass of gray men lay prone on the grass, taking advantage of the shade offered by the oaks, peach, and scruff apple trees rising on the edge of the valley. The sounds from the far end in the other direction of the line, where the battle had been raging earlier, were now silent.

"Hell," the captain continued, his eyes still on the troops below, "the entire South depends on what we do here today, I reckon."

"It's been a long time, Lieutenant," the captain continued. "Too damned long. I was with General Jackson at First Manassas back when this all started. What a glorious day that was, when we still believed the war would be just a matter of weeks. Never thought we could be so wrong. Maybe today, with the grace of God, we'll put an end to it."

"Yes, sir."

To the north of the battery and the troops massed below came the blasts of two cannons. Napoleon ten-pounders from the sound of them, Lewis felt certain. The Napoleons were ancient but effective cannons. He would gladly have traded the two in his battery, though, for Parrott guns or Whitworth rifles. Puffs of smoke from fired cannons drifted down from the ridge, suspended briefly above the valley before a breeze came up and carried them away, and pleasant musings on cannons Lewis didn't have became of no importance.

"Well then, Lieutenant," Captain Harker said, "it begins."

The Napoleons and the Whitworth were already primed and loaded. As the captain rode off down the line Lewis gave the order to fire. The ground-shaking roar of the cannons took him by surprise, almost took him to his knees. But as he straightened up again he realized it hadn't been the sound of the three guns of his battery that had been so shattering, but the noise made by all one hundred seventy Confederate cannons blasting their deadly loads at the same time. The roar reverberated off the ridges surrounding the valley, a thick pall of black powder smoke hung over the field like the brimstone of Judgment Day the Primitive Baptist preacher at home spoke of on Sunday mornings back home.

Then he was back in command of the battery, barking out orders to Cuthbert, Boggess, and Zink to swab the cannons, reload, and be ready at his command to fire. The unit had learned well over battle-hardened time to function as one and without instruction, but he yelled the orders, anyway. Cuthbert had the breech of the Whitworth open, wisps of spent gunpowder smoke drifting out of the open slot. Taking the shell and charge Lewis handed him, he put them in the breech and slammed the chamber shut. Boggess, having swabbed the rifled barrel of the Whitworth clean, was with Dixon and Zink on the two Napoleons, the five men of the battery doing the work of the standard eight without complaint.

There were no replacements for men lost. He counted out to himself, *one, two, three,* in an easy cadenced breath, the time, according to Captain Harker, necessary between each discharge to create a steady, rippling barrage from the Confederate lines. The battery commanders knew how every shot fired was important, given the limited ammunition left to them. The targets on the far ridge, Captain Harker had emphasized, and the rocky hills flanking that ridge, had to be destroyed. Failing that, at least severely damaged.

The battery fell into an easy rhythm, and Lewis was proud to see that though it may be difficult for the men doing the work of eight with only five, it was not impossible. The second hand of his tarnished pocket watch swept to twelve and Lewis, grateful for what he had that day, once again yelled, "Fire." The two Napoleons, one after the other, followed. Then it was quiet for a moment, the quick silence broken by the four guns of the unit thirty yards down the line.

"Lieutenant, sir," Cuthbert yelled above the noise of the cannons. "We're shootin' wide of the mark. Do ye see it?"

"You're right, Sergeant."

Lewis had seen it. Seen how the second round fired from the Whitworth had exploded in a puff of harmless grass and dirt twenty yards to the right of the Federal artillery placement that was the intended target.

"Swing the gun left and see if we can't put one in their laps."

"Yes, sir. To the left. But begging your pardon, sir. Only one? In their laps?"

"Aye, Sergeant. Just a tad. And yes, more than one for their laps. At your pleasure." Lewis watched for the next explosion, straining his eyes to see through the haze created by the humidity and the cannon smoke hanging over the valley. He couldn't be sure at first, but he thought he saw more than dirt fly up when the Whitworth's shell struck home. For sure he saw the startled jerk of a mule still harnessed to a limber just to the rear of the Federal battery. *Much better*, he thought. *We'll blow this battery to Kingdom Come and then turn on that hill to their left.* Lewis couldn't see them, but he felt certain Federal troops were massed beneath the cover the rocks afforded. If he was right, those men would be hard on any assault coming across the valley. Very hard.

We will do as the captain ordered. As General Longstreet had ordered Colonel Alexander. *Blow them all to Kingdom Come. And if not that, then make them wish we had. That is what we can do. What we will do.*

"Lieutenant, sir." Private Boggess interrupted his attempt to see the effect of his cannons. "Damn powder won't fire, sir. In either gun."

Boggess stood next to the first Napoleon, a look of disgust on his face. In the next moment Lewis heard the whistling sound of something heavy flying over their heads. Lewis and the private ducked instinctively as the Federal shell exploded in the rear, destroying a limber and the mule tethered next to it. The enemy was firing back. *A duel of the big guns*, Lewis thought as he waved exasperatedly at Boggess. *Ours against theirs and though outgunned, as usual, we'll just see.*

"There's dry powder in the remaining limbers, private. Avail yourself of it."

Boggess could be trying in the heat of battle, in need of orders, when another would have known the simple solution to the problem and done it. Boggess needed telling and Lewis needed Boggess just as he needed the others now that the battery was down by half. Federal shells were beginning to explode all around them. The returned fire from the enemy batteries spurred Boggess into action, and Lewis was glad to see that in just minutes both Napoleons had been loaded, fired, and loaded again.

The action of the batteries on the ridge firing in turn, one after the other lasted longer than any prolonged cannonade he had been a part of so far. Below the ridge, massed in the peach orchard and along the road, the men in gray awaited their turn to participate. With the Yankee cannons on the other side of the valley returning the fire, Lewis began to wonder if the Confederate guns were doing enough, that when those men below stepped out into formation they would be met with certain death and destruction.

Just focus on the job at hand, he told himself, trimming the fuse of a shell for the Whitworth. The last round fired hadn't been seen to explode. Shortening the fuse might solve the problem. Unless they were firing high and behind the enemy guns. More than a half hour now by his watch and the ammunition appeared to be holding. They would need some in reserve, though. To cover the charge. And God forbid, a retreat, if it came to that.

And still, no order to cease fire came. Lewis shoved his thoughts aside, handing the corrected shell to Cuthbert to put in the open breech of the Whitworth and slam home.

"They're payin' fer it now, Lieutenant," Private Zink called out.

But Lewis didn't hear him; a Federal shell had exploded in front of the Whitworth and suddenly he was thinking once more of Osgood. Of how he had wanted to comfort his dying friend that day when both the Whitworth and Osgood exploded into nothingness. But there wasn't any part of the man left living for Lewis to comfort. They had promised one another that if needed, the survivor would inform the other's family. Lewis had written that letter, imagining the looks on Osgood's Ma and Da as he called them, when they opened it in their house in London and found that their only son was dead. Osgood, the tall Englishman with his wispy blond hair, aquiline features. and quick blue eyes who could discuss the works of Victor Hugo and Nostradamus as easily as he could Stonewall Jackson's treatise on the uses of field artillery. Who had said to Lewis at Marye's Heights when they were blowing the Yankees to hell, "Isn't this smashing good fun?" Who at Chancellorsville that second day when the Yankees tried to flank Jackson's position had said, "I dare say, old boy, but that's not quite cricket, is it?" Osgood, who having crossed the ocean to assist the Southern effort and have a grand adventure in the process before settling quietly into the family's barrister firm, not only learned what the price of a grand adventure could be but paid it in full. *Now*, he supposed, *it will be left to the Captain to write that letter for me if I fall.*

"Yes sir,' Private Zink continued, "them Yankees are payin' top dollar now. Wouldn't you agree, Lieutenant?"

"I do, Private," Lewis answered after a while, the memories of Osgood put away, and his attention back to the task at hand. "That, I do."

He yanked the lanyard of the Whitworth, felt the recoil of the cannon against his leg. In the next instant the Napoleon Boggess and Zink were manning fired, and they switched to help Dixon on the other, and it too went off and then the guns of Lewis's battery fell silent again as the men rushed to reload, the others down the line firing and carrying on the fight.

How easy it would be, he thought. *To get lost in the constant of this great battle. To forget that life hasn't always been this way.*

Private Zink's voice carried out away from the now silent battery. "The bill's come due, now, you blue-bellied bastards. Past due." He laughed and Cuthbert, not knowing the joke but always capable of enjoying one, laughed with him.

Across the valley on the high ground where the Union army had taken position, everything he could see appeared to be in flames. Visible through the summer haze and cannon smoke, Lewis could make out blue-coated soldiers running about, trying to catch panicked horses and mules, other soldiers scuttling supply caissons to safety, and houses the Yankees had commandeered for headquarters, burning brightly in the hazy light of the day.

At least, that was what was visible to the naked eye. But when he brought out his field glass he was amazed to discover, that after nearly an hour of steady cannon fire, most of the Federal batteries were still intact. Lifting the glass higher to see beyond the gun placements he saw the proof of what he had worried about earlier. They had been firing high and past the targets all along. The pounding damage of the last hour was only to the Union rear. When the Confederate troops marched out into the open valley, they'd be at the mercy of the Yankee guns.

"Boggess," Lewis called out, "go find the Captain and tell him we're missing the mark. All of us are missing the targets."

"Sir?" It was no time for Boggess's act of confusion. "I can't be leaving this Nappy gun. Zink and Dixon can't han'le the two of them without me."

"Don't worry about the guns, private. Just do as I tell you."

"Yes sir."

Lewis watched Boggess's scarecrow-like figure set off through the hanging pall of gun smoke covering the ridge, down the line in the direction Captain Harker had ridden. He hoped Boggess wouldn't be too late. That there might still be time and ammunition left—after the proper adjustments were made—to inflict the damage necessary for the success of the charge. Surely, he wasn't the only battery commander who had seen the mistake? he thought. Colonel Alexander had to be aware of the situation. Had to be already issuing orders to set things right. The men massed below the ridge depended on this—the South depended on this. Yet the troops were moving now, forming up with their units, and the color bearers running to get into place, as General Pickett came riding up on his charger, golden curls waxed and falling from beneath the officer's hat. *Now? It was going to begin now?*

An unheard signal seemed to pass along the line, the last of the cannons fired and the others fell silent, the only sounds left to be heard were that of men shouldering arms, buckling on sabers, and fixing bayonets. Then the sounds of the drum and fife corps marching out of the peach orchard, followed by what looked to be the entire Confederate Army.

***

It rained hard that night, stopped at dawn, then came on again just before noon and stayed, a sheeting rain that quickly turned the ground into a sodden mess. Gully-washers flowing off the hills and ridgelines flooded the road south toward the Potomac River, delaying the start of the wagon train carrying the wounded away from that place. It was hard enough for the living on the road south, with the mud and the rain and the memories of what had happened on the field of battle just a day earlier. But adding to the misery were the cries of the wounded and dying in the overloaded wagons. "Oh God, let me die. Please let me die," seemed to be the common refrain from the injured. Those like Lewis, able to walk and carry on his duties, were charged with the protection of those who had fallen but did not perish in the great defeat.

Gene Lee

"Good Lawd, Lieutenant," Sergeant Cuthbert grunted as he helped Raines shove at the wheel of an ambulance mired in the mud. "If that man caterwaulin' so bad to die wants to, I say let him. Chuck him out of the wagon and let him. Lighten the load so we can get on with it."

But Cuthbert's ragged grin belied the hardness of his tone—though Lewis had to admit there was a certain element of truth to what the sergeant said. Jettison the sick and dying so that the strong and living could get away to fight another day. No, as enticing as such an idea could be, Lewis knew the Army would never allow it. They were civilized men, after all. God-fearing men. Most of them, anyway.

"You could exchange places with that fellow, sergeant," Lewis said to Cuthbert, as with a final push and groan the wagon came free from the mud. "Take his wounds and bandages and show him how a Confederate soldier carries his injuries properly off the field of battle."

"No sir," Cuthbert said, smile still on his face as he fell in step with Raines behind the wagon. "I don't believe I'll take you up on that. Never thought I'd turn down a free ride, what with all the marching we've done over the past two years. But today I will. Not if bein' shot all to hell and back is the price of that ride."

"I reckon you're right, sergeant. Hell, I bet even Captain Harker would agree with you on that one."

"He never had to walk, sir," Cuthbert reminded Lewis. "Always had that horse of his. He wouldn't have the bona fides to argue the case one way or the other."

But the talk of Captain Harker put an end to their joking. Like all the other deaths of the day before there had been nothing funny about the captain's. When it became very clear that Pickett's brave division had entered a hell-storm of certain doom without further support, Lewis' battery and two others limbered up and moved out behind the charging men. Lewis was proud of the way his men never faltered.

"C'mon men, pour it into them," Harker yelled while Lewis and Private Boggess were reloading the Whitworth, a task made harder than normal by the nervous mule straining in the harness, the confusion of wounded men streaming by the other way, and the explosion of Union shells in their midst. "Fire, I say," Harker commanded again, holding tight to the reins in the one hand as his charger reared up at the nearby explosion of another shell. The captain raised his sword as he gestured at the enemy to the front of him. "Fire, Goddamnit," he yelled, the last words the captain ever spoke. Lewis turned to acknowledge the order just in time to see the captain catch full in the stomach a Union cannonball that bounced once on the ground before rising up again to lift Harker clean from the saddle and throw him, dead, into the backs of the retreating men. Lewis pulled the lanyard of the Whitworth and yelled at his men to hurry and reload but before they could the cannon, and the ground around it erupted at his feet and there was no more fighting for him that day.

The look of surprise on the captain's face stayed with Lewis all through the rain-filled night following the battle. There were other faces of men he had been with that day that knocked him awake just as he was drifting off to sleep. Boggess was gone, struck down by an exploding Union shell as he was helping with the Whitworth in the first wild moments the battery headed out behind the charging men. The Whitworth, too, gone, blown up, much like Osgood at Chancellorsville, the explosion and up-heaving ground taking the cannon and Private Zink with it. Somehow Lewis had been spared, though the explosion sent him sprawling backwards into the wide-spread arms of a dead Confederate lying on the ground. All of them gone, cannon and men. Harker, Boggess, Zink, corpses lying on the field. Dixon was absent as well though no shattered body was left behind anywhere Lewis could see. The private had just disappeared. When he thought about it longer, Lewis wasn't sure if Dixon had followed the battery out onto the field at Harker's command. Not all the batteries had obeyed that order. Not when the men manning those guns saw what was happening to the troops coming up to the ridge on the other side of the valley.

And where was Cuthbert? No sign of him, either, and now the stream of men returning from the line and the dismantled charge flowed heavier around Lewis and the dead men. But turning to go with that stream of men he saw Sergeant Cuthbert limping toward the rear, his face to the enemy in front of him. Filled with a joy that took him by surprise at seeing the sergeant, Lewis turned back to face the clump of trees and the rocky ridge. While enemy fire continued to rain down on the retreating men, he walked backwards to the rear, following his sergeant's lead and not the other way around.

If death comes now, for what it is worth it won't be by a Federal bullet in the back.

They were almost to the lines when a strange noise came from behind, a strangled cry from the throats of many men, and Lewis turned to see General Lee coming out onto the field atop his iron-gray horse. While retreating men streamed by, the commander of the Confederate forces rode among them, hat in one hand so that the sunlight breaking through the clouds lit up his white hair, the general stopping often to lean over the neck of his horse and talk to his battered troops. Even from where he was, Raines could see that Lee was not berating the men or urging them to turn back and finish the task. Instead, he used a soothing word and a tired smile for his defeated soldiers heading to safety. In another moment Lee was in front of Lewis and Cuthbert, the sad smile still on his face as he as he leaned forward to address them.

"Are you men hurt, Lieutenant?" The sorrow in the general's eyes seemed almost overwhelming. *More than any man should bear.* But though he was sad for the general, Lewis was grateful the overwhelming sorrow was not his to carry. "If so you will find comfort in the rear."

"No sir," Lewis answered. "I'm fine and so is the sergeant here. But the rest of my men are gone."

"You're not safe here, Gen'ral," Cuthbert spoke up. A shell exploded nearby as if to emphasize his point. "Them Yankees done enough damage today without adding you to the list, sir."

"This is my place, sergeant," the General answered. It seemed to Lewis that the weariness lifted from his smile for just a second. Cuthbert had that effect on men. "I'm where I should be," the general continued, sweeping a gloved hand out in front of him at the carnage across the valley floor. "This is my fault." He straightened up in the saddle and put his hat back on. "All my fault. You men did all you could today. Those people," and Lee pointed now to the two rocky ridge tops on the far edge of the field, "had much to fight for, and fight they did."

"I'm sorry we failed you, sir." Lewis could feel that failure in his bones as he spoke.

"No one failed me today, Lieutenant, except myself. I thought you men were invincible." The General tapped gently at the horse's side with his spurs. "I forgot you were only human."

He was gone, down the field to the next group of men reaching the rear lines, leaving Lewis and Cuthbert to continue their journey, to find the battery amidst the chaos and noise of the defeat.

But there was no battery to be found. In the confusion of the first wave of wounded men heading back to the Confederate lines and then the artillery charge, the remaining two guns had disappeared. Like Dixon, Lewis thought. Simply gone. He gave up the search as night came on. He and Cuthbert were making their way back to where the division should be when a major rode up on a frothy-mouthed horse and put up a hand for them to stop.

"You there," the major said, his voice dry and hoarse from the business of the day. "Your insignia says you are artillery, Lieutenant. Is that correct?"

"Yes, sir."

The night was closing the day down quickly. Suddenly, Lewis discovered he was tired, the energy left from the excitement and confusion he had known the last few hours, evaporated.

"Yes sir. The sergeant here, and I, are with Colonel Alexander's artillery. I can't find the division, though, sir. My battery appears to be shot out," he added, as if that might explain the problem.

"Follow me, then," and the major turned his horse back up the ridge the way he had come. "General Lee has ordered General Imboden to take the wounded out of this place back across the Potomac into Virginia. General Imboden needs guns to protect the rear of the column. We have the guns but not the men to man them. Come along, now."

"Sir?" and it was Cuthbert who spoke up as Lewis fell in behind the major. "Begging your pardon, sir, but what about our division?"

A good question, Lewis thought. One he should have asked, what with his rank and all. The sergeant, for the second time that day, had done what he, as lieutenant, should have had the good sense to but had not.

"We can sort that out later. But time's wasting now," the major said, spurring the horse into a slow trot.

"Yes sir," Lewis and Cuthbert answered in unison as they fell in behind the officer. The sudden appearance of direction amidst the groans of the wounded and the shell-shocked men wandering around aimlessly was a relief for Lewis. "Yes, sir," he repeated, saluting the major. "Yes, sir."

But the direction and order didn't last long once the train of wagons carrying the wounded began the trek south. Lewis blamed its loss on the rain and the mud they had to endure. Not that he and the rest of the men had not endured such elements before, but this was the first time they were marching under such a cloud of defeat. They reached the town of Williamsport after two solid days of being bogged down in downpours and mud-filled roads. It was good for a while in Williamsport, though, as it turned out, only for a day. General Imboden wasted no time in commandeering the quiet town and though it was clear the townspeople had heard of the great battle and the Southern defeat, they accepted the occupying forces peacefully. The women, especially, went out of their way to help the wounded, providing them with food and fresh bandages until supplies of both ran out. With the rains stopped, and not occupied with pushing and pulling wagons out of the mire, Lewis allowed himself to feel a glimmer of hope again.

Their bellies full and their tattered clothes dried out, the men had the strength to voice their anger, their bewilderment, at what had happened. Around the campfires that night loud voices could be clearly heard exclaiming how the whole thing was a fluke. If Pickett's glorious charge had been properly supported with reserves and artillery like it should have been, it would have succeeded. The Yankees got lucky, was all; that if Stuart and his free-wheeling cavalry had been where they were supposed to be, by God it would have been a different story. And where the blazes was Stuart, anyways?

They were conversations, arguments of military strategies that Lewis stayed away from. The belligerent voices only served to bring back the weariness he had felt before reaching the limited comforts of Williamsport. The end of the rain, enemy gunfire, and the hot food he was eating were the things he wished to hold on to. Perhaps even more so because he knew how good things didn't last. Soon, no doubt, it would be like before. If it satisfied the men to carry on with their what-should-have-been's, well then so be it.

For the most vocal of those men, their chance for revenge came sooner than expected. In the middle of a hot and humid afternoon the following day, the Union troops caught up to the rear. The sudden attack was a complete surprise and should have overrun the Confederates. It was only General Imboden's quick and fierce action that saved them from another utter ruin when the general, at the first sound of gunfire, came running out of his command post. Calm and collected, unlike most of the other officers, Imboden mounted his horse and proceeded to rally his men while a tremendous fire from Union cannons and muskets raked the streets. Fortunately, the men, resting in the heat of the day, were just as quick to react.

Sergeant Cuthbert ran next to Lewis down the main street of the town. "By God, Lieutenant, we'll settle their hash this time." In another instant the two men had joined the others manning the Parrott gun of their new battery and together they turned the gun and attached it to the limber. "Yes, sir," Cuthbert yelled, leaping onto the back of the mule harnessed to the limber and jabbing at the beast's sides. "Yes sir, we're gonna settle this once and for all."

Lewis saw the first of the Union troops entering the town at the end of the street just as one of those skirmishers' shots cut Sergeant Cuthbert down. The Yankee Minié ball tore the front of Cuthbert's face away and there was no time for comfort or a farewell for the last of Lewis's original unit. Lewis helped the two men left in his new battery to turn the gun into position and they were able to fire a load of canister into the oncoming men and horses. That action, along with the simultaneous blasts of canister from the other guns of Imboden's rear guard, decimated the lead riders, the Union troopers blown from their saddles.

The canister wasn't enough to stop them from overrunning the cannon placements and plowing into the midst of the Confederate soldiers, forcing the men on both sides into hand-to-hand combat in the streets of Williamsport. It turned quickly into a clatter of musket and small arms fire, the jangle of spurs and tack and horses and men grunting, some of them screaming or groaning softly when they were hit. In the madness enveloping him and the battery, Lewis worked to keep the Parrot gun firing canister into the Union troops coming out of the woods surrounding the town. The private taking Cuthbert's place with the swab was shot down not much later and then it was just Lewis and one surviving gunner, the two men working feverishly to keep the gun loaded and firing. He was shoving another can of the deadly shot into the breach of the cannon when he happened to look up in time to duck the slashing saber of an eager Union captain on horseback who had leaped the gun to cut at both Lewis and the private. Without thinking of how the Colt Dragoon pistol his father had given him had gotten into his hands, Lewis turned and fired. It was the first time in two years of warfare he had fired that gun and he watched in amazement as the Yankee captain fell backwards off his mount. But it was not the time, or place, to savor the amazement washing over him. General Imboden suddenly appeared in front of Lewis and yelled, "Get that goddamned gun turned around gentlemen and kill those goddamn Yankees."

Lewis and the private reloaded and fired the Parrott until the limber was empty of shells and the barrel of the gun too hot to touch. As the afternoon began to wane a cool breeze blew across the men. With the issue still left to be resolved, the Yankees unexpectedly backed out of the town to form a line in the trees on the outskirts of Williamsport. Suddenly, it fell quiet, as if both sides needed to take a deep breath and see what would happen next.

During this quiet Lewis's concerns about the empty limber were eased by the arrival of an ordnance train from Winchester. Crates of shells for cannon, musket, and pistols were ferried hurriedly across the swollen river beyond the town and the men under General Imboden re-supplied all under the watchful eyes of the Union soldiers. Given this opportunity to regroup, Lewis tried to be optimistic.

If only it weren't for the cries of the wounded in the makeshift hospitals scattered through the town; the newly dead lying in the streets, Lewis thought. *How long would it all go on? This constant advancing and retreating and the killing involved with it? How long?*

And then the Union line poured out of the trees, firing as they came, and it all started up again.

The second attack threatened to be more than the battered Confederates could handle as the Bluecoats advanced through the sheet of canister and Minié balls Imboden's troops poured into them. They still came on until it was once again fierce hand-to-hand combat in the streets, alleys, and doorways of the shops on Main Street. It was a combat Lewis didn't see how anyone could survive. The soldiers, both North and South, were enveloped in a haze of smoke. Everything living and not, became lost in the smoke and the screams of horses and men and the steady pounding of gunfire.

Afternoon turned to evening. Lewis's new battery, along with the rest of Imboden's division, pulled back deeper into the town, a move that finally convinced the Union gunners to cease fire with their cannons and avoid further destruction to civilian buildings and lives. In the fighting Lewis had taken a ball through the fleshy upper part of his arm. It went all the way through so no bones were broken, the flow of blood staunched by the remains of a handkerchief he took off a dead Confederate soldier. It hurt but after a while the pain grew into a steady throbbing that finally went numb and he forgot the wound was there. He hoped the falling night would put an end to the Yankee advance, but they certainly seemed determined to press the advantage of their will and greater numbers. Lewis couldn't understand how the Southerners were holding out, but he held on with them. He didn't want to die. None of them wanted to die. Not at this place so far from home. Not at this age when the rest of their lives should have been stretching out ahead of them.

At dusk there came the sounds of far-off guns from the north of the town along Hagerstown Road. At first Lewis thought what he was hearing above the constant fray around him was the certainty of their defeat, the sound of Union reinforcements coming in for the kill. Instead, what he heard was victory. In another moment the right flank of the enemy crumbled into disarray under the pounding charge of Stuart's cavalry slashing their way through the Union line. But it was more than just Stuart and his troopers. The men fighting in the streets of the town, soldiers both north and south, watched in amazement as the left flank of the Union line suffered the same fate, from the furious charge of Fitzhugh Lee's troopers roaring up Greencastle Road, firing side-arms and cutting with their sabers at anything in their path. A loud yell rose up around Lewis, his own yell a part of the whole. In danger of being enveloped the Union men broke and ran and the battle, for that day at least, was over.

Except for Union cavalry harassing their rear as the train of wounded headed for the Potomac, the Yankees didn't return. At this Lewis was much surprised. Even a lowly two-year Second Lieutenant Artillery man such as himself could see the vulnerability of his army despite the addition of Stuart's and Lee's cavalry. One more strong push by the enemy, with everything they had, would be enough to finish the Confederates off.

No big push by the armies of the North was forthcoming, though, and on a hot and humid, sun-shining day in the middle of July, Lewis Raines crossed the Potomac River via a rickety pontoon bridge into Virginia. Waiting behind him for the wounded to make it across first was what was left of the Confederate army. Men, who just a month and a half earlier had crossed that river going the other way, jubilant with the victory of Chancellorsville, and ready to bring the Union to its knees.

A soldier in front of Lewis, guiding a mule pulling a wagon of wounded, set foot on the dry river bank and throwing his threadbare forage cap high into the air yelled out, "Hooray boys, we're back in the South. We're home!"

As he stepped off the creaking bridge and onto the bank, still muddy from the recent high water, Lewis Raines wondered if that were indeed true.

Part Two: Back Home

At the end, Lewis Raines swore he would never take another human life if he could help it. On a cold day in April of 1865, along with what was left of Lee's army, Lewis walked away from Appomattox. Defeated, gaunt and hungry, he wondered if he were truly alive. Some of those with General Lee at the bitter end—though they cried and pleaded for their commander not to lay down arms—were glad for the final defeat, the surrender. They would have fought on. Lewis would have, too, but he was damn glad he did not have to.

April moved on, the days began to warm with spring, and Lewis walked the dusty roads of Virginia. The sky cleared and stayed that way until the winds and cold and defeat of the month were blown away. He passed by farms and homes, people, men and women weary of war, coming out to plow wasted fields. They hoped they could coax something to grow from the barren ground, repair wounded barns, and round up the few malnourished beasts of burden still left for them to use. If they had asked—the questions on those people's lips as the straggling men in gray passed by their farms—Lewis would have answered. Yes, it's true. He surrendered. It's really over. But they didn't ask, and as he walked, Lewis stayed silent.

At night he slept in abandoned barns, hay ricks, oak hummocks, or bare fields by the side of the road, cold in what was left of his uniform, the only cover other than his clothes a frayed Union blanket he found as the army fled Petersburg. Finally, after many days he acquired a horse of his own for the first time since leaving home in the summer of 1861.

A farmer who lived on the edges of what Lewis came to learn was the Dismal Swamp sold him the gelding. A transaction that began when the farmer called out as Lewis was almost past his place, "Ye look a little footsore, Johnny. Why don't ye set a bit with an old man? Have a sup of cool water. If ye care to, that is."

Lewis was taken aback by the stranger's kindness, the genuine look of concern in the man's weathered eyes. If the farmer had been wearing an old battered beaver skin hat he would have been a dead ringer for Lewis's father, what with the fading hair atop his head, the same sort of steely grey eyes, the red face from years of life outside, the strong stance never bent for any man or trouble. Even with what the war had taught him there was still a little trust left in Lewis. A fortunate thing, too, or he'd have continued on foot all the way to Charleston, the destination he had finally decided on a few days back. Nor would he have been as well fed and strong when he arrived, having missed out on almost a year's recovery from the war, courtesy of that old farmer's kindness and good food.

But there was trust was in him yet. Lewis said, "Thank you. I think I'll take you up on that. And my name's Lewis, sir. Not Johnny."

"Hell man, all ye boys who went off to fight are good Johnny Rebs far as I'm concerned. If we'd had more of ye we might've whipped them Yankees, too."

Maybe. And maybe not. Lewis didn't want to ponder such a notion. He said nothing as he walked up to the old farmer's front porch, sat down in the shade it provided, and drank the fresh, cool water the man gave him. It had taken four days after the surrender for him to realize he had been walking east instead of south toward home. Toward the ocean, he guessed, something he had never seen before but had heard men talk about. Time for something new, and the ocean appeared to be it. Once he had seen that, breathed in the sights and smell of it, seen with his own eyes that it truly existed and was not just the talk of men around a campfire, perhaps then he could go home.

But he wasn't ready for the ocean. Not yet. He stayed with Tom Harrell on his hundred acres, helping with the crops, the tobacco, hay, vegetables and feed corn they planted in the spring of '65. He stayed, as well, for the harvest in the fall—then did it all over again for one more year. Spring and summer were spent working hard in the sun next to the old man, plowing rows, planting seed, removing the sticky suckers from the tobacco plants when they started stalking up; then pulling the healthy leaves from those plants and hanging them on sticks to dry in the barn. When the tobacco leaves were what he considered to be properly cured, the old man liked to break a leaf up here and there for smoke. Lewis rolled clumsy cigars for himself and at night he and Tom Harrell sat out on the old man's porch smoking.

Occasionally they drank whiskey that was home-made, lovingly tended to just like the crops, in a still the old man kept tucked up in the woods. "Away from four-and two-legged varmints," he liked to say before sipping from a fruit jar he used for a glass, jars left from when his wife was alive and put up her own fruit. Lewis asked Tom Harrell about his wife once as he and the old man sat out drinking, but Harrell only said she had died. Said, "Son, I don't ask ye 'bout the war. Don't ask me 'bout my missus." They left it at that.

It was a good time for Lewis, that year and a half away from the war. A time he spent healthy and safe. Some nights, as he sat with Tom smoking cigars and drinking whiskey, Lewis thought of his home. *Of how his folks were doing.* He didn't know why he wasn't ready to go home yet. He just knew that he wasn't. Just like he wasn't quite ready to ride all the way east to the ocean and see what he had never seen before. Or so he told himself on those nights when thoughts of Ware County and what he had left behind came to mind. When it was time he would go. To the sea first. And then home. When it was time.

He left Harrell's place astride a dappled gelding. He offered Yankee greenbacks for the horse, but Tom refused and said, "Take it. For pay for helping me all this time." The horse had been for his son, a gift ten years before, when Tom Jr. left to study under Professor Jackson at the Virginia College. The boy had gone to school by train, leaving the horse behind. At the school he took to his studies well. Too well, his father said, or he might be alive today. But instead, when war broke out and Professor Jackson left to fight, the boy, like most of his classmates, went with him—some like Tom Jr., to die at First Manassas, a battle the Yankees called Bull Run and where the professor earned his nickname of "Stonewall." Now the horse was there, and his son was not. When Lewis protested the gift, the old man confided that he was plain tired of looking at that horse every day and being reminded of his boy.

"So take it, durn it. Ride it in good health. Good luck to ye, Lewis, and don't be a stranger if ye find your way to these parts again."

Lewis rode off, east again, hoping the old man wouldn't be offended by the twenty dollars he left under the whiskey jug. Gift or no, he couldn't just take the horse, He felt good for what he had done and how he had been with Tom all that summer, thinking as he skirted the edges of the swamp like the old man had instructed and then making a turn for the south when he was well clear of the danger, that yes, he would see that ocean now and then go on home.

Lewis broke his vow of war's end that he would never kill another man one night in Charleston. There was a fellow from Mississippi he worked with on the docks of that port town, a rough and tumble man in his early thirties by the name of Rafe. According to Rafe, he had fought with Hood in the west. Lewis had no reason to doubt this. But he couldn't shake a funny feeling that came over him when Rafe talked of the war, that he was leaving something out. Lewis believed this to be the fact that Rafe deserted that theater, though he couldn't be sure. Even with the war over, this was not something one accused a man of lightly. Especially a man that he drank, ate, and whored with in the taverns along the waterfront where Lewis and Rafe found themselves at the end of each working day.

Lewis woke suddenly in his bed one night to find Rafe standing over him, knife in one hand, a wad of Yankee greenbacks that had come from Lewis's knapsack in the other, and no good intention to be seen on his drunken face. In the next instant Rafe reeled back from the bed, clutching his throat which Lewis's own knife had just slashed wide open. It got very quiet in the room after that, after Rafe's death rattle faded away. In the quiet Lewis dressed in a hurry and gathered up his things, knapsack, money, and the Colt Dragoon pistol his father had given him to take to war. Excitement and anger drove him down the stairs of the boarding house and to the stables where he boarded the gelding.

Goddamn, was all Lewis could think as he walked the quiet night time streets of the town, knapsack nudging at his back and the Colt in its holster heavy on his hip. *Goddamn, but he hadn't wanted to kill that man.* Not that Rafe had left him much of a choice. *Goddamn, deserting, back stabbing thief who had left Lewis no other course of action to take than the one he had.*

Lewis rode out of Charleston like a thief in the night. He ended up in Savannah. The city where the war had begun for him and where he worried at first that he had not put enough distance between himself and the killing of Rafe. After a while he discovered no one cared where he had been before. The War was a simple enough answer for any question put to him, no details required, thank you very much. He found a strange peace in that city by the river—and a woman.

Lewis met her one evening as he was making his way home from the docks, where once again, as in Charleston, he had found work. There was a dry goods store on the corner of a cobblestone road by a carriage park. Seeing it that afternoon he thought of his sister Cordelia; thought of how he should buy a gift of some sort to bring her when he finally returned home. The woman was behind the counter. Confused by the array of linens and bonnets and fabric on the many shelves, all of them dim and unknowable in the soft light inside the store, Lewis approached her and asked for help. The woman behind the counter said, "Yes? What is it you are looking for?" Lewis was struck by the sound of this woman's voice—a soft lilting tone with just a trace of a Georgia accent, as if she had lived elsewhere for a while and been influenced by where that was. Recovering himself he said, "Well, I'm not sure." The woman behind the counter laughed. It was because of the look on his face that she laughed. She laughed because beneath the face of a hardened man she could still see a little boy. Lewis fell in love with her when she told him this. He couldn't see that boy, or feel him, anymore. But if she could, then perhaps there was still hope. Perhaps he was still a human being.

Her name was Sarah, a widow, her husband having died at the Battle of Franklin. She told him every time they met over the next two weeks that she wasn't ready for a man in her life, that they could be only friends and nothing more. Still they met, usually in the Carriage Park where it was cool and quiet, especially in the evenings when the sun was down and the breezes from the river three blocks away came up. Her hair was blonder than he had ever seen on a woman, hair that hung down past her waist and he marveled at the richness of it. Finally, one night, she allowed him to kiss her and when he thought the kiss was done and pulled back, she laughed.

"Who taught you to kiss a woman, Lewis?" she asked, and he would have been put out were it not for the way she looked at him.

"A girl back home, I guess," he answered, thinking of Mamie Hewitt, the preacher's daughter in Pendleton and how very long ago it seemed when he had been with her.

"She must not have known how."

"It was before the war," Lewis said, and then realizing that didn't really explain, added, "We were both pretty young."

"Are you grown up now, Lewis?"

"I think so."

"In some things," Sarah said.

This time when they kissed he understood what she meant. It wasn't too long after that when she let all that beautiful hair down and they lay on cool cotton sheets in her bedroom in the house by the river, windows wide open to let the night air in. The lovemaking left them warm and damp, the cotton sheets no longer cool, but a wadded-up mess at the end of the bed. Laying with her, the two of them breathing hard and the soft hotness of her hands on him still very much a living sensation on his skin, Lewis was grateful for the fresh night air blowing over them. "Sarah," he said into her ear.

He wanted to say more, felt that just her name could not possibly say what he meant. But other words didn't come, all meaning, all thought, lost in his amazement that such an act as they had just known could be a part of living in the world.

"Lewis," she said. When she said his name, though, for him it was more than enough—and as if to prove it was the same for her she pulled him back into her arms.

They were happy together for a little while, and Lewis believed that the peace and love he had found with the woman, after all the killing of the war, would last.

But it was only to be for a little while. Pneumonia took it away. One night when Sarah came home from her work, her face was flushed, her body shaking with a chill no amount of blankets could relieve. The chill was replaced by a fever, Sarah's face pale and shining wet under the cold compresses Lewis kept pressed against her forehead. Finally, all the ministrations of the doctor ended, she was dead, quiet, and still in the bedroom where they had first loved one another just two months before. As she had asked him to do, Lewis buried her next to her husband in the veterans' cemetery on the road east out of Savannah. That part of his life ended.

***

He rode south out of Savannah in the fall of 1868, everything dead inside him once more as he followed the coastal rivers until he came to a small town called St. Mary's. He paid a ferryman there to take him and his horse across the river to Cumberland, an island that lay between the ocean and the small town. Once ashore, he rode the dappled gelding across the sands until finally there was the ocean, stretching out to where he could not imagine. Birds of a kind he had never seen before wheeled and dove along the water's edge. As he watched these birds at work, Lewis realized that it was time. He had been to war and at the end of it swore he'd kill no more men. Yet he had. As if to make up for that, he had found love with a woman. But now, all of it was gone. He turned the dappled gelding's head west toward Pendleton.

***

What was left wasn't much. Not what he had expected, at any rate, or what he had thought of often over the time and long miles it had taken him to return.

That his mother passed away came as no real surprise, what with how weak and sickly she had been before Dawes and he even left. The last letter he had received from her was in the spring of 1864. In the letter she gave no indication her health had improved, only news of crops, who had died, been born, or married, and did he have any idea when the war might be over.

So, Lewis was not surprised that his mother was gone. What he hadn't suspected—indeed had never thought possible—was that Edwin Raines was dead. He was taken from this world on a bright spring morning while he was going about the business of preparing a field for a new crop of corn. As Edwin urged mule and plow down the first furrow, according to Jared Dancy, Edwin dropped to his knees behind the plow. Before Dancy could reach him, Edwin keeled over in the unplowed furrow, dead by the time Dancy could lift him up from the dirt and ask what was wrong.

His father had always loomed so large in Lewis's world, tall, strong, and unbending to any difficulty the frontiers he had chosen to live in threw his way. Immortal, Lewis supposed, was how he had seen his father. Not the immortality of a god, perhaps, such as the Greek or Roman deities his mother had taught him about when he was young, but always alive. Deep down inside this was how Lewis expected his father to be.

Yet they were gone, both mother and father dead and buried, the two graves in the withered cemetery behind the Primitive Baptist Church on the road to Ruskin, proof plain and simple. Lewis had gone straight away to see for himself, having heard of his parents' deaths in Pendleton as he rode in on his way home. The news had come from Dag

Shorter, the same old timer whose sharing of facts gleaned from a three-week-old Atlanta newspaper had begun Lewis's journey to war. Miraculously, the old man was still alive and still just as grizzled looking, his face covered with scruffy whiskers and red splotches from years of hard drinking. He could always be found in a rocking chair on the porch of the general store.

"Hey there, boy," Dag called from the porch as Lewis trotted down the main street of town that afternoon in late June of 1869, "hold up a minute, Raines, 'fore ye go traipsin' out to the home place. I best warn ye first."

The word "warn" got Lewis's attention. That and the fact the day was hot and still and the dust from the dry road west out of Savannah had covered him and the gelding in a fine sheen of faint red powder. A drink of cool water for both man and horse was called for, Lewis figured, both available from the big rain barrel in front of the store. While they were slaking their thirst, he let Dag Shorter say what was on his mind.

"Might want to swing by the church on your way in, boy," is what the old man told Lewis, Dag Shorter's voice low and somber and weighted with import after relaying the details of his parents' deaths. "Get yourself right with your folks 'fore ye see what happened to your home."

"Thank you kindly, Dag." And there it was. Lewis's insides lurched with the sudden knowing. "I appreciate it."

"Aw hell, boy, I couldn' let ye hear bad news like that from some stranger."

The headstones for Edwin and Ella Raines sat stark and gray in the little cemetery behind the church. No breeze of any kind stirred on the hazy afternoon and the green leaves of the oaks surrounding the grounds drooped on the branches. Clouds building to the west held promise that the listlessness of the day would change. But that would be for later, not now, Lewis thought as he knelt in the sandy grass before the markers.

Such a hard place to lie for all eternity. Not a place, he decided, he would be in any hurry to reach since there was no reason to rush one's end. It would come for certain and there was plenty of room in the family plot for him when it came. *More room than there should have been,* he thought as he looked around. For they were one headstone light. The one for Dawes. Nothing to mark his brief existence on earth but the memories Lewis carried in his head. He supposed that would have to be enough.

The three pages of rough paper containing the words his father had written concerning Dawes' death, the knowledge that Edwin Raines had to work hard at composing what needed to be said, had somehow given Lewis the strength he needed to stay alive until war's end. *Yes,* he thought, as he turned from the two graves and walked out of the cemetery to the horse grazing in the dry grass of the churchyard. *That letter certainly helped me to survive until the fighting was done. To survive and when it was over, walk away intact.*

Wanting to be home, he urged the horse into a trot. Turning on the road to Pendleton he realized that perhaps what had carried him for three years away from home *was* gone. Gone, and replaced by the fact that all his family were dead, and no one was left to welcome the Prodigal Son home except his sister and her husband, Jared Dancy.

***

On a hot and still morning in mid-August, when Lewis had been back close to two months, Jared Dancy rode into the yard. Lewis had been working since sun-up that morning, taking advantage of the cooler temperatures available to repair the hog pen. Almost done, hot and thirsty, he sat in the shade of the porch with a dipper of cold water in a bucket, pondering the next repair on the fallen-down farm he had to attend to.

"'Lo, Lewis," Dancy said. "Care to offer a drink of that cool water to a parched man?" Dancy pointed at the dipper in Lewis's hand and when Lewis made no reply, continued, "A man who is not only thirsty, but family, I might add. Seeing as how I'm married to your sister."

It was pushing noon and between the blazing sun and the hard work of the morning Lewis had worked up a body soaking sweat. And yes, the cool water from the well was satisfying. Like the work he'd done and the shade he sat in enjoying the water and the fruits of his labor visible from where he sat. Until his brother-in-law rode in, that is, demanding water and acknowledgement.

"'Lo' Jared." He moved off the porch, stretching his arms over his head in the noon sun. He didn't want to, saw no way around it though, and said, "Let me get you some of that water. Seeing, like you say, you're family and all."

Dancy started to dismount but seeming to hear the tone in Lewis's voice, stayed in the saddle.

"We heard you were back," he said to Lewis who bent over the bucket by the well. "Cordelia's been wondering when you might join us up at the Landing."

"I haven't been asked."

Moving to stand beside the man on the horse, Lewis handed the dipper of water to his brother-in-law. It was a fine-looking horse Dancy rode these days, he thought. Not many of the good stock left after the war. Leave it to Dancy to have one. The mare—bright red in color, redder than roan, and a color Lewis hadn't seen before—certainly had spirit. A very proud horse as well and she had let Lewis know it, giving him a warning snort and baring her teeth as he approached with the water for her master.

A pride you can believe in, he thought as he backed away to give her room. *Unlike the man astride you.*

Dancy drank from the dipper, and then removed his hat. Taking a handkerchief from the breast pocket of his duster he poured some water onto it and began mopping his forehead. That hair had been redder before the war, Lewis remembered. Not streaked with gray, his sideburns, too, so that the man whom everyone had considered to be the darling of Ware County, no longer seemed as much so.

And he hadn't even gone to fight. That being the case he didn't deserve such a fine-looking horse. So tall and proud, that horse, Lewis thought. She should just throw the bastard and be free. That horse. It was what she wanted, what with the way she snorted and flared her nostrils when Dancy jerked the reins back. She wouldn't run from a fight. Not that one. Not like the man upon her back.

"Consider yourself asked, then," Dancy said after a bit. He put away the handkerchief, taking one last sip from the dipper before handing it back to Lewis. Apparently realizing that no invitation to dismount would be forthcoming, no invitation to sit awhile with Lewis in the shade of the porch, Dancy said again, "Yes indeed, sir, consider yourself invited. Your sister and I will expect you this coming Saturday. Cordelia will be delighted, I'm sure."

"And you, Jared?"

Lewis finally took the water dipper from Dancy's outstretched hand and put it handle end first into the back pocket of the frayed pants he'd worn to work in that morning. A far cry from the clothes his brother-in-law worked in, he thought. Black riding breeches. The white silk shirt. If you could call it work. Now that his niggers were gone, who *did* do the work? Certainly not Dancy.

The sun had reached its noontime peak and it was very hot it in the dusty yard. Lewis had much left to do, and no inclination to do it. There would be no escape from the summertime heat that afternoon. Not for a while at any rate — not until five or so at least when the sun would start its slow descent and a breeze kicked up out of the east. If he was even luckier, that breeze would come from the northeast and be even cooler. Being August, though, no one in Ware County, or the entire state of Georgia as far as that went, could count on that sort of luck. Either way, he'd put off finishing the pen until then and would rest in the shade on the porch reading a volume of his mother's Lord Byron.

Pleased with this decision, like he had been about keeping Dancy uncomfortable on his horse, Lewis asked again, "How about you, Jared? Will you be delighted?"

"Why, sir, I will be there." A meager, tight-lipped smile broke Dancy's red features as he turned the horse's head roughly with the reins. "I imagine that will be the extent of it."

He spurred the horse into a gallop, out of the yard, and onto the road towards Ruskin. As he watched Dancy disappear down the dusty road, Lewis thought how atop a horse like that, even a man such as his brother-in-law, could still be proud.

***

Blackshear Landing, like everything in the eight years Lewis Raines had been gone, had changed. His first thought, when turning down the lane off Ruskin Road leading into the plantation, was that his memory must be at fault. He had certainly seen his share of the ruins Sherman and the war had left behind. Why Chandler Dancy's dream should have been any different, should have been spared the same fate as the others, was beyond him, he supposed. For as long as he could remember, the big white house, columns gleaming in the sun, had risen from the earth, surrounded by cotton fields stretching off into the distance. On both sides of the lane off Ruskin Road, north, south, east, and west, grew Dancy cotton. The fields were worked by the multitude of slaves who labored for the family, year in, year out, into eternity and beyond, it had seemed to Lewis' young mind. He thought that way when he was young, when nothing and no one ever died and everything lasted.

But the ways of the Dancys were no longer alive and well, Lewis saw as he came closer to the house at the end of the lane. In the past, the house had been hidden by the oaks and the last curve of the dirt road, invisible from Ruskin Road. As it came into sight now, Lewis could well imagine that Chandler Dancy, lying peacefully in his grave, could not be happy in his eternal rest. The splendor of the plantation was no more. The massive oak trees shielding the house from view were gone as were the pine trees, fields of cotton, and the slaves that sustained the Dancys.

Rounding the last curve of the lane he rode into the yard where he saw the ruined house. The east wing had been burned out by accident or Union depredation. Charred timbers lay collapsed around each other in an ashen heap and soot smeared the once all-white walls of what was left standing.

The west wing of the big house seemed intact, though, when he looked up towards the second floor he could see some windows with shattered panes. A once majestic oak now leaned against the building, its branches sweeping across the roof, the thick trunk nestled peacefully into the gash it had created in the walls of the house. It all seemed very sad to Lewis as he walked up the steps leading to the front door, if only for his sister's sake and nothing else. Hard as it was to believe, the war had come even there.

"So, you decided to honor the invitation," Jared Dancy said as he opened the door. "I made a slight wager with Cordelia that you wouldn't," Dancy continued, his voice thick from bourbon, a time-honored tradition of the Dancy family as everyone in Ware County well knew. "I'll pay up gladly, though. The happiness your visit will bring your sister is worth it."

Lewis didn't believe him, about the wager or about how the happiness he brought, but he followed him inside the house. Lewis had been in the foyer only long enough to hang his duster when he heard a bustling behind him. In another moment his sister, all a rustling of skirts and petticoats and hair ribbons, was in his arms, her face buried in his neck, her tears warm against his skin. She said, "Lewis." And said again, "Lewis."

She pulled away finally and in the awkward silence between them Lewis told her, "It's good to be home, Cordelia." But the words rang hollow, mostly because of the starkness of the lie. She knew it, had to see it in his eyes. He said before the awkwardness could go on any longer, "Yes indeed, dear sister, I have missed you." He was grateful that at least that much was true.

Cordelia had changed, and he had changed. Yes, his hair was still very black, and the dark orbs of his eyes still shone bright and clear, but the skin of his face was weathered and hard, and like his sister's, tight around the eyes. His shoulders might be just as broad as they always were, and he could still work all day and hardly feel it at night, but he wasn't the boy who had gone off to war eight years before.

Dancy broke the moment by tapping his wife on the shoulder. A shy suitor asking for the next dance, Lewis thought as he looked over Cordelia's white, bare shoulder at the man who had taken her away from her family. A shy suitor, who by virtue of possession really didn't need to ask even if he *had* come down much in the world, judging by the state of the rich broadcloth jacket and Sea Island cotton shirt Dancy wore. Both had been new a very long time ago but not worn in a while or attended to. In the twill trousers and ivory colored bib shirt he wore—both reasonably new, having been bought in Charleston for occasions such as this—Lewis felt suddenly out of place.

"Come, my dear, let's sit and have dinner."

The smile on Dancy's face, flushed by the bourbon, was only an attempt to hide the faded elegance of his home, Lewis saw. All for show as if none of it had changed when all of it had.

"We can catch up over that."

In the soft light of the dining room it was easy to overlook the condition of the linen upon the table, the silver, the china, and the heavy curtains covering the windows. Even the platter, containing a pullet that would have been lost in the cavernous plate except for the half-dozen early season quail flanking it, the carrots, squash, and three small potatoes alongside served not by a Negro in white livery but by Cordelia herself. Her look of embarrassment at being seen in such a position was plain upon her face.

"Well, Lewis," Cordelia said, putting an end to his reverie, "please, help yourself. I'm sure you're not feeding yourself properly out at that lonely house. Not like our mother would have liked."

"I think I'm doing okay by myself in the grub department," Lewis said. "One thing soldiering taught me was how to shoot better."

"Pluggin' all them Yankees improved your aim, did it?"

His little joke brought a laugh from Dancy, a smile he didn't try to hide, though Lewis felt if the man had any decency he would have.

"Among other things. Yes."

"Let's not talk about that over dinner," Cordelia said. "Please."

"Certainly, my dear." Dancy's grin had faded at his wife's reprimand. "And you're right. We don't want to do anything to spoil this splendid repast you so graciously laid out for our *wayward son*."

Like the embarrassment constantly on his sister's face, Lewis didn't understand the look that passed between her and her husband.

"I swear, though, Lewis, other than being shy a few pounds, you haven't changed at all."

"Nor you, dear sister."

A flush came on her face then and Lewis was grateful she was pleased with his compliment, truthful or not.

"I could always count on you to say nice things, Lewis."

She bent to her plate and when she looked up again the color was still in her cheeks. For the first time that night she looked healthy, looked somewhat like her old self.

"I hadn't realized how much I missed that, and you, until just now. How I've really missed you in my life."

It was good of her to say, and honest. For a moment, Lewis almost felt the same and that some part of "home" was coming back to him. Not that it could last. Not with the truth of how they both had changed over the years so evident. The last time he had sat at the table at Blackshear Landing had been a month or so before he left with Dawes. That night he had noticed for the first time how his sister was growing older, the pain of miscarriage, of living with a drunkard and rake like Jared Dancy, plain upon her then and Lewis had been shocked. Now the tightness of the skin around her eyes and nose and lips, the graying of her once jet-black hair, were even more so. And instead of the thirty she was, Cordelia Raines Dancy looked to be fifty.

Their father should have forced the issue that night. Called Dancy out and on the appointed morning shot him dead. At least Cordelia wouldn't have had the additional burden of Jared Dancy on her hands during the years of hardship that came with the war. Edwin Raines could have put an end to one part of it, at least.

With a start and a forkful of food halfway to his mouth, Lewis wondered if that were the way he really felt about that night when Edwin Raines had as much as accused Jared Dancy of being a coward and the man had shrugged it off. No good could come from dwelling on that now, though, he decided. Pleased with the look on his sister's face he said, "It's true Cordelia, you know. Looking at you, and seeing how you are now, I have to say again, you're just the same."

"Why Lewis Raines, I thought Father taught you never to lie and yet, here you go, in the space of only two minutes or so, spouting fibs as natural as could be."

The smile and flash of her bright green eyes showed a glimpse of the sister he had once known. "No fibs, Cordelia," Lewis told her, wanting to keep his sister in this familiar light. "Besides, any changes time may have worked on you and me can't be visible to the naked eye. Our family is made of stronger stuff than that."

"Ha, and the Dancys as well."

Cordelia's husband, content with the food and the wine, sat quietly at his end of the table. Finding an opportunity to join the conversation, he spoke up.

"Yes, indeed, brother," Dancy said. "How true that is. Well said, sir, and like a true gentleman. A toast to you and your return." He raised his half-empty glass high and ignoring the fact the other two didn't join him, drank what was left. "Men and women can hide the damages done to them. Women with a little rouge and face powder, both commodities hard to come by these days, though not impossible." The smirk and conspiring glance he gave his wife was not to Lewis's liking, but again, nothing of the man was. "And men? Well, we hide our wounds with our strength. But the land? Our great Southern land? Now there's a different matter. Only time will heal and cover up the scars inflicted on it by those Yankee curs."

Bold talk, Lewis thought. Almost unbearable to take from one who had seen little of what the war had really done to men and the land. The privation and sufferings had been real, perhaps, in Ware County. But much worse elsewhere. Lewis could vouch for that.

Alerted by the flush on her husband's face, the slurring of his words, to where the conversation might head after this outburst, Cordelia changed tack.

"What I want to know, Lewis, is where on earth have you been? The war's been over three years and you've just come back."

"The war's not over," Dancy said, slopping more wine into his glass from the decanter he kept close at hand. "Will never be over. Not if I have anything to say about it."

More bold talk from a drunkard. Much the same as I had heard ever since Appomattox. From both drunk men and sober ones. Either way they were mistaken. Lewis believed that. Had to believe if he were to stay sane.

"I suppose you could say I got a little side-tracked."

Lewis hoped his smile was sheepish enough to give him time to compose himself while he found a way of explaining to his only living relative the why, and where, of what had happened to him at war's end.

"Just took me a little longer than I expected to find my way home I guess," he said.

"I'll say." Dancy's face, red in the yellow light of the chandelier, reflected what the wine was doing to him. "Long enough to let the place go to rack and ruin with no help from you whatsoever."

"Nor you," Lewis said, the tightness inside him loosening just a little as he held his eyes on Dancy's. "Judging by the looks of the Landing, you haven't done much yourself to stop, as you say, things from going to 'rack and ruin.' And you've been here all along."

"But really, Lewis." Cordelia tried one more time to keep the evening and her husband intact. "You really must tell us where you've been all this time. And what have you been doing?"

But what could he tell her? Nothing, really. Nothing that would make sense to her or her husband who hadn't been a part of it. Tonight was not the time to talk of it, not when he could still see vividly in his mind's eye the color of human blood, how easily it could be spilled, how fast it could flow.

"You should've been home," Jared said suddenly. "Fall of '67 your daddy was still alive. Still struggling to keep the place going."

"Like I said before, Jared." Lewis had to work very hard then to let the drunken man's slurred remarks go. "You were here all along. You could've found some time to help Pa. It would have been the family thing to do."

"Sorry, old chap." Dancy sat up straight at the table, his eyes full of something Lewis didn't understand. Judging by the hardness in them, he decided he didn't want to understand. "But I was busy with the Home Guard. All through the war and beyond. Taking care to see no harm fell on the folks left behind while the rest of you went off to glory. So you see, sir," and Dancy spread his hands wide over the faded linen covering the table, "I really, as you say, didn't have the time to help your father. To plow his fields. Or slop his pigs. All jobs, I mind you, meant for his sons. His *real* sons."

What was left of the evening turned into a jangle of quick images and sounds for Lewis. When he had the time to go over it all, he could only blame the wine and Jared for what happened next. The sound of Cordelia screaming high and tightly in the big dining room, capable of feeding thirty or more and only filled with the three now, stood out large in his memory. That, and the way his vision seemed to narrow into a field half of what was normal, focused only on Dancy, whose face turned a ghostly color when the flush from the wine and bourbon suddenly drained from it as Lewis leapt up from his seat. The Bowie knife he had grown accustomed to wearing at all times tucked in his boot was now held tightly in his right hand. Later, he couldn't recall drawing the knife or the low growl that issued from his mouth. But the thud of the heavy blade jammed deep and hard into the mahogany table stayed clear in his mind for days afterward.

"Lewis! No!"

He was cognizant of his sister's screaming, could hear it through the sudden roaring in his head—but as he reached for the hasp of the knife jammed in the table Lewis said, "One more word, coward. Come on, Dancy. Just say it. Let me hear it. Please. One more word and I'll finish what my father didn't."

Cordelia's screaming turned into a low wailing as she buried her head in her hands. Dancy tried to stand up but couldn't. He was able only to scuttle backwards from the table in his chair—like a crab at low tide, Lewis thought. Just like one, scurrying across the mud flats left behind on the shores of Charleston Bay when the tide went out. But it was time the man stood up and gave Lewis the opportunity he wanted so badly. *God yes. Please.* He could taste that wanting like copper in his mouth. The excitement was almost akin to when he had gone to bed with Sarah the first time in Savannah. When it was all new to him. Now that copper taste was in his mouth again, not over a woman, or some unknown excitement—for Lewis nothing was unknown about killing. The war had taught him all that.

God yes, he thought, though did not say it again. Please, Dancy, stand up so I can kill you.

But the only man standing in the dining room of the Landing that night continued to be Lewis. Jared Dancy never uttered the word Lewis was looking for. Other than the sound of Cordelia's low moaning, the only other thing Lewis heard before he left the crumbling mansion that night was the soft sigh of the knife when he pulled it free from the table.

***

Winter came late that year, the steady and bitterly cold days not showing up until after Christmas. When winter arrived, though, it stayed, the days a hard grey, chilled by a wind out of the north that seemed to know no other direction. By the end of March of 1869 Lewis had grown so used to frost on the ground that the first day it wasn't there it took him until early evening to figure out that lack of it was what had been troubling him all that day. Many nights that winter he lay huddled on the floor by the fireplace with his Union blanket thrown over him, wishing that instead of staying when he finally came home he had kept on going, further south, all the way to Florida and where it ended in Key West. Hell yes, he thought one night when he had allowed this delicious dream to take him deeper and deeper into it. *I should have just kept on going and when the land ran out, hopped a boat to the islands.* Negros he worked with on the docks in Charleston came from what they called the Bahamas. Sunny islands where it never got cold, the people worked and fished and played in the sun all day, drank sweet wine at night, ate fresh fish, sang songs, and made love to their women. God yes, I need to be there. Right now.

He had heard, as well, in Charleston, that the Bahamas the Negroes spoke of was very real. That indeed, a band of Confederate officers, faced with the subjugation of the conquering army of the North, had gone in boats to those islands. Lived there now, free of defeat and the oppression of the Reconstruction Act that held all the South hard in its yoke.

A sweet enough dream, Lewis told himself more than once before falling asleep in front of the fire. But he wasn't there and needed more than a dream to keep him warm. The Union blanket, along with a ragged quilt he found in his mother's chest of drawers, would have to do. The walls and the fire would have to be enough to keep him from the howling winds outside.

He worried more about the horse than himself; hoped he had spread enough hay in the stall, that the thin blanket he had attached to the horse's back would bring a small comfort to the gelding. When it was really cold and he couldn't sleep and the concern for the horse was too much, instead of sloughing it off, Lewis would go to the barn. Invariably, he discovered his concerns were for naught. Usually the barn, warmed by the piles of hay thrown about and by the breath and being of the gelding itself, was warmer even than the house. More than one night Lewis stayed with the gelding, sleeping in the hay not far from the soothing sounds of the horse breathing. After a while he made this a steady habit, having discovered after two nights in succession that he didn't dream there. At least not the dreams that kept him awake like those of killing Jared Dancy, or Yankees attacking, or the moaning and screaming of men dying.

When spring came, it came quickly. On a morning in early April when Lewis awoke and decided it was time to get to work, he saw the evidence of its sudden arrival on the ride into Pendleton for supplies. Live oak trees stood tall and green, their willowy arms waving in the slight breezes blowing from the south. The bigger oaks appeared to have grown even taller and wider, the Spanish moss hanging from their branches and almost touching the ground. Stopping for a minute in the middle of the wooden bridge over Ruskin Creek, Lewis looked up and down the creek at all the river birches lining its banks, the pale bark suffused with the shadows made by sunlight pouring through their green leaves. At that end of the creek, the birches were replaced by swamp cypress. He had hunted and fished along the banks of that creek as a child and a young man, yet it was as if he were seeing all of it for the first time. Lewis realized how everything was new to him once more.

Lee had surrendered four years ago, he thought. Damn near to the day. It was about time things seemed new again. Alive and well. Instead of the steady destruction of war, and then afterwards, the people lost and adrift. He had been one of those people. He took a deep breath of the fresh air and rich with the smell of spring, slapped the gelding lightly on its rump with the reins, and said, "Giddap!" The sound of his own voice, the first human voice he had heard since dinner at his sister's house, surprised him. He was suddenly eager to be amongst people again and hear what they had to say.

The rest of that morning and the better part of the afternoon were spent taking care of supplies in Pendleton. There were seeds to buy, hogs to be ordered, coffee, molasses, and a few other personal items to be purchased for Lewis's own needs. Due to the dwindling of the

Yankee dollars he had come home with, credit also had to be established, a task he didn't look forward to. The Raines family had done business with Crueller's General Store for more years than Lewis had been alive, the arrangements made by his father and Dawes. To Lewis's knowledge, no bill had ever come due without being paid. Hopefully, it would only be a matter of re-establishing the old arrangement. But the war had changed so much that had gone before one couldn't be sure of anything anymore. Either way, it galled him to ask for help, a character trait inherited from his father and all the Raines men before him.

It was no surprise that old Dag Shorter was on the porch when he reined the buckboard up in front of Crueller's store. A difference Lewis couldn't help but notice was that instead of sitting in his customary place in one of the three rocking chairs, Dag Shorter had a broom in his hand. Not only that, he was using it, sweeping the porch free of the dust and dirt tracked there by human feet and the wind drifting it along the wooden sidewalks.

"Ye don' have to look so shocked," the old man said, a slight grin almost hidden by the drooping mustache concealing his crusty lips. "I know it's a stunner seeing me up an' moving about. But it ain't the end of the world by a long shot."

"No, no, not at all, Dag,' Lewis said, doing his best to stay straight faced as he shook the old man's proffered hand. "It's just good to see you."

And it was true. The old man was one of the few things, minus a few more gray hairs and a pronounced bend to his shoulders, that hadn't changed since the war.

"I hope Mr. Crueller is paying you a good wage for your hard work."

"Nah. He ain't paying me a dime." Dag leaned the broom against his shoulder, pulled a crumpled rag out of his overalls pocket, and wiped his forehead. "And this ain't 'xactly hard labor, boy." Putting the rag back in his pocket he waved the broom to demonstrate how easily he handled the equipment. "I done a ton lot harder back when I was a younger man and still had the farm."

Two ladies passed by on the sidewalk in front of the store, their bonnets bright blue and pink. Dag tilted the broom stick their way in greeting, saying as he did so, "Mornin' ladies," and receiving a turning away of their faces in reply.

"Some folks gone an' forgot the good manners their mamas and daddies taught them, I guess," Dag said with a grunt of disgust. "Now those two? They come here after the war. Their husbands is Yankee officers of some sort. One them runs the Freedman's Bureau an' the other that Military Tribunal of theirs. Those ladies don' know a damn thing about the Shorters and our good name in these parts, I suppose. Still, that's no excuse for purely bad manners."

Lewis laughed at the old man's sudden tirade about the manners, or lack thereof.

"Ye think that's funny do ye?"

But Dag was laughing, too. Lewis let it wash around him and down along the street thinking how it had been way too long since he had known such a thing.

"Anyways," Dag said, bringing them both back to where they were. "Like I was telling ye. Since his stroke, I been helping old Ed around the store. Was even working some inside. 'Til the younger boy came home. Once he healed up enough from his wounds he took over. Now he's running the whole works an' ain't got much use for an old man like me. If ye were to ask me I'd tell ye that boy don't appear to have much use for his daddy, either. But that ain't my business. Between him an' Ed, I reckon. That's okay. Ed give the boy strict instructions to mind my tab down the street."

Dag pointed with the broom at the salon and billiard hall on the corner of Main Street and Ruskin Road.

"As long as he does that, I'm happy to do what I can 'round here."

It was busy inside the store. Like Lewis, men were intent on purchasing spring supplies, the staples that had provided a living for them and their families. Women—wives of farmers, of businessmen in Pendleton or Ruskin—were making their own purchases. Bolts of cloth were handled and surveyed with precision, colors approved or disapproved, decisions made, some wives taking longer than the husbands.

Store-bought hats were much admired and then hung back up on their hooks, sometime with an audible wistful sigh. One older woman whom Lewis couldn't place, her name just on the tip of his tongue but never revealed, preened herself in a mirror nailed to a post by the hat racks. Whether or not she ended up buying the bonnet Lewis didn't know, but she was enjoying herself in front of the mirror and that made him feel good. Like the laughter he and Dag Shorter had shared outside.

For the most part, though, the men and women inside the store moved with a purpose and, unlike the two women outside, good manners prevailed. When situations arose that could have led to dispute, Lewis noticed how one or the other of the parties involved quickly made a decision, backed off, and if needed, made a timely apology. It was not a time for argument, but for getting the job done. To further that purpose, two sturdy young blacks stayed busy running bags of grain, seed, farm implements, and the like, through the rear door where wagons waited in a line to be loaded.

While pondering a new axe, hefting it in his hands to get the feel of it, Lewis happened to look up as Mamie Hewitt entered the store. He hadn't seen her in some time. The time had been when Lewis, and most everyone else in the area, assumed he and Mamie would marry. Of course, that had been before the War. His return showed him that, along with everything else, his relationship with her had altered dramatically. He had gone to the Hewitts' a week after the dinner at the Landing, but the raw taste of that earlier dinner party was still heavy in his mouth and he excused himself from the table early. He was not yet ready for the company of good people—hadn't been back since. Hadn't even written Mamie a letter to explain his actions, something he had fully planned on.

Now, there she was in Crueller's doorway, framed by the day's light and the shadows of the store. His heart froze for just a beat as he saw clearly how beautiful she still was, the remembrance of the time they had kissed as real and new as it had been then. Over-riding this sweet thought of Mamie's lips on his was his abrupt departure from her home five months before. Ashamed, instead of calling out to her, Lewis watched as she crossed the room to the counter where Cal Crueller worked the till. Young Crueller stopped what he was doing when

Mamie approached. He noticed the look on his face as he saw her, the smiles upon both, and the light touch of her gloved hand on Crueller's bare arm. He placed the shiny new axe back where he had found it, and he knew he didn't have to worry about writing that letter of explanation. He wasn't sure if he was sorry or relieved.

Finally, everything he needed had been purchased, his buckboard loaded and brought around front of the store by one of the Negro hands Cal Crueller had working for him. Before climbing into the wagon and heading home Lewis bought two glasses of ice cold lemonade at the counter inside the store, and, handing one to Dag Shorter, sat down next to the man. By this time, Dag was in his customary place on one of the rocking chairs on the porch.

"Thank ye kindly my friend," the old man said. "Not my beverage of choice, ye could say, but I s'pose beggars can't be choosy."

"You're welcome, Dag." Lewis laughed at the crooked grin slipping across the old man's face as his lips puckered with the cold tartness of the drink. "But give me a minute to cool off after loading that wagon. Maybe then we'll walk down the street and have something more to your taste."

Lewis saw his mistake as soon as he said it. Dag Shorter's eyes brightened with the sudden thought of free alcohol. He'd have to get around what he had just promised or hope the old man forgot it entirely. Knowing how Dag was about liquor, though, Lewis didn't think that likely.

"Yessir, now yore talking." Dag sat up straighter in the chair. "Thank God the old watering hole is still open for business. We had some of them Temperance folks from up north come through here shortly after the war. Came in on the coattails of them carpetbaggers. Between them, the scalawags an' their niggers full of religion up there in the state capitol running things, we almost lost our right to drink whiskey. Hell's bells, man, can ye imagine such a damn fool notion?"

Lewis wasn't sure he could, or if he even cared one way or the other. He enjoyed a drink on occasion and felt a man's decision to do so should be his alone. The outlawing of hard spirits could be a blessing for those like Dag Shorter, perhaps. But Tom Harrell in Virginia hadn't needed a saloon to get a drink of whiskey when he felt like one. He had enjoyed his home-made for a long time. Outlawed or not, men like Dag who wanted a drink would always find a way.

Dag's eyes narrowed as he looked to Lewis for comment. When none was forthcoming, after a furtive glance down the street towards the saloon that Lewis chose to ignore, he continued on.

"But good God, man, he fought for the Confederacy. He warn't really a Northerner at all. Not at heart, he warn't."

Lewis didn't know who the old man was referring to, but he was beginning to think it might be for the best to go ahead and take Dag down the street to the saloon. Buy him a couple of drinks, let him ramble on, and once he had a few, find a polite enough way to make an escape. The afternoon was wearing on and if he did not get out of town soon, it would be well after dark when he got home. But thinking further of the long ride home and the work of unloading the wagon, Lewis decided he had had enough of conversing with the old man.

"We'll talk more of this another time, Dag," he said.

Lewis stood up out of the chair abruptly. Too abruptly, as the quick rising, coupled with the exertion of the day and afternoon heat made him light headed. The porch, the sounds and sights of the street, the people passing by, old Dag looking quizzically at him, swam dizzily before his vision.

"I can see," he said, after catching his breath and the blood had returned to his head, "I've a lot to learn about the current politics of Georgia. But I've got to be heading home."

"I'm the man that can learn ye, lad." Dag was on his feet as well, staring wistfully down the street where whiskey awaited him. "Yessir, I certainly can."

Lewis told the older man that he bet he could and thanked Dag for the good talk. Pressing a fifty-cent piece in the older man's hand, he stepped off the porch towards his wagon. Lewis was just slapping the reins against the gelding's rump when Dag yelled out to him from the porch.

"Ye coming to the meeting tonight, lad?"

"What meeting is that?"

"It's right here, in the back room of the general store. For them's that's interested. I was thinking you might be one. But there's some boys in these parts taken to riding out at night looking for wayward niggers. Call themselves the Knights of the South. Been lynching any niggers they caught. Not so much around here mebbe. But they's been riding something fierce up in the north end of Ware County. Now some of the local boys are meaning to change that. Get in on the act for their own selves."

"Don't think I'll be there, Dag. I've done all the fighting for the Negroes I'm going to do."

Lewis thought of his sister, the plain food she had served up that night and the weariness in her features from doing work that had previously been done for her by others—those others mostly black. Had that truly been what he and the other white men of the south had been fighting for? To keep some in chains so that they would be free of the drudgery that so much of life was? God, but he hated to think so, but said, "It's a free country now. For everyone, white or black. Aren't those 'boys' you mention, Dag, aware of that?" he asked

"That's right, lad. So it is. A free country as ye say."

The old man's eyes were tight against the afternoon sun glaring down on the street, his whiskers a faint white in that sunlight, his face red beneath the battered hat atop his head.

"Seems like it's only the niggers 'at are free, though. Yessir, that's the way it seems. Maybe them Knights of the South can change that some."

The old man shuffled on down the street. The last Lewis saw of him before wheeling the wagon around and heading back home, Dag was hesitating at the entrance of the saloon, pausing a moment to hitch his trousers up around his waist and run a bony hand across his whiskers to smooth them into place. Then he disappeared through the open door where the comfort of whiskey and a darkened room awaited him.

It was just on the farm's side of Ruskin Creek that Lewis came upon three men on horseback in the middle of the road, the barrels of drawn guns flashing in the waning light of the afternoon as they rode in a tight circle around a black man. Lewis couldn't hear what the men were saying but the upraised hands of the black man told him enough. Taking the Colt Dragoon pistol from the holster on the wagon seat, he fired two quick shots in the air before slapping the gelding into a fast trot and bearing down on the men.

Lewis's gunshots, his sudden appearance as he barreled down in the wagon, clearly spooked the three white men off. Cowards, Lewis thought. *They won't dare fire on a fellow white man. Not in broad daylight. Even if he were coming to the rescue of a Negro.* That wasn't entirely true. One of the men—in a fit of bravery, or maybe all-consuming anger that his sport had been ruined—*did* raise his pistol at Lewis. Lewis fired a quick shot at the man that whirled the edge of his grey canvas duster as if a slight breeze had lifted it with its wind. Thinking better of it, or simply being a coward, that man, too, put spur to his horse and rode off with the others.

After brushing the dust kicked up by the horse's hooves off his clothes, the black man simply said, "Thank you, I think I will," when Lewis offered him a ride. When asked if the men had hurt him he said he was fine.

***

By the passing of the brutally hot days of August and early September most of the hard work of living on a farm during growing season had been done. The two men, Lewis and the black man, were mainly waiting to begin the harvest. Lewis figured they'd start after the first cool snap of the fall. The black man said, no, it would be best to begin a week before then. When Lewis asked how they would know that far in advance, the black man said not to worry. He'd know.

Sometimes when Lewis came out on the porch in the early morning just before sunrise, before the scraggly rooster the black man had procured with the wages Lewis paid him began to crow, he was amazed at the changes wrought upon the once dilapidated homestead. Corn rose up in the fields to the east of the house, the stalks tall, green, and wet with dew on the days when no rain was in the offing. North of those fields were rows and rows of tobacco they had struggled with all summer to keep beetles and sucker plants from draining away the quality of the crop. Finally, August and the weekly harvests had come. He and the black man walked slowly through the rows pulling leaves that were ready, stringing these leaves together on thin poles the black man had cut, and then hanging them in the rafters of the barn to cure. Lewis had high hopes for that first tobacco crop. As he worked the rows, he thought often of Tom Harrell in Virginia, of how the old man always said tobacco would be the cash crop of the future now that King Cotton was dead. The tobacco was of good quality. Lewis knew this from the crude cigars he and the black man rolled at night and smoked after dinner on the porch. He expected it to fetch a good price at the auction house in Savannah the last week of September.

To the south of the house two fields of hay had been planted, the grasses waving green and ready. The grass would go brown in the field when it was mowed. What he didn't need for the gelding Lewis would sell. And to the west, a curling plume of gray smoke was rising from the chimney of the black man's cabin. Once Dawes's cabin, it had been restored to a livable condition earlier in the spring. The black man was usually two hours earlier than Lewis. He'd appear shortly, now that Lewis was awake and about, at the front door with hot biscuits, side meat, and his invariable question of, "What's the work for today, Boss?"

One of the few things Lewis didn't like about the black man was his calling him "Boss." He didn't see it that way. What with the man's education, his command of the English language, and the mechanical skills he possessed, it seemed against all nature for the black man to assume a subservient manner around him. Of course, when Lewis thought about it, he realized there was the fact of how little experience he had of being around Negroes. Slaves seen from a distance working the fields of the Dancy plantation, servants who had gone with their masters to the war, the blacks he'd worked with on the docks of Charleston and Savannah, that had been the extent of it. When he finally asked the black man to call him something other than "Boss," it had been the last time he made that request.

"Okay, Boss. I can do that," the black man said as the two of them sat in the shade of a big oak tree bordering the field where they had been busy all morning hoeing furrows for the corn seed. "How 'bout 'Massa?' That sound better to you?"

Though the black man smiled when he said this, the joke sounded ugly to Lewis instead of funny.

"Just call me by my name."

"Would that be Mr. Raines? Or Master Raines?"

"Lewis is fine."

"I don't feel like I know you well enough yet to do that, Boss."

When I know more about myself. And what I'm doing, Lewis thought, *I'll tell him. If the chance comes. If I'm ready.*

That had been the end of it, the black man, still smiling as he rose to his feet, went back to the hard work of hoeing. Lewis supposed it was true enough, what the black man said. That afternoon on Ruskin Road he had probably saved the man's life. Without putting any thought into it at all afterwards, he had brought him back to his house. Now the man lived and worked on the farm without Lewis knowing any more about him than his first name, Waller.

Because of this, Lewis asked Waller what his last name might be.

"Isn't one."

The day had been long, hot, and oppressively humid under the May sun. A thick blanket of gray clouds had moved in around noontime, stayed, and then never yielded the rain Lewis expected. But the corn fields had all been planted and now the two men rested in the shade of Lewis' porch, the air turning cooler with the evening approaching. It was a good time to talk, to enjoy a shot or two of the good bourbon that Waller, like the scraggly rooster, had procured from somewhere.

"Just Waller, then?"

"Yessuh. Just Waller."

It was silent on the porch for a while after that except for the calling of the bobwhite quail that lived on the edges of the newly planted cornfield. The whiskey, the weariness from the day's hard work, evening falling, and the unseen quail out in the field, brought back for Lewis memories of other evenings with his father and Uncle Dawes after a day of work. Or better, hunting, the men going over the details of the day as if by doing so the good and the bad of what had transpired would stay with them, instead of fading away into memory.

"They were Carltons," Waller said, taking Lewis by surprise. He had assumed they would have one more shot of whiskey, he'd go inside for the night, and Waller would head off to his place and do the same. "My owners. Come down from New York, originally. It was the cotton that brought them to Charleston. Not to grow it, mind you. He was a broker for some folks from England, so my Momma told me. I was just a young'un when Mr. Carlton bought my Momma and me to work for them."

"So, Carlton is your last name?"

"No. I never saw it that way. Not after Momma told me I had a daddy. Just like those other white kids I use to watch from the windows of the big house on Crawford Street. 'Cept she didn't know where he'd been sold off to. Or even his last name. I always figured if he didn't need a last name then I didn't, either."

Waller took a long pull from the bottle and Lewis saw how his rough hands were shaking a little as he held the bottle to his lips. The thin, hard features of his face were almost lost in the shadows on the porch, and when he spoke again it was as if his voice, unattached to anything Lewis could see, was a soothing presence coming around just before dark.

"It was Missus Carlton taught me to read. And write, too. Said the slave laws prohibiting that were ridiculous. That sooner or later slavery would be a thing of the past. Damned if she wasn't right. She was a good woman. The Mister, too. Most of the time. In his own way. I never knew him to beat a slave or sell one off when he got mad at them. 'Course, he was new to it and it might have been different if he were a planter.

"Course," and Waller chuckled again as he handed the bottle to Lewis, "I might be different my own self if I'd been a plantation nigger. Out in them fields. 'Stead of a comfortable house boy for Mister and Missus Carlton. Yessuh, it surely would have been a different life."

Lewis didn't know about the rules of slavery, who was picked to do what, why some went up to the house and others to the field. He asked Waller as much.

"Hell, man, I don't know." There was a touch of exasperation in Waller's chuckle this time. "I know my Momma and I were plain lucky to be where we were when we were. I know that. I met some of those field hands after the war and they didn't have nothing nice to say 'bout their lot in life. Shit, the hardest work I've ever done I been doing with you right here!"

The two men laughed together now, the joke neither ugly nor misunderstood by Lewis this time.

"Yessuh, I've always been one lucky nigger, though. Slave or free. Just one lucky nigger."

That couldn't help but be true, Lewis figured. How luck had played a part in the black man's life. He had gone from the confines of slavery, growing up in chains, so to speak, into being a free man. Years of wandering had led him to a dusty road halfway between Pendleton and Ruskin, surrounded by three white men on horseback with nothing but bad intentions toward his welfare. Now he was here, on another white man's front porch, as safe and secure as one could be in this world, his stomach full, bones tired from a day's demanding work, while across the fields the comforts of a cabin he could call his own awaited him.

"I guess we're both lucky men," Lewis said as he stood up and stretched his hands out above his head, feeling the kinks and strains of the day's labor easing away. And though Waller only knew a little of what Lewis's life to that point had been like, he said softly in the dark, "Uh huh,' and the two men left it like that.

If Lewis was fine with the way he and the black man lived on the old Raines place, he was not foolish enough to think that everyone in Ware County felt the same. His suspicions were proved true on the crisp morning in November Jared Dancy rode into the yard for the second time since Lewis had returned. When he heard the barking of Waller's mongrel dog out in the road—the mottled hound had appeared out of nowhere—Lewis came out to investigate. Discovering who was riding up, he went to get the Colt Dragoon hanging in its holster on the wall peg. But like the one white man on the road that other day, he decided against the gun and instead walked back out into the sunlight to greet the intruder in his yard.

"Hello, Jared. Come to invite me over for Thanksgiving next week?"

The redder-than-roan proud horse hadn't lost a step, Lewis noticed, and he enjoyed the way the mare pranced in the cool morning as it fought against the man's grip on the reins. It was still a sad waste of good horse flesh, Lewis thought, being saddled by that man.

"No. I haven't come to do that."

Another thing Lewis enjoyed about this visit of his brother-in-law's was how Dancy kept his distance, perhaps hoping the twenty or so feet away was out of Lewis's knife range.

"This is about that nigger of yours," Dancy said, his face a shadow beneath the wide brim of the planter's hat he wore. "I was wondering if you knew he was wanted in the Carolinas?"

"Well, howdy-de-do to you as well then, Jared. If that's all you came for you have certainly wasted your time. I don't particularly care what the Carolinas want or don't want."

Lewis backed up on the porch, closer to the open door, if needed, closer to the pistol still hanging on the wall just inside that door.

"How's my sister doing by the way? And that *nigger* you referred to? He's not mine, as you say. No sir. That Waller's as free as you and me. Free to come and go as he pleases. And certainly no longer subject to any fugitive slave laws. We lost the war, you may recall."

For a moment Dancy slackened his grip on the reins. When the mare pranced into the open sunlight his face was revealed. He had aged hard since Lewis last saw him, grown even more dissolute. The flush on Dancy's face, it was true, could be explained by the coolness of the morning, the wind on him during the ride from the Landing to the Raines farm. Lewis was surprised he came alone, had to give him credit for that even if it galled him to do so. But Lewis didn't think that was the whole of it. He believed that like the other men he had come to know in his travels, his brother-in-law was probably drinking around the clock now. Lewis was willing to bet good money a few stiff belts had preceded Dancy's getting on the horse and leaving the safety of the Landing.

"Cordelia's fine." Dancy had the horse under control again and pulled her back to what he thought a safe distance from Lewis. "And though she begged me to reconsider, I held my ground. So there'll be no invitation to holiday dinner next week. No sir. Not after the way I was treated last time."

Lewis wanted to laugh at the man's self-righteous indignation, thought better of it, then went ahead and did it anyway.

"That's rich," Lewis said when his laughter faded away. In the absence of it he could hear Waller's dog barking out on the edge of the harvested cornfield. At some varmint, he thought. Hell, the biggest varmint is standing right here in front of me. "Yes indeed, that's a good one all right. It appears you and I are finally coming to understand one another. That's good. Very good."

"That's neither here nor there." Dancy's voice rose up hot and shimmering in the cool air of the morning. "I'm here now because of the nigger. The fact he's wanted in Charleston. For murder, mind you. It'd be best for you and him if you turned him over to the proper authorities."

"Would that be you?" Lewis wondered if he was going to need that pistol after all. "Those *proper authorities*?"

"In my capacity as Grand Chevalier of The Knights of the South, I suppose the answer is yes. The sheriff in Pendleton will serve as well."

"I see."

The silence after this was such that even the horse felt it, enough to cease the constant prancing in place that Dancy's tight grip on the reins hadn't been able to control. In the distance, Waller's dog had stopped its barking. Above the silence the door, in Dawes' old cabin could be plainly heard as Waller shut it behind him and began his morning stroll across the field to Lewis's.

"I s'pect that's him coming now," Lewis said. "The nigger you're thinking of turning in."

Dancy jerked his head around to where the sound of the closing door had come from, where Waller had yet to appear out of the heavy stand of oaks bordering the far edge of the harvested field.

"I might as well take him with me now," Dancy said, looking back to Lewis. "Take him on into Pendleton and turn him in."

"You won't like what happens if you try it."

The hardness in his voice surprised even Lewis, but it served to stop Dancy, who had started off across the field. *He remembers that night well,* Lewis thought. *Knows what I'm capable of. Even when I'm not sure myself.* At that moment Waller came out of the trees and into the clearing, stopping a moment before slipping back into the safety of the oaks when he saw the stranger in Lewis's yard. Dancy had seen the black man as well. He inched his hand slowly toward the holster attached to his saddle horn.

"Yes sir," Lewis said. "Go ahead and reach for that pistol. It'll make killing you that much easier."

"It's murder we're talking about here, Raines." Though Dancy's voice carried a certain conviction, he still pulled his hand away from his saddle horn and the pistol in the holster. "The nigger killed his owners, man. A man and a woman. Killed them in their sleep, I'm told."

"Well, if he did it then, I imagine they needed the killing."

Lewis's breath felt tight in his chest from not knowing if he was going to have to kill his brother-in-law or not. Just like before a battle. Just like when he awoke that night in the rooming house to find Rafe standing over his bed and knew he had to kill him.

"If Charleston wants him," Lewis said, "then they can come and get him. But not you."

That heavy silence came on again, almost enough to suffocate him. Clearly, enough to freeze Waller where he was in the uncertain safety of the trees on the edge of the field. Lewis wondered if the black man knew that what the two white men were engaged in concerned him, wondered just as quickly why he would even think such a foolish thing.

"No sir," Lewis said when he could talk again, when the silence and the suffocation it brought had lifted and it was a crisp day in November once more with everything clean and fine and as it should be. "No sir," he repeated. "Not you, Dancy. Not today."

Dancy, lips set tight and fast, like his hands holding the reins, wheeled the horse around suddenly and galloped out of the yard. His leaving empty handed like that was certain to mean trouble. Of that, Lewis had no doubts. But he said nothing. Only walked out into the field to meet Waller coming towards him. When the two men met in the middle of the mowed ground he took his friend's hand and asked, "You ready to get to work?"

***

On the Sunday night before Christmas Lewis lay buried beneath the comfort of a store-bought quilt, tired from a day of hunting, but not finding a turkey for Christmas. Well, that was how it was. There were three days left before the holiday. Still time to secure a holiday dinner.

And if not? He and Waller would come up with something. So far they always had.

He was dreaming beneath the downy covers of being with his father and Uncle Dawes. In this dream Lewis was younger, maybe twelve, and they were hunting for bear along the edges of the creek off Ruskin road. That's what they were hunting, for bear, with their two dogs—George and Washington, big blue-tick hounds that Dawes had named—baying from somewhere far away. Riding up from the dry bottom of the creek bed, Lewis could see clearly how the two dogs had a bear up in the branches of an old oak on the ridge above the creek. He could see that as well as Uncle Dawes riding next to him and drawing his rifle from the scabbard as he rode. The sound of the shot rang loud in Lewis's head and rang all the way through the dream as the bear toppled out of the tree and hit the ground. The dogs were on the crumpled brown and both Dawes and Edwin were yelling at the dogs, *Back off, goddamnit.*

Then Lewis was awake and sitting up on the edge of the bed and it was no dream. The dogs barking so vividly were only one dog, Waller's. Just as the dogs in his dream had stopped suddenly with the sound of Dawes's rifle going off, so had Waller's stopped its barking, the gunshot quieting the dog as Lewis came fully awake.

He scrambled into his pants and ran out into the yard, Colt Dragoon in one hand. In his haste and confusion, he was unable to determine where the smoke, the yelling of the men, were coming from. But after taking a deep breath, pausing to rein in his senses, it didn't take long to figure out. In fact, he probably knew all along and simply wanted it not to be so. He only had to go around the side of his house to find the truth, to look to the north past the border of oak and pine trees against the clearing there and see the orange flames and smoke rising from where Waller's cabin stood.

Lewis was running, barefoot, across the field toward the trees and beyond them where the smoke poured up into the sky. The grass in the field, cropped short by the two milk cows that grazed it freely, felt wet and cold. He wondered why he hadn't bothered to put on his boots. No time, he thought. As he burst out of the trees on the other side of the field into the rough yard Waller had cleared around his cabin, Lewis saw his friend. Waller, in just his nightshirt and that was ripped to shreds, tied to a pine tree standing just on the edge of the cleared yard. The black man's hard face was drawn tighter by pain, his fear terribly plain to see in the orange light cast off by the cabin fire. Muscles in his arms and thighs strained against the ropes holding but these efforts were futile, and Lewis felt certain the black man knew that. Any possible escape could have only come from Lewis and he was only one man. One man against four men on horseback, weaving in and out of the firelight.

"Lookee here, boys. The nigger lover finally decided to show up for the party."

The harsh voice of whoever spoke these words was the last conscious thing Lewis heard. Before he could raise the Colt and fire at the nearest intruder, a hard blow on the back of his head sent him to his knees amid the sound of men laughing.

He came to sometime later, tied, like Waller, to one of the pine trees ringing the yard. Unlike the black man, the only harm done to him had been the blow to his head. The night riders hadn't been as kind to Waller. In the orange light of the still-burning cabin Lewis couldn't hide from what they were doing to his friend.

One of the men was busy pressing a hot iron into the flesh of the black man. Lewis could see from the burn marks on Waller's face, neck, and arms that they had been at it for a while. The man with the hot iron seemed familiar to Lewis, but only from the way he moved, since his face was covered by a dark, almost metallic looking mask. The other three men wore the same sort of mask. The horses were covered as well by the same dark material as their riders. The effect was that of medieval knights, such as the Black Knights Walter Scott had written about in the books on King Arthur's court Lewis had read long ago.

It was happening now. When he looked again at Waller his stomach turned upside down and he felt all his self float away in a sickening lurch. Another of the men had dismounted and approached the black man. A skinning knife in one hand glistened in the light of the fire as he cut into Waller's leg and then drew it slowly, cutting the black skin away to reveal the pinkish membrane and veins hidden inside. *Why doesn't he scream?* Lewis wondered if *he* would. Stronger, braver, men than he had certainly screamed in pain and fear on the battlefields of the war. His question, though, was answered in the next moment when, hypnotized by the methodical cutting, Lewis followed the blade down and saw a dark mass of something laying on the ground at the black man's tied feet. In another sickening instant he realized it was his friend's tongue.

"My fellow Knight learned that little trick out in the Territories."

The voice, gruff and muffled from beneath the man's mask as he reined up before Lewis, was the voice he had heard right before being knocked unconscious. Had this man delivered the blow, or one of the others? Lewis supposed it didn't really matter.

"Fighting with Stand Watie and his half-breed patriots."

The man on the horse laughed, one gloved hand pointing at Waller tied to the tree and the man busy defiling him. The laugh wasn't much of a laugh; more a guttural snort smothered by the heavy cloth covering the man's face.

"If fighting is what you want to call it. Robbing and raping's more like it from what I heard. But it's a good trick he learned. That skinnin' a man alive. Wouldn't ye say?"

But Lewis said nothing—stared instead at the man and the horse before him, glad for something to focus on besides what was being done to Waller.

"Ah, I see. Cat's got your tongue. Be glad it was the cat and not Skinner over yonder."

He laughed a long time and when the laughter came to an end the man's muffled voice almost sounded sad beneath the mask.

"Well, it's a good trick. Whether ye think so or not. Skinner swears it's the best way going to get useful information from an otherwise close-mouthed individual. Not that there's anything we need to know from the likes of that one. That's why I let him lop the nigger's tongue off." The gloved hand pointed at Waller again. "Lying murdering nigger pretty near says it all. We didn't need to hear anything else. There's a thing or two ye might want to learn, though."

The man leaned over his saddle horn, his voice low and serious now from behind the mask. "Skinner wanted to work on ye a bit. But the rest of us said no. Said you was a white man. Even if ye didn't act like it at times. Said your family's name was still a good one in these parts. I told them—and I surely hope you'll be grateful for this—all ye needed was a good lesson. Make ye see the errors of your ways. So, here's your lesson. Ye best learn it well, Lewis Raines."

The man's voice rose so that even the mask couldn't muffle it anymore, loud and clear over the sound of the fire burning down Waller's cabin and the life being taken from him.

"If we have to come back here we won't go so easy on ye. No sir, we surely won't."

The men freed Waller, briefly, and only to hang him from the branch of a sturdier oak tree. Before untying him from the pine, though, they took the time to prepare the makings of a good bonfire. They hoisted Waller up, lit the wood, and left the black man dangling by his neck over it. His feet, while he was still alive and the breath not quite choked out of him, kicked vainly above the flames. It took longer than Lewis thought possible for Waller to die. But he did, his body hanging limply over the fire until the skin caught and the blaze consumed what was left of him.

Lewis watched it all, the men made sure of that, one of them coming up and with his rough hands twisting Lewis's face back when he tried to turn away once. Watched Waller die in agony, the two friends' eyes locked on each other's as the last of the black man's life expired. It was only after Waller was dead that the men rode off, firing their pistols in the air as they galloped away. The first light of morning broke to the east. With the smell of burnt flesh strong in his nostrils and weak from a shock he hadn't known since The Wilderness, Lewis passed out.

A boy, perhaps fifteen or sixteen years of age, found Lewis the next morning. Lewis came to when the youth stumbled into the remains of the carnage, the two living humans on the dismal scene staring suddenly in surprise at one another.

"Goddamnit, mister. You surely look like hell. What'n the world happen'd here?"

The boy was tall, gangly, and scarred, a musket slung over one shoulder, the game bag tied to his waist heavy with a turkey.

"A man died, boy. Now cut me loose with that Bowie knife of yours and help me get him down."

The back of Lewis' nightshirt was so sticky with resin from being held tight against the pine that when the boy cut the ropes, the cotton fabric ripped away in places, the sudden cool air on his exposed skin a hard slap to his senses.

"Well, shit, Mister," the boy said as he sawed at the heavy ropes with his hunting knife. "I can see 'at. Like ye said, how a man died and all. But it sure ain't saying much."

"That's saying plenty," Lewis said. Wanting to believe it himself that it was true, he said again, "Plenty."

Lewis and the boy buried Waller in a copse of live oaks on the edge of the cleared field. He shoveled dirt and red Georgia clay over Waller's ruined face and covered him up for good. With the boy's help they gathered up rocks from the edge of the clearing and made a rudimentary cairn over the rough grave. It was plain he had done a poor job of protecting his friend from two-legged predators, Lewis felt. Maybe he could prevent four-legged ones from disturbing his remains.

Yet when he went to say a few words over the grave none would come. All he could think of was a man atop a horse, the identity of the man hidden beneath his dark mask. But the horse's prancing, sideways step had been a dead giveaway, Lewis thought as he turned away from the grave. He knew that horse. As he walked across the field to his cabin, Lewis thought of that horse prancing in the firelight.

Yes, I certainly know that horse.

He didn't understand any of what had transpired during the long hours of the night. But he knew that horse. Knew the man who rode him.

***

"'Lo, Lewis," Jared Dancy said to him that morning. "This is an unexpected visit. Though I suppose it *is* Christmas."

"Unexpected, you say?" Lewis drew the Colt Dragoon pistol from the waistband of his canvas trousers and leveled it at his brother-in-law. "Don't know why you'd think so."

Dancy was backing toward the door when Lewis shot him, the ball tearing into his groin, the force of it enough to blow him up against the door of the house he had hoped to escape behind. With both hands clutching at his wound Dancy slumped heavily down on the floor of the verandah.

"What have ye done, man," he moaned, his face pale with shock and the blood pouring out of him. "He was only a nigger." Dancy paused, reaching for breath, and then asked again, "What have ye done?"

"Not near enough," Lewis said. He dismounted and in a few quick steps was on the verandah and crouching over the wounded man. The rage was almost gone from him; Lewis could feel it slipping away. But there was one last thing he wanted to do. Drawing his knife, he said again, "Not near enough, Dancy. But this'll have to do."

He had just cut his brother-in-law's throat when Cordelia burst screaming through the front doors like a howling banshee from hell with her long-unbraided hair flying around her shoulders.

"I'm sorry," he said, looking up from what he'd accomplished. "This should have been done a long time ago. Our father offered him an honorable way out of this life, but he refused. I would have liked the same chance, but he wouldn't let me."

Lewis saw how his sister didn't understand. Perhaps she couldn't remember that night at the Dancys' dinner table when all of them were still alive and their father had challenged her husband. It had happened, and Dancy had refused. It *had* happened. She just couldn't remember. It was just as well she didn't. Didn't know her husband preferred to let others do his killing while he stood back and watched like the coward he was.

"I would have liked the chance," Lewis said once more.

That was the end of it. He only looked back once as he rode up the lane away from Blackshear Landing to see his sister kneeling down and cradling her dead husband's head in her lap. It was a shame, Lewis thought, turning his attention to the road ahead of him. It was a pretty dress Cordelia wore that Christmas morning. The blood would surely ruin it.

Part Three: Florida

Hatred was never a part of what had happened. Lewis refused to believe that. He had killed too many men during the war and had never known hate to be a part of it. He didn't like the sour taste in his mouth when it was over, that much was clear. One night over a campfire and a meal of jerky, the little fire barely enough to keep him warm against the damp December air, he realized that sour taste was with him before—well before he turned the dappled gelding up the lane leading to Blackshear Landing.

The horse carried Lewis at a steady pace out of Georgia and away from his home into Alabama, across Mississippi, and finally, to the eastern banks of the great river that state was named for. He had read about the Mighty Mississippi as a youth. Later, during the war, he had been told stories about how it was living along its banks from men who had before conflict called them away. Still, the river took him aback, the immensity and flowing strength of it more than any river he had encountered before. Much wider than the Potomac, the last river he had forded. Like then, with the shattered army retreating from Gettysburg, he was fleeing for his life. Once he was on the other side of the muddy river that might not be the case. It was a big country, getting bigger all the time. Once west of the Mississippi, Lewis was willing to wager if a man wanted hard enough not to be found, he wouldn't be.

There was no going back east. The good citizens of Ware County would require his neck for what he had done, of that he was positive. Yet he never hurried his pace, but held the gelding to its natural steady gait, the constant rhythm of the horse's hooves against the ground calling out to Lewis that yes, he may be fleeing for his life, but he was not running.

A ferryman—a rough cut man with a crooked back and an ageless expression on his tooth-missing grin—took Lewis and the gelding across the river at a nameless crossing. Winter had set in properly, bitterly cold with snowflakes whirling against Lewis's face. Everything had gone gray that January, both sky and earth. With his back bent so badly, Lewis didn't see how the ferryman could actually pull the flat-bottomed barge over the surging river to the other side. He was partially right. The man had a sure grip on the rope and it was not until they were mid-stream where the current was the strongest, that the ferryman asked for help. The wet hawser, attached to a solid oak on the far bank, felt rough and heavy in Lewis's hands and they quickly lost feeling from the cold water they pulled the rope through. Occasionally, the barge was assailed by floating logs in the river and clumps of earth with uprooted trees still attached to them.

Once safely on the other shore he paid the ferryman, asking as he pulled a fresh bill from his leather pouch, where, and how far, the nearest town might be. It had been a hard three weeks of riding and sleeping out in the cold. He was tired, wanting only a comfortable place to rest for a few days. He needed supplies as well, for both him and the horse, for whatever the next stage of their journey may be.

"El Dorado ain't too far." The ferryman's words came faint in the northerly wind and Lewis had to strain to hear what the man was saying. "Not more than a day's ride. Other than that, the next town be Texarkana. A good five days. Maybe more. Depending on the weather I imagine."

"*The* El Dorado? The streets really made of gold there?"

The joke didn't take, the blank stare he received from the boatman evidence of that. He tipped his hat to the man and rode on. That night he slept inside four walls for the first time since leaving Blackshear Landing on Christmas morning. Everything in his life had changed since Waller's killing. Lewis remembered the event as he drifted off to sleep in the warmth of the meager room in the El Dorado Hotel.

***

By the spring of that year Lewis was in Ft. Smith, Arkansas. Noticing a handbill drifting along the sidewalk, he picked it up, followed its instructions, and come mid-July, along with a band of grizzled fur trappers, he was deep in the highest range of mountains he had ever seen, the "Rockies" as they were called by the trappers. July found him astride what one of the trappers said was the dividing point of the whole continent. It was from here, the trapper went on, that rivers ran east one way and west the other. Standing atop the Continental Divide with all the mountain ranges stretching out above, below, and around him, the highest and furthest away covered in low-hanging cloud banks, Lewis decided he had had enough of the east. More than enough.

The following spring the trappers and Lewis returned to Ft. Smith with their pelts. They were paid well for the furs and after a week of drinking and whoring in Ft. Smith, Lewis returned to the mountains. He repeated this cycle—going it alone from then on—for three years. He grew lean and grizzled like the fur trappers he first set out with, grew a full beard as well that needed to be shaved by the town barber before he went visiting the saloons and whorehouses. One spring when he rode into the town he found it was deserted. The fur buyers were gone, and except for the proprietor of the general store, so was everyone else. When asked, an excited man out in front of the store busy packing an already over-loaded mule with further provisions, told Lewis how Custer and his men had discovered gold in the Black Hills. The pelts Lewis had worked so hard for were worthless. Gold was now the going commodity. Lewis didn't know where, or what, the Black Hills were, but the next day he turned the dappled gelding's head west once more, figuring to find out.

***

On a damp morning in early October eleven years later, just as the sun was beginning to burn off the fog he had been riding through since dawn, Lewis reached the end of the line—or dry land at any rate. To go further would require a boat. Or wings, he thought ruefully as he stared out over the expanse of water putting an end to his travel for the time being. At first, he assumed the body of water to be the Gulf of Mexico— he had been riding along the outside edges of that gulf for the last month without ever seeing it. But as the fog burned off and his surroundings became more evident, Lewis saw that it was a bay which led into the gulf, judging by the peninsula points almost encircling it and the wide open sparkling water off in the distance visible between the two points of land.

He had reined up in front of a train depot on the outskirts of a small community built out of the pine woods in a past of indeterminate time.

Some of the houses and other buildings showed different stages of painting and maintenance. Coming across railroad tracks earlier in the morning, Lewis had figured they'd lead him to civilization sooner or later.

"What town might this be?" Lewis called out to a young man coming out of the depot office. The black vest, white shirt, and visor atop the youth's head indicated he must work there, was probably telegraph operator and maybe depot manager all rolled into one. "I saw no notice on my way in."

"We had to take them down," the young man said.

The youth stopped on the platform, a sheaf of papers in his hand, to stare at the stranger. Lewis knew he had to be an oddity to the young man, what with the trail-grimed duster and chaps he wore. A common enough sight in Texas, perhaps, where Lewis had come from. Maybe not so common in the little town he now found himself. The same could probably be said for his horse, the big palomino. And the horse *was* big, almost eighteen hands high, broad-backed and with strong legs. Though he was certainly ungainly looking, the big horse was fast with a rough grace and surprisingly gentle gait that had served Lewis well over the four months it had taken him to ride from Texas. He had traded two mustangs for the big yellow horse. Uncertain as to his future livelihood, Lewis wanted a horse that could pull a heavy load, a plow, and if needed, cut cattle. He called the palomino, "Horse," or "Boy," and it responded well enough to both that Lewis decided they were name enough.

"We were known as Black Point up until last week," the youth continued, his expression indicating he had appraised and then made a favorable decision about the sudden stranger in his town. "Then Mr. Plant decided to change the name to Port Tampa." The youth laughed. "He must know something the rest of us don't. I don't know about you but it sure don't look like much of a port to me."

The morning fog was almost completely burned away and down by the water Lewis could see two long docks running out into the bay, two wharf areas at the end of the docks, and behind them two small warehouses.

"No," Lewis said. "I have to admit it does not. Your Mr. Plant must be a rare man of vision."

"If he's half as good with ports as he is railroads we should be okay." The young depot manager's smile seemed to spread even wider, apparently with confidence that what he had just told the stranger in town was the truth.

I was like that once, Lewis thought. When I rode off with Dawes to see what the war, and the world, had to offer. Daddy's pistol stuck in my waistband and feeling finally like I was a man.

"Anyway," the boy's voice intruded on Lewis's thoughts, "We're waiting for the new signs Mr. Plant ordered from the home office in Jacksonville. Should be in tomorrow afternoon according to Mr. Plant. If you stick around long enough, you'll be witness to the big celebration."

"Celebration?"

"Yessir! Mr. Plant says there'll be reporters and dignitaries of all kinds from as far away as Atlanta and St. Louis when he cuts the ribbon to open the new port for business."

The Black Point Inn, just down the street from the depot, had a room for Lewis at one dollar a day, fifty cents extra if he wanted board. Lewis assured the plump, florid faced woman who ran the inn that he'd require board for as long as he stayed. She showed him to a room upstairs with a window that opened out toward the bay. "It will be more comfortable up here," she told him as she took a week's payment from him. Hot as it's been lately at least on this end of the house you'll get the breeze from the water." He thanked her and when she had left he put his saddle bags in the one chair provided with the room and sat down on the bed. Along with the chair and the single bed, a dresser was pushed up against the wall; atop the dresser was a china pitcher and basin for his wash-up needs. There were two privies out back of the house, "For when Nature calls," the landlady said. Told him there was a bigger wash tub downstairs in the laundry room if he needed. "Just let me know if you'll be wanting that," she added. "I'll have hot water for you."

Yes indeed, a comfortable enough place to stay for a while, he thought as he pulled his boots off and set them by the bed. Suddenly,

Lewis felt weary, a body-numbing tiredness that started in his shoulders and spread down all along his back and legs. He lay back on the bed, thinking of how badly he needed some rest after the days of being in the saddle—not to mention the nights of sleeping on hard and either damp or cold ground.

But the afternoon was too hot to sleep. To cool down he stripped off the canvas shirt and britches and lay on top of the sheets in just his long johns and cotton undershirt, savoring the small relief the clean and cool sheets afforded. Muted sounds of men working down in the rail yard and the wharf drifted through the open window, reminding Lewis he'd have to find work soon. The cash reserve from the sale of his herd and small place on the Sabine was almost gone. Not that finding work had ever been a problem. He was willing to work hard, even at jobs that some men wouldn't do. Either the rail yard or the docks would have something for him, he was sure. Or, one of those boats he had seen while talking with the young man at the train depot. He had never worked on the water—only by it, as in Charleston and Savannah those long years back. Maybe this place, soon to be Port Tampa, held a new kind of work for him. That would fit in well with the idea of the clean start he had carried with him as he rode away from the cattle ranch he had struggled to build along the Sabine River. Time would tell, he decided.

It had been a long and varied road he had taken to reach Black Point, Lewis thought as he lay on the sheets damp, his body cooled by his sweat and the little breeze through the window.

The Black Hills had certainly been a bust for him and thinking about the traveling he had done to get where he was now, he couldn't help but remember those godforsaken mountains. At the end of his time in those hills, he had found himself back on the plains with no horse, clothes in tatters, and possessing only a bag of gold dust the Cheyenne hadn't taken, the Colt Dragoon, and wondering what in the hell he was going to do next.

Survival seemed as good a plan as he could come up with then, and to do so he walked south on the hot prairie. It was cold at night. A freezing cold he was barely able to shelter himself from with the small fires he managed to build and the underbrush he covered himself with in lieu of a blanket or bedroll. He drank water from the scattered sump holes he came across and was able to catch rabbits and prairie dogs with a crude snare an old trapper had taught him how to make during his days in the Rockies. It wasn't much, but enough to keep him alive.

Lewis didn't begrudge the Cheyenne the dappled gelding—he was lucky that was all they took. There were three of them in the raiding party that stole into his camp that night and Lewis, alerted by something he could not put a name on, saw them in a slip of moonlight falling through the aspens and lodge pole pines as they came in. One of the braves shot at Lewis as he rose up out of his blankets with the Winchester in his hand. The shot missed him but spun the rifle away into the darkness. Relying on instinct, he fell back as the warrior that shot him came in for his scalp. Lewis was ready for him, Bowie knife in hand, thinking he'd at least take this one with him. But something spooked the other two braves and they hollered out in Cheyenne to their fellow warrior. With no time to scalp his kill the brave settled for taking coup instead and the blow from the brave's war club knocked Lewis unconscious. When he came to, the morning light was just filtering in through the trees. He found the dappled gelding gone, along with his rifle. The gold was of no use to the Cheyenne, but the horse and rifle were.

He certainly missed that horse on his lonely walk. After five days he stumbled upon the stage and freight line to Edgemont, the little supply post at the foot of the rail line to Deadwood. Sooner or later one or the other would come by, a stage coach or a train of freight wagons, and Lewis sat down by the worn ruts of the road to wait. He didn't have to wait long; a day later a train of empty wagons heading back to Ft. Kearny picked him up.

One week later, rested and fed, Lewis arrived in Ft. Kearny. He cashed his gold dust in at the assayer's office, spent two nights in the hotel, got drunk, and lay with a woman upstairs of the saloon. Once his senses were sated he purchased a horse, new clothes, a rifle, and mounted the new horse and began heading south.

Neither Kansas nor Oklahoma appealed to Lewis—the month of steady riding it took him to cross the hot plains of both convinced him of that. A saloon keeper in Sherman, Texas, told him that if he were looking to either farm, or graze cattle, there was good country down along the Sabine River. He couldn't swear to it personally, not having been there his own self.

Come a warm and humid day in late August of 1874, some two months after the Cheyenne left him for dead, Lewis found himself following the banks of the Sabine. When he first emerged from the pine woods he had ridden through for most of the day, he was greeted by vast fields of waving brown switch grass, dotted here and there with wild pecan trees. Off along the edge of the river, stands of cypress trees rose up from the muddy banks of the Sabine. For a brief moment Lewis was overwhelmed by a feeling of having been at that place before—of being miraculously back in the red clay pine and oak lands of southern Georgia where in his youth he had thrived until the war changed everything.

The feeling passed as quickly as it had come, and Lewis decided that it *was* good country. Rich, black soil lay beneath the top grasses of the prairie, a condition Lewis discovered when he dismounted from the horse and scooped up a handful of grass and soil. He let it sift slowly through his fingers. Good country indeed. Rich soil for crops. Plenty of grass for grazing livestock, as well as for hay when the winter came. A flowing river, that he could hear running its course on the other side of the cypress trees, would be able to provide the water needed for both animals and crops. He camped that night in a high hummock set back from the river and slept soundly for the first time in a very long time. In the morning he knew he would stay.

It was a good life along the river and for the first time he was pretty much alone—just him, the two hundred acres he homesteaded, the cattle, the corn, and beans and other crops that he raised. After a while others came and he had neighbors. Soon there was a thriving community, a town with a church, saloon, bank, and sheriff. A fine life indeed. Until one night as he lay in his bed in the two-room cabin that served for a home and had a sudden desire to move on. To go even further south. A desire that stayed with him all the next day and for the day after that—stayed with him until he could ignore the desire no longer.

As he fell asleep on that hot afternoon in Black Point, Lewis wondered if he would settle here or travel again back to Georgia.

***

Sick with some sort of ague, Lewis missed the big event, the renaming of the town from Black Point to Port Tampa. He could hear the celebration coming through the window, could hear through the haze of fever and chills racking his body, the bands playing marching songs, *The Star-Spangled Banner, God Bless America* and *Dixie*. Cannons were fired out over the bay and in the lull after each cannon volley the roaring of hoarse voices drifted up into his room. In his delirium he mistook the yelling and the cannon for Pickett's men moving out into the valley below the ridge where he stood with his artillery unit. Even in the haze of sickness, Lewis hated the thought of those men marching into the teeth of the blazing Yankee cannons—cannons his and the other batteries had failed to silence. The war was with him again. The same as that day atop the ridge Lewis tried to stop it and called out for Captain Harker to keep the troops from marching to their doom. Then the sickness overtook him, and he drifted away.

He had been ill like that only once before, as a child. Both he and his sister, Cordelia, had lain for days in their beds with some un-named fever while their mother tended to them. For a while, amidst the chills, the fever, the soaring pain ripping through his body, his mother was with him again. He could hear her voice, low and soothing as she placed cool wet cloths against his face and chest—could feel her hands easing the illness away. "The fever will break soon," he heard her say. "It's almost there and then the crisis will pass." He had always believed his mother. "There, there," she said. "There, there."

It was not his mother at the dresser preparing cool poultices Lewis saw when he was finally past the point where sickness and reality joined. "Senora," he said to the woman. "Gracias."

"Si," she said, coming over to the bed with a fresh cloth in her hand. "De nada."

"Que?" He pointed at himself and then the bed and repeated, "Que?"

A little slip of what seemed to be a grin spread her lips as she leaned forward over him. The wet fabric of the cloth she put to his forehead was cool and refreshing against his clammy skin. A secret, he thought. That little grin. Some kind of a secret.

"Quattro, Senor."

"Quattro?" Four days? He had been in bed floating in and out of this world for four days? he asked himself.

"Si," she answered when he asked again just to make sure. The woman had a full smile and before he knew, or could understand, the room was filled with her laughter, clear and rhythmic and as tonal as the happy bells of Sunday mornings Lewis could remember of his youth.

"What's so funny?" Having run through his limited amount of Spanish, Lewis had no choice but to speak in English and repeated, "What the hell's so funny?"

But it was beyond him and he was laughing, too, along with the woman, though he was damned if he knew why.

"You thought I was Spanish." She was leaning up against the closed door of the room, a hand across her breast as if to keep the laughter from flying further away.

"That broken lingo. I'm sorry, but I played along as best as I could. But the look on your face when I said you'd been down for four days was too much for me. I'm sorry."

Listening to her talk, even through the gasps of broken laughter, Lewis could see how obviously he had been wrong—in English all trace of a Spanish accent was gone, replaced by the soft, long drawl of someone from South Texas. Lewis knew the accent from hunting mustangs with his neighbor from the Sabine, Ed White, and Ed's brother who owned a small spread along the Rio Grande. He saw as well she was not that far removed from being a girl.

"I was mistaken," he said. To make light of it some he added, "Senorita." Then spoke again when his breath had returned, "Actually, I thought you were Mexican. I don't believe I've ever met a genuine Spaniard."

"I see."

Her face fell for a moment and he worried that without meaning to he had offended her. It was true, though, he had believed her to be from below the border. She had a thick mane of black hair falling upon bare, light brown shoulders as she prepared the cloth in the basin of cool water. Her dark eyes and the colorful flowing dress and white low-cut blouse she wore were the visible things that had created his mistaken notion.

"For your sake, Senor," she said as she crossed the small space of the room to the dresser and basin where another of the cotton cloths lay soaking. He couldn't see her flashing eyes and wished that he could. "It's very good my grandfather is not here to hear you insult his family so. I'm afraid you would have to answer for that.

"Yes indeed, fine sir, my grandfather would have surely demanded blood for callous remarks such as yours."

Half-expecting the room to be filled again with laughter, he was disappointed when it wasn't. Her smile said much, though, and was almost as enveloping as the laughter had been. Lewis found himself smiling again and suddenly glad to be alive.

The next morning when he awoke the chills and fever were gone. Yet he was still weak, and when he tried to get out of the bed a wave of dizziness stopped him. If the girl hadn't come into the room just then and taken him by the arm he would've fallen.

"Not quite ready, Mr. Raines, I see."

Nodding his head in agreement he allowed her to help him back into bed. The peasant clothes she had worn the day before had been replaced by a simple white cotton dress that made her seem more a professional nurse. The rich, dark hair and flashing eyes were the same he saw. She can't hide that beauty, he thought. No matter what clothes she might choose to wear.

The nearness of her as she fluffed the pillows behind his head, her face, the fullness and clean smell of her body, was powerful and he closed his eyes as the faintness washed over him again. It had been a long time since he had been that close to a desirable woman and this one was certainly desirable. None of the women of his recent and not-so-recent past came close to this one nursing him back to health. Whores, all of them. Or saloon girls pretending they were not.

The woman with him in the room now seemed real—seemed certain of her place in the world. Like Sarah, he thought suddenly, in Savannah after the war.

Thinking of Sarah, of how she had been in his arms when they lay naked together at night, Lewis groaned.

"Now I know for a fact, Mr. Raines," the woman said when she heard him moan, "You definitely aren't ready to be out of this bed."

"No, I suppose you're right."

He was embarrassed, knowing the groan for what it was, and was tempted to keep his eyes closed until the woman left the room. But he couldn't and when he opened them she was still standing by the side of his bed, arms folded across her breasts, a concerned look on her face. The morning sunlight coming through the open window lit up dust motes in the room caught in the breeze off the bay. The woman looked to Lewis as if she were some sort of ethereal entity. An un-earthly being such as the ones his mother used to read to him about when he was a boy. But a cloud came back over the sun, the light in the room dimmed, and Lewis saw that she was a woman and not some spirit from the beyond.

"You have me at a disadvantage," he said when the faintness had passed and he could speak.

"Oh, I do, do I? And why is that?" That little slip of a grin was back on her lips. "Perhaps because you're ill and at my mercy?"

"There is that. But more because you know my name. Yet, I don't know yours."

"I see. You're right. I'm not being fair to you. Mi llama Inez."

"No," he said with a weak laugh. "No more Spanish."

"Dixon's my last name," she said. "Is that English enough for you?" Once again it appeared he had offended her, for the secret grin was replaced by a frown that was not so secret. "Dixon is my married name. I was born a Strater."

"All the Dixons I knew were from Georgia. You don't talk like you're from Georgia."

"No, no, I'm not from Georgia. My husband was. Might even be there now. Or someplace else. I wouldn't know. Wouldn't care to know."

"Sounds like a sad tale."

"A very sad tale. One you wouldn't be interested in hearing." She came over to the bed holding a water glass filled to the brim with a brown, noxious looking liquid. "Here," she said, holding the glass out. "This will make you feel better. Even if you won't believe it. But drink it you must."

Accepting the glass from her he took a tentative sip. It was no lie what she said about the liquid in the glass. It was hard to believe such a nasty beverage could make one feel better.

"C'mon, cowpoke. None of that sissy lady sipping stuff. Drink it down like it was some of that fine rotgut you men like to indulge in on a Saturday night."

As he drank there was that laughter he so wanted to hear—just having it with him in the room seemed to change the day completely.

He dreamt that night he was back in the Black Hills. The snow was still on the mountain tops and a cold wind from Canada roared down from the white frosted peaks through the tree line where the snow ended. He didn't know if it was winter or perhaps early spring, but he was cold. He had a feeling in the dream that it was late afternoon and night was coming on. He shivered against the approach of it as he stood out on a rocky promontory, staring into a ravine that ran beneath the peak. There was movement in the ravine below and straining his eyes, he saw the dappled gelding come out of the tree line. The horse was all mottled white, clear and alive again in his dream. The Indian who had tried to kill him sat atop the gelding, wrapped in a bearskin against the cold. Turning slowly, he looked up toward Lewis and raised something in his hands. It was Lewis's blanket and bedroll, the two things he'd need most for shelter against the cold of the night. With an angry gesture, the brave tossed both blanket and bedroll on the ground, then shook his fist defiantly at Lewis. Lewis knew it was too far to go down into the ravine to get what would save him. He was weak, and it was too cold. He awoke to find the window of the room wide open. It was much cooler now, with a strong wind from the north howling outside. Shivering, Lewis hobbled from the bed to the window and closed it. When he was back in bed he closed his eyes and hoped to dream of the dappled gelding again—but did not.

The day broke clear and much cooler than it had been, a welcome relief after the hot humid end of a summer that had stayed on too long. Lewis was able to get out of the bed on his own and when a light knock on the door came he was standing by the window, washed, dressed, and looking out at the sparkling bay.

"You've never knocked before, Senorita," he said as Inez came into the room carrying a silver tray with what appeared to be breakfast.

"Up until yesterday you haven't been awake to know if I knocked or not," she told him, adding, "Senor."

That curious, half-twist of a grin of hers did something to his insides—much like when the ground had exploded at his feet that last day of the battle when the war had ended. Powerful like that but in a different way, a much better way. Confused by the sudden emotion he turned away.

"Four days you said."

"Yes, that was the worst of it." She set the tray on the dresser and motioned for him to sit on the bed. "I think you're ready for some solid food, Mr. Raines."

On the plate she handed him was a mound of steaming scrambled eggs, slices of hot bread, and grits with butter melted all over them, the sort of breakfast Lewis had not eaten in a very long time. He was immediately ravenous but when he picked up a fork and started in on the food, Inez cautioned him.

"Easy now, Mr. Raines. You've had nothing but liquids lately. You'll have to eat like a gentleman if you want to enjoy this nice breakfast I made."

"Not sure if I know how it is exactly a gentleman eats."

"Perhaps along with the language of my grandfather I can teach you the ways of polite society. Grandee style. Sort of like it was down in South Texas when my grandfather was in his prime."

"Perhaps. The language, maybe. The other I doubt."

It was quiet in the room as he ate. The food was good, and he was surprised how famished he was. But he did as the woman said and ate slowly. He tried to remember when a meal had tasted so good. The other surprise was how much stronger he felt when he was finished. Afterwards, the two of them did something that unknowingly became a part of their daily routine for a while—at least until he was well enough to find work. They left the inn and walked down to the wharves by the water.

A train, open freight cars stacked high with coal from Pennsylvania, sat at the end of the rail line. A crew of men, their faces and arms black and lined with coal dust, were busy unloading the coal into one end of a warehouse on the wharf. At the other end of the warehouse men rolled wheel barrows filled with the coal down to a steamship waiting at the end of the pier. Train, men, the black coal, all stood out in contrast to the blue-green of the bay and the clear sky above.

Lewis breathed in the fresh clean air, the sights and sounds of the men working, the woman next to him on the quay, all bringing back to him that he was alive.

"Your husband was from Georgia, you mentioned," Lewis said somewhat nervously to the woman after a long silence between them as they sat.

"Yes."

She didn't look at him as she spoke. She seemed focused instead on the water rippling away from the dock in the offshore breeze. Lewis took the opportunity to marvel at the richness of her dark hair lying against her neck.

"From Atlanta," she continued. "His family had no name left in that town and he had to seek his fortune elsewhere. From the war, you understand."

"I do."

"Being of age and with the doors closed to him in Atlanta, Clayton went to Texas. To Laredo. Where he met me."

"I understand about the loss of a good name in Georgia," Lewis said. "Better than I'd care to."

She turned and looked into his eyes and he hoped very badly that none of what he was remembering was visible on his face—it must not have been for the woman smiled.

"I can't imagine a strong name such as Raines wouldn't be respected in most places."

"Most places, perhaps. Certainly not in Ware County, Georgia."

Was it something she saw in him, some darkness on his face? He couldn't tell, but she abruptly put an end to the talk of the past.

"This is probably enough for today," she said, standing up from the bench. "Your first day up and about and all." She reached her hand out to help him up and he surprised himself by taking it. "You were very sick, you know, Mr. Raines."

"So you keep telling me."

They walked in silence back to the inn, Lewis full of curiosity about the life the woman had lived before becoming his nurse and hoping she'd tell him—hoping as well she didn't hold the same curiosity concerning him.

He never knew how she was able to do it, but Inez managed to have the time for both him and all the chores of the inn. Her energy seemed limitless. He supposed the age between them—she could not be more than twenty-five or so, he figured, making him a good twenty years older—had something to do with it. Between them, Mrs. Baker, the widowed landlady, and Inez, they kept the place spotless, along with the three meals provided daily. Lewis hadn't lived under a woman's roof since leaving home with his Uncle Dawes. Over all those years he must have forgotten how nice it was to have clean linens, windows not spotted with dust and grime, fresh flowers in vases adding delightful aromas, fresh, nourishing meals at a regular time each day. It was a far cry from the life he had known, the only home of sorts he had been able to call his own since leaving Pendleton being the roughshod cabin by the Sabine River. That cabin had suited his needs at the time, and if he were to return, which he could not, having sold his holdings to Ed White, it would do so again.

As for their separate pasts, over the course of the next few weeks he and Inez shared their stories. Little by little he talked to her of the war, of after, of how it had been in Ware County when he returned. At first, he skirted around Waller and the killing of Jared Dancy. After a time, with her gentle urging, he told it all and felt better for the telling.

Her life, she insisted, was a simple tale. For Lewis, after hearing what she had to say, it did not seem that way. Her father, Rowell Strater, was a man of means from a New England whaling family who, against all family tradition, contrived to marry a Mexican beauty by the name of Fonda Herrera in Laredo shortly before the Civil War broke out.

"It's funny," Lewis interrupted her.

"Funny?"

"Yes. Your father's being a Yankee means you're part Yankee. The only Yankees I ever had anything to do with were trying to kill me."

"My father may have come from the north originally, Mr. Raines. But Texas cured him of any sympathies he once held for New England. If he could have, he would have gladly fought for Texas. Or so I've been told. His health didn't permit him to fight. He died a year after the war began. A year after I was born. Tuberculosis. The reason he came to the desert in the first place. When he met my mother, the doctors had told him he was better. It didn't last."

"I'm sorry," Lewis said. "I didn't mean anything by it."

"I know you didn't."

After her father's death Inez grew up on her grandfather's hacienda outside of Laredo. Eloy Herrera was the last of a long line of Spanish grandees who had been instrumental in what he called the "civilizing" of Mexico and Texas, when it was still a part of that country. Inez grew up with all the privileges and protection that wealth provided. It was not enough.

"I met Clayton Dixon the year I turned eighteen at a ball held in my honor. My life changed drastically that evening."

If everything she told him next were true — and Lewis had no reason to doubt her — saying that her life changed drastically upon meeting Clayton Dixon was an understatement.

"There were good reasons the Dixons had no name left in Atlanta," she told Lewis when she came to the end. "Men who were willing to look the other way after the war, and accept money for doing so, made fortunes. Clayton's father was one of them. When the time came those such as him were no longer tolerated in Atlanta, his grown son had to look elsewhere to make a living. With his strong frame, wavy brown hair, and honest eyes he could take anyone in. Myself included. As it turned out the letters of introduction he brought with him to Laredo were forgeries. As were the ones he showed to Mr. Plant here in Black Point. He is most likely doing the same sort of thing wherever he is now."

"Why didn't you just go back home?"

It was one of those nights after dinner when they were outside on the verandah talking and while Inez told the story of her past she stood by the porch railing, looking out into the darkness that had fallen over the bay. A half-moon hung overhead, pale slivers of its light the only available illumination.

"I could have. It would have been hard facing the recriminations from my mother. My grandfather, fortunately, did not live long enough to see my downfall. The people here know I was as much a victim of Clayton Dixon as Mr. Plant and the others in this town who trusted him. Mrs. Baker," and she pointed a hand at the inn, "has given me a chance for a decent life. Without my husband. Or recriminations. I decided I preferred that to what I have would have found at home."

"Well, you said it was a sad tale and you were correct."

He stood beside her and tossed the stub of his cigar out into the dark where it sparked once when it hit the dirt road before going out.

"Not so sad anymore," she said.

Without being aware he was going to do such a thing, Lewis put his arm around her.

"Yes, you seem to be doing fine."

"Do I?"

Her face tilted up to his in the pale light and they were kissing, her lips soft, yet demanding against his. He had demands of his own—it had been awhile, and embarrassed he tried to pull back but she would not let him.

"You're no stranger to women, Mr. Raines," she said when she finally let him go.

He thought at first she was mocking him, what with that secret grin of hers. Mocking or not he wanted her, had not wanted a woman like that since Sarah. Any needs of that nature were taken care of on the occasional visit to town where the saloons offered relief for all aches.

"You were married, Inez. I'd say you were no stranger to men."

"He was a lying thief." There was nothing light-hearted or mocking about the look in her eyes then. "And not much of a man in any way that mattered. So no, Mr. Raines. You're wrong. I'm a stranger to men, still."

He remembered what she said that night—remembered it when they were done lying together for the first time and he knew that if she allowed it, he wanted to be a part of her life. Lying entwined with one another on the wet sheets of her bed Lewis said, "Now we are no longer strangers to each other."

"No," she agreed as she reached up to kiss him softly, unlike the kisses they had just shared. "No, not strangers."

***

He loved her. Lewis could think of no other way to explain it. When he was with Inez he felt at peace. He had loved Sarah with the intensity of being young and knowing a real love for the first time. He thought he'd never love another. Mamie Hewitt, before Sarah, before the war, had been a boy's infatuation. Though he certainly didn't believe that at the time he had told his father it was true love when Edwin Raines questioned him about his feelings toward the girl. Now, twenty-odd years later, his loves of before and after the war were gone. Inez was there, now. He couldn't imagine it being any other way.

She was so different from the other two women in her humor, her flashing eyes, and her quickness to take Lewis into her arms and tell him that she loved him, too. In one respect, Inez did share something with Sarah: that same sort of sadness. It was understandable, Lewis reasoned. Both women had lost something before he met them. Lewis surely would have married Sarah, had every intention to do just that.

The truth of what Inez had lost was brought home to him the day mail arrived for her from Laredo. A letter from the family attorney notified her of the death of her grandfather, Eloy Herrera. With her grandmother, mother, father, and now grandfather gone, Inez was alone in the world. Just in from another day of looking for work down along the wharves, Lewis found her reading the letter on the verandah of the inn, a blankness in her eyes when she looked up at the sound of his footsteps.

"It's all gone now," she said. "That life I knew before."

"*Was* it a better life?" he asked, unsure of what else to say.

"Different. Not necessarily better. Just different. I miss my mother, of course. And my grandfather. I miss my horses. Should I be ashamed of that? The horses?"

Judging by that little smile of hers he did not believe she was ashamed.

"I have a horse. We could go riding anytime you like," he said.

She threw her arms around him. Sweating and dirty as he was from the heat of the day he tried to pull away.

"Let's do that, Lewis," she said without letting him go. "Let's ride tomorrow."

The big palomino was eager for the exercise. Inez rode behind Lewis in the saddle, her arms around him, the fullness of her breasts pressed into his back, feeling as natural to him as the easy gait of the big horse beneath him as they trotted out of town. The morning sky was cloudless, the air cool, and the day just breaking when they set out. As the sun came up over the eastern horizon the winds would rise in the southwest, blowing hot and heavy as they had done all that month of April. But for now, it was pleasant enough and they rode to the northeast, away from the small town and the water, for over an hour, through pines and oak hummocks where birds called out in alarm from the trees and the overgrowth protecting them.

Around mid-morning the horse suddenly snorted and reared back before coming to a complete stop in the dusty path. A creature slunk out of a clump of palmettos. When the animal came clear of the unruly growth Lewis saw it was a panther. The big cat stopped, long, tawny tail twitching back and forth in the dusty road as it stared at man, woman, and horse, its green eyes never wavering from the sudden threat before him.

But when Lewis drew the rifle from its scabbard and took aim, Inez stopped him.

"Don't kill him, Lewis. Let's not hurt anything on a day as beautiful as this."

"Perhaps you're right. He's probably more scared of us than we are of him, anyways."

He fired a shot into the air and the panther crept away. Proud, and refusing to run, Lewis thought. *Like I've been known to do a time or two in the past.* He slung the rifle back into the scabbard and they rode on until reaching a higher hummock of oaks sitting above a natural prairie where tall switch grass waved in the breezes from the southwest.

"Why don't you ride him a spell?" Dismounting he handed the reins to Inez. "He's plenty gentle. Nothing to be afraid of."

"You think I'd be afraid of a horse such as this, Senor?"

"I suppose not. I suppose, too, you're going to tell me you're not afraid of anything."

She was smiling as she took the reins from Lewis and mounted the horse—that smile that seemed to mock him at times and that he never minded.

"That would be a lie," Inez said.

Laughing, Inez dug her heels into the horse's flanks and galloped the big palomino off across the grassy prairie, the hem of the riding skirt she wore and her long black hair flying out behind her in the sunlight shimmering off the brown field. She rode on her own for what seemed a very long time, though it was probably no more than fifteen minutes or so. When she came back, her face and eyes lit up from the riding, she jumped down from the horse and kissed Lewis hard.

"Thank you so much, Lewis. Thank you for this." She drew back. Staring up into his eyes she waved with one hand at the horse, quietly grazing on the switch grass now that he had been turned loose. "Thank you for this."

She kissed him hard again. Using her long riding skirt for a blanket they made love in the oak hummock with a sense of freedom Lewis had never known before.

A few weeks later Lewis found work, oystering out in the bay. His boss was a man named Jacob Laws who kept a big ungainly-looking work skiff pulled up on the banks by the wharves. Laws had another boat that he lived on, a sloop anchored in the bay. Every day after dropping Lewis at the pier, Lewis watched the man row the skiff out to his floating home. Laws was a burly, rough-skinned, red-faced man, originally from Tennessee, who had come south to Florida after the war. He was around the same age as Lewis and had also fought for the South. A limp on Laws' left side, from a wound received at Chickamauga, gave proof to his service.

"That damned sawbones wanted to take my leg," he told Lewis.

For such a rough-looking man, Jacob's voice was surprisingly soft. So much so that Lewis had to listen hard to make out what the man was saying on the occasional times that Laws cared to talk.

"But I said hell no! He said I'd die for sure. Looks like I got the last laugh. Took me a little longer than some others, but I walked home just fine when the fighting was done. Been using that leg ever since, too."

Beginning at daylight each morning the two men rowed out to the oyster bars scattered throughout the bay. It was hard work Lewis came to learn. The sharp edges of the wet oysters could slice one's skin like a razor if you weren't careful. But after a while, the cuts and blisters on Lewis's hands hardened into rough calluses so that he didn't notice them anymore. He stayed with it, Laws was a patient instructor, and by the end of the third week of working, Lewis was as adept at raking up oysters out of the bay as his boss was.

It was hot back-breaking work with the summer sun burning down on the Gulf Coast. But it wasn't long before Lewis found he looked forward to being out on the water, watching the sun come up over the bay, the sea birds wheeling and diving and screaming at one another as they searched for their morning meal. He liked how on some days the breezes came up early, almost enough to cool one's body from the sweaty work. Other days there was no breeze at all and he sweated so profusely his clothes became soaked immediately, his hair matted to his skull, and he needed a rag close at hand to keep his hands dry enough to work.

Sometimes in the afternoon, storms would build up in the west. When the stronger winds in front of the storm blew up, the two men would row the skiff in—if they were lucky, making it to the wharfs in time to unload the day's loads before the weather broke. Other days they weren't so lucky, and Lewis had to run up to the inn, soaked to the bones in the hard driving rain. He didn't mind too much when that happened—the cooling rain was a welcome relief from the heat of the day.

Though he did not mind the daytime, it was the nights Lewis looked forward to. The nights were for Inez and him. At first, she had pulled back from his touch when he went to caress her soft skin with his cut and blistered fingers after that first day of working with Laws. Before they went any further she cleaned the cuts and abrasions, soaked his hands in Epsom salts, and then bandaged them as best she could. Later, after the cuts had turned to calluses, she continued to soak his hands in an effort to keep the rough edges smoothed. He enjoyed her ministrations to his work injuries—enjoyed even more the love-making they shared when the oil lamp was put out and they lay together on her bed.

It was a good life. He couldn't imagine wanting more—until the time came that he did.

"Do you ever think we should do something about this?" Lewis asked one night toward the end of July.

They had finished a fine meal of fresh red snapper Lewis had caught on a hand line while working that day. Along with the fish, Inez had steamed vegetables and new potatoes she had gathered from the small garden behind the inn. It was a Friday evening and neither of them was working the next day. They planned to take the palomino for a ride again. In honor of the occasion Inez served the meal on the good china and linen tablecloth she had received as wedding gifts when marrying Clayton Dixon.

The day had been a hot one on the bay. Until very late in the afternoon there had been no cooling breezes to offer relief from the unrelenting sun. July had not been a very good month for oystering. Lewis had been manning the long-handled oyster tongs when a squall brewing out in the Gulf began to push in. The winds in front of the squall started chopping the calmer waters of the bay into a froth. When one of the swells rocked the side of the skiff, Lewis, caught off guard, let the slick tongs slip from his grip. As he watched in disbelief they slid beneath the surface in the fifteen feet of water they were working. Jacob Laws cursed and was over the side after them immediately.

After what seemed longer than a man could survive underwater without air Laws surfaced, his face even redder than usual. Breathing hard, he held onto the gunwales with one hand and with the other shoved the tongs into the skiff. "You better never let that happen again and just stand there," he said after clambering over the side into the boat. "Hell no! You drop them, you fucking best go after them!"

Laws had never spoken a word in anger to Lewis, much less curse him. Before Lewis could do, or say, anything, Laws was back at the oars. "We're done for the day," he said as he stroked hard against the water. "Least, I know I am."

Now, after a good meal, he repeated his question. "You know. Maybe it's time we changed our situation?"

"And how do you propose to do that, Senor?"

Her eyes were hard and tight, the little mocking grin that normally accompanied her use of the word, *Senor*, not mocking now, but something else.

"We could start with you and me getting married. If you'll have me. Be better than this sneaking around we've been doing."

The smile widened on her lips, enough to ease the sudden tension he felt between them.

"I'd hardly call what we're doing 'sneaking around'," she said. "There's not a living person in this town who doesn't know where you sleep at night." Her smile opened all the way. "And with the noises you make when you do sleep here, probably some dead ones know as well."

As it had the very first time he ever heard it, her rich laughter swept him up and carried him along.

"That doesn't answer my question," he said when the room was quiet again.

"I can't marry you, Lewis. Besides, I already have you."

He stood up from the sofa with his back turned to her, the answer she gave cutting as deeply as Jacob Laws's curses had earlier in the day.

"I'm already married," she continued.

"He's nowhere around, though." Lewis couldn't believe how harsh he sounded. "You can get a divorce. Be finally done with that bastard and marry me."

"Divorce is no easy thing, Lewis. I was married in the Church."

"Then goddamn your church." He wanted to stop the anger rising in him. Wanted badly to put a hold on what he felt building. He hadn't felt like this in a very long time. Since I rode to the Landings to kill Jared Dancy. Yes, he wanted to stop the anger. But he couldn't. "Goddamn all of it, then. If that's how it is with you," he said instead.

"I'll live with you as your wife, Lewis. Gladly. Go wherever, do whatever you wish. But I can't marry you."

"Then what good is any of this?"

He was on his feet, hands clenched, head throbbing. It must have been the heat of the day, he thought. Or the look on that damned Jacob Laws's face when he came up over the gunwales.

"You and me?" he asked. "What's the good?"

"I know the answer to that, Lewis." She hadn't moved from where she sat on the sofa. "But perhaps you don't."

"I guess I don't."

The sound of the door slamming behind him had to be loud enough for the whole town to hear, he thought as he crossed the courtyard between Inez's cottage and the back door of the inn. He didn't care if they heard—told himself as he entered the building that it was perfectly fine with him if they got an earful.

He slept that night in his room on the second floor as he had not done in a long time and found he didn't care about that either. The next morning, after a night of little sleep, Lewis strode down to the wharves to work. There, Jacob Laws mentioned that since oyster hauling was doing poorly right then, he was considering sailing down to Key West. He might try his hand at fishing between there and the outer islands, the Dry Tortugas. Come back in late fall when the cooler waters would be better for the oysters. He could fish on the way down, sell the catch at the fish house on New Turkey Key in the Ten Thousand Islands and then head on for Key West. Did Lewis want to come?

Lewis said yes.

The next morning after packing his bag, Lewis left money for three months' rent, along with a note for the landlady, and without saying goodbye to Inez set sail with Jacob Laws.

***

Anger, as well as the wind and the tides, carried him all the way to the very end of Florida. It was a five-day sail to Key West in the little sloop, a shallow draft boat well suited for the waters of the Gulf of Mexico. At the helm, Laws let the variable winds set the pace. They had good weather for the most part, sailing during the day, and then anchoring the boat before night fell in small bays at the mouths of rivers carved out eons before. After anchoring for the night, the two men used the skiff to set out long trot lines that they hauled in before pulling anchor the next morning. As they sailed to the southeast on the blue-green waters of the Gulf, Lewis sorted through the catch on the stern deck, cleaning the fish good enough to sell, packing them into casks filled with salt, and then storing them below decks. They would sell the fish on the docks of Key West once they reached that port.

The steady sailing and the work of the day kept Lewis's mind from going where he didn't want it to. At night, as he lay in his berth listening to the slap of water against the hull at anchor, he had no such reprieve. His thoughts then were of Inez. Of how she had told him she couldn't marry him. Of the hurt and surprise on her face as he went to slam his way out of her house. A face so lovely then, despite his anger.

He couldn't understand why his thoughts of the woman he loved kept getting crowded out by memories of Georgia. How it might have been for him there with the war over. If not for Waller, the night riders, and Jared Dancy? If not for the violence, the killing, he had learned so well during the war, and then taken home with him? They were thoughts that invariably led to Cordelia, the only one left in his family except for him. He wondered if she had forgiven him—if she ever could. He never had the chance to explain, to tell her the why behind what happened on her front porch that morning. He owed her that explanation. And maybe she owed him a listening as well. Maybe she'd be willing to hear his side of the story if she were still alive. If he ever went home. But that was doubtful; he wasn't sure, still, if he would ever return.

They fished out of Key West the rest of that August and all through what Lewis didn't believe could be possible, the even hotter month of September. The work plan was simple. After three- or four-day outings between the tip of Florida and the Dry Tortugas, they'd return to port to sell the catch, get drunk in the bars of the town, load up supplies for the next outing, and take off again. As they had on the way down, Lewis and Jacob set out long lines holding many hooks. It was a different sort of work from the oystering they had done out of Port Tampa and Lewis was content with the change. Different sort of work or not, it was still hard, hauling in the line heavy with fish. They never knew what might be on the long trot line when they brought it in: pompano, big red snapper, maybe a grouper, other species of snapper, strange colored fish even Laws had never seen before. He just did not know what to expect, and Lewis liked that aspect of it very much.

The Atlantic was different, as well, from the shallower Gulf. For fishing purposes, Laws preferred the skinnier waters to the northwest of the Florida Straits. The ocean was never far from sight, though, and for some reason Lewis found a comfort in gazing out on that vast ocean where he could never see the other side. How different it was from the bay of Port Tampa and the water they had fished on the way down to Key West where a shoreline was always in sight. He liked even more how the easterly breezes came across the Atlantic. From Africa, Laws said. No matter from where, the steady winds went a long ways toward keeping Lewis cool and comfortable on the deck of the sailboat after hauling in the lines and then getting down to the cleaning of the catch, the gutting and filleting. While he worked with the fillet knife he tossed the offal overboard where gulls and other sea birds clustered around the boat, clamoring for the leftovers and fighting one another for them.

The fish houses on the quay at Key West were always eager for the fresh fish Jacob, Lewis, and the other fishermen brought in. One of the better buyers was a Negro by the name of Tom Lewis. Their similar names created a friendship between Lewis and this man. Tom Lewis was friendly and easy-going to all on the docks, those who made a living selling their catch to him, and those who bought in turn from him. The black man was a fixture on the docks. He told Lewis once that he had come from the Bahamas in the 1870s, and he made a good living from buying the fresh fish and then selling it to his neighbors in the colored quarters at a modest profit. Like Lewis, he was in his mid to late forties. Unlike Lewis, he was a family man, his wife a tall, broad-shouldered woman with the darkest skin Lewis had ever seen. She always wore a colorful turban wrapped around her head and spoke with an accent Lewis had trouble understanding. There were two children. The girl was five and very shy. She clung to her mother's skirts when Mrs. Lewis brought her husband's lunch down to the docks. The oldest was a boy, perhaps twelve or thirteen, lean and well-muscled like his father. He helped his father with the heavy casks of salted fish as easily as a man much older could have. Helping the two Negros unload the catch from Laws's work skiff the first time, Lewis was struck by how the sheen of sweat on their skin glinted in the hard noonday sunlight. They looked like Waller had looked in the fields when he labored with the planting or harvesting of the crops, Lewis thought.

By mid-October Laws had had enough of Key West and the fishing between there and the Dry Tortugas, seventy miles to the west. He had wanted to make at least one trip to the Bahamas, perhaps even Cuba, before heading back to Port Tampa, but told Lewis it was too dangerous now. That late in the season there was always the risk of a hurricane, of being caught in the open water in the small sloop by one of the big storms. Lewis had no opinion on the matter, having no experience with hurricanes, and said so—said he was willing to go wherever the captain and the winds and the tides took them.

The next week found them fishing off the beaches flanking the mouth of a river that Laws said was named the Lostman's. Having explored upstream one day, rowing the skiff in on the incoming tide, Lewis found the name apt enough. After they crossed a wide bay just inside the river's mouth the water channeled into a narrow ribbon. A natural canopy, created by the overhanging branches of mangroves lining both banks, blocked the sunlight, so that the two men in the skiff moved through a jungle of wild growth in what seemed to be a perpetual twilight. Further upstream the river narrowed even more and now, as they rowed, they had to be mindful of the sawgrass growing along the banks. The green thin stalks of this plant were razor sharp, able to slice your skin if not careful. Coming back downstream on the falling tide when the muddy banks were exposed to the air, they saw big alligators sunning themselves in the available light. Threatening looking creatures, sure enough, but they slid silently off the banks into the water when the skiff drifted past.

Lostman's River, indeed, Lewis thought when they reached its mouth, the afternoon sun shining brightly down on the green water of the Gulf, a welcome relief from the twilight jungle they had emerged from. As best Lewis could tell there was only one hospitable bit of land by that river. It was a tiny strip of beach on the edge of a small key at the river's mouth, the beach partly shaded by a few scruffy-looking trees and bushes of a sort Lewis had never seen before. There was evidence—burnt logs in a crude firepit, some weather-beaten planks scattered on the sand—that people had lived there once. But how they could survive for long on that barren little key, Lewis couldn't imagine. He had judged Jacob Laws's twenty-five-foot sailboat to be cramped quarters. But that night, as the two men stretched out on the stern deck with coffee after their evening meal, Lewis felt like he was in a mansion.

It was a good life and Lewis was in no hurry to get back to Port Tampa. Not now, when the constant thoughts of Inez had finally receded a little and he was able to sleep through the night, the constant gentle slap of water against the hull no longer the irritant it was at first, but instead a lullaby—one that sang him into a sleep where his dreams were no longer of the past and all the bad that had been part of it.

One morning, though, as they lay anchored off the fish house on Turkey Key, the day turned grey with clouds and the breeze faded, so that the Gulf lay at a dead calm.

"I don't like the looks of that," Jacob said as he came up on deck with a cup of coffee in hand. He pointed at a line of flat, grey clouds well off to the east. "Those clouds, this sudden lack of wind? Tells me, my man, there's a storm coming, sure."

"Hurricane?" Lewis had been coiling lines up on the bow, getting ready to lift anchor when Laws said it was time. Now he joined Laws at the helm, looking out to where he pointed. "That what you're thinking?"

Lewis was familiar with the thick, heavy thunderheads of the prairies. In comparison, this weather seemed innocent enough.

"Might be." Laws drained his coffee and then motioned Lewis back up to the bow. "Either way, hurricane or just bad storm, I don't want to be here when it comes. There's a better harbor up Chokoloskee way. We best make for it."

It *was* a better harbor, just as Laws said it would be, well inside from the open Gulf and reached by a twisting pass lined with marl, oyster bars, and mangroves. By the time they reached the mouth of the pass, the winds had started to pick up and the skies go dark with heavy clouds. As they made for the inside of the pass, Lewis saw a small wooden cabin built on the eastern most point of the island at its mouth. A man and a woman were busy out in front of the cabin gathering up loose items and hauling them inside, doing their best to make ready for the bad weather. Both man and woman were young, Lewis saw, maybe in their late twenties.

The woman caught his attention—the way her rich, dark hair blew away from her shoulders in the rising winds.

Like Inez when she galloped off on the big palomino that day they went riding.

Looking again, Lewis realized the woman was pregnant. Very pregnant, judging by the swell of her belly when she bent over once to pick up some cooking utensils lying by the fire pit. A hell of a time to be having a child with all this weather on the way. Not much to be done about it now. And maybe they'd be lucky. Maybe the child would hold off until the storm was past. Maybe the storm wouldn't come at all.

As the boat breasted the point the woman looked up and waved, her black hair shining in a bit of bright sunlight. Up on the bow, Lewis waved back, started to call out something, thought better of it and turned away.

But the storm *did* come. Lewis and Jacob were both glad when it did that Laws had made the decision to ride it out in Chokoloskee Bay. A small fishing village had been carved out of the mangroves and wild palms on the shell mound that made for the higher ground of Chokoloskee Island. There was a cluster of little homes there, the most prominent being a two-story house built on stilts just up from the water's edge where a long pier, cut with slips for boats, ran out into the bay.

"That's Mr. and Mrs. Smallwood's place," Laws said, pointing it out. He was up on the bow with Lewis, helping him with the anchor. By then the winds had picked up and the bay roiled with whitecaps pounding against the boat at a furious pace. Between the hard winds and the rocking of the boat in the swells, Lewis found it difficult to keep his footing on the narrow bow. He was grateful that Laws, seeing the straits he was in, had come up to give him a hand.

"Once we get everything lashed down proper here, we'll go ashore," Laws said. His soft voice, hard to hear in normal conditions, was almost lost in the wind and the sound of the swells rocking against the hull of the boat, "See if Mr. Smallwood will let us sit the storm out in his place. Be a damn sight more comfortable and safer."

It appeared that the other residents of Chokoloskee had the same idea. Twenty of them, men, women, and children of varying ages, huddled around a wood stove in the center of the ground floor of the store. Mr. Smallwood, a tall, lean, bespectacled man in overalls, answered the door when Laws knocked.

"Always room for one or two more," he said as he swung the door wide and ushered the two men inside. "Especially on a night like this one promises to be."

Standing behind her husband at the door, his wife led the two men over to where the others sat by the stove. The gracious smile of greeting on Mrs. Smallwood's bright rosy face was the first, Lewis realized, he had seen on a woman since leaving Port Tampa. And though it shouldn't have, that smile tore at him.

The storm lasted all night, its hard winds and rains lashing against the walls of the house and making conversation impossible. Above the wind and rain came the occasional loud thumps of something heavy, solid, hitting the sides of the house or the roof. Early in the morning of the next day, perhaps three or four, the winds seemed to rise to some sort of howling crescendo. With the others gathered around the stove, he watched as the wooden walls of the building seemed to breathe in and out, the winds putting pressure on all sides. Judging by the tight set of their faces in the small light given off by the stove, that was the only time those gathered inside seemed concerned. Apparently, they had seen worse. Mr. Smallwood said as much when the crescendo of wind began to fade and they were left with only a gentle, steady, rain.

"I thought she might go worse for us, Mrs. Smallwood," the bespectacled man said as he poured a fresh cup of coffee for himself from a pewter pot he had kept full and going all night. "A little rain. A little wind. That seems to be about it. Not much of a hurricane if ye ask me."

The other residents of Chokoloskee seemed to agree, most of them nodding their heads as Mr. Smallwood spoke.

Only Mrs. Smallwood had any objections to her husband's observation. "You sound disappointed, Theodore. Maybe you've already forgotten what happened 'round here when the 'canes blew through, two of them, one right after another?"

"No ma'am, you're right." He lifted his cup to his wife in acknowledgment. "I haven't forgotten. Your point is well taken, and I am truly grateful the storm wasn't worse than she was. I truly am."

The others around the wood stove agreed with this as well, and Lewis decided that if hurricanes could be stronger and more dangerous than the one he had just experienced, he didn't want any part of them.

Come sunrise, the storm had blown itself out completely, the remnants of it visible only as faint dark clouds and drizzling rain moving to the west across the mangroves and marsh between Chokoloskee and the Gulf of Mexico. Everything seemed brown and dead to Lewis when he ventured outside with the others. Like winter, he thought. Except it was hot and very humid in the sunshine streaming down now that the clouds had moved off with the storm. With a start, Lewis understood the reason why: the wind had blown all the trees bare of their leaves. Only naked branches remained, stark and empty in the morning light. Bits and pieces of what once were houses lay scattered about the empty dirt streets of the small town. Out in the bay two tin roofs, ripped clean from the houses they had sheltered, floated on the calm water. The wooden skiff Lewis and Laws had pulled up on the bank for safekeeping was still there, though filled to the gunwales with water from the bay that had flooded in over the stern when the tides rose. The sailboat, too, was where they had left it, the only damage Lewis could see from the shore being the mast, snapped off so that it lay across the bow at an unnatural angle. For a not-so-bad storm it certainly had done more than enough damage. The thought only served to strengthen Lewis's newfound resolve never to be around when another one came ashore.

Other than the wreckage of their homes, everyone on Chokoloskee Island was safe and sound. No one had died or even been injured during the blow. But while helping Jacob repair the mast later that afternoon, Lewis saw something odd out in the bay floating in with the tide. He didn't pay much attention to it at first—there had been snapped off trees and portions of buildings and other debris going by with the currents all day.

But when he happened to look up from his work again the object had floated closer to the boat. In the bright sunlight of the afternoon he saw that it wasn't a tree branch or other debris, but a body. He recognized the young man from the island at the mouth of Chokoloskee Pass. Behind him came an overturned skiff. And behind that came the woman, on her back, dead, black hair trailing out in the water, pregnant belly bare to the sunlight, her dress in tatters, like her hair drifting out behind her in the moving water.

Everything inside of Lewis turned over, the same as it had when the Union shell blew up the world in front of him so long ago. He felt powerless to do anything as first the man's body floated by, then the boat, and then the woman. Suddenly he wanted to weep. He wanted to, but no tears came.

On a very clear and pleasantly cool October morning eight days later, Lewis Raines strode up the graded road from the wharves of Port Tampa. The sailboat was safely anchored in the bay. The fish caught on the way back, sold, and Lewis paid for his efforts. Now, he was about to do what needed to be done. There was something he had to say. A place he had to return to.

His heart began pounding hard in his chest when he spied Inez. She was on the verandah of the inn, sweeping away the dirt and dust left there by the nighttime breezes. Her black hair lay along her shoulders, gently moving back and forth with the motion of the broom she held. He was not sure what he was going to say as he crossed the street in front of the inn. But he was going to say something, and it was going to matter. Of that he *was* sure. At least, if his pounding heart didn't blow his chest to pieces before he could do so.

"I know now," he told her as he came up on the verandah.

"Know what, Lewis?"

She stopped what she was doing and turned to face him. Her flashing eyes and that damnable secret grin of hers that did things to him nothing else ever had, seemed to bore into him.

"I know what the good of it is. Between you and me."

"Well it's about time, Senor. I've known it all along."

Though he was weary from the three months away, the hard time on the water with Jacob, the two dead bodies floating in Chokoloskee Bay, Lewis Raines was still able to be swept up in the laughter of the woman he loved.

BOOK TWO ~ JOHN

Part One: Georgia

Though the day started the same as every day had since the boy's mother died, it didn't end up that way.

"Get up," his father said. He was tall, gaunt of face, grey eyes hard and staring, dressed in canvas overalls and a white, cotton shirt, and standing over the bed the boy shared with his two brothers.

"Plenty of work to be done today and here you boys are, burning daylight. If you think I'm going to stand for it, you've got another think coming."

Every day the same and like he always did, RL, at seventeen and the oldest of the three brothers, said, "Okay, Pop. We're coming."

RL stood for Robert Lee. A name fit for any man, the boy had heard his father say once. This was shortly after TJ, the baby, had been born. He hasn't quite lived up to that name, the boy's father continued. But he's young yet. Pop was smiling when he said that, like he always did right after the baby was born. When instead of dying then and there, as the midwife had claimed she would, the boy's mother pulled through. It was early evening when TJ was named. Supper was over, the night air was crisp and cold after the sun set the way it was in January. As usual, RL sat in a chair in the corner of the parlor room, curled up with a book. Pop and Mom were sitting on the loveseat in the other corner of the parlor, Mom cradling the wrapped-up bundle that was the baby in her arms. The boy lay on the floor at their feet, playing with the lead soldiers Aunt Cordelia had given him for Christmas, everything fine and normal like it was always after Christmas, after New Year—the only thing different this time around being the baby, whose arrival had been difficult. That's what Aunt Cordelia had said. So the boy had heard for himself. His mother's screams echoing through the house, painful sounding enough to make the boy wish he could die.

"This little fellow," his father said that evening, "had such a rough time just getting into this old world. Coming in feet first like that. Hell of a way to start out in life. Hell of a way for us to be starting a new century, come to think of it. But he's going to need a good strong name to get by with. I was thinking Thomas might be a good one. Thomas Jefferson Raines. Has a good sound to it, don't you think? How about we name him that?" And they had.

But when considering the boy's name, no well-known personages had come to mind and they settled simply for John and Rowell for a middle name. When he was old enough to wonder—maybe four or five—and after hearing RL one time bragging to the Hicks boy how he was named after a famous general, the boy had to know. He asked his mother what famous general *he* was named after. His grandfather, Mom said. My father's name, she said. No, not a famous general, she answered when John asked. But a man famous to me. Her mouth was set in that little smile. The one the boy knew was only for him. Not for RL. Famous name or not. I have nothing to remember him by because he died when I was very young. Now I have you, she said, and hugged the boy tight. He didn't squirm away. Felt proud, in fact, as she pulled him against her bosom that his name did stand for something.

His father called the boy and his brothers by just their initials. Where Pop acted like it was a waste of time and breath for him to expend their proper names, Aunt Cordelia, on the other hand, did not. When addressing her nephews, it was always with both first and middle names. "Would you please give me hand with this heavy old laundry basket, Robert Lee." Or, "Now come along over here, John Rowell, and tell me just what it is you thought the minister was sermonizing about this morning." Except for TJ, who was still a baby. Besides, the boy reasoned once when he was thinking about the matter, a middle name like "Jefferson" was simply too much to say. Either way, it struck him as odd. Especially when he considered the fact that all the other adults he knew, the teacher at school, the minister at the church, the Widow Crueller in town, the rare neighbor who stopped by to chat with his father, always referred to the boys by only their first names.

"Get these boys dressed and fed, RL," the boy's father said.

"I will, Pop. Right away."

"See that you do," his father said.

"Okay, Pop," RL said again, and then the boy's father was gone, the room silent and empty once he left.

Pop or Lewis. Lewis is what the boy's mother had called him. And sometimes Senor, the boy remembered. Said this in a playful kind of way when her husband came in from the fields, hot and tired and wondering aloud, Where in blazes was something cold and refreshing for a working man to drink? Her teasing, "Senors," always made Pop smile. Something he didn't do anymore.

Every day now was the same. Hot or cold. Rain or shine. Pop standing over the bed ready for work and demanding his sons be, too.

This day looked to be a hot one. The sun wasn't even fully up and already the air in the room was wet and still. It had been cooler only an hour or so back. But the little bit of sun creeping up to the east had vanished the night time coolness and the boy was sorry for it to be gone. "Goddamn July," Pop had said just yesterday. "Only July and hotter than hell already. Can't imagine what August's going to be like." The boy couldn't either—thought instead that with some luck August would come and go quickly. Then it would be September and school, an escape from the daily all day work of the farm. He was twelve and would be attending the secondary school in Pendleton instead of the elementary class at the Baptist Church in Ruskin. As he pulled on his pants and went to get his younger brother up and out of the bed, the boy thought how nice that would be.

The smell of side meat frying in the pan on the stove, the sound of eggs sizzling when RL plopped them into the hot grease, drifted into the bedroom as the boy helped his little brother get dressed. There wasn't much involved in getting dressed other than to pull some pants on. That time of year there was no need for a shirt. Or shoes. Not that any of the boys ever wore shoes, for the most part. They wore them to church and sometimes when it was very cold. Not like the boys and girls who lived in town in sparkling white homes in Pendleton. They were clean houses with clean white fences running around the edges of green lawns and flowers blooming in orderly rows. Clean houses where life had to be nothing like it was at the boy's place.

Five now, TJ insisted he was old enough to buckle his own belt. In a hurry to sit down and eat, the smells and sounds of food cooking suddenly making him very hungry, the boy let him.

"All right, then. Do it yourself. Just be quick about it. But don't blame me if your pants fall down in the fields and Pop yells at you."

"He won't," TJ insisted, his little square face twisted in a stubborn grimace.

"Suit yourself, then."

Aunt Cordelia claimed that TJ, being a towhead, with a square set face and his stubborn ways, was the spitting image of his Uncle Dawes, a man none of the brothers knew, who their aunt said was killed in the War.

"RL takes after his father," Aunt Cordelia went on to say. "His hair may be a deep brown now. But as he gets older, like Lewis's did, I bet RL's will change. Thin out some. Go a little gray. He'll always be tall and lean like his father. Thank God he inherited his mother's brains. Now you, young man," she said, ruffling the boy's hair with one bony hand. "You take after your Momma. At least that fine head of black hair does. Your skin tones. Sort of brown, like Inez's was. Your face is like your Pop's, though. Especially those grey eyes. Hard to say how you'll look when you're his age. I won't be here to see, so I guess it doesn't matter much to me."

The boy liked his Aunt Cordelia—liked her a lot. If he had his way they would all be living together in her house like they had before. She was a good cook and always had a kind word to say when his father was in one of his harsh moods. With her wrinkled face, twinkly green eyes, and gray hair tied up in a bun, Aunt Cordelia looked like the pictures of grandmothers in the Boy's Adventures books the elementary teacher let him read at recess when it was too hot to go outside and play. He didn't have a grandmother, not living at any rate, but his aunt seemed to serve him as good, or better, than the ones he read about.

She had been firmly against their leaving her house after the boy's mother died. Had argued with his father about it, with a sternness in her voice the boy couldn't connect to the gentle woman she normally was.

The day before this argument they had buried his mother in the little graveyard to the west of the big house. The cemetery was marked off by a wrought iron fence and shaded by big oak trees on the corners of the fence. A quiet place for one's eternal rest, Aunt Cordelia had said as she and the boys and their father walked over to the cemetery. "A little too early to suit me," the boy's father had replied.

"It's God's will, Lewis," Aunt Cordelia said. But the boy's father only snorted. "If you say so," he said. "But I'm not buying it."

The minister from the Baptist Church in Ruskin where Aunt Cordelia went on Sunday morning spoke some words from the Bible over the grave. Then Pop and the minister lowered the coffin into the ground. A stark white tombstone lay at the head of the grave. The boy had read it before the minister arrived: *Inez Raines. Loved by all. Loved more by her husband.* There were other markers in the little plot of ground, all bearing the name of Dancy engraved with a flourish into the stone. One of those graves contained Aunt Cordelia's husband, Jared. A man his aunt and father never talked about. Jared Dancy had died a long time in the past, judging by the dates chiseled into the stone. These dates were all the boy knew about the man who had been his aunt's husband. That cool, sun-bright morning when they buried his mother, after the dirt had been shoveled over the new grave, Aunt Cordelia had knelt in front of her husband's stone and said a prayer, the tears streaming down her pale cheeks making her seem even whiter and frailer than she really was.

"What can you possibly be thinking of, Lewis?" his aunt had said the day after the funeral, while John sat out on the front verandah playing jacks with RL. Even though that morning in March had been two years back—even though the time that had passed since then seemed even longer—the words his father and his aunt spoke to one another coming plain as day through the open windows of the house, stayed in the boy's mind.

"You can't take them boys of yours and move into that old cabin. It's not right."

"The hell I can't," his father had said, and hearing the set of his father's voice the boy didn't doubt him.

"That's Errol's old place, if you haven't forgotten. The Dancys' overseer. Where he kept his women and did what-all with them. The last time I was down to that place, when I went to nail the doors shut so the varmints wouldn't get in, you could still smell him in there. Smell what he did to those poor unfortunates."

"I haven't forgotten who used to live there. When was that, Cordelia? When you was there shutting the place up? Twenty years ago? Thirty? Hell, I been down there every day for the last week. Cleaning it up. Airing it out. Making it livable again. I didn't smell anything in there other than dust and mold. What do you think? That there's some evil spirits in there? Going to make me and my boys want to go seeking out Negro women and having our ways with them?"

"Lewis Raines! I never!"

It was quiet between the two adults for a moment before the boy's father spoke again.

"I guess you haven't, Cordelia. But I can't live here, now. Not with her gone. It's too close. Too damn close.

"I've got her laid to rest in the Dancy graveyard, against my better wishes, and mainly because you and her were so close," the boy's father continued. "At least she's near enough to where I can go visit every day. But I can't sleep in the same room. Can't walk the same hallways every day. Thinking I'll hear her call out to me. Not now, Cordelia. You've got to understand that."

"Well," Aunt Cordelia said, a sigh of surrender in her raspy voice. "I sure hope you're right about all this. I surely do. I just think you and the boys would be a darn sight better off staying put. Right here, where I can help out. Just like it was when Inez was still with us."

"We'll be fine," the boy's father said. "We'll be just fine."

If they were fine in that little four room cabin, after being used to the big comfortable house of Aunt Cordelia's, then it was a funny sort of fine. But he knew better than to say anything like that to his father. He certainly knew better than that.

Now TJ came trailing into the kitchen behind the boy and they sat down at a plain table in the center of the room. RL slid two eggs apiece onto their plates out of the big cast iron skillet, following the eggs with pieces of well-cooked bacon, along with a heaping spoonful each of hot grits. RL was a good cook and the boy was glad for it. Pop didn't seem to have the skill or patience to cook and it showed in his efforts. When RL began pitching in with the cooking and the other chores of the house, everyone involved seemed happier for it. The boy felt bad for RL, being stuck with both his work in the fields and the burden of keeping the cabin clean. Sometimes the boy tried to help his older brother with the household chores, but invariably RL got mad and told him to go on. Said he was only getting in his way. The boy, his conscience clear, once he had at least tried to help, was always glad to do what his brother asked.

Every so often Aunt Cordelia came down to offer what she called "a woman's touch" to the hard cabin the boys and their father lived in. This wasn't very often—only on the days her arthritis or rheumatism allowed. She did her best, but she was old and stove up some, and even the boy could see her attempts at straightening up the place were feeble.

"Why your father doesn't get a woman in here is beyond me, John Rowell," she said once when her nephew was helping her shake out the one rug the cabin was adorned with. "Get one of those Nigra women in here and give this place a thorough going over. God knows he's got the money to pay one. Let your poor brother have a day off. Let you boys just be boys."

The boy didn't know anything about having a "Nigra" in the house, or boys being boys, and said so.

"No," Aunt Cordelia said as she helped him carry the rug back inside. "I imagine you don't." Her face was pale and sweaty from shaking the heavy rug out. Once they had the rug spread out on the floor she sat down in the rocker his father usually occupied at night. "No, I imagine none of you boys know anything about that. It's a crying shame, too, if you ask me."

"Go on and eat, TJ," RL told his little brother. TJ had been pushing the eggs and grits and bacon around on the pewter plate, trying to form them up into the shape of a little pyramid. "No time today for any of your baby foolishness. When you're done, John Rowell, you two shake your butts down to the field. Pop's in a hurry to get started this morning."

"He's always in a hurry," the boy said.

"That's right." RL grabbed up the boy's empty plate and put it in the sink by the stove. "And he always gets mad when we don't hop to. As you well know. Now wash that egg mess off your face, grab TJ and get moving. I'll see you two down there."

He helped TJ wash up after the meal and then splashed cold water from the sink on his own face. He thought of how nice it would be if this Saturday was one of the rare ones where they stayed up at the big house with Aunt Cordelia rather than going back out into the field. If they had one of his aunt's Saturday meals—fried chicken, potato salad, biscuits, and slices of dripping cold watermelon—rather than his father's plain lunch, he'd be happy. If he was allowed to play a game of checkers with RL, or play soldiers with TJ, or go into Aunt Cordelia's library and pull down a book and sit on the settee to read, he'd be grateful.

Pop wasn't one for reading. Not now at any rate. His mother had taught him when he was just TJ's age, five. Taught him with primers she ordered from a catalogue, that arrived in a box all wrapped up like presents on Christmas day, though without the colorful paper and bows. Back then Pop had helped her with the boy's reading lesson, even liked to read himself. At night when the family sat after supper in the library, they all talked and laughed and read and then talked about what they were reading. Pop liked to read the old poets: Keats, Byron, and Shelley. Said that his own mother had taught him with those poets. The boy's mother liked them, too, but also liked this new fellow, Walt Whitman she said his name was. One night she read aloud a long poem of his about President Lincoln. It was a sad poem. At the end of it there were tears in both his mother's eyes and Aunt Cordelia's.

"All those poor boys dead," Aunt Cordelia had said, "because of that man."

Pop snorted at that and said, "All dead because they wanted to keep their slaves you mean."

"Don't you two ruin this lovely poem," the boy's mother said quietly from where she sat next to Pop on the love seat. "All that was a long time ago and done with now."

"Damn straight it's done with now," Pop had replied.

"I don't know," Aunt Cordelia said. "I just don't know."

But that day wouldn't be one of food and rest at Aunt Cordelia's. The boy was pretty certain of that. Not with the way Pop had come into the room earlier ready for work and demanding the same of him and his brothers. Not this time of year when the tobacco needed so much tending to. But wouldn't it be something, he thought.

If I played a little trick on them. If when I get to the end of the lane, instead of heading off to the tobacco rows on the right I point my finger out in front of me at the road to Ruskin. Go eeny, meany, miny, mo and go wherever my finger ends up pointing at. It darn sure won't be the tobacco rows. I'll make sure of that. Maybe Pendleton. Or Ruskin. Either on, don't matter.

As long as it was far away from home. As long as it was somewhere folks didn't have to live like he did.

It was pleasant enough to think so, but the boy knew it wasn't going to go like that. Not today; probably not any day.

***

By the time his younger brother and he reached the tobacco fields down by the road to Pendleton the boy was in a full sweat, one that ran wet under his armpits and that he had to brush out of his eyes with the back of one hand. The big wicker basket resting on the ground beneath the two oaks on the west side of the field put the final nail into the coffin of any hopes the boy still had of a peaceful afternoon at his aunt's. From experience, John knew the basket contained their noontime meal, plus water, and whatever other refreshments the boy's aunt had managed to sneak in. Resigned to his fate he looked around for TJ, who had wandered off. Finding him kneeling in the grass trying to squash a grasshopper with his thumb, the boy took him by the arm and dragged him over to the field where their father and RL were already hard at it.

"Don't just stand there looking dumb, JR," his father yelled over one shoulder without even looking up from his work. "Get in here and get busy. TJ, just try not to hurt yourself. That's all I ask."

John did as he was told, starting at the head of the next row over from where his father and brother were working. With the summer heat and steady rains, the tobacco had grown tall and green. The leaves were starting to flower off at the top, healthy and bushy, and very near ready to be picked. Working on his knees in the dirt at the base of the plants only served to intensify the heat of the morning. It didn't take long for his hands to be covered with sticky sap from pulling moist green suckers off the tobacco stalks. He had learned a long time ago not to bother wiping his hands on his trousers to clear them of the sap. It was a useless task, only to be done before they sat down in the shade to eat the noon meal. Then his father would take a damp towel from the wicker basket and they would take turns cleaning their hands as best they could. Which usually was not very good.

How in the blazes, the boy wondered for what he figured to be at least the ten thousandth time, could you clear the pesky suckers from a row of healthy plants one day, only to come back two or three days later and find things looking like you had never been there at all? That's what working like the most common sharecropper got you. And for what reward? A slapped-together cold supper. Followed by precious few hours of restless, weary, sleep in the bed next to TJ, who cried sometimes as he slept, and if not that, wanted to crowd in tight to his brother's warmth, adding even more to John's restless sleep, especially on the hot nights of summer when the idea of another hot, sticky body almost on top of him was close to intolerable. And yet he had to. Just as he had to tolerate the fact of the next day being the same. Just one of those mysteries—and there were quite a few of them—John imagined he would most likely never understand.

"Oww, owww," he heard coming from somewhere in the bushy green plants. Just like he always did, TJ must have gone and wiped his sweating eyes with a sap-covered finger. Now the baby's eyes were stinging and smarting as he stood unseen in the rows, crying out for help.

"Goddamn, JR," Pop called from the row over. "Go and wipe the baby's eyes best you can. See if you can't find something less troublesome to keep him occupied while we work."

"I can take him down to the creek," the boy offered up hopefully.

"You do that and leave your brother and me with this suckerin', you won't be happy with the results. I can guarantee you that."

"Yes, sir."

"And hurry back. We ain't got all day for the baby's fun and games."

"Yes, sir."

He found TJ sitting on the edge of the field in the grass, crying and wiping his eyes with both hands now.

"Cut it out, TJ. You'll only make it worse," he told his brother. "Let's get the towel and clean you up."

After TJ's face was clean, they both took a long drink of water from a jug in the wicker basket. The water was still good and cold, wrapped as it had been in another wet cloth in the bottom of the hamper. The boy thought about bringing the jug with him back to the field for his father and RL and decided against it. If Pop wanted a drink he knew where it was. That's what he deserved for making them work all that hot day. He felt bad for a minute about RL. Too bad, he thought as he took another long drink. That's just too darn bad.

He left the baby sitting on the grass under the oak trees with a couple of the lead soldiers. In the past, the toy soldiers had proved helpful. Hopefully, they would be enough to keep the baby occupied until the noon meal. Afterward, RL could put him down for a nap and the rest of them could work in peace.

It was mid-morning. As the boy started back across the rows of tobacco he could see dark clouds forming up in the sky to the east. The rain had been pretty good about coming in the early evenings of late, though much too late in the day to be of help to someone hoping for an early end to the day's labors. Staring up at the distant clouds the boy could tell there was not much chance of the storm breaking sooner. Too bad, he thought. He hadn't done much this morning and already he was sick of it.

He heard a faint rumbling from the east just as he was starting into the row of plants where he had left off when the baby began crying. It was not the rumbling of thunder, though, but that of wagon wheels on the hard clay road leading from Pendleton. In another moment the wagon hove into view, the Widow Crueller's wagon pulled by a dray gelding that looked to be almost as old as its owner. Above the rumbling of the wagon wheels came the laughter and happy squealing of children at play. As the big wagon came closer the boy could see why. The bed of the wagon was occupied by about a half dozen boys and girls from town, children he knew from school and the occasional Sunday when the family went to church in Pendleton instead of the Primitive Baptist Church of Ruskin. On the front seat of the wagon sat the widow, reins in hand, her head covered by a wide brim hat such as a man might wear when working outside in the sun.

"Morning, Lewis," she called out when she brought the wagon to a stop. "Morning, boys."

A look passed between the Widow Crueller and the boy's father—a look the boy had noticed one time before, wondering then, as he did now, what it meant. John could never see the widow without remembering the first time he'd seen that look and what she had told him that day. This was two years back and his father and he were at the general store in Pendleton, laying in supplies for the spring planting. While his father was examining some new plows the store was promoting, the widow took John by the hand and pulled him aside. When he protested that his father wouldn't like it, the widow told him not to worry, that Pop wouldn't mind if it was her he was with. The boy didn't believe it but still let her lead him into the back office where over cold lemonade and shortbread biscuits the widow explained how his father had been a different man once. A good man, kind and God-fearing. With a full head of black hair and a heart full of courage. Until the War, the widow said. And some terrible things that happened afterward.

The boy wanted to hear about these terrible things but never got the chance. His father's knock on the door put an end to that. In another minute the boy was on the wagon seat next to Pop. He and Pop rode home in silence.

"Morning, Mrs. Crueller." The boy's father touched the brim of his hat with one sweat-grimed hand. "Where y'all headed on this fine day?" His eyes never left the widow's, the boy noticed. Out of politeness or because of the other—that "other" the boy couldn't explain?

"I believe we've known one another long enough, Lewis, for you to call me Mamie," the widow said. "Like you used to do. If you can remember that far back," she continued, ending with that same nervous little laugh the boy had first encountered in her back office that morning.

"I do remember," Pop said, quietly now, in a manner the boy had known him only to use with his mother. "Mamie it is, then. But you haven't answered my question."

"Why, I'm taking the children for a swim over to the creek." She pulled the wide-brimmed hat off her head and ran a hand through her graying hair. "It's so hot today I just might join them myself. Perhaps your boys would care to join us?"

Pop hesitated for a moment—long enough for the boy to wonder if he were really considering the widow's invitation.

"I suspect not. Not today. Too much to be done here, as you can see."

"Yes, I do see," the widow said. "That's too bad. But maybe another time."

"As you say, Mamie. Maybe another time."

John knew better, though, as the widow slapped the rump of the old dray with the reins and said, "Giddap." As the wagon full of laughing children moved off down Pendleton road toward the turn-off to the creek, he thought again how there wouldn't be another time. Not on Lewis Raines' farm. Not as long as there was work to be done.

***

Toward noon the sky turned an ominous gray and a stiff wind rose up, rustling the branches of the pine trees down by the creek. But though it seemed a storm was coming, it never did. From where they sat in the shade of the two oak trees on the edge of the field eating the lunch, the boy could see it raining far off to the east, a thin gray wall slanting down from the sky that refused to come any closer. He kept hoping all the while that it would, but it never did. When Pop awoke from the short nap he was accustomed to after his noon meal, it was back to work.

With the passing of the distant rain the air grew still and heavy and so wet the boy thought that if he were to reach out he could just wipe it away. As he knelt at the base of the tobacco stalks pulling off suckers he could hardly breathe, the air was so thick. His father claimed that men got used to the heat and the moisture summer brought to their part of Georgia. Said that a man just had to put up with some awful conditions at times if he wanted to make a good living. It seemed like a high price to pay to the boy, and he had told his father that once. He wouldn't do it again, though. Not after the look his father gave him in return.

In need of fresher air than was available to him on his knees, John stood up. All across the field running west, away from Pendleton Road and down to the creek, the air above the grass shimmered and danced in the hot wet of the afternoon. He stared so long at this moving air that everything went blurry. For a brief moment, it was as if he had simply melted away into the shimmering heat. It was a peaceful feeling—one that didn't last for long.

"JR," Pop yelled, bringing him back to where he certainly did not want to be. "What the hell are you doing?"

"Nothing, Pop!"

"A blind man could see that, boy. Now get to it. I'd like to finish up sometime today."

"Yes, sir."

Not long after that, TJ woke up from his nap; sooner than either the boy, his father, or RL would have liked.

"JR, JR!" John heard his younger brother calling out. "Looky what I found!"

TJ came crashing through the planted rows holding aloft in one tiny hand a bright green, wriggling garter snake. The boy stood up so fast he went dizzy for a second. He had to put a stop to the baby's foolishness, though. And quickly, before there was hell to pay with Pop.

"Stop it, TJ," he yelled out to his excited little brother. "You'll get us in trouble with Pop."

"But lookit, JR. Look what I found."

In the dash through the plants TJ had trampled down some younger stalks. Now, seeing that he had his brother's attention, he began running even faster. But in his haste TJ tripped, bowling into John and sending both of them to the ground in a swirl of dirt and dust and more crumpled tobacco plants.

"Lookit, JR," TJ repeated as he scrambled back to his feet, a flowering leaf of green tobacco stuck in his belt and still holding tight to the wriggling snake. "Lookit."

The boy was on his feet, too, praying that somehow their father hadn't heard the commotion—and better yet, not seen the damage to the crop.

"That's real nice, TJ," he said as he took his brother by the hand not holding the snake. "Now let's get you out of here before Pop sees the mess you made and we both get a whipping."

But it was too late for that. Their father came striding through the trampled plants and the next thing the boy knew was Pop's rough hands on him.

"For the love of sweet Jesus, JR," Pop yelled. John was yanked up hard so that he was suddenly face to face with his father. His feet dangled in the air between him and the ground. "Have you no more sense than that? Look what you've gone and done."

His father shook him like a rag doll before tossing him, as easily as he would a child's toy, to the ground. He landed hard, the wind knocked out of him by the contact with the sandy soil, where he lay struggling to regain his lost breath as Pop turned to TJ.

"And you," Pop yelled, his full wrath now turned on the baby. TJ stood opened-eyed and frozen in the row of tobacco plants, the wriggling snake still there in his hand. "I've just about had it with all your goddamned baby nonsense. I most certainly have."

While the boy watched, wide-eyed and frozen much like his little brother, Pop advanced on the smaller child. John thought his father looked intent on murdering his own flesh and blood. A murder prevented when out of nowhere—like one of those avenging angels in the Bible, RL flew out of the tobacco rows behind his father, striking a blow on Pop's back that sent him sprawling face forward into the dirt.

"Goddamn you, old man." Now it was RL who yelled. His anger was almost a match for Pop's, something the boy would never have believed possible. "They were only playing for God's sake. They were only playing."

With a quickness John had never seen before, Pop leapt to his feet and raked a lashing blow across the side of RL's face so hard it sent him reeling sideways into the tobacco plants. RL crumpled to his knees, one hand clutching at a clump of tobacco stalks, the only thing that kept him from sprawling all the way out. As RL slowly got upright again and turned to face his father, the sun broke through the layer of gray clouds that had lingered overhead all that afternoon. Suddenly, from where the boy stood still frozen in place, everything appeared bright and real and full of uncertainty.

boy stood still frozen in place, everything appeared bright and real and full of uncertainty.

"You think you're old enough for this?" Pop stood squared off on both feet in front of RL, his hands still clutched in two balled up fists.

"Yes," RL answered through tight-set lips, his hands too clenched into fists. "Somebody's got to stand up to you. It might as well be me."

"Might as well be," Pop said.

They closed on one another like two brown bears they had come upon fighting one spring when they were turkey hunting. Instead of the two bears, though, now it was two people swinging their fists at one another. Both of them landed fierce blows that thudded against strained flesh. First RL, then Pop, reeled back from the force of them. The success of one of the blows was visible in the blood streaming down RL's right cheek from a gash above his right eye. A red pool coagulated on Pop's neck from a similar gash across his bottom lip. It was loud and frightening, and the boy hoped it would all end soon. He couldn't see how RL and Pop could continue pummeling one another that way without one, or both of them, ending up very hurt. Or worse. The thought of "worse" of either his father, or unlikely though it was, his brother, killing the other, was more than he could think of.

"Stop!" He wasn't aware that he was going to cry out. The sound of it was almost as startling to him as what was happening between his father and older brother. But he yelled out again. "Please. Stop it. You're gonna kill one another."

RL must have heard his little brother. He suddenly pushed Pop away from him. Pushed him hard enough that Pop fell backward on his feet. He stumbled once, then twice, couldn't help himself, and then to the ground.

"That's enough," RL said. "I'm done."

"You are, are you?" Pop asked as he regained his feet. The white shirt he always wore to work in was ripped open on the one side. Blood still streamed down his neck from the cut on his lip, the cut puffed up and blue in the dull sunlight, the blood an ugly reddish hue on the ripped shirt. "I've got some news for you, son," Pop continued. "So am I."

The two of them stood apart from each other, their eyes looking out with a wary stare from their strained faces. They were both covered with sweat, as well as the blood from their wounds. RL's hair was wet and matted down on his forehead; the little hair Pop had left was matted, too, in stray wisps of gray across the bald spot above what used to be his hairline. Who was the winner? The boy couldn't tell. He wondered, too, if either one of them thought that he was.

"So now what?" RL wiped his hair back, trailing a streak of blood from the cut above his eye along his wet forehead. "Any ideas?"

It all had been one big surprise for the boy, the fighting and the grim determination of his father and brother as they did their best to pound one another into the ground. Now there appeared another surprise, just when he thought there could be no more, a tight smile played across his father's bruised lips. And the same sort of grin on RL's face.

"Well, son," Pop said after a bit, his breath apparently coming at a more normal pace as he stepped towards his oldest boy. "I think we both know what comes next."

"Yeah. I guess we do."

Suddenly, the hot, wet, air that had hung heavily over the field all the day, was filled with laughter, a full, honest roar of sound that as best the boy could figure had no place there at all.

"So that's it, then," Pop said.

His laughter had faded away. The only thing to be heard now, other than the labored breathing of the two men, was two crows squabbling somewhere off in the pine trees in the distance. In the little bit of silence John felt something in his hand. Looking down, he found that TJ was holding tight to him with one little wet hand of his. The snake that had started all this trouble, the green wriggling delight that had so intrigued the baby, was nowhere to be found.

"You'll be leaving?"

"I reckon so," RL answered. "If that's all right with you?"

"Hell, boy," Pop roared out again, not with anger, but with that hearty laughter RL and he had just shared. "It's got nothing to do with me. You're your own man, now. Yes sir. Damned if you didn't just prove that. Standing toe to toe with me out here in this Godforsaken patch of ground that don't mean much of anything when you get right down to it. No sir. It ain't up to me at all whether you stay or go. Hell no. That's your call, now. Yours and only yours."

It was the longest speech the boy had heard from his father since the day they laid his mother to rest in the little cemetery up behind Aunt Cordelia's house.

"In that case," RL said, "I'll be going."

There was a longer silence then. Pop clutched his side as if it still hurt, which the boy imagined it must. Suddenly though, he straightened all the way up in the trampled rows of tobacco and was again the man the boy had always known.

"How you planning on doing that?"

"My feet, sir," RL answered, standing up as straight as his father. "I'm a good walker."

"Ain't no son of mine starting off in this world afoot. Take the mule. If I had a horse, I'd give you that."

"You'll be needing the mule, Pop. Come planting time next spring."

"The hell I will. He's worthless behind the plow. Always has been. Maybe he'll ride better than he pulls."

"I'll take him, then. With thanks."

"I guess I owe you this." Pop reached in his pocket, a struggle because of how his hand was bruised and swollen from the fight, and pulled out a coin that shone clean and gold in the afternoon sunlight now that the grey clouds had finally drifted away. "Your month's wages."

"The month's not over, sir."

"We'll pretend it is. Hell, call it severance pay if it makes you feel better."

The surprises were to be never-ending that day. All this time he had never known RL was paid for the work he did around the place. Yet the evidence glinted bright and shiny in his brother's fist before he shoved the coin down into his pocket.

"Good luck to you, son," Pop said. "You'll be needing plenty of that. The luck, I mean. I know I sure did when I left home."

Suddenly the boy's older brother and their father were hugging one another in the row of tobacco plants. The sun was shining along like always as if nothing world-changing had just occurred in the boy's life—in that of his family's life, too.

It was very quiet as RL strode off to the house. Pop busied himself pulling some of the trampled plants until they stood upright again. The boy and his little brother stayed out of his way, still holding hands, while John's brain raced with questions he dare not ask.

He heard something coming from the old barn that housed the mule at night, as well as tobacco hung up to cure. There was no tobacco in the barn now, but in normal times they would be about two weeks away from changing that. Not that these were normal times.

As if to drive this point home, RL atop the bony old mule, came riding out of the open barn and away from the house. And behind the house, up at Aunt Cordelia's place, there she was, standing out on the front verandah looking small and frail. Even more so, John thought. The four of them watched RL ride out onto Pendleton Road heading in the direction of town, waving as he rode by. John could see his brother had washed up and put on a clean shirt, the dark blue one their mother had given him the Christmas before she died. RL waved again and the last the boy saw of him that day was when he hit the big bend where the road curved and then he was gone from sight. The boy wondered if he would ever see his brother again.

"You want to go with him?"

The boy turned and looked up and found that his father was standing by his side—had been there all along, the smile on his father's face almost enough for him to want to like the man again.

"No sir. I don't."

"You will, boy. Sure as I'm standing here, now. You will."

The boy wondered if he were supposed to say something to this. If so, he had no idea what that might be.

"Well," Pop said. In what the boy hoped was to be the last surprise of the day, Pop put a gentle hand on his shoulder. "Well, if you're staying then come on. There's work to be done yet."

It was true. The one certainty of life still left on Lewis Raines's farm was work. But now there was a new thing for the boy to consider: the idea that one day he'd ride away from the farm just as RL had just done. Of course, seeing as how Pop had given RL the mule, the boy figured when his time came he'd be going on foot. Where would he go, he wondered. When that time came, what sort of life awaited him?

It was just too much to consider. Instead he walked with his father and TJ through the rows of tobacco, pulling out plants too far gone from the recent struggle, shoring up others that had a chance to make it. Though all the while one idea *did* run through the boy's brain. If and when he did leave, and if that leaving ended up with a wife and family as Pop had, then he'd be goddamned if they would ever have to live like they had all been living on that farm since his mother had died.

No sir, no wife—or child—of his would ever live like that.

BOOK THREE ~ HILTON

Part One: Florida

Hilton Raines spent the week leading up to Labor Day of 1935 fishing with his father, John Raines, and his father's two brothers, RL and TJ, in the Florida Keys. A tall and lean boy for his age, with dark brown hair swept back from his forehead and deep brown eyes — features befitting of a Roman senator of old, his mother liked to say — Hilton was fourteen that summer. He was leaving the grade schools behind, and at summer's end, going on to the upper classes. The end of summer, the beginning of school, was the reason for the trip. At least part of the reason. The Raines brothers were eager for any excuse to set off in John Raines's boat, the Mari-Lyn. They had seized on far flimsier excuses in the past.

Hilton was no stranger to the sea or to his father's boat. He had spent considerable time on both since he was eight years old. He was ten when he caught his first sailfish, a "whopper" of one as his dad had said. He didn't know who was more excited, his father or himself. Young as he was, Hilton still suspected it might be his dad, judging by the way the older man restrained himself from grabbing the bucking rod from the boy's hands. Twice the elder Raines *had* gone to take over when Hilton was lunged forward in the fish chair, his arms straining just to hold onto the bent-double rod. Both times his dad stepped back, standing again behind the boy, lightly squeezing his shoulders with those big, sunbrowned hands of his.

As his son battled the big fish, John Raines told him, "It's okay, Hilly. You're doing fine. Just let the fish run. He'll tire, and your turn will come. Soon. I know that, son. Even if you don't."

The first time his father said this Hilton turned to look over his shoulder at the man, surprised to see his father not looking at him, but out over the water — the ocean blue and luminous that day, billowy white clouds overhead and the winds chopping the Gulf Stream to the east. Following his dad's eyes Hilton saw the sailfish clear the surface of the sea, a blue and silver form shaking its magnificent head back and forth, water flying every which way and the fish's dark sail spread fully along its back. At that moment Hilton was very glad his father had reassured him he'd have his turn. Otherwise, he didn't see how it could be so.

The trips on the Mari-Lyn were always good, full of fine fishing, adventure, and plenty of laughs, especially if TJ was along. Another side of his father seemed to show up on board the Mari-Lyn. Not the trial lawyer known for taking his legal opponents by surprise; not the stern disciplinarian quick to apply the rod if he felt the offense called for it; not even the man who sometimes looked at Hilton when he didn't think the boy knew, and who, when caught, drew up startled as if he were somewhere else. Instead, this John Raines could smile freely, joke affectionately with his son, tell off-color stories with his brothers as they drank bourbon and smoked cigarettes deep into the night. It was only on these sea journeys or around a hunt-camp fire that Hilton ever heard his father sing. For a hardened man, John Raines had a soft, melodious singing voice. When Hilton listened to his father croon old Stephen Foster tunes or gospel songs, he sometimes felt sad. It was a sadness he couldn't place, one he saw reflected on his uncles faces as well as they listened to their brother sing of times past and the glories to come when they all went to the Great Reward. At the end of these nights all of them—John Raines, his two brothers, and Hilton—joined in for the singing of "Dixie." Their boisterous voices rang out loud and clear, until the last verse of the song, "Look away, look away, look away... drifted off into the night

There was no singing, though, no telling of off-color stories, or the drinking of raw whiskey, when they set out for Marathon. The three Raines brothers were all business, stowing rods, metal ammo boxes full of supplies, and coolers loaded with bait and ice below decks of the thirty-two-foot Parker fishing boat. Hilton was busy along with the two oldest men while the youngest brother worked at prepping the diesel engine that powered the Mari-Lyn. TJ popped his head up through the hatch once, a wrench waving in one hand, his face grease-stained, a goofy smile spread across his lips.

Spotting Hilton staring at him he told the boy, "Don't ever learn the fine art of mechanics, Hilly. If you do, that son-of-a-bitch you call your dad'll stick you down here every time." With that, TJ dropped down out of sight again, his laugh and the sound of his wrench on metal all that remained of his sudden visit from the depths.

When he was done helping with the supplies, Hilton started rigging baits, sitting in the stern of the boat with his Uncle RL, who was doing the same. John Raines had been readying the cabin of the Mari-Lyn, but once finished he came out with a set of rolled-up charts that he shoved in the pocket on the cabin door. All that morning he had barked out orders as he worked alongside the others making the boat ready for sea. Now she was—the joy this gave his father plainly showing for Hilton to see. It inspired him to work even harder with rigging the baits, wanting to know that joy for himself.

"It's a down-right glorious day, Johnny." TJ was out of the engine hatch and standing next to his brother at the wheel as he took the Mari-Lyn out the Fort Lauderdale inlet to sea. "Shoot, diggity, dig, but we're gonna have some fun now." He bowed his head for a minute—the back of his neck sticking up through the collar of his white cotton shirt—stroking his chin thoughtfully. Riding in the stern and staring out past the cabin and bow of the boat at all the open water ahead, Hilton watched his uncle raise his head again and turn to face John Raines, that looping grin of his covering his entire face. "And some damn good fishing, too. Right, Johnny?"

"I imagine you're correct on that, TJ."

The older brother draped his arm across TJ's shoulders, one weather-browned hand reaching up to tousle the loose, straw-like blond hair flopped on top of the younger man's head. Hilton had never seen his father hug the other brother, the eldest of the three. Both were attorneys—one the mayor of the small town he lived in on the west coast of the state—and affectionate enough toward one another, if in a wary way. Considering his father was in his early forties, RL a little older than that, and TJ in his mid-thirties the baby of the family, Hilton supposed it was only natural they treated him differently. They worried about their younger brother, Hilton knew. Just as he, too, worried about his little sister, Marilyn, at times.

TJ was no attorney. In fact, he didn't do much of anything that Hilton knew of. He was prone to long stretches of being absent—

"riding the rails," he'd heard his father say once. Then he'd show up suddenly at the big white two-story stucco house on 9th Street that was John Raines's home. For months on end TJ would stay with them, doing mechanical odds and ends, as well as whatever carpentry jobs needed to be done for his older brother and his family. Then one morning he'd be gone, and the cycle would begin anew. Hilton supposed TJ had a similar arrangement with RL over in Ft. Myers. But it had never been spoken of. One time when Hilton was twelve, he helped his father and TJ hunt stray cows out of the palmettos and pine scrub at the ranch. On the little sorrel that was his favorite of the horses John Raines owned, TJ was ranging far out in front. Watching his uncle on the sorrel weave in and out of the thick palmetto clumps Hilton told his father that one day, when he was grown up, he wanted to be just like TJ.

"You may want to give that some further thought, Hilly."

"Why do you say that, Dad? You love TJ."

"I do. But he'll never be more than what he is now. And that isn't much. I hope I've raised you better. My father gave up on TJ. Gave him the reins, if you will, way before he should have."

Hilton didn't understand it at the time. But he didn't discount it either. Not if his father said it was so.

***

RL stood on the bow of the Mari-Lyn for a long time that morning, holding onto the railing with one hand, his eyes looking south and east as the Parker chugged steadily across the surface of the rippling sea. His uncle could be a figurehead for the boat, Hilton thought, he stood so still at the bow. His father and TJ were talking and drinking beers TJ had dredged up from one of the ice-filled coolers. They paid no attention to their brother at his post. Hilton couldn't figure out what RL was so focused on. They were looking out at the same ocean; all Hilton saw was the sunlight reflected off the water and the occasional sea bird wheeling overhead. Here and there the bow of the Mari-Lyn flushed up a flying fish, its tiny pseudo-wings beating rapidly in the air before the fish dropped back down into the sea and was gone.

Three hours later they came up on Miami. The eight- and ten-story buildings in the business heart of the city rose up glinting in the late summer haze drifting off the ocean. There were some hotels scattered along the shore. Using his father's binoculars, Hilton scanned the tourists gathered on the beach, men and children splashing in the waves breaking against the sand. A few women were in the water as well, their hair bound up out of view beneath tight bathing caps. More women clustered in small groups under beach umbrellas where they chatted to one another while keeping an eye on their respective broods.

Then Miami was gone. The Mari-Lyn was cruising south at a steady eight knots when RL decided to come aft and have a beer like the one his two brothers were enjoying.

"We'll need to keep a sharp eye to the east the next couple days, John," RL said as he took the brown bottle TJ handed him. "That sky doesn't look right to me. Not like I'd like it to look when I'm in a small boat on a big sea at the height of storm season."

It all looked good to Hilton, the sky and the water. But he also knew his uncle was good with the weather. RL smiled a lot, smiles much like those of his youngest brother, though they seemed to get lost a little in RL's rounder, florid face. He was a softer man than his brothers, with a bit of a paunch overlapping his leather belt and a chubby face beneath the same sort of receding brown hairline as John Raines's. But RL's softness was deceiving—like his brothers RL was strong. Hilton knew this full well.

"Well then," John Raines said, looking toward where RL had pointed. "If you say so. I don't see it, RL, but I certainly value your opinion."

"She-et," TJ snorted in an exaggerated drawl. He was busy in the cooler again, coming up with another bottle of beer for himself. Before popping off the metal cap he set it down on the console and thrust a lean, muscular arm back into the metal ice-box. When he pulled it back up he held a bottle of Coca Cola that he handed over to Hilton.

"She-et," TJ said again. "RL worries too much, Johnny. That's why he never has any fun."

It was RL's turn to snort. "I've had my share of fun, as you call it, little brother. Just ask some of the ladies over in Ft. Myers. Or those boys who lose their money to me on poker night."

The two older brothers laughed. Not knowing any reason not to, Hilton laughed with them.

"That's a sure load of hoeey if I ever heard it. Like I said, RL, you worry too much. That storm talk and all on a beautiful day such as this one. Seems to me sometimes like you want to live forever."

"I don't know about that, TJ" RL said. Hilton saw a frown come across his uncle's face. "But I'd like to find out. Besides, what would my faithful constituents do without me?"

The sound of their laughter drifted out behind the stern of the boat as she cruised south. Drinking from his own brown bottle, Hilton felt glad to be a part of it.

By mid-afternoon they were deep into Biscayne Bay, a quarter mile west or so of Elliot Key. As they came up on two small islands, split by a deep-water cut running between them into the ocean, Hilton saw a spiraling plume of blue-gray smoke rising from the center of the island on the northern side of the cut. Soon he glimpsed a dock leading from the water up to the shore. Inside the cover of the mangroves and coconut palms lining the shore of that island, there had to be a dwelling of some sort.

"Hey John," RL said from the stern where he was busy rigging two stout boat rods for the next day's fishing. "Why don't you go and see if Mr. Henry'll let us tie up to his dock? You know, so you can pay your respects and all." RL's round, sunburned face was split in a wide grin. Sitting next to his brother, and also engaged with a rod, TJ burst out laughing.

"Yeah, Johnny. That sounds like a capital idea."

"No, sir." John Raines fell silent. Standing at the wheel with his dad, Hilton waited for him to say something more. But John Raines stayed quiet until after he brought the boat around, turning the bow until the Mari-Lyn faced into the wind blowing west from the mainland. "No, sir. As much as you two might enjoy it, I doubt today is the day for me to go calling on Mr. Henry. That day may come. But not today. We'll anchor here, tonight."

At his father's nod, Hilton jumped up to the bow to help TJ with the anchor. It took a bit for the steel hook to grab hold satisfactorily in the sandy bottom of the bay. The man and boy strained at their task, Hilton's hands slipping some on the wet line as they let it move through their fingers. At the wheel, John helped with the throttle, easing the boat forward or back as needed, until finally the anchor took good hold.

"What's all that about with Dad and Mr. Henry, Uncle TJ?" Hilton asked.

"Ah now," TJ said. "That's something you'll have to ask him." He pointed at his brother, who was helping RL with the rods in the stern. "It ain't really my affair to discuss." Then TJ's young face spread wide with the smile that was always threatening to break out, his straw-like hair lifting slightly in the breeze. "As much as I'd like to."

"Do you think Dad'll tell me?"

"Nope."

When all was secured on the boat, TJ dropped the dinghy over the side and motioned for Hilton to board. The boy and his uncle set off for the cut with TJ at the oars. At the other end of the cut Hilton could see the Atlantic Ocean. Gray waves rose out from the cut in the wind, blowing stronger now as the day shut down, their tips shining dully in the receding light. They trolled back and forth with hand lines set out behind the stern of the dinghy. Tied to the end of these lines were shiny metal spoon rigs, garnished off with the fluffs of brightly dyed deer hair TJ had wrapped around them. Hilton enjoyed watching his line trailing out behind the little boat, the subtle tugs signifying a cooperating fish — perhaps a mangrove snapper or its bigger cousin, one of the red variety. There were stronger takers, too. A gag grouper, perhaps seven or eight pounds worth of fish, came out of its hiding place in the rocks to strike TJ's lure. Hilton heard his uncle grunt at the oars and turned to see him un-wrapping the end of the hand line he'd strung around his belt while he rowed. There was a wild glee on his uncle's face as he slowly hauled the grouper in. Finally, the mottled brown fish lay flopping in the bottom of the dinghy. His hair blown back from his face and that grin stretched as wide as it could go, TJ yelled out, "Now goddamn, that's gonna be some fine eatin'. If that don't tickle your daddy's palate, nothin' will." With TJ's loud yell of triumph reverberating off the water and the mangrove-lined sides of the inlet, Hilton didn't care what his father had said about the uselessness of his younger brother's life. He only hoped that someday he, too, would know that kind of joy in a simple thing.

The sun was slipping away. While TJ fought the grouper, leaving the oars unattended, the tide going out the cut had pulled the dinghy almost into the ocean.

"Shit, boy," TJ said, grabbing at the idle oars. "With this grouper and them snappers, we got more 'an enough to feed us for the night. Heck, might even be some left over for fish and grits in the morning. Uh-huh. We'd best head back."

TJ pulled hard, his face and muscles drawn tight as he rowed against the tide. Hilton drew his line in and then stowed both rigs, coiling them neatly like TJ had shown him on one side of the deck. Above the sound of the oars slapping the water, Hilton could hear the rhythmic flopping of the dying fish against the wood. He looked forward to the eating of those fish even if their dying at the end always disturbed him.

Finished with the hand lines, Hilton straightened up on the bench. They were coming even with a long dock reaching into the cut. Behind this dock, set up in a clearing obviously made by the hands of man, sat a neat little cabin constructed of white painted Dade County pine and topped off with a tin roof. A brick chimney rising up one wall issued the curls of grey smoke Hilton had seen earlier. On the end of the dock a man stood, tall and white haired, his face uncovered, forehead burnt red and freckled. From long years in the elements, Hilton guessed. Like the way his father's skin would look when he was that age, he thought suddenly. How his own would be too if he chose that sort of life.

"That your boat yonder?" the man called out through cupped hands. He gestured at the Mari-Lyn riding her anchor in the bay.

"It surely is, Mr. Henry," TJ answered the man.

"Then you go to hell and take that John Raines bastard with you."

The raw anger in the white-haired man's voice stunned Hilton, but TJ only laughed.

"I'll be sure to do that, Mr. Henry. And I'll tell Johnny you send your regards."

But the man on the dock had turned his back on them and was walking rapidly up toward the house. Having lost his momentum against the tide during the exchange, TJ grunted again and bent to the oars. Soon TJ, Hilton, and their fine catch were pulling up alongside of the Mari-Lyn and the others waiting for them there.

***

It was a long haul after leaving Elliot Key. By the end of it, all four of them were glad it was over. They were also grateful for the light seas and a wind from the east blowing on their stern to help them along. Eighty some land miles of keys, broken up by the endless water, had to be traveled; with a head wind and rough seas it would have been close to intolerable. John Raines's face was set at the helm. His brothers and son knew by this look his mind was made up. He had announced Marathon the goal that morning over coffee, informing his crew they'd be there by nightfall and make it their base, "come hell or high water."

"Well, actually," he continued, rolling up the chart and placing it by the wheel. "We'll anchor behind Boot Key. If you want to be exact about it. That's close enough to Marathon, I suppose."

"Hell, Johnny," TJ piped up. "We all know you're only hankerin' for another crack at the sailfish 'at broke you off in front of Sombrero Beach last year. You ain't foolin' nobody here." TJ paused a second, looking around the table until his eyes set on Hilton. "'Cept maybe the boy. And heck, *anybody* could fool him."

All that day the Mari-Lyn steamed west, her diesel engine chugging steadily below decks at eight knots. At the wheel of his craft, John Raines steered her past the watery line of the Florida Keys. Hilton spent most of the morning by the wheel with his father, the chart spread out on the console as he stared out the window at the ocean unfolding before them. His father tested Hilton's chart reading ability, periodically asking him what he thought the land mass they were currently passing might be. It was good when he knew the answer. After a bit it felt to the boy like he was back in school. He read the chart, then with John Raines's binoculars, scanned the coastline they were approaching. Soon, he was calling out the place names with confidence; so that if it were a school, Hilton thought once, it was a better school than any he'd yet attended.

After Key Largo they chugged past Tavernier and Plantation Keys. Past small, barely perceptible strips of land where it looked like no one could, or would, live, strips of land with names like Cotton and Wilson Key. The bigger land masses of Windley, Islamorada, and Upper Matecumbe Key slipped by the boat as she headed west, steaming on by Lower Matecumbe, Layton Key, Fiesta and Long Key. All the way down this line of land and water, one thing remained the same: the railroad Mr. Flagler had built. On both big and small key the iron rails Flagler's men had laid, gleamed dully in the sun.

Hilton had ridden those rails once to New York—though not in the manner of his Uncle TJ, who jumped box cars to get where he wanted to go—the summer when he was five. His father had business to conduct in that city and at his wife's urging decided to bring his family along. What Hilton remembered of the trip was how his sister Marilyn, still a baby, cried for most of the long train ride to New York. Now, standing at the helm of the Mari-Lyn with his father, he thought of how those strips of iron stretched from where the land ended at Key West to a noisy metropolis Hilton could barely recall. It seemed impossible, the fact of those rails and the course they covered, but it was so.

As John Raines had predicted, the daylight was ending by the time the Mari-Lyn slipped past Marathon Key proper, past the southernmost point of Sombrero Beach, and around Boot Key into the narrow harbor laying there. A few faint lights winked up on shore, shining out from the windows of people's homes. As he helped TJ again with the anchor, Hilton wondered what it would be like to live in such a remote and watery region. He thought it could be grand.

It wasn't long after the boat was secured that TJ was in the small galley preparing "boat chow for dinner." John Raines and RL sat out on the stern with glasses of what RL called "bourbon and branch" while Hilton helped with the meal. A sense of comfort settled over the boy as he set enamel plates and pewter silverware on the cabin table. A soft light glowed from a lantern TJ hung on the hook above the table. In that light Hilton felt that everything was just as it should be. For an instant he wished that it would all remain forever just as it was. But just as quickly, he decided it might be best if it didn't.

The next day, the day after, and the one after that evolved into a pattern. Not so much a plan of John and his two brothers, Hilton thought, but a course of movement that had been there all along waiting for them. They fished. It was that simple. The boy fell easily into the rhythm of manning the rods: rigging dead mullet upon the sharp hooks attached at the end of thin wire leaders TJ had wrapped up; tying this tackle to the sturdy line coiled on the big reels; dropping the baits into the water off the stern at RL's word; and once the baits were at the proper distance behind the boat, setting the drag on the reel and then jamming the rod butt into the holder. Atop the cabin TJ did the work of two men, placing rods into makeshift holders he'd built there, so that instead of two lines they could run four to double their odds and their catch. Hilton liked to watch his uncle at his work, the way TJ's lean frame moved in a rhythm of its own, fluid and sure, so unlike Hilton's own, which was awkward and lacked confidence. Once again, as he watched his uncle move through life, Hilton thought that his father was wrong about his younger brother. It was rare, to Hilton's knowledge, that his father was mistaken about something. But as far as Hilton was concerned, regarding Uncle TJ he was.

They encountered schools of dolphin, brightly colored fish, aqua and yellow, which slashed eagerly at the rigged mullet the Mari-Lyn pulled in her wake. Once hooked, the dolphin fought hard, with line-searing runs and sky-walking leaps. There were sailfish, too. Hilton landed one of them after a struggle that seemed to last an eternity but was only twenty minutes or so according to RL. And though his uncle RL stood by him during the battle, no words were said, nothing offered to Hilton on how to deal with the beautiful swimming creature on the other end of the line. Finally, the sailfish was boat-side and TJ, with the long-handled gaff in his right hand, leaned over the gunnels and snatched it aboard. With the engine in idle and the boat dead in the water while TJ and RL unhooked the flopping sailfish on the deck, Hilton turned and saw his father at the wheel. What Hilton saw on his father's face suddenly caused him to feel different inside.

"You did good, Hill." John Raines put the boat in gear and eased the throttle forward. "You learned well from that first sailfish. The one we caught together that day. It's fine to see." Then John was busy with the wheel for a bit. When he was done he looked back again at the boy, who with TJ and RL's help was holding the dying sailfish in his arms. "You did real good, son."

Saturday was the last day of the fishing. The next day would be the first of September. John Raines planned to turn the bow of the Mari-Lyn east and take her home. School awaited Hilton and the office and work for the grown men. A strong wind from the southeast had risen in the night. When they came out of the harbor they discovered the ocean was too rough for comfortable fishing. The moderate chop they had known for the last week was gone. In its place, sparkling in the sunlight pouring out of a blue and cloudless sky, was a steady stream of heavy swells crashing into and rolling over one another.

"It'd be a good day for the sailfish, Johnny," RL said. "Rough like this. Maybe even a marlin. One of those big blues."

The boat rounded the leeward side of Boot Key and came into the Atlantic. All up and down the coastline Hilton watched the breakers pound into the beach. The Mari-Lyn rocked awkwardly in the swells. Hilton had to grab hold of the console rail at times as the boat shuddered and shook coming up over the top of the oncoming waves, and his feet grew unsteady on the rolling deck.

"It's too rough, RL. We'd pound ourselves to death chasing a blue in this water." John leaned into the wheel, both hands gripping the chrome to keep it from wavering in the rollicking sea. His morning mug of coffee was in the holder on the console. Once he'd turned the boat around so she was riding with the swells instead of into them, he lifted the mug to his lips. Hilton watched as the steam rose up around his father's ruddy face. "Let's go into the bay and do some easy fishing. We've got a long ride tomorrow. No sense in getting beat up today."

RL nodded in agreement, his face looking redder in the morning light than usual. Hilton knew the men had stayed up late the night before, drinking the bourbon RL had brought along. It appeared his uncle had what TJ called a "whiskey burn." All of them were sunburned, though. The first few days Hilton had had a hard time sleeping, what with the way his back burned against the sheets. His father had brought some leaves from the aloe plants growing on the side of the house. The lotion he squeezed from these leaves and rubbed into Hilton's skin had helped ease the sting some. Now the burn was gone. As was the summer, Hilton thought, suddenly remembering what day it was.

"Aw, you boys just lost your spunk is all." TJ came lurching into the cabin from the stern where he'd been busy stowing loose objects. "That goddam' easy livin' in the courthouse and your office have ruin't you two. I never thought I'd live to see the day I had to say such a thing, but I guess I have. A little sea like this shouldn' put us off our game."

But TJ was smiling as he grabbed the table for support when a heavy swell thudded into the stern of the boat, sending it skidding sideways before John could straighten the wheel.

"That's a bear I see no sense in chasing today, Tommy. But you're welcome to the dinghy if you wish. RL and Hilly and I will be anchored at the same spot tonight. We'll expect you for dinner."

"Expect me for dinner?" TJ snorted. "Heck. You expect me to *cook* your damn dinner."

"I do."

"I swear, Johnny. Good thing our Daddy ain't alive to see this." TJ's grin was just a sheepish, half-smile on his lips. "The way you treat your poor younger brother and all."

"It's a good thing our Daddy hasn't been alive to see a lot of things."

Hilton expected a loud laugh from the men with his father's last statement. But it didn't come. In fact, the cabin was suddenly quieter than it'd been all trip.

John Raines took the boat around Knight Key and into Florida Bay. The Mari-Lyn slipped under the railroad trestle built by Mr. Flagler's crews. Beginning at Pigeon Key, Hilton remembered, it stretched seven miles west across the water until reaching the next patch of dry land. As they steamed beneath the railroad bridge Hilton looked up through the tracks, wishing a train were roaring by overhead. He wanted to hear the noise of something other than ocean and the sound of men talking. Wanted to see the sparks flying from the rushing wheels of the train as it headed east, or west, whatever the case might be. But there was no train, only the steady hum of the Mari-Lyn's engines and the heavy surf crashing into the beach of Boot Key behind them.

The water was calmer in the bay. John allowed the boat to drift with the remnants of the wind in the shallower water there. Four feet beneath the hull, in some spots even less, were vast stretches of grass flat that Hilton could see when he shaded his eyes with one hand and leaned over the gunnels. Flashing streaks of silver darted here and there just above the waving grass, their shadows showing dark against the sand in the places where the grass cleared away.

They fished with TJ's spoons and handmade jigs for the spotted sea trout and redfish that roamed the vast grass flat. By day's end they had filled the metal fish box with their catch. Though the sky remained cloudless and a deep blue, by then the wind had finally caught up with the bay, blowing from the south hard across the tiny keys to chop up the surface of the shallow water.

Hilton and TJ wanted to stay longer and fish more, what with the day being their last. But John said no. Hilton, and he guessed TJ as well, knew better than to try and argue. All that day Hilton had noticed how quiet RL was; noticed how he kept looking to the south where the Straits of Florida and the Atlantic Ocean had been unbroken white foam shining in the clear light of the morning. The boy remembered the day they left home. RL had stood at the bow for hours staring south then, as well, with what his dad called his "weather eye." RL had seen something that day. Hilton wondered as they returned to the harbor if his uncle had seen that something again.

But though they could hear the wind howling outside the harbor, the boat rode easy at anchor that night. TJ busied himself with the fish in the galley and the smell of breaded fillets frying in oil soon filled the cabin of the Mari-Lyn. The men were drinking RL's bourbon. John surprised his son by handing him a bottle of beer from the cooler. Hilton sipped at the beer, wanting the yeasty flavored brew to last as long as possible. But it didn't work; the cold, bitter beverage tasted better than he thought possible and before he realized it, he'd drained the bottle.

"Uh oh, John," RL laughed, noticing the empty bottle Hilton was holding. "Your boy drinks the way you used to."

"Fuck," TJ grunted, from where he was standing over the skillet flipping the frying fish. "Nobody drinks beer like Johnny could in the old days. Lord knows I tried. But heck, even I couldn't do it."

"I'm not worried." John leaned back against a cushion he'd propped up against the wall as he sat at the small table beneath the hanging lantern. In the soft light, Hilton noticed that his father's hair had thinned out even more of late, the wispy brown strands still left above his forehead almost invisible now in the lantern light. A weary smile was on his dad's lips, but he looked comfortable where he was, sipping at the glass of bourbon RL poured out for him. "Hill's got too much of his mother in him for the sort of foolishness I was prone to."

Hilton said nothing, just felt surprised again when his dad rose up suddenly from his comfortable spot to get the boy another of those cold brown bottles. As he handed his son the beer, John's eyes held the same look Hilton had seen when he caught the sailfish two days earlier.

"Here, Hilly. I guess if you're old enough to sit around men jackin' their jaws, you're old enough to drink with them." John leaned up against the cushion again, the glass of bourbon raised to his lips. "Just don't tell your mother." Then he drained the contents of the glass in one quick swallow.

"Oh, I won't," the boy blurted out. The men all laughed, his father the hardest of the three.

***

The following morning came up gray and raining. The sound of the early storm pouring down on the deck woke Hilton. It was dark and comfortable in the cabin, with the splatter of the rain falling outside and the random snoring of his two uncles in their berths. When he woke fully enough to realize where he was, what day it was, Hilton was glad. There would be no church to attend aboard the Mari-Lyn, unlike at home where rain or shine, his mother made sure her flock was counted amongst the faithful come the Sabbath. Happy with this, Hilton burrowed down in his bunk, falling back asleep to the sound of the rain.

It wasn't a long sleep. The sound of TJ making coffee in the galley and the waking men made sure of that. His father came out of the forward berth, already dressed in his customary khaki pants and long sleeve shirt, saying, "C'mon and get up, Hilly. It's no day to be sleeping in." Soon Hilton was at the table with the others, in the T-shirt and chinos he pulled on, his berth stowed away, a steaming mug of TJ's coffee in one hand to help hasten the waking process.

"Well, gentlemen, we've got our work laid out for us today." John sat across from his son, with his own mug of coffee and a chart spread out in front of him. "I'm afraid the run home's going to be considerably different from the trip down."

"Now there's an understatement, John, if I ever heard one." RL's face looked pale in the gray light of the cabin. Hilton saw that his uncle's hand shook holding his coffee cup. "There's no inside cut to Elliot Key. With the wind out of the south the way she is, that outside's going to be a real bitch."

The men shook their heads in agreement and following their lead Hilton did the same.

"A lot of ocean'll be washing over the stern all the way up," RL continued. Hilton noticed the color slowly returning to his uncle's face. TJ's coffee was getting his insides working. Hilton figured it must be doing the same to his uncle as well. "Maybe we can make it as far as Key Largo. Snug up in Blackwater Sound for the night and pray it all blows over by morning. It'll be a long haul home the next day but might be for the best." RL finished the rest of the coffee and put the empty mug down on the table. "Just my thoughts on the matter, Captain."

"Good thoughts, RL. I was thinking Blackwater Sound myself." John hadn't paid much attention to his coffee. His eyes were focused on the chart as he traced a finger over the spread open sheet of paper. "If we had a smaller boat we could run the bay back. But you're right, RL. It'd be impossible with the Mari-Lyn. Damn. I was hoping to have the boy home in time for the first day of school."

"I don't envy you any, facing Miss Sadie if the boy's late." RL chuckled, the color completely back in his face. "There're few good things to be said for bachelorhood, but at the moment I do believe I'm seeing one of them."

"No," John said quietly. "Sadie won't be happy, you're right. But there's nothing to be done for it." He looked to his son then, a slight grin playing across his lips. "How 'bout you, Hill? You don't mind missing the first day, do you?"

"Hell no." TJ's voice rang out in the cabin as he set plates of steaming grits and fish fillets in front of his two brothers. "'Least, that's what I'd say. If I was Hilly."

"Yes. I imagine you would, Tommy." John's ghost of a smile was trained on his younger brother. "But you're not him. Thank God. I've got enough to contend with at the moment."

"Aw hell," TJ snorted, sitting down with plates for him and Hilton. "A man like you, Johnny? You got no worries. That's a charmed life you live. Yes, sir, a flat-out charm."

An hour later they had the boat ready for the run home. All the fishing gear, coolers, metal tackle boxes, and other non-essentials, were carefully stowed away. Hilton worked along-side TJ putting the ammo boxes that had contained food and bait and the like, down below. When they finished there, he helped his uncle button down the galley and cabin, making sure all the pots, pans, plates, and silverware were in the proper cabinets and drawers and the cabinets and drawers latched shut. John worked at the helm, going over the chart as if he might find something he missed, another way home not readily apparent, yet there. Hilton saw his father look up once and shake his head, then get busy with compass and pen setting down course headings on the chart.

RL stood out on the bow, protected from the blowing rain by a light windbreaker and watching the weather coming from the southeast. He was waiting for his brother to start the engine and give him the sign to hoist anchor. It was an urgent hour or so of labor Hilton thought, very different from life aboard the Mari-Lyn on their usual fishing trips.

Then the diesel engine was humming, the anchor up, and everyone back inside the cabin as the Mari-Lyn moved slowly out of Boot Key Harbor. Hilton stood at the wheel beside his father as John steered his boat abreast of Pigeon Key, with its long railroad trestle to the north, into the pass. The water rolling through the channel was a seething mass of pounding white caps driven hard by the wind and the incoming tide. A mass of water suddenly slammed the bow of the Mari-Lyn, smashing sheets of foaming white water over the decks where Hilton was glad no one stood. Ten minutes later they were around Boot Key and in the

Atlantic Ocean proper, the boat rocking with the wind and waves coming at the stern and starboard side. The Mari-Lyn rode with the violent movement, but Hilton didn't see how she could do so for the long hours it would take to get home. Not and still be in one piece.

"RL," John Raines said when they cleared the southern point of Sombrero Beach. "What's that flag blowing yonder?" He pointed toward the land at something Hilton couldn't see. Then, straining his eyes through the mist-covered windshield, he saw a long pole standing up from somewhere in the middle of Marathon Island.

"It's too far for me to make out properly." In the gray light of the cabin, Hilton saw a fine sheen of sweat on his uncle's forehead. "But it's got to be the flag pole in front of the post office."

"Use the binocs."

"Have the boy do it, John. I'm having trouble with my eyes this morning."

"Gee, I wonder why?" TJ was sitting on a bunk playing solitaire with the Mari-Lyn's lone set of cards. "Wouldn't have anything to do with all that Black Jack you were pouring down your gullet last night would it, RL?"

Hilton didn't wait for his father's command. He took the heavy pair of German binoculars from their place on the console and trained them on the far pole. It took a little bit to get the glasses focused right. Through the sheeting rain he saw the American Flag attached to the flag pole streaming out in the wind washing over the island. Below the large, national flag was the state flag of Florida, and below that a smaller flag flapped in the wind, as well.

"What color is the bottom one, Hill?"

"It's a red square, Dad. With a black box in the center."

"You sure, son?"

Hilton felt the tension in the cabin of the rocking boat, felt the eyes of his father on him as he looked again through the binoculars.

"I'm sure, Dad. It's like I said, large red square, small, black one in the middle. Here. Look for yourself."

"No." John was silent for a moment. "I believe you, Hill." It was quiet in the cabin of the Mari-Lyn, except for the noise the wind and rain made outside.

"Fuck." John spoke after what seemed a very long time to Hilton. It was the first time he'd ever heard his father use that word. Even more surprising was the sudden fear he felt—a fear that didn't lessen any when his father said again, "Well, fuck it all."

"Damn, Johnny." TJ's loud burst broke the strain in the small cabin. "I'd have never in my wildest imaginin's thought you knew such a word, big brother."

"Oh," and John was smiling for the first time that morning. "There's lots of things I know, Tommy. But right now, we've other concerns."

"Well, it's what I've been pretty much expecting." RL had left the cabin and gone out into the weather for a minute to smoke a cigarette alone on the stern deck. Now he was back, thinning hair wet and plastered on his head, his cotton shirt soaked through. In his hands were three bottles of beer, two of which he handed to his brothers. "We might as well enjoy one of these while we can." RL tilted the bottle to his lips and drank. "It's letting up some out there, but it won't last."

"Not according to the warning posted there on Marathon."

"Goddamn, JR." TJ stood up from the bunk, the beer in one hand and his other brushing the tousled hair back from his forehead. "If a hurricane's coming, your polite 'fuck' don't come close to describing our situation."

"Let's settle down here, boys." John Raines took the beer RL opened for him and drank. "We don't need to scare Hilton any."

"I'd be a lot less scared if someone told me what's going on." The boy looked at the three men drinking, feeling left out of a sudden. "Where's my beer, Uncle RL? Seems to me I'm in this thing as well."

The three brothers laughed, their laughter making Hilton feel even more left out.

"Well, son," and John Raines turned from the wheel to look at the boy. "Somebody's got to stay sober today. By virtue of seniority, I suppose, that'll be you." He was smiling again, but the bow of the boat slashing through a rolling breaker coming across the starboard side demanded his attention. When it was over, the last wild spray of water sluicing down the scuppers and back into the sea, John looked at his son again. "Hilton, there's a hurricane bearing down on us. That flag you saw through the glass is a Coast Guard hurricane warning. It means the storm'll be here in twenty-four hours or less. That's what's going on. If we get through today, into a safe harborage somewhere tonight, you'll get your beer. Perhaps something stronger. I promise you that."

"Oh." There had been a lot of surprises on this trip, Hilton thought. The newest one being this. Now that he knew what had his father and uncles so concerned, he was no longer scared or feeling left out.

"It doesn't change anything," John said. "We'll still head for Key Largo and Blackwater Sound. Maybe the storm'll hit well west of us. Maybe we won't get any more than we've got now."

Hilton looked out the window past the bow, at the churning sea, and the way the gray rain sheeted sideways with the wind across the deck of the Mari-Lyn. The boat rolled and vibrated in the heavy swells pushing from behind and on the starboard side. What they had now, as his father said, seemed pretty bad.

"TJ," and John looked at his younger brother. "Best break out the slickers. We're going to need them."

"Aye, aye, Captain." With a crisp, military style salute TJ was out the cabin door.

***

The heavy squall slacked off after a while. For the rest of the morning the skies remained gray and threatening, the rain pouring down. The sun came out sporadically. When it did, beams of light shone on the wind-blown sea and the Mari-Lyn pushing through the rough swells. They left Key Colony Beach behind. Used to the rolling ride of the boat by now, Hilton thought that maybe his dad would be right: the hurricane would hit somewhere else, far away from where they were. He was in no hurry to get home or to school the following day, it was true. But he didn't want to be in the boat with a hurricane blowing through, either.

Hilton had been in hurricanes before, as a child of four and seven respectively, when the bad storms of '25 and '28 came roaring in. The storm of '25 was the one most affecting his home that he could remember, a strong hurricane that came ashore between Miami and Fort Lauderdale on the day of his sister's first birthday. It was a long time ago and hazy in his memory. But Hilton could still recall how the storm blew all night, objects banged against the shuttered windows, and the walls of the house moved in and out as if they were breathing with the pulsing winds. Thousands of people died in that storm because of the rising waters, although Hilton only knew this as being something his father and mother told him later—whenever the talk turned to storms, and stories of what they had done.

They were coming up on Long Key when the engine began to cough and sputter. Then it suddenly died. John Raines cranked the starter. Hilton listened to it whirring and whirring, but nothing happened. All the while the powerless boat drifted in the heavy swells pushing at it. In another moment the motor finally coughed once throatily and fired up. But Hilton could tell it didn't sound right as they began to chug through the rough seas again.

"Shit, Johnny, sounds like somethin' blockin' off the juice." TJ, out on the stern when the motor died, was standing with John at the helm now. "Don' let her die out. She might not start up again."

"I know that, Tommy." John turned to Hilton and the charts spread out on the console. "Where are we, Hilly?"

"We should be coming up on Long Key, Dad." Hilton looked at the chart, then at the coastline they were following. They'd been running for hours, it seemed, but were only at Long Key? Less than twenty land miles from where they'd started? At that rate it'd be midnight before they reached Blackwater Sound. If they got there at all, judging by the sounds the boat's engine was making.

"Okay, son." John Raines pointed out a bridge leading away from the western tip of the key, just visible now as they came up on it. "I'm going to run her in around there. Hopefully we'll find a good lee out of the wind, and TJ can go below and see what's wrong with the engine."

TJ nodded in agreement, and not long after the boat steamed out of the wind and heavy seas into a relatively calm place. Hilton could still hear the wind blowing, could see the force of its movement in the swaying palms and Australian pines waving on shore. Up ahead, when they came in around the point and under the railroad bridge, the land humped out and a long dock jutted from the shore. No landing was marked on the chart, yet, there it was. His father saw this dock as well and steered the Mari-Lyn toward it.

It didn't take long to secure the boat on the leeward side of the dock. It felt good to Hilton to be stopped, out of the rolling sea and with the throbbing engine off. TJ popped the engine hatch and dropped down in to the oily smelling bay. RL sat up on the bow smoking a cigarette, still watching the gray weather moving in from the south, the plume of blue smoke from the smoldering Pall Mall held in his fingers blown away in the winds not fully blocked by the key.

"There's nothing for you and I to do here right now, Hill." John came out of the cabin and draped a loose arm around Hilton's shoulders. The boy was watching TJ at work in the engine bay, his uncle bent over the hulking motor block with his wrenches clanging away. "TJ there doesn't need our help, and if I look at those charts any longer I'm liable to go blind."

The man and the boy walked up the long dock to the shore. A beach made of shell and sand ran the length of the key as far as Hilton could see. The beach was some thirty yards wide, its borders defined by the waters of the Gulf of Mexico. Thick stands of wiry brush and palms grew up where the beach ended. There were hummocks of Australian pines and smaller palms scattered across the key, but no sign of any other life, not even a sea bird seeking shelter from the wind.

Hilton and his father made their way through the brush, and palm trees, no set destination in mind as they followed a fading game trail leading away from the beach. As they walked they flushed none of the varmints, the rabbits, raccoons, and tiny Key deer that had created the trail over time. Their absence was somewhat perplexing to Hilton, but it didn't matter. He was just glad to feel solid land beneath his feet after so many days on the Mari-Lyn.

The trail suddenly opened into a clearing. A burned-out shell of a cabin lay in a heap in the center. It wasn't much of a shell anymore; the timbers, burned down to the sand foundation, were now just gray and flaky charcoal. The base of a brick chimney was all that remained, rising three feet or so from what once had been a wall. Someone's hard work and dreams had ended at that place, Hilton thought. It had happened a long time ago. The charred scattered bricks and cold ash of the cabin remains told that much. Still, an aura of utter defeat seemed to linger over the rubble.

They walked out of the clearing, John leading the way along where the trail picked up again past the burned-out cabin. It wasn't long before they reached another, smaller clearing. As they stepped into the open space Hilton could tell by the wind, the roaring sound of it, that they were getting closer to the ocean. On the far edge of this smaller clearing two faded stone markers rose up from the sand. When Hilton and his father came up on these markers he saw how there were inscriptions etched into the stone, the makeshift tombstones pale above the two graves beneath them.

Mary Cromartie Edwards
B. May 10 1881
D. Jan 1 1906
"Her husband loved her
But her Father
Needed her by His side"

Ellie Cromartie Edwards
B. April 2 1905
D. Jan 1 1906
"Called Home too soon."

Other than the obvious, Hilton, didn't know what to think as he listened to the wind coming off the sea.

"They must have died in the fire. Think so, Dad?"

"I imagine they did, Son."

"It just doesn't seem right. That God would take a child so young."

"You get older, Hilly, you'll see a lot of things attributed to God that don't seem right." John squatted down by the stones and ran his fingers along the rough lettering. "It's the man I wonder about. These folks here," he tapped the woman's headstone, "are beyond pain. But the man's had to live with it. If he's still alive. Lord knows, that kind of misery would be hard to survive."

"You could."

There was a long silence in the little clearing where both man and boy knelt together in front of the graves.

"I don't know, Son," John finally said. "Perhaps I could. I damn sure don't ever want to have to find out." He rose to his feet, brushing the sand from the knees of his pants. "It's a damnable thing at times, Hill. The sadness between men and women. That much I have learned. But come on, now. Let's get back to the boat. I'm hungry. We'll get TJ away from that engine for a while and have him whip us up some grub. Motors and cooking; you'd think with two talents like that a man could get somewhere in life."

Hilton agreed, though he was not really sure. Thinking about the two graves they had stumbled upon, he followed his father out of the clearing, back down the trail the way they had come.

***

Come the next morning there was no more talk of making Blackwater Sound before the storm hit. TJ had finally been able to repair the engine problem. "Carb and fuel lines 're all gunked up, Johnny. That cheap diesel you buy did 'em in. But she's runnin' clean now, brother." It was dark when he was done, and John elected to leave the boat where she was. TJ cooked up the last of the fish. After dinner the three men hunkered down at the cabin table with what RL claimed was the end of his Jack Daniels supply. True to his word, even though they had not been able to make Key Largo that day, John let his son have two shot glasses of the whiskey with the men. The raw liquor tasted hot going down his throat and Hilton gagged on the first sip. The smile on the faces of his father, and Uncle RL, along with TJ's loud whoop of, "Watch out tiger. Don't let it burn ya," led him to stay with it. Hilton liked the warm glow that came over him. He liked how after the second glass everything inside the cabin seemed soft and right. Drifting off in his bunk that night he hoped his father would let him drink with the boys again soon.

The vicious pounding of the boat against the dock woke him in the early hours of the morning, the banging thud of the wooden hull into the wooden pier vibrating through the cabin. The others were already awake, on the move getting the Mari-Lyn free of the dock. When he sat up in his bunk and saw what was going on without him, for a moment he felt the left-out sensation that had bothered him earlier. But he stumbled from the bunk, pulling on the pants he'd tossed on the floor, and staggered out on the deck, where RL was hauling in the lines TJ flung to him from the dock. In the next instant TJ leapt aboard and grabbed Hilton up in a bear hug. "Well now, little nephew, it's gonna be a Labor Day holiday you'll never forget." Just as suddenly, TJ let him go, scrambling up to the bow where he snatched up the loose line laying on the deck and began coiling it up, leaving Hilton alone in the stern. He felt dazed, left reeling and confused from the nervous energy he'd felt flowing from TJ's body into his.

It had all gone different on him, sometime in the night while he slept, or early that morning. It didn't matter. The relative calm of the bay they had steamed into yesterday afternoon was no more. The wind pounded out of the northeast and standing on the stern deck Hilton realized for the first time it was raining. The rain and driving wind from the north had churned the shallow waters of the gulf into what looked to Hilton to be a solid mass of unrelenting white-capped swells. It was these swells, along with the wind, that were pounding the Mari-Lyn into the dock. To escape this vicious beating, Hilton's uncles had cast off the lines so that his father at the helm could take the boat around the island to sea.

But as the boat rounded the point it became obvious that no safe harbor would be found on the sea side of Long Key. All above the ocean the sky was dark with bands of squalls. A heavy swell of gray foaming water ran before the squalls, crashing relentlessly upon the exposed beach of the key. In the distance Hilton saw a solid black wall pouring down on the ocean. Across the southern horizon lightning crackled, and above the sound of the swells hitting the beach came the dull booming of distant thunder. There was no sanctuary anywhere. Standing next to his father at the helm Hilton heard John let out a breath as he turned the bow of the boat away from the crashing swells.

"That dock's looking better and better all the time, John."

RL was on the other side of his brother, both with mugs of hot coffee TJ had somehow found the time in all the commotion to brew.

"None of it looks good," John said, as the long dock came into view. "But I suppose the dock will be the lesser evil." John turned to his younger brother. Hilton saw how his father's eyes had hardened into gray slits, even in the dim light of the cabin. "Get extra lines ready, TJ. We're going to need all the help we can get. Let's just pray it'll be enough."

"You've got it, Johnny. I'm prayin' as you speak."

They tied the boat up again to the wooden pier. Hilton helped TJ with the extra lines, tying the heavy rope around the wooden pilings above the regular bow and stern lines. Hilton could see the value of the extra lines. When heavier gusts came blowing across the bay, the Mari-Lyn, reeling away from the dock in these winds, stretched the four ropes taut. The lines vibrated in the wind and rain, the wooden pilings groaning with the strain placed upon them.

"It's gonna be something," all right, Hilly." They were done, standing on the dock in their slickers, huddled against the rain. "Sad to say though, pretty won't be the word for it." Seeing the look in Hilton's eyes, draping a lanky arm over the boy's shoulders, TJ drew his nephew close to his side. "Now damn, Hilly, don' you worry none. We're gonna be jus' fine. I never been, but I bet your dad's been in worse fixes than this. And hell, look at him." TJ pointed to John's head and shoulders visible through the starboard window, standing square and stern at the helm. "He knows what to do. Your dad'll take good care of us. He always has."

The boy and his uncle stepped back on the boat. As his feet hit the rolling deck Hilton thought about what TJ said about his father and about how he hoped it held true, at least one more time.

***

The storm came on all that day, the wind and driving rains intensifying. The only thing they could do aboard the Mari-Lyn now was sit and wait. TJ kept coffee on in the galley and the men played cards at the cabin table, talking softly about the game. Here and there they told stories of other days, laughing about the antics of one or the other of them, in the times before Hilton was born. The boat rocked endlessly in the wind coming from the northeast. Making the rocking motion even worse was the tide coming in, pushing on the hull from the other direction. By early afternoon it was so dark inside the cabin that TJ lit an oil lamp and hung it on the hook above the table. Most of the time Hilton lay on his bunk with a book of sea stories, watching as the lantern light played back and forth across the faces of his uncles and father at their cards and talk.

As the storm built and washed over them that Labor Day afternoon, there were times Hilton thought about how nice it would be to sit in a calm and quiet classroom. He longed for the low murmur of his friends' talk in his ears and everything normal instead of the howling wind and rain. Periodically, he got up from the bunk and stretched, sometimes crossing the rolling cabin to stare out the starboard window. A wall of rain poured down on the bay, sheeting out on the wind driving into it. The tall palms on the shore swayed backwards in the heavy wind gusts; sometimes so far back it seemed that the tops of them would soon be scraping the ground. Clumps of the wiry brush he and his father had trudged through the day before had been ripped from the sand and blew like tumbleweeds down the beach. Up on the higher ground he saw Australian pine trees down, branches bare, the green needles stripped from the limbs, roots still clutching the earth they had grown down into.

By nightfall the island was devoid of trees and underwater, as best Hilton could make out in what little light remained. The dock the Mari-Lyn clung to was covered by the foaming bay as well with just the pilings still showing. The men had abandoned their cards and talk of the old days. Now the boy joined them at the table, all of them silent as the boat pitched and rolled in the maelstrom. Talk was useless anyway, impossible to hear above the storm. Shouting was the only means of communication. Though it hadn't been said, Hilton was beginning to believe the men were saving their breath, their energy, for something else.

They didn't have to wait long. From somewhere on the other side of the island came a roaring that sounded like locomotives heading their way. Suddenly, the strongest winds they had felt yet were on them. In the next instant the stern of the boat lurched, then swung away from the dock. As if one, the men and boy jumped to their feet, struggling to keep their balance as the boat rolled, the lantern swinging wildly, lighting up their startled faces.

"The stern lines're givin' way, Johnny," TJ yelled above the roar. From outside came the distinct snap of something stretched to its limits. TJ snatched up his slicker and was out the door. In another instant Hilton and the others had done the same.

Everything speeded up after that. And yet somehow, Hilton thought, it remained the same. No one barked out any orders when they scrambled out on deck and saw the stern of the Mari-Lyn connected to the dock by only one wet strand of stretched-out line. They simply acted, moving in the wind and rain beating down on them like so many relentless jackhammers. TJ grabbed what was left of the surviving stern line and hauled the back of the boat slowly to the dock. As soon as he could, RL leaned out and wrapped his burly arms around the top of the nearest piling, hugging it to his body in a tight embrace. Then TJ was next to him and doing the same. John laid his hand on Hilton's shoulder. When the boy turned to look his father pointed to the bow. In another moment the boy and his father had the piling by the bow in a similar embrace.

There was no question of time. It didn't exist. Everything was the storm and the rough wood of the piling chafing his slicker-covered arms. In the dark, and rain, Hilton could barely see his father's face. But Hilton knew he was there. Above the storm he heard John's soothing voice. "You're doing real good, Hilly. Just hang on tight and we'll get through this together. You're doing good, Son." It was hard in all the turmoil, but Hilton willed himself to believe what his father was saying.

Suddenly TJ's voice rang out from the stern. "Get down RL. Get down!" In the rip of jagged lightning searing across the sky, Hilton looked toward the rear of the boat just in time to see something fly out from the island, something gray and heavy. In the same instant the flying object slammed off the side of RL's head, Hilton realized it was one of the tombstones he had seen the day before.

RL toppled over the stern into the foaming bay. In the next frozen moment, before the jagged light disappeared, Hilton saw TJ go over the side after his brother.

***

It was close to midnight when they reached Elliot Key and Mr. Henry's dock. At least, Hilton guessed that was the hour. It seemed that a very long time had passed since he first laid eyes on that dock. A lot had happened. So much so, that it didn't feel out of place at all to pull up there quietly in the dead of night, tie the Mari-Lyn off without permission, then stumble to the darkened house, lit only by the faint rays of the waning moon shining down. It didn't seem odd at all to be following behind his father and TJ up the path from Mr. Henry's dock. Then TJ was banging loudly on Mr. Henry's front door, loud and steady, until finally they heard the sound of someone on the inside grumbling and fiddling with the latch. In the sudden light of the opened door Hilton saw how weary his father looked, how pale and lifeless his uncle looked, unconscious, and held up by his two brothers.

"You're not welcome here, Raines. None of you are."

Mr. Henry looked so gentle and grandfatherly, the boy thought, standing in the open doorway in a nightshirt, a lantern held up in one hand, his thinning gray hair mussed up from sleep and a pair of wire-rim spectacles perched precariously on his nose. How could this grandfatherly looking man hate so?

"I know we're not welcome, Henry."

John voice stopped the older man from slamming the door. For a moment Hilton wondered at the sight his family must make in the sliver of light from Mr. Henry's lantern: their clothes ripped and disheveled, the unconscious and bleeding RL.

"It's my brother. He was hurt badly in the storm. We need a place for him to rest. Just for a bit. Until he's able to travel on."

"I was hoping that hurricane had blown you and yours to hell."

"I imagine you were." RL stirred in his brother's arms, moaning once before his head hung slack again. "I'm not asking for me, Henry. You know I never would. But Robert here didn't do anything against you. Except be my blood."

The old man wavered in the light. After what seemed a long time he stepped back from the door, motioning for them to come in. After what seemed even a longer time, Hilton stood in a dry house on dry land.

All the rest of that night Hilton sat in the living room of Mr. Henry's house while his father and TJ stayed with their brother. Mr. Henry let them put RL in his bedroom. Through the open door, Hilton could hear the low murmur of the two men talking. Occasionally, a loud groan came through the doorway, followed by John's voice. "It's okay Robert. You'll feel better in the morning. You'll see." In the circle of light cast out from the lantern by the bed, Hilton saw his father leaning over RL, patting the injured man's forehead with one hand while the other held a wet cloth to the massive wound above RL's temple. TJ was in a chair he'd pulled up to the bed, his own hands clasped nervously in his lap, a look like Hilton had never seen on his face.

Sitting in the dim light of Mr. Henry's living room, Hilton remembered the apparition of TJ coming back over the side of the boat out of the water, dragging an unconscious RL with him. The boy thought of the panic on TJ's face as he laid his brother on the rolling deck. How awful TJ looked when he opened his mouth, screaming. "RL's dyin', Johnny. He's fuckin' dyin'."

His father tried to put an end to his younger brother's hysterics, telling TJ to shut up, that RL wasn't going to die. But TJ only crumpled to the deck, moaning, "He is, Johnny, he is. Just look at his head. It's gone. Just look at his head." Over and over TJ moaned, "Just look at his head. Just look." Another jagged slash of lightning cracked open the dark. In the ripped light, Hilton saw his uncle laying on the deck, RL's head was caved in on one side. It was just a mass of bloody, sponge-like substance. The only thing to show his uncle was even still alive were the groans coming from his bleeding mouth, the spastic clutching of his hands against his stomach. Suddenly, RL tried to sit up and TJ started screaming again.

In the next instant, John's voice rang out. "That's enough, goddamnit. TJ, shut up and come grab hold of a piling. Be of some goddamned use here and let me take RL below."

TJ did as he was told. John took his injured brother into the cabin while Hilton at the bow and TJ in the stern held the boat to the dock, and the hurricane did its best to rip them away.

In the quiet safety of Mr. Henry's house, Hilton marveled that any of them were alive. He didn't know how long they held onto the pilings, didn't know how he managed to ignore the burning ache in his muscles. He just held on. Like his father told him to. Until suddenly, the wind was gone, the rain let off. An unearthly silence descended over them then. When Hilton looked up at the sky he could see stars shining, could see the full moon.

But this calm didn't last. It was only the eye of the storm passing over. A half-hour later the back side of the hurricane slammed into them and Hilton and TJ were again to the pilings. There was no more rest for their weary arms, just more of that same desperate holding on for dear life. Hilton heard TJ shout out something he couldn't hear over the wind. But he saw where his uncle pointed. Out over the bay. Where, after lightning ripped open the sky once more, Hilton saw the wall of water the driving winds had pushed up into a giant wave coming down on the Mari-Lyn.

"Jesus," TJ yelled. Then the wall was on them, lifting the boat up and away, no matter how hard Hilton tried to hold on, letting go finally, and without even thinking, simply knowing that it was useless, simply knowing instinctively he needed to save himself. And he did, clutching hold of the starboard rail as the Mari-Lyn was lifted by the wave and carried toward the island.

Hilton sat in Mr. Henry's living room remembering it. After the storm it all felt so strange: the soft dark of the room, the comfortable armchair he sat in. He noticed the photographs hung so neatly in their frames. One was a picture of a young couple, a man and woman, obviously taken long ago. The man in a stiff waistcoat, dark and sober, a black top hat held in one hand. The woman in white lace and muslin, virginal and clean next to the man, her hair a cascade of brown curls down her shoulders. It was a photograph of Mr. Henry's parents, Hilton guessed, much like pictures of his mother's folks that hung on the wall in the dining room at home. Which was real? he asked himself. This quiet room? Or the howl of the winds, the constant rain, the sound of everything being destroyed as he held on helpless to the starboard rail of his father's boat?

What happened after the wave lifted them up was a blur in the boy's mind. He knew the Mari-Lyn had come to rest in the shoals on the seaward side of Long Key. The boat rocked and bobbed there for hours until the dawn broke and the storm receded. With the storm eased up and the light of day, Hilton let go of his grip on the rail and made his way back inside the cabin. TJ was huddled on his bunk, his face pale and shrunk into itself. The door to the front berth was open. Hilton saw his Uncle RL laid out there, John hovering over him. The way his father held onto his brother's hand while he washed the blood and gore from RL's face reminded Hilton of old pictures he'd seen in his school books, of nurses and soldiers in past wars caring for their fallen comrades. It *had* been a war of sorts, Hilton thought, they had come through. And they were still together. Because of that, it would probably all be okay again, though he didn't yet see how.

***

As Hilton remembered it, TJ finally came out of his trance. Standing up from the bunk, he motioned for Hilton to come with him. Out on the deck in the new morning they saw the storm moving away. It was like watching the back of a huge, slowly moving dark beast, spewing wind and rain as it headed to the northwest. Left behind were bands of smaller squalls that blew across Long Key onto the nose of the Mari-Lyn, threatening to push the battered boat further out to sea. Hilton helped TJ set the bow anchor, then the one at the stern as well. The boat's two hooks held. The fury of the hurricane had gone to the north now, and they rode at anchor in front of Long Key all the rest of that day and night. The following morning broke clear and bright, the sun's warmth falling on a calm sea. It was like nothing had ever been different. Not long after daybreak John finally left his brother's side, but only long enough to tell Hilton and TJ to pull anchor. Not long after that, the diesel engine chugging steadily as the prow of the boat cut the surface of the sea, John steered the Mari-Lyn around the shoals off Long Key and then turned her bow north, toward home.

Everything was changed, washed clean and away by the storm. John kept the boat close to the shore, except where shoals stopped him. The boy was stunned by what he saw. Most of the trees were gone. All that remained were bare shell and sand beaches. Strangely enough, most of the telephone poles still stood, here and there rising up cockeyed and wobbly on the land, looking like drunken men trying to walk.

Something else was missing. After a bit the boy realized what it was: Mr. Flagler's railroad. It took perhaps an hour for Hilton to figure it out. The once proud trestles spanning the water between the keys were gone. Not only the railway bridges were gone, in some cases it appeared entire keys were, as well. Then the boat came up on Islamorada. On shore they saw a train swept clean of the twisted rails and scattered like a child's toy across the broken land. Only the locomotive still stood on a stretch of intact rails, proud and defiant, its stack rising to the sky and despairing of the mangled cars attached to its spine.

There were people walking along the rail bed by the cars, the first people other than themselves the crew of the Mari-Lyn had seen in days. They were mostly men, though some of these men were with women and children. Hilton watched as one man pointed out something to his woman. Hilton looked where the man pointed up and saw a crumpled body strung across the top of a telephone pole. Then the boat rounded a point and the wreckage was gone. Yet a part of it remained with them, as Hilton discovered when he stepped out on deck and happened to look over the port side. In the water, dark and bloated bodies bobbed up and down in the wake, pushed out to the side by the moving boat.

Suddenly, Hilton wanted to throw up, and he wanted to cry. He wanted to be anywhere but where he was, most preferably at home.

Sometime in the early afternoon, while Hilton and his father stood watch at the helm, RL called out softly from the forward berth. "John? Are you out there, John?" His voice was faint and raspy, not the voice of any man Hilton knew. "I need you, John."

"Here, Hilly. Take her." John Raines stepped back from the chrome wheel, gently nudging Hilton forward. "Don't worry about the charts for now. Just keep her on a straight line and look out for floating debris and shoals. You know what to look for. You'll be fine." His father's voice brokered no argument. Hilton did what he was told as John ducked through the hatch into the room where his brother lay.

Hilton could hear the softness of his father's voice when he told RL, "I'm right here, Robert." They were always so formal with one another, the boy thought, and yet so easy with the others around them. Then for a while it was quiet again. Alone at the wheel, Hilton concentrated on the task at hand and the water ahead.

"John." It sounded suddenly to Hilton like the RL of old, the faint rasp gone from his uncle's voice. "I need you to do something for me."

"Name it."

"Find me a dry bed on solid land. I don't want to die on this boat."

"You're not dying, RL."

There was a long silence.

"Well. I hate to be the one to prove you wrong on this, John." Now Hilton could hear how the weakness was back, how it was an effort again for RL to talk. "I just don't see how it can turn out any other way."

"I might know a place." His father's voice sounded weak as well.

"Then take me there. Please."

After another long silence Hilton heard his father's voice rising from the berth, this time strong, just like it always was.

"I will."

***

The room grew lighter as the day came on. From outside came the shrill cries of sea birds over the cut. Hilton pictured how those birds looked wheeling through the morning sky in search of their first meal. The boy was tired, bone weary from the long haul of the day before, the even longer period without sleep. But his tiredness was past any need for sleep. Not knowing anything he could do but feeling like he had to do something, he stood up from the wicker chair he'd been in the last few hours and stretched. His aching muscles resisted at first. Then he felt the blood flowing again into his legs. His body loosened as he walked back and forth across the hardwood floor, debating whether he should go in and see his uncle. He hoped someone would come out before he had to. Come and tell him it was all okay. Or all over. He didn't think there would be an in-between. It would be one or the other. Remembering what RL's head had looked like when TJ dragged him out of the water and over the stern, Hilton felt certain he wouldn't be hearing that everything was okay.

He had made up his mind to go on in, was at the door even, when something on a small table halfway down the hall caught his eye. Whatever it was it shone a little in the faint light of the hall. Hilton saw that it was a photograph encased in a brass frame. Before he knew it, he had gone down the hall and picked the frame up from the table, holding it in both hands as he stared and stared. The person in the photograph was a woman. Not only that, the woman was his mother.

"She was a beauty, all right." Absorbed by what he held, Hilton hadn't heard TJ come up beside him. "Not that she isn't now." The youngest of the Raines brothers sounded more like his old self now. When Hilton turned to his uncle he saw that yes, though the man's face was drawn and haggard, a trace of a grin cracked his lips.

"I tell you, boy," TJ continued, "your dad was hooked the second he laid eyes on her. Yes sir, he was gone, by God. Not that I was there to witness firsthand, mind you. But that's what your dad always told me, and RL, and anyone else he could get to listen."

Hilton never thought of his mother as a "beauty." She was simply his mother. But staring at the fading photograph of the young woman he saw that she had been. Tall, she had clean, swept-back features like mine, he thought. He had always felt he was the spitting image of his father. Her long hair was put up in the fashion of that day, covered by a wide-brimmed hat, her eyes dark and staring out from the glass as she stood on a boardwalk. In Tampa, Hilton supposed, and only because he knew that was where his mother and father met. She was wearing a high-waisted dress and a puffy, long-sleeved white shirt with gathers at the breast, her face smiling as she looked at the camera. But the photograph didn't do her right; it didn't capture the rich colors of hair and skin and teeth that made up the woman he knew as his mother. Not that any of that was important. Not when things were all jumbled up in his mind like they were then.

"You gotta tell me, TJ."

"What?" TJ looked at his nephew. "About your momma, and dad, and Mr. Henry?"

"Yes."

"Yeah." TJ turned away from Hilton for a moment, back toward the open doorway where his two brothers were. "Well, Hilly, like I told you before, it ain't my place to tell. 'Specially at a time like this." He draped an arm around Hilton's shoulders and steered him toward the front door. "Let's go down an' sit on the dock. Say a prayer or two for RL. God won't listen to me, but he might to you."

***

But before any prayers could be said, and just as Hilton and TJ were going to sit down on the end of Mr. Henry's dock, Hilton heard the sound of someone stepping onto the wooden pier behind them. He and TJ turned at the sound to his father coming toward them. Behind him, standing in his doorway, Mr. Henry watched John go to his family.

There was a look on his father's face. Hilton knew, without knowing, what was about to be said.

"He's gone."

It was really that simple? How could that be? Hilton thought as he stared at his father, at the grim smile on his face when John Raines said nothing more. Hilton let his eyes wander out over the cut. A flock of gulls were wheeling and screaming above two porpoises herding a school of silver mullet up against the bank. Suddenly, the water exploded around the gray backs of the big fish as they inhaled the panicked baitfish, the gulls screaming louder and diving down frantically to snatch up the bits and pieces of the dead and dying mullet left in the dolphin's wake.

The eldest of the still-living Raines looked at his watch. "He died at ten-twenty-five, to be exact. He went easily, though. Thank God."

"Damn it, Johnny, it just don't seem right." TJ stared silently for a moment up the dock at Mr. Henry blocking the doorway to the house where his brother lay dead. "Goddamn if it does."

"Your brother lived a good, full life. That's the main thing."

"Maybe. Still seems too goddamn short. If you ask me."

Hilton watched as his father suddenly wrapped his younger brother up in his arms, the two men swaying back and forth silently on the wooden pier for what seemed a long time.

When John let go of his brother, he hooked his thumb back in the direction of the house and Mr. Henry standing in the door.

"I imagine that man there wishes it was me lying dead in his bedroom."

"She-et, Johnny." TJ burst out laughing, his face broken open in that wild smile—a smile that to Hilton seemed so very wrong for the moment. "You're gonna outlive us all."

"I surely hope not." John started back up the dock. "Let's get Robert and go home."

***

In the years after, Hilton often found himself thinking about the fishing trip to the Keys he took with his father and two uncles right before Labor Day of 1935. He remembered all the good and all of the bad. The hurricane, and how his Uncle RL came to die in a stranger's house. Except the stranger really wasn't one, except to Hilton. He sometimes thought, too, of how life appeared to be a long line of connected events he didn't know anything about.

But that came later. For now, Hilton stood out on the bow of the Mari-Lyn as his father eased her away from the dock and out to sea. The boy wished he were home. Not so much longer after that, he was.

Part Two: Manila

As dawn was breaking over Lingayen Gulf at 0700 hours on a day in early January of 1945, the invasion began. Hilton massed with the rest of his artillery unit below decks of the LST, couldn't see the start of the action, but he could certainly hear it. The roar of the big naval guns firing from the seventy warships spread out across the bay reverberated violently through the hull of the ship and the ears of the men waiting to go ashore. The sound of the bombardment was like nothing Hilton had ever heard before. At least not at the artillery range in Brisbane where he joined the division and his new crew and first became familiar with the 105 mm howitzer. Not on Mindoro, where the action, except for one brief skirmish, was mostly over when his battery arrived. The firing of the naval guns was louder even than the loudest noises he had heard during the hurricane of 1935 when the storm had come howling in at night and killed Uncle RL.

The order to stand down came through the ranks at 0745 hours. Though the men waiting to go ashore were at ease, the barrage continued, leaving Hilton wondering what could possibly be left for the guns to destroy. Shortly after the stand down, Hilton saw Sergeant Jesup elbowing his way through the ranks of men.

"C'mon, Corporal," the sergeant said when he came up on Hilton. "Let's go topside and see the show."

"What about our stations? Our orders were to stay here at the ready."

"Not to worry, my boy. Scuttlebutt has it we'll be among the last to go today. The infantry has to get ashore first. Might not be until tomorrow for our turn. In the meantime, I'd like to see what we're missing out on."

The sergeant ran a sweaty hand across his flushed red face. It was warm and airless below decks of the landing craft. The men of Hilton's division had been issued the new herringbone twill uniforms designed specifically for use in the Pacific Theater.

At first Hilton had been glad to get his. But after wearing it for the last two weeks aboard the LST he had come to miss the lightweight khaki they wore before. The herringbone stuck to his thighs and arms when it was damp and aboard the ship it was damp most of the time. Sergeant Jesup didn't look any too comfortable in his uniform, either, though Hilton imagined he was probably uncomfortable in just about anything he wore.

Jesup had huge biceps and muscular thighs that stretched everything he put on. A couple of inches shorter than Hilton, Jesup had a physique that would've been almost grotesque on another man. Somehow, he managed to carry it well. Hilton had been witness to what happened to men who made that mistake. One night a sergeant from another company, meeting Jesup at the NCO club in Brisbane, had called out, "Good God man, are you some kind of giant dwarf or something?" After a long hard silence in the crowded club Jesup had proceeded to pound the daylights out of him. He had earned a night in the stockade for his efforts but told the men later he would gladly pay that price again for the opportunity to, "Stomp the shit out of that loud-mouthed asshole." Admittedly, both men were very drunk at the time.

"Well," Hilton said now, "If you think it's all right. Then sure. Let's go."

"It's okay, kid," Sergeant Jesup said, patting Hilton's shoulder with the big hand. "Like I said, not to worry. Now, c'mon."

"Right behind you, Sarge."

"That's the spirit, Corporal."

It was natural to follow the sergeant's lead as Hilton discovered on Mindoro. His unit had been assigned to cover an infantry action against a small detachment of Japanese trying to overrun an airfield the US had commandeered shortly after the initial invasion. Though the men had been trained for just this sort of situation, there was a moment of confusion when the battery arrived at the airfield.

"Shake it out, you damned galoots," Sergeant Jesup had yelled. He jumped out of the rear of the big GMC truck that pulled the howitzer, the ammo, and carried the men of the unit. "Corporal Raines. Back this fucking gun into position. ASAP."

Hilton, at the wheel of the deuce-and-a-half, as the big trucks were called, snapped out of his hesitation and did as the sergeant ordered. By the time the gun was in place to Jesup's satisfaction and Hilton was out of the truck in a line passing shells to the gunners, Jap mortars were exploding on the airfield, blowing holes in the tarmac and the P-38s lined up there in formation. The three platoons of GI's guarding the airfield against just such a maneuver had spread out across the field, returning the enemy fire as best they could from the protection of the parked planes. The Quonset huts and the crude barricades made out of packing crates the men had erected as part of their defensive perimeter also served as protection.

"Goddamnit, boys," Jesup called out when the howitzers of the battery were ready. "Pour it into 'em."

In the next instant the roars of the 105 mms drowned out the small arms fire of the combatants on the airfield and hidden in the jungle, drowned out as well the steady *crump, crump, crump,* of the Japanese mortars.

"Keep it coming, boys," the sergeant yelled out. Hilton looked up as he was handing one of the explosive shells to the gunner and saw the sergeant standing right next to their howitzer, one hand waving his helmet in the air, the other hand gesticulating wildly at the enemy's position. "Get those little bastards!"

The fight lasted less than an hour, but it was fast and bloody. The sergeant was always in the thick of it, keeping his crew and the guns firing at a steady pace. Under his direction the howitzers unleashed a barrage of shells over the heads of their own troops into the enemy.

"Another day, another dollar," was all the sergeant had to say as he helped his men hook up the howitzers to the trucks and head back to the base. "Anyone besides me ready for a beer?"

The afternoon had ended with the edge of the airfield strewn with the remnants of a final, desperate *banzai* charge by the Japs and wounded GI's straggling back to the rear. But the ease of Jesup's tone was more than enough to dispel the ugly images of the battle from Hilton's mind. *It was war after all*, Hilton thought. *Men were going to get hurt. Were going to die.*

In the excitement of his first taste of combat, Hilton hadn't had time to be afraid. That only came when it was over. When he was driving the men and the gun back to base and he noticed how his hands trembled as they held onto the black steering wheel.

"We done good today, Corporal," Sergeant Jesup said. He was sitting up front in the cab of the truck with Hilton. Hilton wondered, *Does he know? How does he know?* As if in reply Jesup only repeated, "Done real good."

Hilton told himself he had been in good hands that day. Told himself that no matter what, he would do as the sergeant ordered, no questions asked.

Sergeant Jesup led him away from the bow staging area, down a narrow passageway toward amidships. The passageway was lit badly by small yellow bulbs spaced every twenty feet. Though it wasn't crowded with men like the forward area had been, still, it was hot and confining. Between the long, boring seasick voyage that began a year ago in California and now the claustrophobic waiting aboard the LST to go ashore, Hilton was thankful again he hadn't joined the Navy. The Army wasn't all bad, he supposed. The food was pretty good, and he had won a sizeable amount playing poker at night. It was true he had always enjoyed being on the open water back home. But to make a career of it? No, that wasn't for him.

"Sarge?" Hilton asked as they reached one of the three circular stairways leading topside.

"What is it, Corporal?"

In the dim yellow light Hilton could see the amused grin that seemed perpetually frozen on Jesup's face—even in the thick of the firefight on Mindoro.

"You think we'll see action today?"

"If we go ashore today, as opposed to tomorrow, why then I imagine we will. Depends on the timing, I suppose. On how boys do on the beach. On how strongly the Japs defend their little piece of paradise. On how well our boys make the Japs regret their decision to even be there in the first place." He pointed up the stairs where the roar of the big guns, funneled as it was down the narrow stairway, seemed even louder than it had been below. "Depends, too, on how well those cannons do *their* job."

"You think we'll be okay?" Hilton regretted the question as soon as he asked it. But it was too late. His words seemed to hang for a long time in the yellow light of the gangway. "You know? When we *do* get ashore."

"Hell yeah, we'll do okay."

Jesup snorted, like he was prone to when something took him by surprise, so perhaps this little habit, along with the grin, were two of the things that always made Hilton comfortable in the sergeant's presence.

"Why, Corporal? You scared?"

"Yes," Hilton answered. "I am."

"Good. Me, too. Maybe a little case of the fears will keep you and me alive. Get us through the coming mess."

Fear—the word that none of the men liked to talk about. Though judging from the expressions on their faces as they waited clumped together below decks, Hilton was not the only man feeling it. The way none of them wanted to meet the others' eyes was proof enough of that. But having the sergeant admit to it as well, and say that feeling it was to the good, helped Hilton to believe that when it was his turn on the beach he'd do what was required of him.

Then they were topside, out in the light of the morning and the warm, humid salt air where everything had exploded into the sights and sounds of the invasion. The sky was overcast, the bay calm and serene as it rolled up in gentle swells upon the beach a mile distant. The same sort of easy swells slapped softly against the hull of the ship on the side away from the roaring guns. The beach shone white in the early tropical light, wide and sandy and rising up toward a jungle of coconut trees, vine-laden palms, and leafy, green jungle shrubs.

Suddenly, five Japanese Zeros burst through the layer of clouds, flying in tight formation low across water toward the LST. Just before it was either crash into the ship or bank high into the sky, the Zeros all let loose at the same time with their .50 caliber machine guns. In the same instant the sailors and GI's lining the port rails dove for the deck. All except one, who lurched forward in the hail of gunfire clutching his stomach and toppled slowly over the rail into the water. All this happened in only a blink of the eye. The Japanese planes had come, and one man was dead, along with several others wounded that Hilton could see and hear. The Zeros banked high, disappearing just as suddenly as they had come.

But not for very long—they came again, firing as they flew in over the water. Hilton was back on his feet, watching as other Jap planes off in the distance attacked the American ships, his attention suddenly diverted by the cracking of the ship's anti-aircraft guns finally opening up on the enemy planes. Red tracer shells arced into the sky while the steady *ack-ack-ack* of the anti-aircraft guns kept up a staccato firing. The sound was punctuated by black puffs of smoke when the tracers fizzled out, like fireworks back home on the Fourth of July, most of the fire missing the target because of how the Jap pilots banked and swerved to avoid it. One Jap was not so lucky, or perhaps not so skilled. As Hilton, the sergeant, and the others looked on, the Jap banked into the light and came back for another deadly strafing run. But before he could do any damage the ship's guns caught up to him. One of the Zero's wings exploded, then the other, and the plane was a bursting fireball. As it hit the water and slowly sank, the troops cheered. Hilton heard Jesup yell, "Ah, fuck yeah. Fuck yeah."

Turning to the sergeant Hilton joined him and said, "Fuck yes."

The Jap planes continued the attack, strafing the troop ships and dropping bombs, some of which hit home. A destroyer not far from Hilton's ship received a direct hit below the forecastle that sent flames, heavy black smoke, and pieces of metal flying into the sky. His mind flashed back to Sandy Nininger who had been two years ahead of him at school. Sandy had been the first American hero of the war, decorated posthumously for his actions saving his wounded fellow soldiers during the Japanese invasion of the Philippines. His death and military honors had been front page news back home. Receiving the clippings in the mail while he was at school in Columbia, Hilton had been deeply affected by the news. He had wanted to quit school then and there and enlist. It was only his parents' pleas to finish his four years first that had made him change his mind.

Now he was part of the American attempt to reclaim the islands where Sandy had died — not only reclaim physical territory, but perhaps avenge the deaths of Sandy and all those others who had died in the early days of the war. Four years had passed since Sandy's death and here Hilton was, a former classmate, preparing to land on the same soil.

The remaining planes seemed to have backed off on their attack of the crippled ship. The destroyer was listing heavily in the bow and flames belched up from deep in its hold while a series of smaller explosions — from ammunition catching fire, Hilton supposed — rocked the ship. But as the Zeros banked away from the sinking vessel, another came streaking down out of the sky, the surviving anti-aircraft guns of the wounded ship all firing at once at the oncoming attacker. To help them bring the attacker down, some of the sailors had picked up Tommy guns and were firing in a frenzy. None of them hit the mark. The Zero should have leveled out, released his bombs, or at the least, opened up with his machine guns and cannon, but the plane continued.

"What the hell?" Sergeant Jesup said. His question was almost a whisper, barely heard above the resounding explosions of the naval guns still pounding the shoreline. "What the hell is that goddamn Jap doing?"

The answer came very quickly then as the Zero, at the last possible moment when it could have pulled up, banked away again into the safety above, then nosedived instead straight into the command tower of the crippled destroyer where it exploded into the biggest fireball yet. The concussion rocked the ship and the men aboard her as Hilton and the rest of them stared on in disbelief at what they had just witnessed. As the LST began to sink, men frantically got the lifeboats over the sides, ship horns blared out in alarm, and all was pandemonium. Others, not willing to wait their turn for the lifeboats, dove over the side of the vessel into the waters of the bay.

Now that one of the American ships was down for the count, a formation of Zeros began to re-group for another deadly attack. Before they could do so, though, a squadron of P-38s burst out of the clouds high above the bay. A new battle was joined at high altitude, the acrobatics of both friend and enemy dazzling to watch. The aerial drama stirred the men aboard Hilton's ship into a frenzy of cheering and back slapping as they yelled out, "Go get 'em, boys. Get those yellow bastards."

"You see that, Corporal?" Jesup's punch in the side of his arm rocked Hilton back a step. But he didn't mind the sudden pain as he stared into the sergeant's excited face. "Goddamn, son, do you see that? That's Americans up there, man. Americans! Let's see how those fucking Japs like *them* apples."

And yes, Hilton *did* see. He saw very well how the bay roiled up with the firing of the naval guns and the explosions from the ship sinking. Behind the lifeboats the mother vessel was up-ended into the sky. It wouldn't stay there long and soon it would slip beneath the surface of the bay.

***

But the scuttlebutt Sergeant Jesup had heard and then repeated to Hilton was wrong. Their howitzer platoon did not go ashore that day, or the day after. On the morning following the first phase of the invasion a tropical downpour started soon after daybreak. The storm continued all that day and through the night, slowing the movement of men and war machines to a grinding near-halt. The only advantage of the heavy rain and squalls was the absence of Japanese resistance. It was as if the enemy had shot their wad the day before with the attacking Zeros and suicide dive-bombing of the destroyer.

Not that anyone thought the enemy was defeated. The lack of opposition to the landings was probably a trap of some sort. This idea rippled through the GIs and artillery men waiting to go ashore, creating a nervous tension Hilton thought even higher than the first day of the invasion. At least then, with the bombardment and then the Zeros, they had known they were in a battle. Now, the strange quiet of the beach, pounded by a drenching rain that made visibility near to impossible, just didn't seem right. Not to Hilton, at least. Nor to the men around him.

Two days later the rains came to a drizzling end and "The Guns of Dixie" went ashore. The men had chosen the name for their platoon because nine out of the twelve who manned the howitzers were from the South. The three northerners had put their heads together at an impromptu meeting called by Sergeant Jesup. After a few minutes of talk those three had come up with an alternative: "The Avenging Angels." Privates Mathers and Hackett were both attending divinity school. Private Timothy James, the other Yankee in the unit, went along with his fellow northerners, but with a disclaimer.

"Wasn't my ideas, boys," James, a skinny, kid from Lake George, New York, told the others. "Being out-numbered and outvoted," he continued while pointing at the two divinity students, "I just went along. Hell, I joined the army mainly so I could get away from home, drink some beer, and maybe get laid."

"Good lord, man," Sergeant Jesup spoke out. "You can't get laid in New York State?"

"No, sir."

"Well hell, man, I'm not sure joining the army, and pardon my expression you two," and Jesup bowed to the divinity students, "is going to be the answer to your prayers. Look around, son. You see any women here?"

"No, sir," James said. The goofy grin on his face, all spotted with freckles of varying sizes, made Hilton laugh. He wasn't the only one. "Perhaps I made a mistake?"

"I guess you did, boy. But don't despair none. There's hope yet. You stick with me, son, and come liberty I'll take you to a little place I know."

Hilton knew of the place Jesup referred to, a shack on the edge of Port Moresby run by a heavily rouged madam from Australia. Hilton had never been inside. His love for Gwen kept him from nighttime forays with Jesup and the others. True to his word, Jesup had taken James there when the opportunity arose. Though both men paid a price for their adventure, courtesy of the gonorrhea they came down with shortly after.

The vote being mainly a formality, The Guns of Dixie won out, with no hard feelings around. Once the vote had been taken and the result announced, Jesup exclaimed loudly enough for the whole base to hear, "Well goddamn, it's about time the South won something. Now, who's joining me for a beer down at the EMC?"

Everyone except the two divinity students took Jesup up on his offer. With Private James leading the way, they marched together down the graded main road of the base to the big barracks tent that served as the enlisted men's club. That night the new name of their platoon was toasted and drank to until "Taps" rang out over the base.

Now, just shy of a year later and in a place very different from Port Moresby, Australia, three of the men gathered that afternoon to name their artillery unit were gone. Two of them were dead: Mathers, one of the divinity school students, and James, who had joined up for the drinking and the "getting laid." Tropical illness had killed them on Mindoro before they even saw combat. The other man, Private Robert Hardin from Mississippi, was missing, presumed dead, after a drunken, midnight trip to the latrine from which he never returned.

For a long time, Hilton had wondered what really happened to Hardin. A tribe of native headhunters were rumored to live on

Mindoro. Either headhunters or the Japs had captured him. This became the common consensus of the rest of the Guns of Dixie, and that was that. But as he drove the truck pulling the howitzer down the wooden ramp leading out of the open bay of the LST, Hilton looked toward the jungle at the top of the beach. The green palms and banana trees waving in the drizzling rain, for some reason, reminded him once more of Hardin.

Up and down the beach that gray wet morning, Hilton saw the dull army green of uniformed men and painted vehicles stretching out for what seemed miles. Tanks, trucks, two-and-a-half-ton GMCs, like the one he was driving, other trucks carrying ammunition and food and all the accoutrements of the campaign to come piled out of open LSTs. At the crest of the beach where temporary bases had been established by the first to go ashore, lines of GI's walked a defensive perimeter.

All of them were on high alert, waiting for a repeat of the first day of the invasion. As it had been below decks of the LST, the tension was a palpable force, rippling through the air and echoing in the shouted orders of the officers overseeing the off-loading of men and equipment. Caught up in the tension, Hilton expected at any minute to hear the muted throbbing of Japanese Zeros breaking out of the cloud cover to bomb and strafe the army coming ashore. Following the planes' deadly fire, would come an immense wave of enemy soldiers in a banzai charge bursting out of the jungle. He not only expected that attack, but just as he and the sergeant had talked about on the LST when the invasion began, Hilton realized he feared it. How else could he explain the trembling of his hands?

But there was no attack. No dreaded overwhelming banzai charge, no screaming Zeros with their machine guns and bombs. Only the thud of the flat bows of the LSTs hitting shore where they opened their bays to disgorge men and machines on to the island.

"Goddamn, son, you daydreaming or what?"

The back wheels of the truck had buried themselves in the wet sand. No matter how much he raced the engine and shifted gears, Hilton couldn't get enough traction to move forward. They were stuck. Jesup had pushed his beefy red face into the window of the truck. When he received no answer, he asked again. "Did you hear me, Corporal? If you're daydreaming, it's high time you snapped out of it."

"Yes sir, I guess I must have been."

Hilton felt sheepish. His mind had wandered and now the truck was stuck in the sand because of it.

"Sir is it?" Jesup's red face looked puzzled for a moment, but only for a moment before he burst into that infectious laughter of his. "Since when, Corporal Raines, is a non-com like me a *sir*?"

Before Hilton could answer Jesup's question, another one came down from above.

"Why're we stopped, Sergeant?"

Private Hackett, the divinity student and brewer's son from Pennsylvania, was riding atop all the gear and ammunition piled into the back of the GMC. "The back wheels are just spinning deeper and deeper into the sand. Any Japs decide they want to come in about now and start shooting, we'll be sitting ducks," he yelled. After a minute, as if remembering where he had come from, Hackett added, "God help us."

"Well now, Private Hackett." Jesup jumped off the running board of the truck. "I hope God does decide to help us. In the meantime, give me a minute here with Corporal Raines. Maybe we'll come up with something to do while we're waiting on Him."

Though they were spoken in a light-hearted manner, the sergeant's words carried weight. Hilton knew better than to say anything more and judging by their silence, he guessed that Reeves and Hackett felt the same.

"Now then." Jesup was back on the running board, his face stuck again through the open window. "What're we going to do about this mess we're in, Corporal?"

Hilton was glad Jesup hadn't put the blame entirely on him.

"I guess the only thing we can do, Sarge, is dig out the back wheels, get Reeves and me and Hackett to put our backs to it, and while you drive we'll push her out."

"That's exactly right, Corp. That's what we're going to do. Except you stay here at the wheel. No offense, boy, but my back's probably better at pushing than yours."

There was no doubt of that, Hilton thought. Jesup had muscles like nobody's business. Muscles Hilton lacked. When some of the men were talking about their sergeant, Reeves said once, "Shit, that old boy's got fucking muscles on top of his muscles." Besides, it was hard to be offended at anything Jesup said with that grin of his spread all over his face.

"By the way, Corporal," Jesup said as he stepped off the truck's running board one more time. "That's a good plan you came up with. Even if it means I have to wield a shovel in this soggy-ass sand and get my nice clean uniform all muddy. Hell, son, you might make officer yet."

Hilton laughed, though he didn't agree with Jesup. He had no desire to be an officer. Getting home in one piece when the war was over would be enough for him.

After a long day of slogging guns and supplies up the beach, followed by a cold meal of K-rations for dinner, their reward was perhaps the most beautiful sunset Hilton had ever seen. The drizzling rain nagging at them all day had finally come to an end. For what seemed a very long time, the sun hung just above the water line turning the fading light of the day into a pale-yellow shining over the Pacific. Then, as the sun began to slip below the horizon, the pale light turned into a deep crimson, which in turn blended in with the dark of night falling over the beach and jungle where Hilton and the rest of the troops were eating their evening meal.

The damp and muddy foxhole was a cold reminder for Hilton, sunset or not, that he was still very much at war. The Japanese were famous for night attacks, so the orders were to sleep but be on alert. After an hour or so Hilton didn't see any problem with being alert. Sleep was another matter. He shared his muddy station with Reeves, who promptly nodded off, his muffled snoring was just loud and constant enough to be annoying. How anyone could sleep in those conditions was beyond Hilton. The mud walls of the hole seemed to grow wetter and colder as the night went on. Hilton was as cold as the muddy hole he sat in.

Hilton leaned back against the side of the foxhole and shut his eyes but sleep still didn't come. Not only Reeves's snoring, but the strange sounds of the nighttime jungle fifty yards away prevented it. Birds called out to one another from perches in trees visible only as giant black forms rising in the dark. The loud screeches and cawing might have been crows, but Hilton wasn't sure if crows lived here. He heard moving through the branches and underbrush of the jungle, chattering at one another as they went. Monkeys, Hilton figured, much as he had seen on Mindoro. Not Japs. No threat. Only monkeys and birds and nothing else.

He finally dozed off and he dreamed. Of Gwen. Of a night right before he left for basic training. They were in his father's new car, a big four-door Dodge sedan, at the beach. They were finally alone after a day of celebration and the engagement party Gwen's folks had thrown for them. Being alone he could hold her close, tell her how happy he was, how much he loved her, could reassure her that yes, God willing, he wouldn't die and when he came home they could start their lives together, have children, and put war and all its horror behind them.

He dreamt of sitting close together on the front seat of the Dodge, arms around one another, kissing, their breathing steaming up the window of the car. A strange sort of light seeped through the fogged-up windshield, bathing Gwen in a pale-yellow glow when she pulled away from him and asked, "When do the submarine races begin?" Then the top of Gwen's dress was unbuttoned, her breasts laid out before him all milky white and lit up by that yellow light, the smile on her face lit up too as he bent to kiss her hard nipples.

There came a loud cracking sound against the driver's window. The nighttime Home Watch, Hilton knew, knocking, knocking, and interrupting them just when—but it wasn't the Home Watch at all.

"It's the Goddamn Japs!"

Reeves was standing up in the foxhole, firing his M1 at something Hilton couldn't see, even though he was wide awake, his own rifle in hand and every part of his being wanting to know what the hell Reeves was shooting at.

"Goddamn Japs," Reeves yelled out again and then fired another round into the dark, the sharp cracking of the rifle so close to Hilton that he jerked back as if the recoil had been against his shoulder and not Reeves's. There was enough light for Hilton to see a wild grin on his fellow platoon member's face—for him to wonder if Reeves had cracked up from the strain. There was nothing to be seen out on the edge of the jungle. No enemy soldiers returning Reeves's fire.

But visible or not, other GIs down the line were shooting into the jungle as Reeves was. Just as he was shouldering his own rifle, Hilton heard a loud hiss rising into the night. A flare burst into a bright light, bathing everything below it in a strange incandescent white.

"What asshole shot off that goddamn flare?" Jesup's voice rang out loud and clear above the scattered shooting. And then there he was, in front of the line, one hand waving his .45. "I find out who it was I'm going to court martial his sorry ass!"

The firing stopped. In the last burst of the flare, the men of The Guns of Dixie saw a wild pig rooting around in the scraggly bushes just where beach met jungle proper.

"There's your goddamn Japs," Jesup said.

The pig stood frozen in place, apparently as surprised as they were by the sudden commotion. As the flare finally died out, Jesup turned and shot the pig dead.

"Battle's over, boys," he said. "Any of you yahoos know how to dress a pig? Maybe we could have barbecue tomorrow night instead of those sorry ass K-rations."

The sergeant strode off in the dark. There were no more dreams for Hilton that night, no more Japanese scares, just the beginning of another day.

***

Nine days after the invasion began orders to move out were issued. To where no one was sure. Orders were orders and Hilton's artillery division fell in behind the rest of the 37th Infantry to head into the jungle beyond the beach.

A rumor that Manila, held by the Japs since the early days of the war, was their target affirmed something Jesup had said two days before the troops moved out. Hilton and the sergeant were coming back from morning mess when a jeep roared past them on the sandy road cut to serve the needs of the temporary base. Bright American infantry stars were painted on the sides of the jeep and flags attached on both ends of the windshield waved in the breeze. An older man in officer's khaki sat on the passenger side, a corncob pipe in his mouth, a jaunty military cap perched forward on his head.

"There's Old Mac," Jesup said. His pale eyes were bright beneath the fatigue cap covering his mass of curly red hair. "General Douglas MacArthur to you, son. Or as some of us call him, 'Dugout Doug.'"

"Maybe he's here to tell brass what our next move is," Hilton said as he and Jesup watched the jeep come to a stop in front of the tent serving as HQ.

"Oh, I imagine you're right, soldier." Jesup snorted and shook his head. "I bet he's fixing to give Griswold and Krueger hell for keeping us on this godforsaken beach all this time. He'll light a match under their asses. You just watch."

Hilton hoped Jesup was right. Like the rest of the men, Hilton was ready for a move. Daytime at the base wasn't so bad now that the rains had stopped. Even though the air was humid the temperatures were bearable—certainly no worse than the summer days Hilton had known back home in Florida. It was the nights that were hard on them. The strain of waiting in their foxholes for the Japanese to attack was taking a toll. It was evident in the red eyes of the men, the way their shoulders seemed to slump as they went about their daily chores. Heavy combat most likely awaited them wherever they headed, Hilton was sure. But at least the waiting for it would be over.

"It's about time," Hilton said. The general and the aide driving the jeep had disappeared into the headquarters tent.

"Yeah? What's the matter, corporal?" Jesup swung a beefy arm around Hilton's shoulders as they resumed the walk back to their position. "You tired of crappy rations and sleeping in a muddy foxhole every night? Maybe figure it's about time you got hold of some of that fine champagne and pretty Filipino women those Japs been enjoying in Manila all this time? That about it?"

Again, Hilton was reminded of Uncle TJ. How everything in life for him was just a big joke, one to be enjoyed to its fullest, no matter the circumstance or cost. It was the same way with Jesup. Hilton wished he could share their temperament. But he was certain that he never would.

"Maybe," he said. "Maybe it's something like that."

"Hell yes, it's something like that, Corporal," and Jesup's booming laugh rang out over the beach, startling some men busy cleaning their rifles beneath a copse of palm trees. Even not knowing the joke, they looked up and laughed anyway.

After cutting through the jungle on the other side of the beach, Hilton was surprised when the army came upon a paved highway. It was only two lanes, poorly paved with potholes and chunks of asphalt, but it was a highway just the same. With the infantry in the front and the artillery units, tanks, and supply trucks bringing up the rear, the army headed down the road to the south. In the distance, rising at the edge of a vast plain, was a small mountain range. These mountains were about the size of those Hilton remembered from family vacations in the Blue Ridge, the tops of them covered in the same sort of haze that had given the Smokies their name. The plain they drove across was nothing like the valleys of North Carolina, though. Not with the stands of bamboo, banana trees, and coconut palms growing off the edge of the road. Cattle grazed here and there on the plain, eating the green wire grass carpeting the ground, watched over by bands of Filipino men and children who looked up and waved as the army went by.

At each of the scattered villages they entered it was the same. Made from plywood or bamboo, the simple huts were covered with thatched roofs that reminded Hilton of the Seminole Indian village on the edge of Fort Lauderdale where his father had taken him and his sister once to watch the alligator wrestlers. The Filipinos were happy to see them, waving and calling out to the army, "Victory, Joe. Victory." Hilton was struck by the beauty of the Filipinos. The women's faces were soft and brown, with big dark eyes staring out from equally dark hair that fell on their foreheads. When they looked up at the soldiers they seemed so innocent, yet seductive. Their smiles *were* inviting, and their bodies, covered in thin cotton skirts and colorful blouses, were something he had to turn away from.

The older women showed the hardships of their lives more plainly. As did the men, who came in from the fields where they tended crops or watched over small herds of cattle to greet the soldiers. Though smiling, those men seemed drawn and gaunt and ageless. If they were truly glad for the presence of the American army in their midst, it was hard to tell. It was the children who brought some relief to the soldiers, their laughter and delight over candy bars a break from the somber business of war.

"They probably acted the same way when the Japs came through," Jesup said as he handed out another Hershey bar to a little Filipino girl. "Probably said, 'Victory, Akimodo. Victory Hirohito.' Now can I please have some candy? Or whatever the hell they call the Japs."

Hilton didn't know what to say. Could only look at the sergeant as he, too, handed out another chocolate bar to a clutching brown hand.

"It's a hard world, Corporal, I'm sorry to say," Jesup continued. "And these are hard times for these people. You can't blame them for doing what they have to do."

It was difficult for Hilton to imagine these same people, in this peaceful and timeless village, gathered around the enemy troops and calling out for candy bars. But he supposed Jesup could be right. Hated to think it but supposed it could be so.

The day grew increasingly warm. Even behind the wheel of the GMC Hilton was sweating. Air coming through the open window offered no reprieve. He felt bad for the troops on foot marching up in front. Stopping every two hours for a tepid drink of water from their canteens and a "smoke if you got 'em" break seemed hardly enough to revive anyone from the grueling march. It certainly made Hilton grateful, though, that he had gone into the artillery.

As if reading his mind, Jesup, sitting beside Hilton in the cab of the truck, said, "Riding sure beats walking, don't it?"

Hilton didn't know what to say. He wanted to empathize with the men on foot. Yet, what Jesup had said was true. He only shook his head and said nothing.

"Jesus K-rist, Corporal. Just because you're lucky enough to be in this nice, comfy, old truck doesn't mean acknowledging that fact is lording it over those poor bastards." Jesup pointed at the men marching up ahead of them. "That's just life in this man's army. Some get the breaks. Some don't. Simple as that."

"Yeah, I guess so," Hilton finally said.

"Goddamn right you better 'guess so.' Goddamn right."

Jesup lit another of the Camels he smoked all through the day. Nothing more was said until the troops came to a halt on the edges of a village laying just at the foot of the mountains Hilton had seen in the distance when they started out that morning.

Unlike the other villages this one was strangely quiet. No throngs of happy villagers rushed out of their huts as the army approached. No clamoring Filipino children looking for chocolate and calling out "Victory Joe." Just burned-out houses, silence, and the smell of old smoke and the rotting corpses of chickens and dogs that lay in the dirty streets. Everyone who had lived there was gone, women, children, and men. They found the men on the outskirts of the village, dead, some hanging from trees with gaping holes where their genitals used to be. Others, headless, lay sprawled on the sides of the highway. The stumps of their necks were black in the sunlight with dried blood and buzzed with flies. The heads had been tossed here and there with no telling which head had belonged to which corpse. Buzzards rose up from the bodies as the troops came upon the dead, hovering over the corpses until the army moved on.

"Good lord," he muttered once they rounded a bend in the road, started up into the mountains, and could see nothing but the artillery units coming behind them in the truck mirrors. "Good fucking lord."

"Yes sir, Corporal," Jesup said. And for once, when Hilton glanced over at the sergeant, the irreverent grin usually plastered on his face was absent. "That, my boy, is the kind of animal we're fighting here. Just remember that. Especially if one of them ever asks you for mercy on the field."

"Good fucking lord," Hilton said again. It was the best he could come up with.

***

They found the enemy the next day waiting for them at an airfield on the other side of the mountains. It was bigger than the one on Mindoro where Hilton's unit had their first taste of combat. Instead of American P-38s lined up off the runways ready for action, this base was home for rows and rows of Japanese Zeros, the bright red suns painted on them gleaming in the sunlight. The Japanese were heavily entrenched with pillboxes set up around the perimeter of the base, artillery units in place, and what seemed like thousands of well-armed troops stationed in defensive formations on the outskirts of the airfield. Tall watchtowers had been set up on the corners of the base.

When Hilton scanned one of them with a pair of binoculars, he was startled to see the Japanese sentry in the tower staring back at him through his own binoculars.

"As soon as we get the order we're going to blast the hell out of those bastards, Corporal," Jesup said. "Now hand me those binocs for a second."

It was just after daylight. The hazy sky promised another warm and humid day. Jesup stood next to Hilton, ready to man the howitzers with Hackett and Reeves. All along the edges of the jungle Hilton could see the 37th Division spread out in front of the artillery. Back at artillery school, text books had been clear about what would happen now. The howitzers would soften up the enemy with a steady barrage of high explosive before the infantry went in. It had seemed pretty simple then, but Hilton was anxious, now, to see how it would play out on a real field of battle.

"Jesus, Corporal," Jesup said after scanning the Japanese positions for a moment. "Did you see that Jap up in the watchtower watching us?"

"Yeah, I did," Hilton said. "Guess that puts the idea of a surprise attack to bed, pretty much."

"Pretty much, Corporal. He was jabbering away on his radio. Not that they didn't know we were coming. Not that it's going to help them any." Jesup patted the barrel of the 105 he was standing next to. "Not after they get a taste of what we're serving up for breakfast this morning."

"You seem pretty confident, Sarge." Hackett had pried open a case of shells for the howitzer and was lining them up for easy access. The thin brown hair atop his bony head was plastered with sweat. Judging by the look on his face, Hilton thought, Hackett didn't quite share Jesup's confidence. His lips were pinched tight, his eyes wide as he stared out across the open ground in front of the enemy airbase. "Look at all those planes and soldiers and pill boxes, Sarge. This isn't going to be any cakewalk. God help us is all I've got to say."

"That's right, Private Hackett, that is *all* you say."

Hilton worried for a minute that Jesup might go hard on the private. Jesup could do that with the former divinity student whenever Hackett brought up religion. But the grin on Jesup's face eased Hilton's concerns. "Hell, son, being a pessimist in situations like this ain't going to help none. You've got to have faith, man. Faith in Generals Griswold and Krueger. Faith in these fine cannons we got right here. Faith in those boys out ahead of us ready to give those Japs a taste of death. That's all."

"I have faith, Sarge."

"I know you do, son." Hilton was surprised then by the seriousness suddenly on Jesup's face. "We're probably going to all need it, too, before this is done with."

A round of mortar fire came from the edge of the airbase as the Japanese managed to get off the first shots of the fight. Tucked inside the copse of bamboo they had hollowed out to use as camouflage, the Guns of Dixie were too far away for the Jap mortars to be of danger to them. Still, the walkie talkie Jesup held in one hand began to squawk. After listening for a minute Jesup replied crisply, "Yes sir." He looked at the men in the platoon. "Let her rip," he said, and the edges of the jungle exploded into one continuous roar of heavy artillery fire.

The Japs held out for five days while the 37th and 40th Divisions gave them everything they had. By the end of the first day Hilton's arms and hands were numb from unpacking shell crates and carrying rounds to the gunner. His ears rang constantly, even when the 105 was silent. Not that anything was ever really silent while the battle raged. If it wasn't the rattling of machine guns and other small arms fire, then it was the thumping of mortars coming from both lines. There were planes, too, American bombing sorties, B-52s dropping load after load of heavy bombs on the airbase and the jungle on the Japanese side, their explosions even louder than the roaring of the howitzers. After the first day the planes didn't come anymore. There was no reason. The Japanese Zeros were in flames on the airfield, unable to mount any kind of aerial attack. It was up to the men on the ground to finish the enemy off.

At dawn on the hot and still morning following the bombing runs and continuous cannonade from the American lines, the enemy launched a banzai charge. From his position in the hollowed-out bamboo copse, Hilton watched what seemed to be the entire Japanese army pour out of the jungle on the far end of the base. The soldiers in their khaki and puttees fired as they ran. Mortars ripped shells over their heads as they came; sometimes falling short and tearing holes into the charging line. Japanese machine gun crews dropped to the ground at the end of the tarmac, set up their guns. and began firing into the American position. Suddenly, nothing was safe on the American end as the mortar and machine gun fire began pouring in. Hilton could hear the whistling sound of rounds zipping through the bamboo. Could hear the thumping explosions the mortar rounds made when they hit, could see the sharp upheavals of dirt and grass and leaves and bodies thrown up by the explosions. And then the Americans were firing back. The rest of it that day was nothing like Hilton had ever known before.

At the end of the fighting, the tarmac and the grassy field at the end of it were littered with the corpses of Japanese soldiers. American soldiers, too, who had been forced to come out of their positions and fight hand to hand or risk being overrun. The torn and bleeding bodies from both armies lay sprawled out, quickly beginning to bloat in the heat of the day. With the sun going down and everything as close to being quiet as it possibly could be in a battle zone, Hilton could hear the humming of flies and mosquitoes as they settled in to feed on the dead.

With the night the wind shifted out of the south. The heavy smell of cordite, along with the stench of the bodies, drifted into the American positions and stayed there. Sitting in the little foxhole he had cut out for himself by the rear of the truck, Hilton wished he could wake up the next morning without the numbness in his arms, the ringing in his ears, or the dead out on the airbase.

But that was not to be. The next day it was more of the same. The fighting raged on. On the third day of it Hilton realized he hadn't slept. Some kind of nervous excitement mixed with fear seemed to keep him on his feet. Looking into the faces of Jesup and Hackett and Reeves as they manned the howitzer he saw how he, too, must look—eyes red and exhausted, black from gunpowder around the edges, streaks of grimy sweat running down the sides of his face.

When they were in the thick of it there were no breaks. If a lull came they ate and smoked in shifts, huddling by the side of the truck or the howitzer to scoop out grub from the cans of K-rations, smoking like it might be the last one for a while. The need to be ready at any moment was an urgency Hilton had never known before. He wouldn't miss it when it was gone. If it ever was.

As the sun went down over the mountains on the third day, it seemed as if everyone involved was taking a long, deep breath before doing whatever had to be done next. Hilton had settled into his foxhole hoping to grab some sleep when Jesup came over in the dark and plunked down in the hole next to him.

"Care for a smoke with an old buddy, Corp?"

There was a wisp of light as the moon came up. In that little brightness Hilton could see Jesup grinning at him.

"Sure," Hilton said. Smoking, like foul language, was something he had picked up in the army, another habit neither his mother nor Gwen would be happy about when he returned home. "If you have any. I ran out earlier."

"I got," Jesup said, shaking two Camels out from a crumpled pack he pulled from his top pocket. The two men smoked in silence for a moment, Hilton drawing the smoke deep into his lungs, savoring the hot tobacco taste before letting it drift into the dark.

"They sure didn't teach me any of this crap at Bolles," Jesup said after a bit.

The red glowing end of the cigarette gave his grin a sinister look. Like the trick kids played with a flashlight on their faces at Halloween, Hilton thought. Or around a campfire at night telling ghost stories. A rush of sudden homesickness washed through him. To push it away he asked, "What's Bolles?"

"A school I went to a long time ago," Jesup said, crushing the cigarette out against the side of the foxhole and then lighting up another one. "You know, one of those fancy prep schools? Up in Jacksonville. My folks thought it would give me a better chance at getting into college. They had high hopes for me, my folks did. Wanted me to be a doctor like Dad. Not that they ever asked me what *I* wanted. If they had, I sure as shit would have told them Bolles wasn't it."

"What did you want to do?" Hilton was glad for the talk and the cigarettes, and that the feeling of missing home had left him almost as fast as it had come.

"Shit, all I wanted to do was to hunt and fish and fuck off. Easy enough to do where we lived. Out in the backwoods of Ocala."

Hilton knew that country. He had hunted the woods and forests outside of Ocala for deer and quail with his father and Uncle TJ right before the war, and they had come home well pleased with their efforts.

"Dad had his office in Gainesville," Jesup went on. "Drove in there every morning. Came home in the evenings with never a smile or a good word to say. Just sat down in his chair by the radio and poured himself a drink of whiskey and read the paper until it was time to eat. And that was the life they wanted for me."

"So, you're not planning on being a doctor, I take it."

"Dentist, actually. That's the kind of doctor dad is. And hell no. Can you see these big mitts of mine in somebody's mouth?"

Jesup struck his hands out in front of him. In the little bit of moonlight coming through the clouds, Hilton saw that they were swollen and red from handling ammo for the howitzers all day.

"I take after my mother's side of the family," Jesup continued. "Why I'm so big. My dad's people were all kind of runts. Mom and pop made a real Mutt and Jeff team, you know? Dad told me once that people's mouths all looked the same after a while. But that the money was good. Jesus. That's what he had to offer? I told myself, thank you, but no fucking thanks."

It was the most talk Hilton had ever heard from the sergeant at one time—even when they had drank together at the Enlisted Men's Club back at Port Moresby before coming to this place.

"No sir, that ain't the life for me. I've been saving my army pay. Gonna buy me a piece of good grazing land. Maybe up around Lake George. Or over to Lake Weir. Someplace where I can run a few head of cattle." Jesup's grin was wide open now in the faint moonlight. "And do all the hunting and fishing and fucking off I want." Suddenly he wasn't smiling. "If I make it out of here in one piece, that is."

"Yeah, I hear you, Sarge. Loud and clear."

"What about you, Corp? What you want to do when this war's over?"

"A lawyer, I guess. I'm planning on law school when I get home. I joined up right after I finished my four years of college. With the war going on I figured law school could wait."

"I can see you as a lawyer," Jesup said, with no hint of the usual sarcasm in his words. "You're smart and methodical and take your time until you know what the answer to a problem is. I've seen how you handled it on the range, calling in coordinates and all. How you paid attention to where the shells landed and were ready with the adjustments. The way you were on the beach the morning of the landing and we got stuck." Jesup snorted, that little laugh of his. "Not to mention that a handsome kid like you will look good in a shiny new suit come court day. Hell's bells man, those hick Florida judges won't have a chance against you, counselor."

"Well, it's what my dad does."

If it was the most talking he had ever shared with the sergeant, Hilton thought how it was something even more. Not just war talk, getting laid stories, and the other tall tales of home the men spouted off in nervous breaks between the fighting. No, this was something more— something that made him remember for the first time in quite a while that a life had existed before the war.

"I've spent time helping him out with paper work in his office," Hilton continued after a bit. "Gone to court a few times with him. He likes to help people in a tight spot. Likes to use his wits against people who think they're smarter than him. Not many are."

"If he's anything like you, Corp, I don't imagine they are."

"So that's my plan. Go home, finish law school, marry my girl. You know? Get on with life." He took the cigarette Jesup offered. Hilton didn't want to sour the good mood this talk of life and plans had created, but he couldn't help himself. "Yeah, that's what I'd like to do," he concluded. "But like you said, Sarge. *If* we get out of here in one piece."

"The Japs won't make it easy."

They both slapped at mosquitoes, Hilton wondering if he had taken his Atabrine tablets that day or not. Now that he was thinking about it, he couldn't remember the last time he *had* taken them. The fighting of the last few days had been front and center; the threat of malaria never entered his mind. He would take them in the morning, he told himself as he killed another of the mosquitoes gorging themselves on the back of his neck. But there was something else on his mind right now.

"You ever think you might not? You know, Sarge. Not make it back home?"

"Every fucking day, Corporal. At least once. Sometimes twice, lately, with all this shooting going on."

He wanted to make light of it. Hilton could hear that in Jesup's voice. But it didn't quite come through. The moon slipped behind a cloud. Over the sounds of the jungle behind them, the cries and moans of the wounded drifted by on the night air.

"It's like I told Hackett in so many words the other day," Jesup said. "Fuck all this pessimistic chatter. You and me, Corporal, are both going home in one piece. Going to live out our wildest dreams. Fuck these goddamn Japs if they think they're going to have it otherwise. That's what I say."

"I sure hope you're right, Sarge," Hilton said. "I sure do."

"It would certainly be nice if I was, Corporal."

By the end of the following day the battle for the airbase came to a close. The Japs were dead, dying, or wounded. The living enemy were now prisoners of war or gone off into the jungle to fight another day. According to battlefield rumors, the commander of the Japanese forces had done the honorable thing when facing defeat and committed hari-kari. Whether or not the rumor was true didn't matter to Hilton. He was just glad the fighting was over for now.

Late in the afternoon, after the firing had stopped, Hilton and Jesup walked out onto the tarmac to take a look at the damage. For the most part it was strangely quiet except for the sounds of small arms way off in the jungles to the east and west of the base, or the occasional explosion of sappers detonating mines and other booby traps left behind. Bombed-out planes still smoldered in place. Everywhere they looked the dead lay, both Japanese and American.

Some of the GIs were busy taking souvenirs off the enemy bodies, pistols and the tiny hari-kari knifes the officers carried, along with any other worthwhile trinkets. It was a task Hilton had no stomach for. The sight of the bodies, bloated up and smelling, robbed him of any desire to go nearer to them than he had to.

Just as they had reached the end of the field and had turned back toward their position, Hilton heard a moaning from one of the bodies. It was an American and amazingly, still alive. Hilton didn't understand how. The man's legs were so mangled and blown up Hilton only knew they were legs because legs were supposed to be there.

"Hey Sarge," the dying GI managed to get out as he raised one arm feebly to Jesup. "Can you help me out?"

"I'm sorry soldier," Jesup said. "I'll go for a medic, but he ain't going to be able to do much."

"I don't need no medic," the soldier said. He laid his head and arm back on the hard pavement of the tarmac. "Just need you to help me out."

"Sure then," Jesup said. "I can do it."

He drew the .45 from the holster at his side and shot the soldier once in the forehead, turning to Hilton in almost the same instant as he fired the gun.

"Don't look at me like that, Raines. I did what the poor bastard asked. You'd do the same for me if I were all fucked up like that, with no chance. Wouldn't you?"

"I don't know, Sarge," Hilton said, and it was true. He didn't know.

"By God, Corporal, if it comes to that for me, you damn sure better."

Hilton said nothing. The two men left it at that as they walked back to the bamboo copse where the howitzer and the rest of the platoon waited.

Mail came two days later, a rare reminder of civilization. They were bivouacked in a small valley nestled in the mountains just north of Manila. A long waterfall rushed down the side of a cliff into a lake at one end of the valley. Earlier in the day, in a native canoe commandeered for the purpose, Jesup and Reeves had rowed out into the center of the lake, tossing grenades into the water and scooping up the fish that came floating to the surface.

Hilton read his letters from home after the fish fry the Guns of Dixie platoon fed themselves for dinner. He sat on an empty ammo container in the shade of two coconut palms and opened the packet of mail. There were three letters from Gwen and one each from his mother, father and sister Marilyn. Gwen's letters ate at him as he read about how much she missed him, wanted only for him to come home safe and sound so that they could get married and start a family like they had talked about so many times. He put them aside to read again later, maybe when he was in a different frame of mind.

His mother's letter was about things he didn't really care about. Bridge games, Mrs. So and So had passed away, there had been a big War Bond drive at the Yacht Club, everyone asked how he was doing. Reading her letter, he could see his mother well dressed, smoking constantly, always polite in the society amid which she moved so well. The one from his sister was light enough. She wrote about how happy she was in New York City with her new husband, Tom. Hilton shared the same feelings about her husband his father did and that wasn't saying much. But for her sake he was glad his sister was doing well.

The letter from Pop was all about ranch concerns. Hilton had spent many of the best days of his life on that ranch, and the letter brought that time back for him. He sure missed the fishing, riding horses, running the dogs in search of small game. Many of his best memories involved TJ, and the two of them doing much like Jesup had as a boy in the Ocala woods. Just fucking off and having a good time. Pop ended the letter with his usual advice. "Be careful, son, for God's sake. Keep your head down and take careful aim before you squeeze the trigger, Love, Dad."

Hilton finished with his mail and then couldn't help himself. He leaned back against the palm tree closest at hand, wiped his eyes, and thought, *Goddamn.*

The hard part really came, though, when he took out his pad of military stationary and tried to answer the letters. What would he possibly write about in this place where everything was nothing at all like how it was back home? Not that he could write very much anyway. The military censors deleted any real information. But how could he describe the death and destruction of the last five days? How, after the battle was over, Jesup had put the dying GI out of his misery. How the next day, when the Graves Detail was clearing the area of dead bodies there were too many to bury. To solve this problem the Detail piled them in stacks on the far end of the airfield and set them afire. All that night the smell of burning human flesh, a sweet smell sort of like pork loin on a barbecue spit, blanketed the bivouacked GIs. How could he write home about that? These were the questions that flooded his mind.

He couldn't. Instead, he put the pad on his knee, dated the letter, and wrote, "Dear Mom, got all your fine letters and just want to say, thank you very much. Don't worry any about me, Mom. I am safe and sound and doing okay…"

***

The city was in flames and had been for days. As far as Hilton could see in any direction, Manila lay in ruins. Before the army arrived on the outskirts only two weeks before, Manila had stood proud and shining in the warm sunlight. Palm trees lining wide boulevards waved in the tropical breezes. Tall office buildings rose up from the sidewalks and streets of the business area. The residential sections on the outside of the city proper were clean and fresh, neighborhoods with houses designed in the same Spanish colonial architecture as Hilton knew from back home. The streets in this part of town were bordered by white sidewalks and green manicured lawns. The sort of neighborhoods, Hilton thought, where children should be playing while mothers watched protectively from front porches. Where fathers, arriving from another day at work, would pull into the driveways in the late afternoon, happy to be home with their families.

Because of the war, these neighborhoods were empty. No children playing in front lawns or fathers coming home from work. Not any more, Hilton thought, as he unloaded another crate of ammo from the GMC and walked it over to the howitzer. Not live ones. Dead ones a-plenty lay in the streets, children *and* adults, and Hilton was pretty sure he'd never forget how *that* looked. Although it was true that civilians killed by the Americans had been by accident, those killed at the hands of the Japanese were a different story. Hilton had seen the proof of that, more than he cared to, in the shot and bayoneted bodies of women, children, and men, evidence of Japanese brutality.

It was mid-afternoon when they came down out of the mountains onto the plains at the northern edge of Manila. The air had been clean and fresh in the higher elevations but turned hot and humid and still when they reached the valley floor. As the army reached the outskirts, the sound of distant firing came through the open windows of the truck. Jesup told him that it must be the 129th Regiment encountering the enemy as they approached the southern rim of the town. But everything was quiet there. At first. As they rolled further in small arms fire rang out from the shops and office buildings and restaurants lining the streets. Caught in the enfilade, the infantry column spread out, taking what cover they could as they returned the enemy fire. Hilton instinctively slowed the GMC down. As he did so the truck in front of him, carrying the other howitzer crew of The Guns of Dixie, burst into flames.

"Land mines, Corporal," Jesup yelled. "Back it up, man, back it up."

But Hilton couldn't move, couldn't reach down and shove the gear lever into reverse, couldn't seem to push in the clutch or let up on the gas enough to allow the gears to exchange. He watched frozen at the wheel of the GMC as another explosion of smoke, fire, and body parts, billowed out from the truck in front of him. The four of them in the truck, Hilton, Jesup, Reeves, and Hackett, bringing up the rear, stared helplessly as the blown-apart truck came to a sudden stop in the middle of the street, fire ballooning out from the its body.

"Move it, man," Jesup yelled in Hilton's ear and when he stepped on the gas and began to move forward Jesup yelled again, "Not that way, Corp. I said reverse, man. Goddamnit, I said reverse."

The tanks in the column behind them had rumbled up on the sidewalks and were firing on the buildings where the Jap snipers hid. The other trucks hauling howitzers and the bigger guns had done the best they could to allow the tanks the room they needed to maneuver. In the confusing melee of machine gun and tank fire all mixed together in a tight space took Hilton out of himself in some strange way. It was as if someone other than him was watching a war movie, the likes of which no one had ever seen before. He knew that Corporal Jerrod, the driver of the blown-up truck, and Hansen, riding shotgun with him, were dead. No one could survive an explosion such as that. With the rest of the truck on fire Hilton assumed Privates Thomas, Jackson, and Chancey, were dead as well.

But he was wrong. In the next second Thomas rose up from the back of the flaming truck and was killed by a hail of machine gun fire riddling his body. Right behind him came Chancey, crawling out of the rear of the truck on what was left of the tailgate, one hand clutching what used to be the side of his head, the other probing in front of him like a blind man for any solid purchase. Then he, too, was dead, picked up and blown off the dangling tailgate like so much flotsam in the unending hail of machine gun fire raining down on the streets and troops below. They found the body of Private Jackson later, burned to a crisp in the charred bed of the truck, the skin of his face and arms so shriveled by fire that he was more a skeleton than a body.

For days afterward, Hilton had dreams of the truck blowing up in the center of Manila. Of Thomas being lifted up by the enemy fire like a rag doll dancing on a string in the wind. Of Chancey clutching the ruined side of his head. Unlike any of the men killed in action he had seen so far, Hilton knew these men.

It took the tanks and the infantry going from building to building to put an end to the Japanese that day, some two hours of street fighting so intense that Hilton could never have imagined it in his wildest dreams. When *all clear* came, dead men littered the Manila street, doorways belched out black smoke from having their rooftops blown in, and here and there along the sidewalks, GIs with flame throwers blasted all the places the enemy might be hiding.

In the days following none of those still left in The Guns of Dixie ever talked about what had happened that afternoon as they rolled into Manila. At first Hilton didn't think that was right. But after three successive nights of dreams about his dying comrades he decided that maybe the not talking about it was for the best.

Now, two weeks later, down to just the one gun and with the smoldering city lying to the south of them, they were positioned *en masse* with the artillery units of both the 37th and 40th Divisions on the banks of a muddy river serving as a moat for a fortress on the other side.

Inside the walls of this fort, a walled city within the bigger city of Manila, were the last of the Japanese forces. It was shortly after dawn, the air warm and thick with the smell of the fires behind them. The artillery units had spent the last two days getting into position on the banks of the river, all of them were trained on the little fortress across the water. Judging by what they had accomplished over the last few weeks, there was no doubt in Hilton's mind that the walled fortress would soon lie in heaps of shattered wood and concrete rubble.

"Anybody happen to know the name of this here river?" Reeves, the private from Alabama, spit a long stream of tobacco juice on the ground at his feet. He was kneeling by the howitzer, his stringy blond hair shining dully in the faint light of the morning, his face streaked with black battle grime, the corners of his mouth stained from the tobacco he constantly chewed. "Or maybe this mud hole don't have no name."

"It's got a name, Reeves." Hackett looked up from the pocket New Testament he always read before and after a fight. "The Pasig, I believe."

Hilton agreed with Reeves. The river *was* a mud hole, especially at low tide as it was now. The exposed banks below the gun positions were damp and dark in the early light of the day and the stench of the fallen tide was strong in Hilton's nostrils. He wondered if there were fish in the river, then decided it was certain he'd never have the opportunity to find out.

"You get that out of that little Bible of yours, Hackett?" Reeves asked and then spat out another stream of tobacco leavings. "You telling me God Almighty himself named this stinkhole and wrote it down in the Good Book?"

"You're a real jackass, Reeves. You know that?"

"I do, Private. Know it very well as a matter of fact."

Hilton couldn't help but laugh along with Reeves, whose loud bray of amusement at his own joke drifted out over the water. He lifted one of the heavy shells out of a crate and carrying it with both hands humped it over to the howitzer alongside the others already placed there earlier in the morning. A little bit of humor before what was coming might go a long ways, he thought as he straightened back up. Might go a good long ways, if they were lucky.

"I'm a damn fine gunner, though," Reeves said when he stopped laughing. "For a simple ol' jackass from Alabam'."

Reeves would get no argument from Hackett, or anyone else on that score. Hilton knew that well enough. Not even from Jesup, who always had something to say in situations such as this. Instead, he stood quietly by the howitzer, staring through binoculars at the walled city on the other side of the river.

"Yes, you are, Reeves," Hackett said. "And for that I thank you."

He looked back down at the little Bible in his hands, Reeves spat another stream of juice, and apparently the conversation between the two was over. Though he could've used some help with unloading the ammo crates, Hilton let Reeves and Hackett be. In a very short while there'd be no time for rest for any of them. Not content to sit still, Hilton yanked another ammo crate out of the bed of the GMC—grateful for the work to keep his mind on something other than what lay ahead of them that day.

"Boys, those walls are thicker than hell." Jesup put the binoculars down and turned to the platoon. That smile of his was all over his face. He was the only one of them left, it seemed to Hilton, who could still manage such a thing. With Jesup, irreverence in the face of it all was never-ending.

"Looks like we've got our work cut out for us today," Jesup continued as he joined Reeves at the gun. He opened the breech block of the howitzer and motioned to Hilton to slide a shell into the open breech. "Good thing we've got the big guns to help us out. We'd be in a world of shit without them."

There were certainly plenty of the "big guns" as Jesup called them. Hilton had quit counting when he reached a hundred, leaving probably half again that number uncounted, the row of cannons all trained on the fortress across the water.

The Guns of Dixie's target, like that of the other units on either side of their position, was the main gate of the fort. A bricked road leading off a wide plaza ran over a concrete bridge spanning the river into the fort, and the walls on either side of the heavy gate had already been breached. The bigger cannons had pounded shells into those walls for a good forty minutes the afternoon before, the barrage an effort to soften the enemy up for the assault troops who would have to fight their way inside. Now those troops were massed to the extreme left of the rows of cannon. Like the battle for the airfield before the army reached Manila, Hilton saw how everything was strictly by the book. Once the gates were blown, the troops waiting on the banks above the muddy river would cross the bridge and take on the enemy within the walls.

On the other end of the line of guns, inflatable boats were pulled up on the riverbank. When the walls on that side of the fortress were blown more assault troops would cross the river in the boats. The enemy would be enfiladed on all sides—forced to either surrender or fight to the death. Hilton was fairly certain what the choice would be. In all the fighting they had done so far, he had yet to see the enemy lay down their arms and walk out under a white flag.

At 7:35 the cannons began to fire. As he had at the beginning of the battle for the air base, Jesup told the platoon, "Let 'em have it, boys."

Then the work began in earnest. Hackett was at the breech loading shells, Jesup at the elevation wheel, Reeves manned the lanyard to send another high explosive shell across the river into the walls of the fortress. It wasn't long before Hilton was only aware of what he could see through the gun sight, the smell of cordite, the sound of high explosives hitting a target, the yelling of men with the excitement of battle.

Exactly one hour later a command squawked through the radio at Jesup's ear and they fired a round of red smoke, the signal for the infantry to move in. Hilton and the rest of them stepped back, took a deep breath, and watched as the assault troops dashed across the empty plaza fronting the fort and into the walled city.

Whatever could burn inside the walls of the fort was in flames, even a tall spire rising from what must have been a church in the middle of the little city. Most everything else lay in a heap of smoldering rubble and billowing concrete dust. Expecting to hear small arms fire ringing out from inside the fort, he was surprised to hear nothing. After what seemed the longest time, there came the sustained rat-tat-tat from a GI firing a long burst from a BAR. And then, nothing. While Hilton waited for something more to happen, up on the north end of the fortress the troops in the inflatable boats reached shore and stormed into the gaping holes in the city walls the artillery had made for them. And then again, silence.

A loud cheer erupted from the crews manning the guns down from Hilton's platoon. Turning at this unexpected sound Hilton saw two nuns, each holding a child in her arms, straggle out of the fort's demolished gates. The nuns stopped. In the rising sunlight and the smoke from the recent cannonade they stood staring at the line of artillery, tanks, and mortar units. The troops manning those guns stared just as dumbly back at them.

Where did they come from? How did they survive the storm of fire unleashed on the fort? Were any more still inside?

Hilton's unspoken questions were soon answered when a stream of men, women, and children came pouring through the gates, escorted by GI's with shouldered arms. They were blackened with dust and smoke from the attack; their clothes tattered or in some cases, mainly those of the small children, missing. Many of them had wounds of some sort crudely bandaged. They had to be weary, Hilton thought. Shocked and afraid, too, from what they had gone through inside that fort. But all of them greeted the cheering soldiers with smiles and waving arms.

"Goddamn, boys, look at that," Jesup said. "By God, we did it." He leapt up on the howitzer, his feet planted on the tires so that he straddled the cannon, the barrel of the gun still smoking from the last discharge. "Now one of you sorry-ass gunners just try and tell me different."

He threw his helmet up in the air, letting out a loud, screeching yell that seemed to run out over the water in a rambling wave. Standing next to Hilton, Reeves cupped his tobacco stained lips with his hands and did the same as Jesup. And then Hilton, too, opened his mouth wide, without even thinking about what he was doing, and joined Jesup and Reeves. Hilton knew that Hackett had certainly never heard such a thing before, but he stood up and yelled out with the rest of his platoon a long and loud sustained Rebel Yell.

***

Not that the battle was really over, the mopping-up of Japanese resistance continued all that day. Three tall buildings remained standing in a plaza just to the south of the walled city: the financial office, post office, and another one Jesup told Hilton he wasn't sure of but suggested it might be city hall.

"That's as good a name as any for it. Don't matter. It won't be standing long. None of them will. Just watch."

He wasn't wrong. Shortly afterwards several units of 155 mm howitzers wheeled away from their positions on the banks of the river and trained their guns on the plaza. The Guns of Dixie and the other units that stayed behind became simply spectators as the bigger cannons brought the three buildings down. When the big howitzers were done, assault troops rushed into the doorways and the gaping holes made by 155 mm's, flushing out and killing any enemy troops that survived.

Much the same was going on across the river. Small arms fire rang out all through the day. Not until early the next morning was the "all clear" finally sounded and the battle *really* over. Hilton was asleep in the cab of the truck.

"C'mon, Corp, let's go." Jesup woke him again a couple of hours later just as dawn was breaking. "Let's rustle up some grub and then see what it looks like out there."

The sergeant's face was freshly washed and smiling, the curly red hair slicked down, combed and brought to order beneath the helmet cocked at a slant on his head. Struggling to come awake Hilton wondered where Jesup had found the water to wash and shave with.

"What about our post?" Hilton asked. "We probably shouldn't be leaving our position."

"Give me a break, Corporal." Jesup waved a dismissive hand at the idle howitzer where Reeves and Hackett lay sleeping on the ground on either side of the gun. "You see anything here for us to do? In case you didn't hear last night, the battle's fucking over."

"I guess you're right."

"Damn straight I'm right. Come on boy, let's get. I'm starving. And in dire need of some coffee."

Hilton didn't see how Jesup's smile could get any wider. The sight of it in the dull smoky light of the early morning was enough to bring him all the way awake.

"Don't forget that new gat of yours," Jesup said as Hilton crawled out of the cab of the truck. "We find any Japs not quite dead we'll give them some good old fashioned American *Bushido*. Help them on their way to heaven or wherever the fuck it is they go. Either way, we'll send them there."

Hilton didn't say anything as he straightened up, stretching his arms over his head.

"Of course, Corp, you know I'm only kidding. Right?"

Jesup didn't look like he was kidding, though. Not the way his lips had gone tight, his eyes narrow and hard as he stared at Hilton from beneath his helmet.

"Yeah, Sarge. I figured that."

The new *gat* Jesup mentioned was a long-barreled Colt .38 revolver Hilton had traded a quart of George Dickel whiskey for the day before the army came down out of their bivouac in the mountains above Manila. Hilton grabbed the pistol and holster off the seat of the truck. He hadn't had to use the gun yet and as he strapped the holster around his waist he hoped he'd never have to.

It was a crude mess hall indeed, serving only the same sort of rough coffee, dried eggs, and canned side meat they could have made from their own K-rations. The eggs and sausage were hot, though, warmed over camp stoves the mess crew had set up in the rear of the big tent. Hilton supposed that made a difference. When he mentioned this to Jesup the sergeant only grunted and said, "If you say so, Corp."

By the time they finished the grub the sun was fully up, the light from it filtered through the pall of smoke hanging over everything when they stepped out of the mess tent. Tanks rumbled down the street behind them, their metal treads clanking over the pavement and the debris left from the days of fighting. Squads of infantry patrolled the otherwise empty neighborhood, the point man peering into the windows and doorways of the ruined shops and office buildings with a flamethrower operator right behind him ready for the first sign of trouble. Other than that, it was quiet and still in the ruined city.

With Jesup in the lead, the two men picked their way over the rubble of the main gate and into the fortress. Hilton didn't know what he expected to find inside the walled city and was not ready for what he did.

"Jesus H. Christ," Jesup, whispered. "Will you look at that?"

Hilton didn't want to look, but he had no choice. The dead lay everywhere. Some of the corpses were intact, but many more were not. Torsos without heads, bodies with heads attached but minus arms or legs, or sometimes both, bodies unrecognizable as having once been human beings except for the contorted faces staring out of blank eyes. More corpses were found hidden in the concrete mess. Hilton discovered this by accident when he stumbled over something in the street. Looking down to see what had tripped him up, he saw a foot sticking out from a pile of dusty bricks. A hand reached out from the dusty pile as well, grasping for help that never came.

"We tore 'em up something fierce, eh Corp?"

"Yeah," Hilton said, but he didn't want to say more.

Most of a church by the north wall of the fortress was still standing. The spire Hilton had seen burning during the cannonade was now a blackened stump reaching up toward the sky. Chunks of the red Spanish tile roof had caved in, the edges of the tiles jagged and charred from the impact of high explosive shells. Where Hilton assumed stained glass windows should have been, only gaping black holes looked out on the plaza. There were no smiling angels, chubby cherubs with gifts of flowers, or the grimace of Christ dying on the cross to greet worshippers come a Sunday morning. Only the two big wooden doors of the church, blown off their hinges and wide open for anyone who cared to come inside.

More bodies lay to the side of the church—spilled out of the blown doors and onto the brick walkways leading away from the place of worship. But the very worst of the carnage they found inside was where the wrinkled burned bodies of women and children sat up in the rows of wooden pews before the altar with the huge painting of Jesus behind it. Hilton wondered where the men were, but didn't have to wonder long. They were out in the courtyard, strung together with baling wire in groups of twenty or so, bayoneted and then set afire like those inside.

More stacks of dead Filipinos littered a little graveyard in the rear of the church. A white-haired priest still in his robes had been propped up against a headstone, his eyes wide with death, his hands still clutching the bayonet in his throat.

Hilton staggered back through the church and out into the plaza where he vomited up everything he had eaten that morning. When the retching finally ended he felt better, glad that Jesup had lingered behind in the church and not witnessed his fit of sickness. As he straightened up and wiped his wet lips with the back of his hand, something in the corner of his eye caught his attention just as Jesup emerged from the church, a strained grin on his face.

"Help me, Joe," a woman screamed. The sound of it was loud and piercing in the quiet of the empty plaza. "Help me."

She was a young Filipino woman, perhaps in her early twenties, stumbling out of a doorway across from the church. Naked from the waist down, her brown legs matted with blood, she held something tight to her chest as she came screaming across the plaza. "Help me, please."

It was sudden, unexpected. Hilton barely had time to register the sight or figure out whether it was a baby the woman was holding, when he saw what she was running from—a Jap appeared in the doorway the woman had just come out of, a machine gun in his raised hands.

"Get down, Corp. Get down!"

Hilton turned when Jesup's .45 cracked twice. He both heard and felt the .45 slugs ripping by him. In the next instant the sharp cracking of Jesup's pistol was drowned out by the louder roar of the Jap's machine gun. The woman screamed and was knocked to the ground. Then Hilton had the Colt long-barreled revolver in his hand and he was firing, too. As he walked toward the Jap, pulling the trigger of the Colt as he went, he only half-noticed Jesup's surprised grunt from behind him and the fact that the man wasn't shooting anymore. Hilton stopped firing only when the enemy dropped his gun, slumped back in the doorway, and it was quiet again in the plaza in front of the church.

It was over. But when Hilton turned to Jesup to tell him so, he saw the sergeant on his knees, one hand clutching the side of his head, the other holding his stomach.

"Goddamn, Sarge." Without knowing how he got there, he was at Jesup's side, kneeling down to help. "Goddamn."

"Boy, ain't that a fact."

"Lie back, Sarge and let me take a look."

"I'm glad one of us can see. I sure can't."

Jesup tried to grin, but his lips and face were so covered with blood that if he managed it Hilton couldn't tell. Not only was his head torn open by one of the machine gun rounds, Jesup's stomach had been, too. Hilton hadn't noticed the stomach wound at first, but when Jesup went to lie back he could see very clearly how the only thing holding the sergeant's gray intestines in place was Jesup's own blood-soaked hand.

"That Jap shot me every which way to Sunday," Jesup groaned again, his words and breaths coming shallow and fast. "Goddamn if he didn't."

Hilton wiped the blood away as best he could, but the open wound on the side of Jesup's head wouldn't stop bleeding. His left ear had been torn away and the whole top of his head was laid open. Flesh and hair were gone or covered with blood. Hilton realized with a sickening lurch in his guts that all the blood was coming from an exposed section of the sergeant's brain that pulsed it out in a steady stream. He wanted to stop the outpouring of blood but when he started to put pressure on the wound he stopped, uncertain if it was wise.

"Seems like I'm going to have to call in that favor after all, Corp."

Blood gushed from his mouth, down his chin and neck. Hilton had floated away for just a moment, out of himself, much like he had that day the truck suddenly exploded, and his fellow platoon members had all been killed. But when Jesup spoke he came back to the plaza square, where some GI's, aware that something had happened, were rooting through the blown-up buildings for Japs. Hilton could hear them loud and clear above the moaning of his friend dying beside him.

"I don't think I can do that, Sarge."

"You're going to, Corp. You have to." Jesup tried to sit up, couldn't. "You have to, buddy."

"No, Ray," Hilton said. "Let me get a medic. He can fix you up and we'll get you out of here."

It was the first time Hilton had ever called Jesup by his given name. Now, even if it didn't seem like near enough, he said it again.

"Just let me find some help, Ray."

"You've got all the help you need, Corp." Jesup's voice was getting weaker, the effort it took him to speak all over his face. "Right there in that holster on your hip."

"No. Goddamnit, Ray, I can't."

He stood up, stepped away from his friend for a moment and looked desperately around the square. There was no one around. No one to help him. The GI's who had been seeking enemy soldiers seemed to have given up their search and were looking instead for souvenirs amidst the rubble and the bodies. There was no one to help him.

"I can't do it," Hilton said.

But he pulled the Colt from his holster. It was then, finally, that he could see very clearly through the caked blood that grin of Jesup's, as wide open and alive as his shattered face and mouth would allow. That grin was the last thing Hilton saw before shooting the sergeant once in the forehead. The crack of the .38 rang out in the plaza. And that was that.

There was the woman, though, moaning where she lay on the plaza bricks. Hilton had thought she was dead, but she wasn't. Not yet, anyway, though it was clear she wouldn't survive. Not all shot up like she was. Funny, but she still clutched the baby in her arms. Hilton had one bullet left in the revolver and he shot her, too. It seemed like the right thing. Besides, if it hadn't been for her, running out in the street like that crying for help, Jesup would still be alive.

Hilton pried the baby from the woman's arm, thinking there might be hope for the child. But as soon as he held the infant up he knew that wasn't going to be. The little boy was cut open from below his neck all the way down to his groin. The place where the boy's heart and lungs should have been was an empty, gaping hole, looking faintly brown with dried blood in the fading light of the afternoon; the baby dead, even as his mother ran screaming for help.

All of them dead. Hilton lay the little body down next to its mother. All of them dead and only Hilton there to know.

Part Three: Home

In October, with the war on both fronts over, the 37th Division was separated into those who would go with MacArthur and be part of the occupying force in Japan, and those to be sent home. It was mainly the Regular Army men, soldiers who had been with the army well before the war started, who went with MacArthur. "Thirty-year men" is what the other soldiers called them, even though the old thirty-year career in the army had been scaled back to twenty by that time. Hilton harbored no designs on a career in the service and before the month was out he boarded a troop ship in Manila that would take him to Australia. After a short processing period there—or so the Army claimed—they would board another ship, this one bound for the States.

It wasn't until mid-December that Hilton arrived back in the States. But after a two-week crossing the troop ship he was aboard pulled into sight of San Diego. In another day Hilton was ashore, glad to be off the ship. Even more glad to be finally free of the Philippines and the war.

The bus ride north up the California coast to Fort Ord was a revelation. While the other soldiers on board were laughing, joking, singing dirty songs, and talking about the booze they'd be drinking and the women they'd be with soon, he stared out the bus window, just happy to be once again in America. The air coming off the Pacific Ocean drifting through the open bus window was fresh and clean. Not only that, but it was empty of the sound of booming howitzers, small arms fire, and the screaming of the wounded and dying. It smelled better, too. Much better than the bitter odor of spent cordite that had been such a part of his recent life and the corpses rotting in the humid stale air of the jungles south of Manila.

Hilton's body was being washed with something cool and renewing. *To wash my sins away?* Probably too much to ask for, he thought. Even if Jesup *had* begged him to do what he had done.

He figured to be at Fort Ord only for a short time before heading on east to Fort Bragg where he'd be fully processed out of the army and given his discharge. Since it was December, Hilton held no illusions of getting home for Christmas. Still, he didn't think New Year's would be unreasonable.

But as it had in Australia, malaria had other ideas for him. This bout was even worse than that one, and for three days he lay sweating with a fever rife with wild dreams of bloody combat. If he wasn't out of his head with the fever and bad dreams, then he lay freezing with chills no amount of blankets could keep away. The fever broke on the fourth day, but he was worn out from the attack. It was another two days before he could keep solid food down and get on his feet. As in Australia, during his time in bed, the rest of his division had moved on.

One morning when he was finally able to get out of bed and walk around a little, Hilton decided to go to the canteen. He felt a little foolish in the flapping hospital gown he had to wear as he walked down the hall. Hopefully, conversation with another human being besides a doctor, or an orderly, would take his mind off the silly gown. A pretty nurse in a fresh white uniform carrying a stack of file folders under one arm came down the hall toward him. As they passed one another in the narrow passageway, Hilton's arm accidentally knocked the file folders loose from the nurse's grip. The sudden contact, the surprised, "Oh!" from her mouth when the folders hit the floor, stopped him in his tracks.

She was very pretty, he thought. The blonde ponytail hanging down her neck that swung back and forth as she came down the hall was very pretty. Like Gwen, sort of. It was his fault the folders dropped on the floor. The least he could do was give her a hand picking them up.

But when Hilton turned to help everything had changed. Lost in a sudden loud roaring noise inside his head, his body swayed with the sound. The nurse was gone, leaving him alone in the sunlight splintering down through the pall of gun smoke in front of the ruined church in Manila. The church where the corpses came to pray. Above the roaring in his head he heard Jesup calling out, "Watch it, Corp." But when he turned Jesup wasn't there. Neither was the nurse. Instead, the Filipino woman came screaming across the square, already dead and the baby held in her arms dead, too. Both of them skeletons as the Colt revolver in his hand fired and fired and the dead woman's face blew apart.

The next thing Hilton knew he awoke in a bed in a different wing of the hospital. Like the others he could see when he lifted his head up, he was strapped down tight.

He wasn't alone. A man in a white smock stood next to his bed. A doctor, Hilton thought through the fog in his head. One with kindly eyes and balding hair that reminded him of his father.

"Good," the doctor said. "I see you're awake. It's been a while since you were."

His voice was low and easy, comforting somehow, even as the screaming of a man strapped to his bed at the other end of the ward echoed through the room.

"I guess I'm awake," Hilton said, quickly adding, "Sir," when he saw the major's gold oak leaf clusters showing just above the edge of the white doctor's smock. "How long have I been out? Been here?" He lifted his wrists against the straps holding him down. "Like this?"

"You had a rough time there for a bit, Corporal. We had to keep you sedated. For your own good, you understand?"

"No, not really."

Though he heard clearly everything the major said, Hilton's own voice seemed as if it were far away and not his. From the drugs, he figured. Were it not for the fact he was strapped to the bed and had no idea of what had happened to him, it was sort of pleasant, this feeling the sedatives had given him.

"Yes," the major said. "I don't expect you would understand. When you're up and about again we can talk about it. We'll ease up on the sedatives now and I'll see you in my office in a few days. Until then, Corporal, take care of yourself."

"I don't see how I can do otherwise, sir." He lifted his arms again against the restraints holding him down.

"You've still got your sense of humor, soldier. That's very good. But I'll have the orderly remove the straps."

"Thank you, sir."

"I'll see you soon, Corporal Raines."

The major saluted him, a salute Hilton couldn't return. With his head turned to the side he watched as the major moved down the ward, stopping at each of the beds for a moment to leaf through a chart or talk to the patient if he were awake. Then the ward orderly was un-trapping his leather restraints. Before Hilton could protest the orderly also jabbed a needle in his arm and pushed the plunger down. He wanted to scream, tell the orderly how the major had just said to ease up on the sedatives. But he couldn't—he was asleep instead.

That was the last of the drugs. Four days later at 1000 hours Hilton sat in the major's office, finally out of the hospital gown and in his fatigues, starting to feel like his old self again. The major's office was a sparse, wood-paneled affair. Framed medical school degrees lined the wall behind the desk along with one framed photograph of the Major with MacArthur in Australia.

"As you can see from my photographs, Corporal, I too, did a stint in the Philippines."

The major, looking crisp and clean in a starched Eisenhower jacket, sat behind an equally spartan wood desk. In the middle of the desk, covered by the major's clasped hands, was a file folder—his, Hilton was sure.

"Unfortunately," the major continued, after clearing his throat with a short harrumph that reddened his face, "I wasn't able to return with the general. The higher-ups, in their infinite wisdom, had other plans for me."

"I saw the general once," Hilton said. "On Luzon. Right after the landing, before we moved on Manila."

He fidgeted in his seat, a metal folding chair that was very uncomfortable. He hadn't been given any sedatives now for three days, but the lingering effects caused by them—a numbing, pins and needles feeling in his arms and legs—added to his discomfort.

"Yes. I read your file here, Corporal Raines." The Major shuffled the folder and then put it back down on the desk. "You boys did a good job over there. I commend you for that."

"Thank you, sir."

"Care for a drink?" the major asked, taking a bottle of Old Grand-Dad whiskey out of a desk drawer and placing it with two shot glasses on the desk.

"No thank you, sir. I guess it's a little early yet for me."

"Well, as they like to say in the Navy, the sun's always over the yardarm somewhere in the world."

The major chuckled at his own joke but not for long when he saw that Hilton did not. It didn't stop him from filling one of the shot glasses to the brim, downing it, and then re-filling it, though only halfway, before picking up Hilton's folder again.

"I'm curious, Corporal Raines," the major said, all official now, "as to why you're still a corporal. It says here you were promoted to sergeant after the death of your squad leader, but you refused. Why is that?"

"I wasn't the leader, Sergeant Jesup was. It didn't seem right, sir."

"You don't see a career in the Army as part of your future?"

"No, sir, I do not."

The prickly pins and needles were getting worse and Hilton didn't like this talk of his being promoted after Jesup's death. Of how he had said, no.

Maybe a shot of the whiskey the major was enjoying *was* in order, Hilton decided. Maybe it would help. "Can I take you up on that drink now, sir?"

"Certainly, Corporal." The major's face brightened as he poured another shot out for himself and one for Hilton. "Anytime, Corporal. Anytime. Just stop by my office. If I'm in, just give me the ol' high sign and we'll drink up."

It was the first lie the kindly major had said to him and Hilton was surprised by the sadness it caused. But there it was.

"Well, son, the Army's not a career for everyone," the Major said after tossing off the new drink. "What *do* you plan to do when you're discharged?"

The Old Grand-Dad was hot and strong without water, ice, or soda, to cut it. But as the whiskey burned down his throat Hilton realized it was helping to settle him. Even if the dulling effect of the alcohol hadn't totally set in quite yet, thinking of the coming comfort he pushed his glass across the desktop without saying anything. The major, completely understanding, filled it to the brim.

"I'll be going into law, sir. That was always the plan, before the war broke out."

"Good. Very good. Always room for another lawyer in this country, I suppose." A slight grimace crossed the major's face as if he did not quite believe this to be true. "But I imagine, Corporal, you're more interested in finding out what happened to you on the ward that morning than in making idle chatter about life after the war."

"Yes, sir. I very much would like to know."

The major took the bottle and empty glasses and put them back in the drawer underneath the desk. *Time to get down to business, now.* Hilton suddenly wished he had one more drink of the Old Grand-Dad. Outside, a sergeant led a squad in calisthenics on the common ground. At the sound of his orders, the grunts of the men doing jumping jacks and pushups drifted through the open window. The day was clear and mild, with a morning mist rolling off the ocean. The misty air seemed to bathe the exercising men in a soft light. One suited to the cinema, Hilton thought. More like a movie in a darkened theater than real life.

Just as he had wished for another drink, Hilton wanted to be out on the common area with the others. Working his body through the exercises, breathing the air coming off the ocean, the mist keeping him cool and fresh. He wanted to be just about anywhere other than where he was.

"Corporal, here's the simple fact of it. You seem to be suffering from a condition we call battle fatigue." The major cleared his throat and pushed Hilton's file to the corner of the desk. "You're not alone in this. A lot of the boys coming back from both the Pacific and European fronts are afflicted with it. If that helps any."

"A condition?" Hilton asked. "It's a disease, then? Like the malaria?"

"No, not in that sense it isn't. More of a mental disorder, really. We know it's brought on by the stress of combat. The Brits put a name to it during the First World War. Called it shell shock. They thought at first it was caused by the gas the Germans used. Then they began to find it in other soldiers, too, men who hadn't been exposed to the gas."

"So, I'm crazy? That's what you're telling me?" Hilton paused. "Sir."

"No, Corporal, that isn't what I'm saying. I would think 'disturbed' would be the word best suited."

Hilton supposed this was meant to be reassuring though he didn't see how it could be. "Is there a cure?"

"Rest, a healthy diet, and exercise are helpful. Of course, removal from combat is necessary. With the war over that part of your treatment has been completed. Thank God."

The major started to smile, but perhaps seeing the look on Hilton's face, thought better of it.

"The malaria doesn't help," he continued. "Hallucinations and breakdowns like what you suffered are more common when the subject is weak or compromised by other physical ailments. You'll have to be careful. Attend to the malaria quickly when you feel it coming on. Stop and rest when you're overexerted. If a breakdown does come on or gets violent, well, then, sedatives will probably be in order. And maybe a hospital stay like you just went through. That's about it, Corporal, I'm sorry to say."

"Will I get better?" Hilton asked. "Will it go away?"

"That's hard to say, Corporal Raines. Very hard to say."

Something in the major's tone set things straight for Hilton. Or perhaps it was the way the officer reached again for the whiskey bottle on the desk, though his glass was damn near full.

Hilton was angry. Fuck him. His smiling face that won't say what he means. Hard to say if I'll get better? He doesn't think I will. Why it's hard for him to say. So yeah. Fuck him. Just because *he* thinks that doesn't make it so.

Hilton spent the first three months of 1946 at Fort Ord and though he was anxious to get home he didn't really mind. At the doctor's suggestion he was on a four-month Atabrine regimen for the malaria. This he *did* mind, mainly because of the yellow pallor his skin acquired from taking the drug. As for the other, what the kindly major called "battle fatigue," he did the only treatment possible, at least according to the major—exercise, three healthy meals a day, and rest. The last thing he wanted to suffer was another episode, the subsequent sedation, and being strapped to a hospital bed until it was over.

The Atabrine helped with the malaria, and the exercise and good diet seemed to keep what Hilton came to call the "dead woman" at bay. After the first two weeks of this treatment, being in good enough health,

Hilton was free to leave the base during the day. After morning mess and roll call he took to wandering the streets of Monterey. Late morning, when the sun had cleared out the fog and the air was warm and fresh coming off the water, he liked to walk by the canning factories down by the bay. He enjoyed listening to the loud voices of the men and women bantering with one another while they operated the canning machines, the presses and conveyer belts that were visible through the big open bay doors. The laughter and cursing mingled in with the screaming of sea birds wheeling and diving for the offal tossed overboard by fishermen cleaning their catch, the rumble of the trucks heading up the road away from the quays with their loads of finished product—all of this steady, vibrant sound of life, served to remind Hilton how another world existed outside of the army and the war.

A ramshackle bar & grill sat on a point stretching into Monterey Bay just up from the rows of canning factories. It was called, appropriately enough, "The Cannery," and Hilton liked to go in there after the walking and enjoy a cold beer. Sitting at one of the rickety tables by a window overlooking the bay, he spent the time reading and writing letters or looking over military case law. If he was going to be a lawyer when all this was over, he reasoned, he needed to start preparing himself. Reading military law might help with that. The waitress, perhaps in her fifties and with her hair always up in a tidy bun, reminded him a little of Aunt Mabel on his mother's side of the family. The waitress always had a smile for him and was prone to pat him on his shoulder after bringing his order to the table. Her green eyes, moist and approving in a sorrowful sort of way, made him wonder if she maybe had a son in the army who had gone off to the war. Though he wondered this he didn't ask, not wanting to discover that she did, and they hadn't come home at war's end. But when writing a letter to his mother or his dad, the woman's presence behind the bar seemed to give him a sense of almost home.

***

Hilton left on the troop train for Fort Bragg the first week of April. As far as he was concerned he was over the hump with the maladies he had brought back from the Pacific. At his last interview with his doctor, the major said he was very pleased with his progress. But to Hilton, the major said this in the same tone he had when responding to Hilton's question about whether or not he'd get better.

Hilton was going home. He'd get better. Hell, he was better now. That was all that mattered and for now Hilton believed that to be more than enough.

***

On the Friday afternoon before Mother's Day of 1946, another train, this one from Fort Bragg, North Carolina, pulled into the Florida East Coast station in Fort Lauderdale. Hilton was on the train, having boarded it the morning before, along with three or four hundred other GI's—men mustered out of the Army like he was, finally, and going home. By the time the train arrived in Lauderdale only five soldiers still remained aboard. Four of them were to get off in Miami, the end of the line, including Hilton.

The regular passengers aboard the train had been out-numbered almost two to one by the soldiers, the GI's drunk, or drinking, for most of the journey until they reached their particular stops. It wasn't long before the cars where the soldiers were—which was most of them—reeked of booze and cigarette smoke and echoed with laughter and loud profanity. The war had been over almost eight months by this time, but support for the returning veterans still ran high. Other than a few prim and proper old ladies, no one riding the train that day minded the soldiers' behavior.

Hilton watched the carrying-ons with a rueful eye. If not for a recent bout of malaria three days before he had to board the train, he'd have been drinking right along with the others. *More of that soldier talk*. He'd have to watch that around his mother. *And Gwen*, he thought. But he'd have joined in with the others if he wasn't worried about a return of the "dead woman." Not to mention being still a little weak from the chills and fevers of the malaria that came and went. He comforted himself with the thought that there'd be time later. Time for good whiskey and laughter with those he cared about.

Waiting to greet him at the station were his fiancée Gwen, his mother, and father. The three of them stood in almost the exact same spot they had the last time he'd seen them, three years before. They had been saying goodbye to him then, his thirty days' furlough over before being shipped overseas. It was mid-December, cold and windy—or as cold and windy for South Florida—the morning his girl and his family sent him off to the war. The four of them had been bundled up in coats and sweaters and scarves, and when he hugged Gwen for the last time, he could barely feel her body through the military overcoat he wore. He had felt her warm tears against his face. There had been a lot of tears, from all of them, along with sad, lingering hugs and kisses. And then he had climbed aboard the train and was gone.

It would be different now, he thought. On all fronts. One he noticed right away was the smiling faces of the people waiting on the platform.

It was also a bright, early summer day, instead of the winter chill of before. One difference he hadn't found the words for yet. He just wasn't the same man who had left three years back. Not the optimistic boy in a clean and new soldier's uniform going off to do his duty for country, God, and loved ones. No, that boy was long gone. The war had seen to that.

How Hilton felt must have shown judging by the looks on his folks and Gwen's faces when he walked across the station platform. He knew how they felt. He, too, had stared in disbelief at the face greeting him from the bathroom mirror at the military hospital. It hadn't seemed possible that the gaunt, yellowed face in the glass was his. His parents and Gwen were lucky they hadn't been with him then. His hollow features and thin frame had filled out some since Fort Ord. Hot meals, proper exercise, and rest had brought him a long ways back. Just not all the way. That was clear enough on their faces as he came toward them.

Gwen sure looked great, he thought. Goddamn if she didn't. He had spotted her in the crowd first thing as the train rolled into the station. Even standing next to his mother, a woman taller than most, Gwen stood out. No other woman on the platform that afternoon had hair even close to hers. Long and silvery blonde, styled Veronica Lake fashion with one long bang coming down and hiding her left eye, a style that went perfectly with the brilliantly white summer dress she was wearing. With his reaction to it so obvious Gwen had laughed and said she'd have to remember the effect it had on him for when he came home after the war. They had been in his father's Dodge parked along the river bank making out the night before he had to leave. Gwen had laughed again, then said, "Oh my. Look what I've done to you." Her blouse was open, her breasts white and pale in the moonlight as she leaned over him. I will remember this, he thought. Then she took him in her hand and finished him off as he kissed her wildly, breathing into her ear how much he loved her.

Then he was pushing the others aside until he finally held her in his arms, her bright blue eyes lit up with the sunshine. He was holding her, kissing her, and saying, "Thank God, thank God." And she was saying, "Yes, my love, yes thank God you're home." They kissed and laughed as if no one else, not his parents or any of the others, were there. His father was saying, "Welcome home, Son. How was it over there?"

"Now, John, don't be silly," Hilton's mother said in a throaty Illinois accent. "He's just got home, for goodness sake. He doesn't want to talk about the war. Or any of that other Army stuff you two can talk about some other time. Hello, son."

And then Hilton was in his mother's arms, smelling the Chanel Number Five she always wore and the smell of the Pall Malls she constantly smoked. Tall and straight, she was in the walking heels and navy dress she wore when leaving the house on important daytime excursions such as this. Her hair was up in a bun, covered with a small, straight brimmed hat with frills of lace on the sides. When he pulled away from her, Hilton saw the uncovered wisps of hair visible below the little hat were gray instead of dark brown.

His father, some two inches shorter and slighter of frame, wore the brown suit he always wore for the office. The tan Stetson he favored hid what little hair John Raines had left. Hilton was reminded of how Jesup had once described his own folks as being "a real Mutt and Jeff team." His parents were that, as well. He knew who wore the pants in the family, though, even if Pop never failed to defer to his wife when circumstance, or failed argument, dictated he do so.

Hilton saw that his father had not changed a bit in the time he'd been away. Like always, no matter the situation—hurricanes, war, peacetime—John Raines stayed constant. He was a loving, but stern man, known about town and at home, as a fine citizen who would go out of his way to help a friend or loved one.

"C'mon, son, let's go home," his father said.

Hilton picked up the duffel bag he had dropped and with one hand holding the bag, the other arm around his fiancée, he said, "Sounds good, Pop. Real good."

***

Hilton and Gwen made love for the first time that night. He hadn't expected anything more than a goodnight kiss at the door when he drove her home. It had been late when they finally left the Raines house. He was tired; Gwen seemed tired as well. So it was a surprise when instead of saying goodnight at the door she invited him in.

"Are you sure?"

"Very sure, darling." Tugging on his hand, she opened the door with the other one. "Mom's working the late shift tonight, so we have the place to ourselves. We can have a drink together, just you and me, catch up on things without anyone else around. Then I'll send you on your way. Unless..." But her voice trailed off and before he could say anything they were inside the house, standing in the little hallway, and Gwen was kissing him with an urgency he had never known from her before. "Unless," she said again when they broke apart, "you don't want to go."

She led him by the hand down the hallway toward the two bedrooms in the rear of the house. When she opened the door to her room he saw that the sheets had been pulled down and a soft light glowed on the bedside table. On the dresser across from the bed, a bottle of Jack Daniels and two glasses sat on a silver tray. Everything nice and neat and well planned, he thought. As Gwen sat down on the bed, he stood dumbfounded in the doorway.

"Well?" she asked. "What do you think? Care to pour a girl a drink?"

It was plain, even if she was playing it as brash and cavalier as she could, that Gwen was nervous. Hilton was nervous, too, though he didn't want to show it—more for her sake than his. He crossed over to the dresser and caught a glimpse of himself in the mirror on the wall. The thin, pale, faced man he saw didn't seem like him. At least the hair on his head, still cut military short, was pretty much the dark brown it had been when he entered the service. Though he would never have thought it possible, he knew plenty of guys his own age at the end of the war that walked out of it with gray hair. So there was that at least. Not to mention the fact that he was still alive.

"How about that drink, darling?"

"Coming right up."

Glad for Gwen's nervous reminder of the drink, he turned away from his reflection in the glass and the unwanted thoughts that went with it.

"One or two fingers," he asked, holding a glass and the bottle up for her to see when he turned from the mirror. "I'm going with two," he said, as casually as he could muster.

"Then two it is. Why don't you put some music on, Hilly? Something soft and nice to go with the drinks."

He turned the dial on the radio perched on the corner of the dresser until Glenn Miller's "Moonlight Serenade" drifted out into the bedroom, soft and low, like the light on the table by her bed.

"Here's to ya, kid," he said in his best Humphrey Bogart voice as he sat down by her and together they clinked glasses.

Through the bedroom window light from the full moon washed over the backyard, a soft white that matched the light of Gwen's bedroom. Though he wanted to think and feel nothing but the woman sitting next to him, his nervousness wouldn't quite let him. A faint squeal of dirty brakes on a car coming to a stop at the corner drifted through the open bedroom window. Over the music from the radio Hilton could hear the car's engine throbbing in idle, followed by a throatier rumble as it pulled away from the stop sign. His thoughts ran to the Colony Theater where he and his pals went as kids to see movies on a Saturday morning, and later, on dates with his high school girlfriend, Nearbelle Hunt, where they sat in the back of the theater and when the lights went down, made out more than they watched what was being shown on the screen.

Hilton finished his drink, the Jack Daniels hot and full and burning all the way down his throat the way good whiskey should. "Why now?" he asked.

Before she could answer though they were kissing—but not for long, because he needed to know and pulled away.

"I thought you wanted to wait until we were married? That's what you always said."

"I'm tired of waiting." She tried to smile but it wasn't enough to cover the nervousness in her voice. "You were away a long time. Everything was so uncertain. It was always in the papers and on the radio. Every day there was no news from you, your mother and I read the lists of casualties in the paper. We were so relieved when your name wasn't there, or a letter finally came from you."

"But that's all done now, baby. All done," he said.

"Yes. It is. And you're home, and I don't want to wait anymore."

The only awkward moment came when he was about to enter her, the two of them naked on her bed, the drinks forgotten, the music on the radio there but not a part of it.

"Wait, Hilly, wait."

Her voice was husky, her lips and eyes wet from the kissing. He wasn't sure if he *could* wait, they were so damn close, and he was so damn hard, but he did. He laughed when he saw the reason why—the little tin of Nutex prophylactics she took out of the drawer on the bedside table. He hadn't seen a tin of those since Australia when the Top handed them out to all the GI's departing base on leave.

"Where'd you get those, baby?"

"Nearbelle. When I told her what I had planned for us."

"Of course," he said. "Good ol' Nearbelle. I should have known."

When it was over and they could both draw a normal breath again—still entwined, both damp with sweat, glistening in the little bit of moonlight, he felt himself slip out of her in a sad but good way. Stirring in his arms Gwen said, "Let me up, darling. I'll be right back."

She left to go to the bathroom down the hall. Feeling something warm and damp on the sheets where her body had just been, Hilton rolled over and saw Gwen's virginal blood shining wet and red on the white sheet.

Through the loud roaring noise ripping through his head he saw something else. Something he hadn't seen since Fort Ord and had hoped dearly to never see again. The young Filipino woman screaming across the shelled-out square in front of the ruined church in Manila, her baby that he had lifted out of her dead arms, covered with the brown-red blood left behind from being gutted by the Japanese bayonet.

And then Gwen had her arms wrapped tight around him, the points of her naked breasts pushing against the skin of his back as he sat on the side of the bed shaking and crying. Gwen was asking him, "What's wrong, Hilton? What's wrong?" He didn't know how to answer her.

***

He didn't remember driving home. Had no idea of the time of day when the shaking and the dead woman's face left him, and he was able to get in the car and drive away from Gwen's. At some point later, he awoke in bed in the upstairs bedroom in the house he grew up in. The sheets were soaked with sweat and a dull throbbing in his head beat with the sound of tugboats pulling barges up New River. The Raines house sat on a deep water, man-made canal just off the river and boat noise was not unusual. But now, the steady thrumming of diesel engines coming through the open bedroom window seemed louder than he ever remembered. Even though it was mid-afternoon, judging by the daylight flooding through the un-curtained windows, Hilton rolled over and went back to sleep.

He had a vague sense of the bedroom door opening once or twice, of his mother's voice, seemingly from very far away, asking, "Hilly? Are you all right?" If he had answered her, mumbled something in reply, he later couldn't say. Most of his sleep was racked with half-awake dreams of the war. Of Jesup, his friendly smile that morning when he convinced Hilton to go topside with him and watch the invasion unfold. Of Hackett and Chancey and Reeves shooting at the wild pig that first night ashore. Of the truck on fire that day on the streets of Manila, with Chancey crawling out of the back of it, his body in flames and machine gun fire riddling him as he tried to find some sort of safety but couldn't.

Often, though, these half-awake dreams were of Jesup, mostly of how he looked with the neat hole in his forehead after Hilton shot him.

When he finally awoke, drained and still shaky but no longer capable of lying in bed, Hilton showered, shaved, dressed, and went downstairs. It was dusk, shadows stretched across the darkened hallway and staircase. The only light in the house came from the kitchen where he knew his mother would be making dinner.

She turned to him as he came through the doorway, wearing the faded blue apron he would have been surprised not to see, her graying hair put up in a bun, hands white with flour from the chicken she was frying on the stove, her face knotted with questions she did her best to hide.

"I'm okay, Mom," he said before she could ask. "A little touch of the malaria, I guess. But I'm all right now."

It was the best he could come up with. *She's worried more than enough already over me. Worried over my sister, too, married to that jerk in New York. God knows that's plenty for one person.* She smiled as she turned back to the chicken sizzling in the pan and Hilton was relieved to see his little lie seemed to work.

Gwen was another matter. He needed to call her. He wanted to put it off but knew he couldn't. The phone rang on her end a long time. Long enough for him to think he might be postponing the call after all. But just as he went to put the phone back in the cradle, she picked up.

"Are you sure, Hilly?" she said after listening to his "malaria" excuse. "Sure that's all it was? I've worked with a few malaria cases at the hospital, you know."

He had forgotten about that. And of course, that wasn't all there was to it. But how could he tell Gwen about what had happened in Manila? Even if the major at Fort Ord had said he wasn't crazy, that didn't mean Gwen, or his folks, would agree. Not if he started spouting off about the dead woman. Or Jesup. Or the baby.

"You seemed different from those patients," Gwen continued. "Out of your head like that. Staring right through me as if I wasn't even there. You really scared me, Hilton."

"I scared myself," he said and chuckled. But she wasn't buying it.

"I'm serious, Hilton."

"So am I, darling, believe me. So am I."

"Perhaps you should give Dr. Rocklin a call."

Good ol' Doc Rocklin, Hilton thought. The family doctor who had delivered him, and his sister, and who was always right there at the house when any member of the Raines family was sick. Like the major at Fort Ord, Doctor Rocklin had kind eyes—*the only difference between those two men being the fact that Dr. Rocklin had never lied to him.* Yes, good old Doc Rocklin. He was supposed to tell this kindly doctor how he had shot Jesup, the best friend he ever had, because the gravely wounded sergeant asked him to do so?

"I'll be fine, Gwen. One or two of Mom's good meals and I'll be right as rain in no time. You'll see."

"I hope so, darling. I sure hope so.'

They ended the conversation with an extended series of "I love you's." He promised to call the next day. If he was feeling up to it, they'd have dinner and take in a movie that night.

Within a couple of weeks summer came on fully, long days of hot sun followed by afternoon rainstorms that cooled everything down. When the rain came to an end and the sun came back out, the humid heat rose up in steam from the wet streets. It didn't take long for Hilton to feel nostalgic for the moderate climate of Monterey and the California coast. Even if his time spent there had been under the threat of the dead woman, at least he didn't have to change his shirt and undershirt twice a day or more.

Hot and miserable as it could be during the summertime in South Florida, Hilton soon became grateful for one thing. The roaring noise in his head and the visions of what happened in the church plaza that day in Manila seemed to have left him. Other than the occasional fitful dream of Jesup and the others in his platoon, he was free of the horror. Apparently, what he had told Gwen on the phone was correct and all it had taken to fix him up was a couple of weeks of his mother's home cooking, a predictable daily routine, and the time he spent with Gwen.

He quit taking the Atabrine tablets, replacing them with one or two glasses of Canada Dry tonic a day. That seemed to do the trick as far as the malaria went. The yellow pallor of his skin from the Atabrine went away, his hair grew out from the military cut of the last three years, and he regained the weight lost overseas.

He began working for his father at the law office during the day, running errands such as picking up the mail and taking briefs down to the courthouse to be filed. After a bit his father had him typing the briefs, the two of them sitting in the office on the fifth floor of the Sweet Building downtown, going over the details of the cases and making sure everything was written correctly and in the proper *legalese,* as John Raines liked to say. Looking up case law, correcting mistakes in the briefs, even the mundane task of taking the finished papers down to the courthouse, gave Hilton that sense he had been looking for—of being a part of the living world again.

During a rare moment of free time in the busy office, he typed out a request for an application to the law school at the University of Florida. When he finished that he typed another formal letter, this one to the Veteran's Administration, requesting information regarding the newly created GI Bill. On the ride home from the office that afternoon, cutting through gray rain coming down so heavy the wiper blades could hardly keep up with it, all Hilton could think of was how properly his life was beginning to go, just like he and Jesup had talked about.

"You know, Pop," he said as his father turned the car into the driveway of the house. "I think everything's going to be just fine."

"Me, too, son."

That his father seemed to know without asking exactly what Hilton was talking about didn't surprise him. Then he forgot about it as the two of them made a mad dash through the rain for the dry comfort of the house.

He married Gwen that year on a sunny Saturday afternoon during the Labor Day weekend. The ceremony took place in the little park at Tarpon Bend where a little over a hundred years before, Indians massacred the Dade family and sparked the Second Seminole War. His father stood by his side as best man. After a noisy reception at the Yacht Club, where just about everyone in attendance drank more than their fair share of liquor, the happy couple retreated to the Hollywood Hotel for a week of honeymooning by the sea.

Toward the end of that October Gwen told him she was pregnant, and Hilton didn't see how anything could be better.

And yet, with all this good in his life, come Thanksgiving he was in the county hospital, as sick as he had ever been with the malaria, lost in the roaring noise inside his head and the pleas of the dead woman begging him to help her baby.

***

Fortunately, no one was hurt. They could easily have been, though Hilton only learned that later. After he came to he found that he was in the hospital, chilled to the bone and aching all over. He had a vague remembrance of someone coming in and changing the sweat-soaked sheets he lay on. Now, though the sheets were dry, he still felt cold and clammy. He wasn't alone. Gwen sat by his bedside, the look on her face the same as had been there the night they made love for the first time.

And the dead woman came back.

Malaria seemed a safe bet. *If I was a betting man*, Hilton thought. *Not after the war I'm not.* Judging by the worried frown on Gwen's face there was more to it than just malaria. Before he could ask, a nurse came in and took away his bedpan, an embarrassment adding even more to the misery of what had brought him there.

For better or for worse. They swore this to one another that lovely afternoon in the park. Well they certainly had to be at the worst.

"What happened?" His voice sounded weak and trembling—not his, he thought. *At least there were no straps this time. That had to count for something.*

"It doesn't matter now, darling," Gwen said. She took his hand and raising it to her lips, kissed it once. "The important thing is for you to just get better."

God, but she's so beautiful. Worried look or not. Beautiful, even in the lousy hard light of the hospital lamp overhead. Even within the sterile confines of the faded white walls, he thought. A thin privacy curtain that shielded him from the patient in the bed next to his, was drawn. It made the small, confining space seem even more so. Footsteps echoed from outside of the room from nurses, visitors, and doctors. The loud squawk of the hospital intercom rose over the footsteps, followed by a distorted female voice calling out, "Paging Dr. Mills. Paging Dr. Mills. Please come to the nurse's station on the third floor. Paging Dr. Mills."

It all seemed so unreal. So shining, and harsh, and ugly. Just like how he felt. Certainly, no place for someone as fine and beautiful as his wife. No place at all for her to be, vows sworn during a better time or not.

"It *does* matter," he said, struggling to sit up in the bed. He was able only to make it halfway before having to lie back against the pillow Gwen quickly shoved behind his shoulders. "It matters a goddamn lot."

"At least we know now what the problem is. Dr. Rocklin was finally able to reach a Major Carlson out at Fort Ord. Finally."

She was stalling, and he supposed he couldn't blame her, for it must be very bad.

"The major told him about the battle fatigue?"

"Yes. I'm so sorry, Hilton. I didn't know. I just didn't know, and you wouldn't tell me."

"No. I wouldn't."

He was very tired. From the sickness, he imagined, or the dope they must be giving him. Lying in the bed—not looking at Gwen but looking off at the side at nothing at all—he remembered he *was* home. In fact, he had a new home, with Gwen, and the baby coming, and he didn't feel good at all. Did not feel at all like he was home.

Lying there saying nothing, Gwen must have thought he was still waiting on her to tell him what had happened. Though she had said to him that it didn't matter and that she didn't want to tell him, she went ahead and did so. When she finished he really wished it had been somebody, *anybody*, other than her to tell him. Wished that it had been his father. John Raines, being a man, might have had something to say that would make sense of the whole thing. Like Major Carlson, who reminded him of his father, and who only told the one lie.

Maybe his father could have made sense of it. Maybe. But John wasn't there so Hilton listened to his wife. At the end of it, he thought how much better she'd be if they had never married—how much better she'd be if she were far away from him and all that he had brought home from the war.

The long and the short of it, though, was that on the Monday before Thanksgiving while Gwen was at work on the 4-to-midnight shift at the hospital, he had gone crazy. Major Carlson or not, "disorder" or not, as Hilton listened to his wife tell this sad story, the only thing he could think of was that sane people don't do what he did. They don't go out into their front yard with a Colt .38 revolver and shoot all the windows out of the new car their folks had given them as a wedding gift. Don't calmly reload the revolver and then proceed to shoot the tires of the car. Doing this while still in pajamas that late in the day and cursing and crying all the while.

Hilton remembered being in his pajamas. Remembered giving up the notion that he wasn't getting sick, putting them on, then heading off to the bedroom with a glass of quinine tonic in hope that he could ward off the malaria before it got too bad. Beyond that was just a dark, empty, hole in his mind.

"Sheriff Harker," Gwen said at the end, "heard the address of the disturbance report over the radio and came personally to the house. He told the other deputies on duty that afternoon that he'd handle the situation. As a favor to the family, he told me. Out of respect for your father."

Hilton was able to muster a little smile at this—knowing as he did how any respect between the sheriff and his father was a one-sided affair.

"Thank God," Gwen continued, "he was able to settle you down and get you to the hospital."

"I guess," Hilton said. He wasn't sure any more about the existence of any God. But seeing the look in his wife's eyes he said quickly, "Yes. Thank God."

"Oh Hilton! You don't know how frantic I was when I saw you brought in to the emergency room."

"I'm sorry, Gwen," he said. "Truly sorry. For all of it."

"It's not your fault, Hilly. Not your fault."

It was quiet for a moment between them before Gwen thought of something and spoke up again. "While the doctor was examining you, Sheriff Harker pulled me aside and told me something really strange."

Hilton couldn't imagine anything stranger than what she had just told him.

"He said that when he pulled up in front of the house you were in the middle of the front yard shooting into the ground. Yelling, 'Stay dead, damnit, stay dead.' What's that mean, darling? Do you know? Or remember?"

The nurse came back into the room carrying a tray with two pills and a cup of water, one of the pills the big yellow Atabrine tablet that Hilton was very familiar with. The other white capsule looked like one of the sedatives they had given him at Fort Ord.

"It's time for your afternoon medications, Mr. Raines," the nurse said.

"You'll be better soon, darling," Gwen said after he had swallowed the pills and the nurse left the room.

"Yes," Hilton said, right then hoping just for the numbing sleep of the sedative to come and take him away.

Gwen stayed with him for a little while after that, the two of them not saying anything, the room quiet except for the restless stirring of the unseen patient in the bed next to his.

"You'll be better, soon," Gwen repeated.

But Hilton was half-asleep and didn't really hear her.

***

He wanted a life after the war. As did Jesup and Chancey and all the other poor bastards who didn't come home. But it wasn't going to be possible, he realized. Just as it wasn't for his dead companions.

His wife couldn't help him. Nor his parents. Not even his sister who was far away with her new family in New York, other than the occasional letter full of meaningless news, she was no longer a part of his life.

Not that his loved ones didn't want to help. Their desire to help was so painfully obvious in the avoidance both his mother and father tried very hard to practice—and failed miserably. Yes, they all of them wanted to help, but there wasn't anything any of them could do.

It was as simple as that, Hilton decided on the Monday morning following one of those Sunday dinners at his parents' house shortly after being released from the hospital. He was dressing for work, not at all sure he could make it through the day. Not feeling the way he was right then, alone and helpless, and with the truth of his helplessness staring him in the face from the bathroom mirror.

As he shaved, forcing his trembling fingers to hold the razor and not inflict too much damage to his face, he remembered leaving Fort Ord for home in the spring. He had told himself that no matter what, he was going to get better. The morning he left was cold, and misty, the bay obscured by the heavy fog banks rolling off from the shore. But as the train started to roll east the fog began to lift. It was at that moment that Hilton made vow to himself. The vow to get well again. Six months back, he thought while wiping shaving suds from his face. A lifetime ago and the idea of him "getting well" nothing more now than a horrible joke.

The dinner the night before was a disaster. His mother, being nervous, burned the leg of lamb—a first, as best Hilton could remember. Over cards afterwards, Hilton couldn't focus on his hands, keep track of what cards had been played, or who played them. After a very uncomfortable hour of this, he told his parents that he just wasn't quite up to it yet. Maybe it would be best if they called it a night. He received no argument.

The customary drink with his father on the back porch after the meal had been marred by an uncommon silence. Finally, his father cleared his throat. "Well, Son, I think you're looking better."

Apparently, it was the best his father could come up with while handing Hilton a fresh glass of bourbon and branch.

"But tell me truthfully, Hilton," John continued as he sat back down in his wicker chair, the identical twin of the one Hilton occupied. "How do you feel?"

"Like absolute hell, Pop." It was about as true as he could get, Hilton figured. Seeing how his father's face tightened up, he added quickly, "But I'm better than I was a couple of days ago."

"A new year is just around the corner." Instead of the customary cigar John shook a Camel out of a pack and offered one to Hilton. "Christmas will come and go and then the holidays will be over. We can get a fresh start. All of us. Put the war and your illness behind us and get on with it."

The rich tobacco and the bourbon helped. As he drew the smoke deep into his lungs, Hilton could feel the tension in his shoulders and neck softening. Gwen and his mother were clearing the table in the dining room, and the comforting clink of china and silverware being gathered up and taken away drifted through the open doors of the porch. Outside, a wind blew up out of the east, just strong enough to rock the boat, "Mari-Lyn," at her moorings on the dock behind the house. With this easterly wind the stern light John faithfully turned on every evening became a bobbing dot of white against the dark over the water. A small dot of safety, Hilton thought, that white stern light in a very dark world.

"I sure as hell hope you're right, Pop," he said.

"You'll see. Things will get back to normal. We just need some time."

Hilton saw something else, though. Saw how the bobbing light suddenly resembled machine gun tracers arcing through the night in the jungles south of Manila. That awful place below the mountains with the Japanese dug in tight where no amount of artillery and machine gun fire would budge them. The roaring noise in his head began to rise, the tracer rounds flew fast and furious, and Hilton saw one more time the dug-in Japs pouring out of their holes in a last-ditch charge that filled the night with carnage and the screaming of the wounded.

Then Hilton shook his head. For once the roaring noise receded as suddenly as it had come. He said again, "I sure hope you're right."

In another minute his mother stood in the doorway, waving them in for the card game and saving Hilton from the explanation his father clearly wanted, judging by the puzzled look in his eyes.

For the next few weeks following the Sunday dinner Hilton continued to feel like hell. Maybe worse. Despite Gwen and his mother's best efforts to feed him he lost the weight he had gained back over the summer. The pale, jaundiced skin pallor returned, courtesy of the

Atabrine regimen Dr. Rocklin insisted he follow, bringing with it the headaches and nausea he always knew as side effects from the drug. He was weak and aching all the time and going about his daily business took everything he had.

Christmas came and went just as John had said it would. Clear and cool, blue sky days ushered in the first real cold snap of the season. Just in time for the holidays Hilton appeared to rally, began to almost feel like his old self. But the good weather ended with the beginning of the new year, when hard rains and high winds from the northeast came ripping off the ocean. With the lousy weather Hilton's brief rally vanished. The health and happiness he had known during the holidays quickly turned into a brief memory from another time.

The very worst of it was the roaring in his head. Most of the time it was only a dull throb in the back of his mind. Sort of like the muted sound of grenades going off underwater when they used them for fishing in the Philippines. Other times the roaring came on loud and unforgiving, like the steady pounding of the cannonade unleashed on the walled fortress toward the end of the battle for the city. The only forgiving grace being that loud, or dull, neither the dead woman nor Jesup with the neat hole in his forehead accompanied the noise.

Bourbon helped to keep the noise at bay. Hilton took to making a cocktail first thing he got home in the afternoon. Gwen worked a four-to-midnight shift at the hospital, so he had only himself, the radio, and the whiskey for company after work. It didn't take long for him to discover he liked it that way. Occasionally at day's end he went with his father to the Governor's Club on Las Olas, a dark and cozy retreat favored by John's good friend Tom Ryan, as well as bankers, attorneys, judges, and the businessmen of the downtown area. The Club was three blocks away from John's law office and the short walk after being cramped in the office all day seemed to do wonders for his father. Before the incident with the Colt .38 in his front yard, Hilton had enjoyed walking with his father after work to meet Ryan. It was not the same now. Once inside, the three of them sitting at a table by the window, Hilton could never seem to get comfortable, couldn't shake the feeling that the others in the bar were staring at him.

"Well, Son, we did it," John said one afternoon after a particularly hectic day. "How about taking a walk down the street with me?"

"I'd like to, Pop,' Hilton said. "But I really have to get home."

It must have been the way he said it, or the look on his face. Whatever it was, his father didn't bring up the Governor's Club after work again and Hilton was fine with that.

He drank Manhattans at first but came to believe the sugar, bitters, and sweet vermouth did something to the bourbon that made for a terrible hangover the next morning. Hangovers only served to make the roaring noise even louder. He switched to rye and soda, a drink Tom Ryan favored. But after two nights with this mix, he couldn't understand what Mr. Ryan saw in it. He finally decided his father was right and stuck to bourbon and branch. Like his father, Hilton preferred it with very little "branch." He liked very much how the bourbon, hot at first, burned down his throat. From experience, Hilton knew it wouldn't be long before the melting ice cubes softened the initial heat of the whiskey. Even better, after two or three nice healthy drinks on the back porch, the edges of his world also seemed to soften. Softened enough that he could stand being a part of it.

One night he lost track of how many cocktails he drank. When Gwen came home he was asleep in the chair on the back porch. She told him so the next morning when he woke up in their bed and couldn't remember how he got there. Embarrassed to be found like that by his wife, asleep and still in his rumpled clothes from the office, he promised her it wouldn't happen again.

"Really, Hilton? You promise?"

"Cross my heart and hope to die," he said, and believed it to be so.

There was just something about the whole ritual of the thing, though. Pulling the bottle of Old Grand-Dad out of the cabinet above the kitchen sink. Putting ice cubes in the metal ice bucket. Taking bottle, bucket, and glass, out to the back porch. Tuning in Gabriel Heatter's newscast on the radio. Drinking until well after the sun went down, the newscast was over, and depending on what day of the week it might be, jazz from New York, The Mystery Theater, or some other program. Something about all of this Hilton needed very much. A week later Gwen came home from work and he was asleep in the chair again. But the next morning when she told him what had happened there was no anger in her tone. Only a look on her face he had never seen before. He would've preferred anger—dishes breaking, glasses flying, and everybody crying and cursing at one another over the saddened, furrowed look on Gwen's face.

The drinking helped. Gave him time, even if only a little, when he could ignore the yellow of his skin, the headache and nausea from the Atabrine, and the noise in his head. Gwen didn't like it, true, and Hilton felt bad for that. He loved his wife very much, but she had elected to stay with him, even damaged as he was and of little use for her now. Their baby would come sometime in the summer. With a little luck he'd be better then, finally able to be the husband and father he wanted to be. If he had any luck left at all, Gwen would still be with him when this came about.

Maybe it would've played out that way if one Friday night in the middle of April, Gwen, her stomach swollen with the child, hadn't come out on the back porch where Hilton sat in safety with his bourbon and radio. She lowered herself slowly into the chair next to his, the smile all over her rosy, pregnant face so beautiful it made him almost want to cry. She showed him the magazine she had brought with her.

"Look, Hilton," she said, holding out the magazine. "Pretty soon we'll have one of our own. Just like this little darling. Won't that be wonderful?"

The cover of the magazine depicted a healthy, chubby little baby. Hilton looked. He wanted to say something. Was willing to say anything, but it was suddenly too loud inside his head for him to speak.

When the roaring subsided to a muted throb, Hilton found that he was at the train station, sitting hunched over on a bench at the far end of the loading platform. Beyond the platform it was dark, other than what shone from streetlamps in the neighborhood behind the station. Once past the range of light offered by the station, the railroad tracks disappeared into the night. His hands hurt and looking down Hilton saw the reason why. The knuckles were cut and raw. Not only cut but bruised and swollen and crusted with dried blood that looked more brown than red in the soft light.

Whose blood? The question pounded at him—though with the sickening lurch of his insides, Hilton knew whose blood. Gwen's.

So. It had come to this. He had done something terrible to his wife. Drawn blood from her. Or worse. Could he have taken her life? Killed her while lost in that goddamned roaring noise that wouldn't leave him alone? These fears streamed through his clouded mind.

And now—for retribution of what he had done that day in the city of the dead—had he finally paid the price with his own wife? With Gwen?

He stood suddenly, just making it to the edge of the platform before heaving his guts up in a thin stream of bile, yellow and gleaming as it splattered on the tracks below.

"You okay, young feller?"

Hilton straightened up, wiped a hand across his mouth, and turned to the voice at his back. A man, older than Hilton by maybe twenty years or so, stood in the open doorway of the station.

Everybody asks if they can help me. But no one has been able to. "Thanks," Hilton said. "But I think I'll be all right. It's probably just something I ate."

His voice seemed louder than it should—apparently not only to him, for the man stepped back a pace.

"Thought I'd ask," he said. "If you're here for the 10:05 to D.C., she's running a little late. They called up from Miami a half hour ago. Said unexpected repairs would hold her up a bit."

"Yes?"

Hilton had no idea what the man was talking about.

"The way you drove in here? Like the world was coming to an end and you needed to get out fast? I just figured you were supposed to be on the 10:05 and was afraid you'd missed her."

"What time is it?"

"Quarter past ten."

It was clear now that the man in the doorway must be the night station manager. The night was warm and sticky with the promise of rain, summer not far away, and with fireflies winking on and off in the pine trees on the other side of the train tracks. Everything normal.

"You got plenty of time, yet," the station manager continued. "Fred, down in Miami, said he'd call when she left the station. There's coffee inside if you're interested. Some bandages. How'd you hurt your hand anyway?"

The man's voice was raspy and soft. He coughed as he lit up a cigarette and took a first long drag. There was only curiosity in the man's tone, no accusation or suspicion.

Though his own voice seemed loud and distant and not his own, Hilton felt safe enough with this man that he could tell him the truth.

"I'm not sure."

"About the coffee? Or how you hurt yourself?" The man smiled as he flicked the cigarette onto the tracks, the lit end of it a red spark in the dark. "I need to quit these goddamn coffin nails," he added. "Or so my missus says. I'm almost starting to believe she's right." The coughing fit that racked him served to punctuate his point. "But hell, if you're anything like me, young feller, you probably skinned yourself hurrying to put your bags in the trunk. Being late and all."

"That's probably it," Hilton said.

Not that he believed that was the case. It would've taken more than loading a suitcase in haste and an open trunk lid to do that. He could taste the bile rising in his throat again. Taking a deep breath, he managed to keep it down.

"I think I'll take you up on the coffee," he told the station manager when he could breathe normally without feeling like he was about to vomit.

"Sure thing, young feller. I'll give you a hand with your bags, too, if you need it. The night porter called in sick so it's just me here tonight. Lucky for him we ain't busy."

The man smiled again, a lop-sided grin that cocked his thick glasses to one side of his face. He stepped back in the doorway and waved for Hilton to follow him. Inside, the station was brightly lit with fluorescent lights that made the darkness outside seem very far away. Advertising posters were plastered up on the walls, large photographs of glittering women and well-dressed men, exiting immaculate train stations in places such as New York, Chicago, and Miami, the bold lettering splayed across the photographs extolling the glories of these destinations. On both sides of the glass double doors of the main entrance, smaller train schedules were posted here and there. The advertising posters and train schedules, the hard wooden waiting benches in rows, the ticket counter where the night manager was busying himself with something—all served to keep the darkness outside even further away

"I keep a pot going on a hot plate behind the counter," the man said with a wink. "It's the only way I can make it through the long nights. Especially when I'm on shift by myself."

The coffee was hot and strong, in one of those old speckled enamel camp cups like his father kept up at the ranch. Come break time John would make a small fire and brew the coffee in a pot, also enameled. When it was ready the two of them would sit back, sip the hot brew, and smoke a cigarette or one of Tom Ryan's good cigars. Sometimes his father would talk about what was on his mind, mostly ranch issues. If fall was nearing, John usually expounded on the possibilities, or lack of them, for the upcoming hunt seasons.

Now, sitting in the train station, confused, his knuckles cut and bleeding, and at a loss as to how he had even gotten there, Hilton knew as he drank the hot coffee, that those days were gone for good.

"So, where you headed tonight?"

He hadn't heard the question at first, only became aware of it when the station manager repeated it. Hilton looked up from his coffee at a loss for an answer.

"D.C. or New York?"

"New York," Hilton finally answered, only because he was staring at an advertising placard on the wall concerning that city.

"Taking the late train like you are, you'll get there sometime early in the morning on the day after next. That ol' Big Apple's one big city. Dangerous, too. According to the papers, anyway. Somebody be there at Grand Central to pick you up?"

"Maybe," Hilton said. Seeing the puzzled look come over the manager's face, he added quickly, "Somebody will be there."

At least the coffee was helping to clear away the last fog of the bourbon and the roaring noise that could so consume him and make him do terrible things. With a little luck, now that the noise in his head had subsided, maybe he could piece together what had happened at his house. All Hilton needed was just a little while to figure things out. And then he could decide. Where to go. What he had to do to make it all right again.

"That coffee treating you okay, young feller?" The manager had put down a paper he was reading. Holding his black frame glasses in one hand and tapping them against the counter he reminded Hilton of a professor he'd had at college. "You still look a little peaked to me."

The professor always knew just the right question to pose the class to get their attention. Philosophy? Or world literature? He couldn't remember the subject matter now, or even the professor's name. It was just another of those classes that had lost all meaning with the war. Hopefully, that professor had come up with some new questions for his students. Now that everything had changed so.

"Yes, it's helping," Hilton said. "The malaria I picked up overseas. That's what you're seeing."

He suddenly wanted to talk with his father. Just to hear his voice on the phone would be good. He stood up from the wooden bench, rooted in his trouser pocket, and found a nickel. He was making his way to the pay phone by the restroom doors when the manager stopped him.

"You boys did one heck of a fine job over there. That God-awful war. You fight the Japs? Or the Krauts?"

Hilton realized it was no use. He couldn't call his dad. He hadn't been able to tell him about Jesup or about shooting the dead woman. How was he supposed to tell him now what he might have done to Gwen? Ask for his help? He could just see the look on his face, the disappointment. No. It wasn't possible. Instead, he turned to the station manager who was frowning as he tapped his glasses against the newspaper lying on the counter.

"I wanted to go. Damn sure did. But I have a heart murmur. That's what the Army docs told me. Told me I couldn't go."

"Everybody did what they could," Hilton said.

"I'd have liked to done more."

The words began to reverberate in the empty room. It was funny, Hilton thought, how it had been peaceful inside the station. Quiet in his head, until he started thinking of the war. Until the station manager spoke of it out loud.

"All right if I have another cup of that coffee?" Hilton's hand trembled a little when he held the empty cup out to be refilled.

"Sure thing." As he poured the hot brew into Hilton's cup the station manager added, "I can see how that malaria's got you pretty bad. Way your hand's all shaky like that."

"Yeah. It can get pretty bad all right."

You haven't seen anything. Not by half you haven't.

It was plain the station man wished to talk more about the war, but it wasn't safe to do so. Not for Hilton. He took the fresh cup of coffee back outside, down to the bench overlooking the tracks where he had found himself when some sense returned to him. An easterly wind had come up off the ocean, the breeze strong enough to cut the hot, sticky air of the unusually warm night.

An owl hooted off in the pines on the other side of the tracks. The sound of the living, but unseen, being brought Hilton back to the problem at hand. What had happened at the house? To Gwen?

Suddenly, the difficulty of the task ripped across the top of his head in a searing flash of pain that made his eyes water as he groaned out loud. But in the watery mist clouding his eyes, coming through the burning pain that filled his head, images of earlier in the evening began to unfold.

There was a baby on the cover of a magazine Gwen handed him just as the bourbon was smoothing out the hard edges. It was suddenly too loud in the room. Too loud inside his head. And the baby was no longer just a picture on a magazine.

But there. Cradled in the dead woman's arms as she came screaming across the ruined plaza demanding Hilton do what he didn't want to do. What? Of course. Kill Jesup. His only friend. Kill him when he didn't want to. Even if it wasn't really the woman who asked. Had been Jesup who asked. Still. Her fault. Her and her goddamned baby. But before she could make him do it all over again, Hilton put a stop to it.

Hilton! You're hurting me!

The dead woman screamed in a voice Hilton knew well. And there, trapped between the world he lived in with his wife, and the church square in Manila—Gwen.

No. *You're dead. The baby's dead.*

And—Stop it, Hilton!

His wife. Not the dead woman. Back in the world again, he took his hands from around his wife's throat. To keep from choking her again, he had slammed both fists into the wall behind her. Beyond that he could only recall being in his front yard sucking in a desperate lungful of warm evening air while Gwen stood in the doorway of the house. At least she was safe. For the moment.

Safe from him.

Come back into the house, Hilton, she called out. He could remember this. Could clearly hear her saying, *It's okay. Everything will be okay. You didn't hurt me, darling. Come back inside. Stay here with me.*

But it was *not* okay. And that was it. All that he could recall. But despite the sick insanity of what he had done, there was one thing he had not. He hadn't harmed his wife. Dear, loving, Gwen. The blood on his knuckles came from hitting the wall. He hadn't harmed her. This time. And that had to count for something. For now.

But what about the next time?

A next time would come.

If he knew anything at all, he knew that. He was as sure of it as he was of his own name. Hilton Raines. Son of John Raines and Sadie Doon. Brother to Marilyn Raines, now Mrs. Thomas Alred of New York City. As the son of John Raines, he had been privileged with a safe and secure childhood. For the most part life had treated him well. Until he was grown. Until he was a man. And war came calling. And nothing was safe anymore.

There would be a next time. It would come with no guarantee that he wouldn't hurt her. That being the case, he was of no earthly good to her, or to anyone. Not the way he was now. The way the war had made him.

And there it was. End of story, as his father liked to say. Black and white. Cut and dried. As long as Hilton was around, none of those he loved were safe. It was as simple as that, and he was the only one who could fix it.

He heard a pneumatic swishing sound come from behind him. Turning, Hilton saw the night manager standing half in, half out of the station's two open doors. With the light from inside spilling out around him he looked much as Gwen had in the doorway of their house when she was pleading with Hilton to come inside.

"Miami just called. The train left fifteen minutes ago. She'll be here soon."

As if to confirm that what the station manager had said was true, a train whistle blew way down the tracks.

"You got your ticket, young feller? Everything you need?"

"Yes, I do."

Hilton stood up from the concrete bench. The concern for his well-being in the man's voice was touching. Too late to be of much good. But nice, just the same. The train whistle sounded again, a long piercing wail in the dark. Looking south down the tracks Hilton could see the one big headlight of the train cutting through the night as it came toward him.

"You need a hand with your bags?"

"No. I won't be needing that."

The light of the train was coming fast and closer now. Above the roaring noise and in his head, Hilton thought he could make out the clanging of the iron wheels against the iron tracks—could envision in his mind the sparks flying off the train wheels into the dark.

"Hey now," the station manager shouted out behind him. "What the hell you doing?"

"It's all right," Hilton answered.

"Son, you better get off those tracks. Get back up here where it's safe."

"It's going to be all right," Hilton repeated.

Both train and roaring noise in his head grew louder and louder as he began to walk south down the tracks toward the light coming his way. He felt safe suddenly, with the light of the train rapidly cutting the dark away.

It will be just fine now. For Gwen. For me. For everyone. Just a little way yet to go. And it will be all right.

"Please son," he heard the station manager shout one last time. "Please don't do this."

"I have to," Hilton said over his shoulder and without looking back. "I've got to meet the train."

The roaring rose up louder than he had ever known it before and lost for the last time within that frightful noise, Hilton Raines let the light bearing down on him, a brilliant light against a very dark night, carry him away.

About the Author

Gene Lee has been writing fiction and poetry since he was a teenager. A third generation Florida native, his fiction is derived from family history. His poems have been published in various anthologies and small literary quarterlies, such as *The Cathartic*, The *South Florida Poetry Review, The Kerouac Review* and others. *Men Without Hate* is his first published book and the result of eight years of writing and research. Mr. Lee currently lives with his wife in Sebastian, Florida. An avid sportsman, he enjoys wing shooting and fly-fishing all over the country. "At present, he is developing more stories of the Raines family and expects this task to keep him busy for the next several years."

ALL THINGS THAT MATTER PRESS

FOR MORE INFORMATION ON TITLES AVAILABLE FROM
ALL THINGS THAT MATTER PRESS, GO TO
http://allthingsthatmatterpress.com
or contact us at
allthingsthatmatterpress@gmail.com

If you enjoyed this book, please post a review on Amazon.com and
your favorite social media sites.
Thank you!

www.ingramcontent.com/pod-product-compliance
Lightning Source LLC
Chambersburg PA
CBHW051630260626
47170CB00004B/1109